# Celara Sun

By

Lee McQueen

McQueen  Press
Des Moines, Iowa

Published by McQueen Press
info@mcqueenpress.com
www.mcqueenpress.com
http://www.facebook.com/pages/McQueen-
Press/177434247186

About the Author
Lee McQueen takes on research, data analysis, organization, editorial, digitization, and database maintenance assignments and writes web content, reports, biographical articles, essays, novels, short stories, poems, and screenplays.
lee@mcqueenpress.com
http://www.linkedin.com/in/leemcqueen
http://www.twitter.com/leemcqueen3

Cover design, interior design, and typesetting by Lee McQueen.

Publisher's Cataloging-in-Publication

McQueen, Lee
Celara sun/Lee McQueen
p. cm.
ISBN 978-0-9798515-8-2 (pbk)

1. Renewable energy sources—fiction. 2. Conspiracies—fiction. 3. Suspense—fiction. 4. Business intelligence—fiction. I. Title

# Works by Lee McQueen

## Short Story Collection

Imaginarium

## Poetry Collection

Things I Forgot to Tell You

## Novel

Kenzi

## Screenplay

The Angel and the Lion
Kindred

## Non-Fiction

Writer in the Library!

Empathy is the ability to participate
in the thoughts, feelings,
and ideas of
Another

For the Survivors
Who do what has to be Done

# Contents

# 1 The Idea

This is not a romance. It is not a fantasy. There are no heroes or villains. Just people. This is a story about the choices people make in the real world when situations go extreme and push past equilibrium. Then both the heroes *and* the villains become what they really are.

Survivors.

From a series of terrible events initiated by people of questionable character, the future of renewable energy in Lake City grew stronger and brighter. In fact, Lake City became not so much a fairy tale of green possibility, but rather, an urban legend of green power. As in the days of exploration of uncharted territories and the development of the cotton, oil, coal, rubber, and steel industries... fortunes grew from the pain of others.

Robber barons from Apollo to Zenith slammed cannon fodder like so much artillery through red tape and bureaucracy. During the green revolution, the gods held the sun and wind hostage to their visions.

They pushed the levers of power past all limits of human understanding and decency. They ran the rollercoaster fast and far over the twists and turns of history.

◆ ◆ ◆ ◆

## 2 The Opening

4 years ago

**H**e looked down at the frail man in the hospital bed. Fierce blue eyes glared back at him underneath thick, dark eyebrows in harsh contrast to the wisps of white hair that floated above his wrinkled scalp. Those angry eyes cried their defiance at the position in which life placed him—flat on his back at the mercy and whim of the younger man that stood over him.

Cold, ugly pain ravaged and radiated from his core. It was time for the end of all things.

"Do it!" Despite the skeletal frailty of his dying frame, his voice held a note of clear contempt.

Both knew that soon it would be over. Anything left undone here on Earth would remain undone.

"Damn you!" The whisper-scream seared the younger man's cheek. More curses followed. Death pulled the older man even deeper now.

His eyes crystallized to pinpoints. His breathing slowed. His altered mental state showed him visions.

Not of this life.

Visions of what would be in other places and other times. He swam now, swam towards destiny. He left the past and the future where they belonged—to the man who took it all away. Or did they just drift on the wind, upwards to the sun?

His lips curled.

The younger man closed the door. Left him to his dreams. Casual footsteps walked away from flashing lights, warning bells, and running feet.

Nothing mattered anymore. Fate would see to the remains of the day.

At the doorway to everlasting coma, the man of yesterday's heart beat once. Twice. The shouts and curses floated around him then vanished into smoke.

Once he danced with Celara.

Now Death took the lead. He followed with aplomb. The band played his favorite song.

They circled the room together.

The bloody business of the day came to an end.

❖ ❖ ❖ ❖

# 3 The Interview

Exceptional Boss seeks
Extraordinary Researcher.
Take care of the ordinary crap.
So that I can enjoy my life!

Laid-off from a fifteen-year teaching gig downstate last February, Martina Butler returned to Lake City early one brisk March morning. She bathed then got dressed for her job interview in the bus station's bathroom. Luckily the hair that flowed past her shoulders in dark, luxurious twists was the least of her worries.

She gathered the long curtain into a bun with an elastic band, smoothed her best navy suit over a slender, curved frame. Over that, she put on a hip-length jacket that revealed a narrow waist made narrower by the hard choice between food and shelter. She bought the classic-cut coat in better times but it still worked.

She stroked dark brown mascara over lashes that rimmed sherry-colored eyes. She preferred to leave her reddish-brown skin free of foundation and powder. She finished with wine-colored lipstick over a full mouth that curved into a heart shape. After a critical once-over in the mirror, she repacked her toiletries with an efficiency learned from moves into and out of dormitories during the college years.

But the janitor in the doorway around the corner didn't seem impressed.

"Lady!" he yelled out and rattled the mop handle against the door. "Lady! I gotta job ta do! What're you doing in there?"

She rolled her suitcase past his suspicious glare to a locker, ignored his low mutters.

No one knew she was back in town. If she got the job, she'd move back. If the job fell through, she'd return downstate and try to think of another way to survive the economic crisis. So she'd better land the job. Right?

She remembered her way around the downtown area. She took the correct commuter train but the wrong bus connection to the northwest suburbs. Actually, she never really knew the outlying areas of Lake City. She, her mother, and her brother mostly lived their lives in the Central District, just north of downtown.

But anyway, she came back to her hometown. She took an awkward bath in the bus station.

She got lost in the northwest suburbs. She got off the bus and walked the rest of the way to her job interview.

She arrived late.

◆ ◆ ◆ ◆

Evan Lewis seemed pleasant and deferential. Brown-haired with small, dark-brown, nearly black eyes, he met her in the lobby with a stack of paperwork then ushered her into the conference room. They exchanged pleasantries. Marti didn't have time to form an opinion about him.

Because menace layered over with a thin cover of calm watchfulness stalked into the conference room like a hungry panther. The air vibrated and shimmered around Alexander King. He took the chair opposite her and Evan. Alex sat still, made no movement. Two brilliant blue lights glittered with lighter flecks of crystal and gray beneath raven's wing black hair and strong black brows. She guessed from the self-assured manner that he had to be mid-to-late forties. His eyes pinned her to her chair. Assessed her in return. Measured her. Judged her.

Wisdom of thirty-eight years taught her when to make an exit, when to speak, when to listen, when to take notes, when drink a glass of water to delay an answer, or to decide whether to laugh at a joke that may not have been a joke. But when any of the strategies she normally used escaped her, she maintained one reliable fall back.

*Wait for more information.*

Faced with coiled energy that anticipated the slightest reason to pounce, she wasn't sure of a single thing. She watched Alex as he watched her.

Both of them ignored Evan as if he weren't in the room. Whenever Evan did speak, neither looked his way. She and Alex answered Evan, of course, but kept their eyes on each other.

They went through her portfolio.

Actually, she slid her portfolio across the table to Alex. Alex picked it up. Then he dropped it back on the table with a thud after the briefest flick of his eyes towards it.

"I really don't know if I want to work with you yet. But if you can write all this, you'd have to be a stone-cold idiot not to be able to write what I need you to."

Marti sat still not sure how to react to what might be a compliment, an insult, or a job offer.

"So you're from Lake City?" he asked her.

"Yes, I was born here. I attended Rose Creek University and taught English and Writing at Rose Creek Prep for fifteen years. They had lay-offs this year and so..." she trailed off.

"There's a lot of that going around. Why didn't you look for something in Rose Creek?"

"I wanted to. I've been there a while and I like the community. Employment prospects aren't good though. A lot of people are out of work in the smaller towns and rural regions."

"It's like that in the city too."

"Still, odds are better."

"Your father, is he involved in construction?"

"No, he's a minister." *And my brother's in prison. And my mother's dead. But let's talk about me.*

Alex frowned. Considered that for a moment. Turned it over to examine the other side. Waited for the punch line. The punch line didn't come.

He made up his mind. She was serious. His eyes turned speculative. Marti knew this routine. Minister's daughters either conformed or rebelled. What Alex saw before him was the epitome of conformation. Teacher. English degree. Conservative clothing. And to top it off, a quiet, calm, cool—some say robotic—demeanor. Perfect.

He held the strange moment a while longer. She sensed he enjoyed awkward moments like these. Awkward moments, pregnant pauses, and long silences served his advantage and validated his assurance that he looked the part of an attractive, wealthy, and successful executive. The coiled spring waited for her reaction. An electric current radiated throughout the room.

Marti endured the scrutiny. She kept her eyes on the portfolio abandoned on the table between them. She wanted what he wanted—for her to do the best job she could on his project. As long as she continued to want what he wanted, whatever it was, it would be okay. If ever the case were different, if her will opposed his...

She raised her eyes, at last. Met his.

He said the last thing she expected. "My father passed away a few years ago."

"I'm very sorry."

Alex inclined his head to acknowledge her condolence statement.

"Celara Electric was my father's baby. It's the foundation that made Celara Solar Construction the success it is today. However, Celara Electric's slowly being absorbed by the solar division. Not completely, though. While we maintain a presence in the traditional construction market, we're doing a full-out sprint to lay claim to regional solar energy markets. These days, you have to go green to get green. And that's what we're doing."

Marti pulled out pen and paper. Her hand jerked and twitched left to right. Her eyes never strayed from Alex's.

Though she knew he remained in the room, Evan disappeared. Every space filled with Alex's voice, his eyes, his skin, his hair, his cologne, his charisma. He made the mundane seem fantastic and not the slightest bit over-the-top. If Alexander King said it could happen, it very likely would, if it hadn't already.

"So these days, Lake City goes out of its way to promote a so-called green economy. But what is that?" He ticked the rules off on his fingers. "Efficient use of energy, reduced emissions, renewable power sources. So with that, Celara steps into the vacuum to create jobs, opportunities, and strong communities. So look, we're not talking granolas and environmentalists hugging trees and singing kumbaya. We're talking real men with families who've had technical training who go out there and get the job done. They're wearing hardhats, steel-toe boots, and tool belts, showing up on construction sites ready to go from day one. Blue collar, green collar, whatever collar it's called these days, they're doing it. Got that?"

Marti nodded.

"Alright. Where does Celara fit in? What's our role? We use computer-aided design to build, install, and then service telephone and data cabling. All the infrastructure, and fire alarm and security systems."

Again, he ticked off on his fingers.

"We do fiber optics, wireless communications, voice over IP, medium voltage power distribution, on-site and remote energy management systems, control panels, generators, and lighting systems. We've done these projects for years. With Celara Solar, we're still maintaining the traditional services, but we're also doing photovoltaic systems in various configurations, sometimes with solar thermal, to satisfy whatever the client wants, and of course, city code. Retrofit or new designs. Okay get caught up."

He sat back with a triumphant smile as Marti's pen raced across the page.

"Who are our clients? Whoever. Airports, schools, libraries, hospitals, prisons, casinos, hotels, office buildings, residential, industrial plants. There's not a lot we won't do.

The overall goal for Celara is to deliver solar electrical systems throughout the Midwest region for residential, commercial, and industrial customers. There's all sorts of lofty reasons and rhetoric for doing this—lower carbon footprint, help the environment, make the world a better place for you and me. Da da, da da. On and on it goes.

Look. Here's what we really want. We want it all. We want to take advantage of money allocations by local, state, and federal governments to increase our market share in the emerging technology arena. We want those incentives. Where no one else is, we plan to be."

Marti nodded.

"Keep writing," Alex ordered.

Marti refocused.

"So we're looking for an increase in consumer demand. Despite market fluctuations, competition, and government regulations, we want to be out in front. We aim to be first. We want market share. Whatever it takes to get that, we will do."

She took a break to uncramp her fingers. He raised his voice and motioned with his hand for her to continue writing. She picked up her pen.

"What we've always known as a small company is that larger contractors," she flipped to a blank page and positioned her pen again, "are less adaptable to emerging markets because of the costs associated with retraining a large workforce."

He paused to deliver the sound bite. "We turn on a dime at Celara." Marti remembered the copy from the company's website.

"Though we're relatively small, Celara is one of, if not the largest solar power construction, research, and development companies based in the Lake City area. We've been able to diversify and handle most situations. We do energy audits, paperwork, permits, design, engineering, and installation. We help finance some systems. Start to finish, we're holding the customer's hand the entire way. They love us for that. They come back for more. They tell a friend."

Another pause. "Martina."

She looked up. "Marti."

He inclined his head. "Marti, did you know that silicon is the second most abundant element in the Earth's crust?"

Marti shook her head.

"Silica or sand, which is silicon dioxide and silicates, is over 25% by weight. Silicon gets processed into thin film for photovoltaic cells. They're good conductors for electricity. They're gray-black, crystalline. Lustrous. But also brittle and hard.

*Like your eyes.* Marti bit her lip to prevent the thought from voicing itself.

"Celara's manufacturing partner patented cheaper ways to process silicon to maintain conductivity and increase flexibility. That's our ace in the hole.

But additionally, Celara Solar has been able to acquire large jobs in the Lake City area and the surrounding suburbs. Mostly government contracts to retro-convert traditional power plants into solar plants. Those are very big, very important projects. Lots of money. It means our people are always working. We create jobs. We add to the tax base. We strengthen the economy, and lately, even though it's like treading water, we maintain our financial position and hold our own while other businesses are going under."

Marti nodded.

"But we can always do better, right?"

*Agree, Marti.* "Sure."

"Now. What are we looking for these days? We're seeking additional U.S. partnerships in the areas of building materials, manufacturing, systems solutions, distribution, and installation of photovoltaic products. We want innovation. If one ace is good, three of a kind, or hell, six or seven from up our coat sleeve is better. We're always looking to identify new markets for solar construction. Someday, possibly wind construction as well."

He paused. "I need you to help me do that."

Marti nodded, opened her mouth to assent.

"Tomorrow." He cut her off in a flat voice that dared her to have another engagement. Silvery-blue mirrors revealed icy indifference to her personal life.

"Tomorrow." She straightened in her chair. Tried to look alert and competent. "Of course. Starting when?"

"Come in at nine."

Alex got up and strode from the room. He pulled the pulsating electric current away with him. Released from the gravitational pull of Alex's orbit, Marti sagged back in her chair and turned to Evan.

"Did I just get hired?"

"You did. But I would get here at 8:45."

"And the pay rate?"

"Is the same."

Evan shook her hand, smiled, and hurried after Alex. The fading staccato of additional orders echoed down the hallway from her new boss.

Dazed, she gathered her portfolio, her notes, and purse. She bumbled her way back through the cubicle maze to the front entry.

Along the way, she noticed a woman with red hair who glared angry pale green eyes her direction. The woman held a jar of candy in her hand. A young girl, maybe eleven or twelve dug through it.

Marti smiled at the woman. The angry expression didn't change. *Okay.* In the front lobby, she waved goodbye to the receptionist, a cheerful brown-blonde who waved back.

The incandescent sun of a crystal clear day defied the cold wind to turn her sherry-brown eyes to a fiery gold. Newly-employed, Martina Marie Butler threw her shoulders back. She walked to a nearby delicatessen to buy herself a celebratory sandwich. Her peanut butter and crackers breakfast seemed as far away as last week. Thank goodness she had the rest of the day to put her life together and get established in Lake City before she went on Alex's clock.

◆ ◆ ◆ ◆

"Christian, in another year, you'll be free. Do you have a plan for your life?"

"I'm working on it."

"Because I don't want your craziness in my house."

"I can take care of myself."

"The way you took care of yourself before is what got you here."

Chris stared down at his hands.

"I look at you now at thirty-four with those braids in your hair, that hard look on your face, and those tattoos. You look exactly like what you've become."

"Your son?"

Chris's father tightened an already tight jaw that jutted forward to form a distinctive square. If the thick glass partition didn't separate them, Chris was sure Reverend March Butler would forget his religion and swing on him.

"Don't worry Reverend March, you'll get your chance to show the world you're king of all you survey once I'm released." Neither he nor his sister called the good reverend "Father" anymore.

"You used to be a good kid. When you were at camp, you..."

Chris cut him off. "When I was at camp, the leaders tried to..." He took a breath. "They... they didn't do right by the kids there. Almost all of us."

His father frowned.

"They came after me too."

Reverend March stared at his son with eyes of bitter chocolate, for once, at a loss for words. No biblical scriptures. No homilies. No lecture. Just a blank stare.

"I fought them off me. You remember that summer I got sent home early for fighting?"

His father nodded. "You were thirteen."

"That's why."

"You never said a word. Not to me, not to your sister. She would have told me."

"The camp leader was a friend of yours... Mr. Thompson."

"Roger Thompson?"

"He said you would never believe me and that the people in my neighborhood would call me a sissy boy. They would call me gay if I said anything. We all kept quiet."

Reverend March seemed stunned. He tried but failed to remember the events of that long-ago summer.

"Do you believe me?"

His father shook himself. "Christian... I don't know what to say."

"It's all true, Reverend. Before God and all the angels, it's true."

At this, his father grimaced and paused. He formed his next words with care. He looked down at the table. Chris recognized this display as his father's particular type of fury. In that case, then the good reverend did understand. He did care about his son. Chris waited.

"Christian... your step-mother and I did our best to protect you and to raise you and your sister. We taught you about the world and how to live in it."

Reverend March paused.

"I never thought I'd see the day... when a son of mine... my own son that I raised under God's watchful eye... would..."

Another pause. Chris waited, barely breathing.

"...bear false witness against another man of God."

Chris recoiled from the glass partition in shock.

"*Deacon* Roger Thompson has been my friend for longer than you've been alive, boy. Don't you ever... EVER... you hear me?"

Reverend March's jaw tightened close to the breaking point. He shook his head slowly back and forth. In response, Chris hardened his own features to the prison-style façade he acquired for survival. Vulnerability got you killed behind bars.

Chris sat frozen to the metal folding chair. His father put down the phone receiver then walked towards the guard who let him out. Vulnerability did not work with Reverend March either. The guard on Chris's side of the glass took the phone receiver from his hand, hung it up, and escorted him back to lock-up.

❖ ❖ ❖ ❖

At the public library, Marti sat at a computer. She glanced through her emails. She sent a thank you note to Alex, copied to Evan. Then she scanned some online ads.

Two hours later, she met Augie at a coffee shop who agreed to rent her his couch for two weeks.

At the condo, Augie glanced down her torso, "Or longer." He pretended to fiddle with his watch.

"So, what do you do, Augie?"

"I'm a project manager for Lakeside Power Plant. I want to be my own boss, though, you know? I'm working out a business plan but my cash flow's not where it needs to be."

"I see. So..."

"So among this, that, and the other..."

"The other?"

"I rent space in my place on the low. Gotta do what you gotta do."

"As do we all."

"What about you?"

"Oh. Right. So here's first month's." Marti handed him an envelope. "It's cash."

"Like I said, somebody's already got the extra bedroom upstairs. Otherwise, I'd give it to you."

"No problem."

Augie swept his arm in grand hotelier style. "That's your half bath. That's your couch." He tugged at a wooden screen. "You can pull this around when you want to sleep or get dressed. No one will bother you. I have rules about that."

He took a few steps away then turned. "Unless you want them to." He laughed and answered his ringing phone. Marti took that opportunity to reflect on her misgivings.

"Nope. Sorry. It's already taken," her new landlord said to the caller. That ended her moment of reflection.

She left Augie's condo, walked around the North Central neighborhood and noted some changes for the better. Some for the worse. She ran errands and bought a few groceries. She knew this neighborhood. She visited the Lake City History Museum on a junior high school field trip. And here it still stood.

She wandered into the museum and breathed in its quiet, dusty atmosphere. Behind the front desk, a middle-aged woman concentrated on a stack of papers. Her blonde hair blended into snowy-white waves down to her shoulders. That's how Marti recognized her.

"Beryl... Allen?"

"Close. It's Beryl Aland. Who's that?" Beryl took off her reading glasses and refocused her eyes.

"Marti. Marti Butler. You and my mother used to be friends."

Beryl smile looked a little uncertain.

"You remember Christina Butler? We used to see you once in a while in the Central District, but then, I guess, we lost touch. I came to the museum when I was in junior high, though."

"I remember. Marti!" Beryl hugged her. "You're so grown up now I didn't recognize you. Your hair is so long..."

Marti quickly got Beryl caught up on her life.

"These days, finding a job deserves extra congratulations. Where are you working?"

"Celara Solar Construction."

"Celara?"

"Yes, you know the company?"

"In a manner of speaking." Beryl bumped the edges of her paper stack against the desktop. "We keep track of the local business community and so we do have files on Celara. You know, newspaper articles, press releases, reports, things like that. Celara's pretty important in green energy these days."

Marti laughed as she told Beryl about her job interview with Alex.

"Sounds like you're in for a fascinating experience."

"He's fascinating alright."

Marti caught the briefest flicker in Beryl's hazel eyes. Then Beryl smiled. Once again, the older woman neatened the stack of business literature and ephemera.

"You know that I knew both your father and mother growing up?"

"Yes, my mother told me." Somehow, the mention of her father made the room a little dimmer.

"We all lived in Central District, but we didn't attend the same school. You know how it was back then."

"I know." *Segregated.*

"We used to see each other around because her mother, who would be your grandmother, worked with our family for a time."

Marti smiled at Beryl's polite choice of "with" instead of "for."

Beryl continued. "And your father? Reverend March Butler?"

"He's still on the Internet. Lake City's first Internet evangelist. E-vangelist."

"Oh, that he is. That he is." Beryl smiled. "I remember he used to have coal black hair, but its gone salt and pepper now." She gestured toward her own hair. "And so have we all changed. Still very handsome, your father."

Beryl paused. Looked at Marti out of the corner of her eye. "He was always very fascinating too. He's a pillar of the Lake City community these days. But you already know that."

Marti had no reply for her.

"Be careful on your job, Marti. Very careful."

Marti couldn't read Beryl's expression. "As long as the focus is on work, I'm sure I can handle it."

Beryl nodded. Marti could see it was more to move the conversation along than in actual agreement. "Well, maybe they'll feel the same way you feel about it."

Marti felt prickles under her arms. But that didn't matter. She was employed!

◆ ◆ ◆ ◆

Back in the conference room at Celara, Alex sat with the private investigator and the psychologist he attended college with so many years ago. Opposite the three men, sat Harlan,

Celara's main counsel that Alex's father hired direct from law school about the same time Alex became active in the family business.

"Dutiful," the psychologist concluded after they watched Marti's interview recorded with a discreetly placed digital camera.

"Her advantage is perseverance and effort. She'll do just about anything she's decided to do or feels obligated to do. She keys off logic and reason. In other words, if you give her a satisfactory reason to do something, she won't stop until it's done or until you give her new instructions. She'll be competent and effective. Reliable. She's driven. That's a strong trait that will work to your advantage if you can direct her. If you can't..."

"I can."

"She has a lot of potential. She'll likely achieve any goal she sets for herself or one that you set for her."

"What else?"

The psychologist rifled Marti's paperwork. "She has sharp organizational skills and a high degree of focus and concentration. She prefers order, peace, security, and structure. She's consistent and persistent. In other words, she'd be an excellent choice for the management or executive layer."

"Mmm. Well, right now, she's research."

"You hired a winner."

"Better than a whiner. I already have enough of those on board."

The private investigator lifted Marti's fingerprints and a DNA sample from her water glass. He already knew her phone number so that part of things would be a piece of cake.

Near the break room, Evan scanned Marti's handwriting. He emailed the file to a graphologist.

Harlan drew up papers for Alexander King's newest acquisition to sign.

◆ ◆ ◆ ◆

# 4 The Job

From Augie's landline, she called Reverend March Butler, Lake City's First E-vangelist, according to his website.

"Think you'll keep this one?"

"What?"

"You can't live with me, Martina." Her father refused to call her Marti.

"I already have my own place." *On Augie's couch.* "I haven't lived with you in twenty years, why would I want to now?"

"I'm just letting you know."

"As am I."

"Martina, this back-and-forth has got to stop. Christina was my wife and your and Christian's mother. I loved her. But she was unwell. You know this."

"If she'd gotten the help she needed, the love she needed, she wouldn't have…"

"You don't understand, Martina."

"I was there."

"You were a child, Martina. Yes, you were." He cut her off. "Christina gave up on herself, you, and Christian. And me. That's the only reason why I left our marriage in the first place. She didn't want to try anymore."

"I have to get going."

"Martina, look. You know you're welcome to come over for dinner anytime. It's important that you take care of yourself and eat balanced meals."

Marti held the phone away from her ear and shook it. *Are you kidding me?* Surely he meant to say, "But don't spend the night."

"Yes, I know." She really meant to say, "But don't hold your breath."

◆ ◆ ◆ ◆

Marti arrived to her office space at 8:45 a.m. She waited for a summons from Alex. Evan took off for a week in the Rockies. She fiddled with the copies of Celara's annual reports for the last five years that she made at the museum.

Her mind drifted to Christina's backbreaking work on second shift at the paper factory. Her mother stood on her feet and ran a machine all night. In the morning, she stood on her feet at the restaurant. Between shifts, she was always exhausted. Or asleep. Or tired. Or unhappy. Or drunk. Or smoking. Or depressed. At Marti's age, Christina had two children and an ex-husband—the Reverend March. Martina made it her life's goal to avoid her mother's destiny at all costs.

◆ ◆ ◆ ◆

Alex walked into her cubicle with a large box. He set it on her desk with a loud *thunk* and greeted her with a wicked, tooth-filled grin. "I need you to read through all this material so you can get a fuller background on what I told you yesterday. You have to understand everything here in order to write up what I need. We've got a lot to prepare for the May convention."

Marti nodded.

Alex pulled out folders, books, pamphlets, reports, softback publications, and ephemera. He tossed various computer disks one by one onto the pile in front of her.

"Okay, get started. Take a lunch. Half hour or an hour. That's up to you. I need eight hours every day though. Do you know where the break room is?"

"I can find it," Marti said quickly.

"Come on."

Alex wheeled around and stalked from the cubicle. He didn't bother to see whether she followed in his wake. Of course she followed. Wherever Alex led, she would follow. That was her job now. That's what he would pay her to do.

Alex pointed out various attractions along the way. "Bathroom. Copier, printer, and scanner. Another bathroom. Warehouse. Kitchen."

Marti ran into the break room to catch up to Alex. She nearly bumped into him when he wheeled around again to face her.

"There's everything you need. Lunch in the refrigerator there. Microwave. Dishwasher. Okay?"

Marti nodded, still out-of-breath.

"Okay, you've got everything. I have a meeting so I'll see you later."

With that, Alex stalked from the kitchen at his usual fast pace. Marti helped herself to a donut. She walked back to her desk to get her lunch to put in the refrigerator. This time, a heavy-set man in overalls, maybe from the warehouse, stood in the middle of the room. He drank a cup of coffee. Marti smiled at him. His large jowls remained still and unmoving. Marti put her lunch in the refrigerator in silence. She turned around. The man stared back at her.

"Hi, I'm Marti." She stuck out her hand.

He continued to drink out of his cup.

She let her hand drop. Cleared her throat. "Well, I'll see you around." She walked out of the kitchen. Maybe he didn't speak English. Or maybe he just couldn't stand the way she looked.

"Hi." She spoke to the receptionist in the front entry. "Leslie, right?"

"I am. And you're Marti, aren't you? I handled some of your paperwork." Leslie tended to slur her words. Marti wondered if she had a speech impediment.

"And I thank you." Marti inclined her head. "So I'm settling in."

"Finding everything?"

"The essentials. Kitchen. Bathroom. Fax machine."

"The exit." Leslie giggled.

Marti raised her eyebrows. "The exit?"

"Ah... just kidding, Marti."

Marti swept her arm around. "So what's the story on this place? I mean, solar construction is such a new world. It seems... almost mystical when people talk about it. Does it seem that way to you?"

"Well, in a way, I guess. A lot of people know Celara's work. There's a lot of history here."

"I know a little from what I've read and from what Alex told me. It's so fantastic to think about. I mean, nearly every culture on Earth's worshipped the sun as a god. And it takes a genius to harness the energy of a god."

Leslie raised her eyebrows. "Um. *Yeah.* Well, I will say this. Though Alex is somewhat considered godlike around here by some, he's only one of many geniuses we have on staff at Celara."

"Really?"

"All very true."

"Okay. Let me ask you this." Marti described the sour-faced man from the break room.

"That's Ronny, Marti." Leslie bumped a stack of papers on her desk. "Don't be mistaken by the way he looks or acts. I'm telling you just about everyone here could cut glass with the edge of their intelligence."

"Good to know."

"Good to remember. That's rare air you're breathing."

"Really?"

"I'm serious." Someone walked up to ask Leslie a question. Marti went back to her desk to flip back and forth through discussions of traditional construction.

She ran into Leslie again in the bathroom.

"Look, Marti. I'll tell you what you'll soon see for yourself anyway." Leslie did a quick check of the bathroom stalls. Marti bent to help her look for feet under the doors.

Leslie relaxed and brushed out her hair. "Men usually fill the project manager, estimator, and engineer positions. The women on staff, like me, support the men—accounting, marketing, administrative." She cleaned her brush thoughtfully. "The men look down on that."

"Why?"

"Because they think its women's work and they don't respect women or their work." Leslie got out a lipstick.

Marti flicked at invisible lint on her shirt. "You speak from experience?"

"I'm saying, keep your eyes open."

"But what if a woman wanted to be a project manager?"

"A woman is project manager."

"Here?"

"A.J. You'll meet her."

"How's she doing?"

Leslie shook her head and blew out a breath. "A.J. told me they say things like 'bitchy, castrating,' and 'lesbian' out loud whenever she's near. Not *to* her, mind you. *Near* her."

"That's pretty horrible."

"You have to make up your mind about it, you know? The only way to move up to the top construction positions is through the managers. They're all men."

"So how did she do it?"

Leslie looked at her sideways. "Not how some people like to think. Management knew her father. Worked with him on a few jobs. They knew he trained her well. But even so, she had to deal with a lot of teasing. Intimidation. Negative attitudes. It can be kind of low down. I mean hard to prove. Not that she'd try. She knows better. Basically, she puts up with discrimination and harassment every day."

"I wonder how she does it."

"I wonder how you'll do it."

"Me? What about you?"

"I'm in the secretarial pool. I'm where I belong."

"Leslie..."

"Look, I'm just saying this so you won't be taken by surprise. Don't mind me. For all I know, you'll find your own way and it'll be fine."

"No. I mean, thanks for the heads up. I know I'm not the ultimate in research, but I'm certainly competent and I'm a professional."

Leslie's head listed to one side. "So that should work out just fine, you think?"

"I'm here for quality control on Alex's visions. That's it. I push them forward with logic. Present them in a comprehensible manner."

"Piece of cake." Leslie snapped her fingers and laughed. "Okay, look. I'll just finish by saying 'good luck.' And then that's all."

Marti washed her hands. "I need to get back to it before they notice I'm gone."

"Me too."

Marti opened the bathroom door. "Thanks, Les."

"Anytime." Out of the corner of her eye, Marti saw Leslie's reflection. Celara's receptionist shook two pills into her palm and gulped them down.

◆ ◆ ◆ ◆

Marti typed up her first report for Alex:

> "For green construction, most contractors would do well to consider whether the architect and designer have documented expertise. The contractor should do additional research on suppliers and their materials. Consider the training and experience of staff and subcontractors. Plan for emergencies and delays. Be aware of insurance policies that will cover on-site events. Know green standards and codes. Communicate clearly with lawyers, insurance agents, designers, and clients. Realize that almost all litigation stems from design, construction methods, codes and standards, materials, and job-site accidents. Full project commissioning is required for green construction and operations. With high insurance costs and standards, contractors take ultimate responsibility for project results."

Her mind wandered back to last night's conversation with her father.

He did not watch television talk shows or read self-help books. No one ever explained to Reverend March that victims of domination and intimidation lost a belief in the worthiness of their feelings or perceptions. Or if someone did explain it to him, it didn't "take."

So, for the most part, only two things resulted from such discussions with his daughter. He was right. She was wrong. The conclusion of their conversation the previous evening proved no different.

"Martina, you have to take better care of yourself. You know your mother was extremely irresponsible about her life."

"Well, she was there when you weren't."

"I was always there, Martina. You could have lived with me before things went bad. And let me tell you this. You're going to have a tough way to go in life with that hard edge."

"I'm not a hard edge."

"And defensiveness."

"I'm not defensive!"

Reverend March chuckled.

"Remember your twelfth birthday? Remember that boyfriend you nearly had? Do you actually plan to be single all your life?"

"Why are you bringing up all that old stuff? Nobody cares about that anymore."

"My advice to you... my fatherly advice... is to own up to your mistakes."

"I'm more than the mistakes I made, *Reverend*."

"No. You *are* the mistakes you made, Martina. We all are. And so was Christina."

"You always bring her up. Why do you do that when she's been gone for years?"

"If you did more listening and less talking, you'd realize that I'm trying to help you avoid ending up like her."

Marti slammed the phone down. She covered her face with her hands. It took an hour for the trembles to stop.

❖ ❖ ❖ ❖

After she finished the report, Marti read her copy several times. She closed her eyes, held her breath, and clicked "send" to email six pages to Alex. "Marti to see Alex," echoed over the intercom system,

When she passed Celara staff housed in the cubicle maze, she caught furtive glances thrown her way as though they thought she were about to be devoured alive by a wild animal. Was she?

The wild animal looked up from his desk. "Print all this information right now. Make copies of these extra documents," he tossed them toward her, "by four o'clock. Bind fifteen copies with a cover. Stack it for me. Have a presentation prepared on all that you've done thus far. I need you to tell the group what you've been doing."

"Doing?"

"Tell them about your research."

"About the research?" she repeated slowly.

Alex looked at her as though he wanted to slap her.

Marti drew back. Tried again. "What time is the meeting?"

Alex got up and moved around the office as though restless or as though he were tired of her and wanted her to leave.

"Eight."

"Here?"

"No."

"Where?"

Alex rewarded her with another look. This time Marti held her ground. *No address, no Marti at the meeting.* He bared white teeth into a smile, reached into a desk drawer and handed her a card.

"You can find a map online."

Alex sat down and moved papers around his desk. Ignored her. It took a moment for her to realize the conversation was over.

◆ ◆ ◆ ◆

"Hi, are you doing that for my dad?"

Marti turned to see a young girl with dark hair and bright blue eyes. She had to be Alex's daughter. The girl moved closer to watch Marti's tentative efforts at the bindery machine.

*Yes, Virginia, I am an idiot.*

"I'm Lexa. My dad told me to find something to do because he's busy."

Marti tried to hide her smile. *That's our Alex.*

"Well, I'm making these little books for your father for a meeting." She arranged the pages and pulled the handle. Then she pulled it again. And again.

"How's it going?"

"Uhm." Marti removed the mangled stack of paper. "It's going."

"Can I help? I don't have anything else to do."

"Sure. Just pick up each of those papers in order and make a stack. Then I'll put the binder ring on. Okay?"

"Okay. Like this?" Lexa held up a stack of paper

"Exactly."

Marti turned back around to figure out the binder ring.

"So like I told my dad, my ballet class is doing a recital soon."

"You take ballet?"

That was all Lexa needed. For the next twenty minutes, she discussed her classes, ballet positions she liked and didn't like, and who was the class princess and teacher's pet (not Lexa).

Marti told Lexa about biking and strength training at her gym and how she used to play tennis in high school until she inured her knee.

"Like Venus and Serena?"

"Not quite that good. But I always enjoyed the game. Still, that's why it's important to have more than one interest, you know? Just in case something doesn't work out." *Like teaching.* "Now, I'm a biker."

"Do you have any candy?" Lexa asked hopefully. She quickly added, "I know I'm diabetic, but I can have a little."

"Candy?"

"Yeah, Kate's not here today. She locks hers up when she's not here." Marti remembered the red-haired woman who gave her the dirty look yesterday.

"But Lexa, if you're diabetic then you probably shouldn't be eating candy, right? There's still some fruit in the break room from this morning."

Lexa scowled and made an exasperated sound.

"What did your doctor say? You've seen a doctor, right?"

"He put me on a diet, but I'm not fat."

"No, you're not fat, but you should still listen to your doctor."

Lexa eyed her as if to decide from which direction to launch another go to get what she wanted. Marti gave her the same look she gave her students that mistook final examinations for group study sessions.

"Well, anyway, my dad doesn't mind."

With the impeccable timing of a German clock, Alex strolled by. All conversation ceased. Marti felt two hot lasers hit the dead center of her back. She pulled the lever to bind another report. Thankfully, the machine gave her a break and bound the report. However, Lexa fumbled a stack of papers. The papers dropped to the floor.

Alex walked away without a word. Marti felt bad for his daughter.

Lexa got her apple from the break room, then wandered off somewhere else in the office. At 4:05, Marti again felt two small holes burn between her shoulder blades.

"You almost finished?"

"Umm. It's getting there."

"No. You've still got a ways to go. Look, I'm going to take my daughter to her mother's. She has to get ready for school. So, bring those to the meeting tomorrow. That means you need to be there on time."

Marti felt her face burn from what sounded like a reprimand for her late arrival yesterday.

"I'll be there," she promised.

It took her until 8:30 in the evening to finish the binding. Unbelievable. Christina used to run an industrial-sized printing press and several bindery machines all by herself. Her mother glued, stapled, folded, hole-punched, and whatever else the factory could think to do to paper. Sometimes overtime.

Marti wrote up the presentation. She arrived to Augie's couch at ten o'clock. She shoved a fistful of food into her face, sponged off, laid her clothes out, then closed her eyes at eleven.

◆ ◆ ◆ ◆

Up at five o'clock. Dressed by six o'clock. Downtown by 6:45. No time to take public transportation on the last leg to the far west suburbs. She called a taxi.

Marti arrived eight minutes before the meeting's eight o'clock start time, her long twists raked back into a bun. Fifteen minutes ahead of Alex's grand entrance.

She got through the meeting largely unscathed due to the fact that Alex did most of the talking. She made the motions. Smiled. Shook hands. Nodded and chuckled at jokes. Answered the occasional question.

Celara's silver-haired chief operating officer ribbed her, "Too bad for you Marti, you have to work with Alex. How's it going, by the way?"

She felt Alex's quick glance her direction. "Like gumdrops and rainbows everyday, Kenneth," she smiled.

"Yeah right," Kenneth snorted.

She laughed too. Felt Alex's gaze linger on her. He looked away. Shook hands around the table. She gathered up materials. She wondered if she would do public transportation back to their office. That would take several hours. She didn't know whether to ask Alex for a ride. But then, that didn't matter. By the time she turned back with an armful of paper, he disappeared. She could hear his voice. It echoed down the hallway with a few of the other executives on their way to a power lunch.

She caught a ride with one of the secretaries as far as downtown. She used the opportunity to learn a little bit more about her new boss. Rich. Divorced. Ruthless. Easily bored except when focused on the bottom line. No surprises there.

She pulled her lunch out of her satchel and ate it on the steps of the art museum in the warmth of the midday sun. Then she squared her shoulders and finished the last two legs of her journey to the northern suburbs to for the afternoon shift.

◆ ◆ ◆ ◆

Days passed. One by one, the few females on staff found her either in the bathroom or in the break room for quick snatches of conversation.

"Well, I'll just say, look out for Alex. He has a temper worse than his father's."

"Seriously?"

"Oh yes," Leslie nodded. Her voice drawled and while Marti liked Leslie and truly wanted to believe she was a Southern transplant, she sensed the receptionist's happy pills induced the easy like Sunday morning demeanor.

"I'll keep it in mind. Hopefully, I won't give him a reason."

"Honey, he doesn't need a reason." Leslie smiled, finished with her lipstick and left. Helena, one of the administrative assistants, walked in and spoke to Marti from a stall. Marti fiddled around at the counter. She pretended to straighten her clothes to keep the conversation going.

"Oh, you and Alex were out of the office one day last week. How are things going?"

"Well, it was my first meeting, so everything was new. All the people and the conversation."

"Strange things happen when you go out on the town with Alex."

"Well, I don't know about that. I mean, I've never been out on the town with him. Just that business meeting."

"Well, just so you know, it does get unusual."

"Unusual?"

Helena didn't elaborate further.

"I'll take your word for it." Marti made that her exit line. She remembered Helena almost always brought her lunch to the office in a bag from a popular lingerie store.

Marti continued her rounds around Celara's offices. She interviewed project managers about their philosophies on the direction of solar construction, in general, and Celara, in particular. Two weeks passed before she met A.J., Alice Janson, a project manager for the solar division who'd been with Celara for almost three years.

"I realize you're busy out in the field, A.J., so I'm going to get right to it. You already know what it's about, right?"

A.J. wore her brown hair in a no-nonsense short, chic style. On the tall side, she dressed in the basic business casual uniform of most project managers—a button-down shirt and khaki pants.

"You need information on what we're doing so Alex can make plans to expand Celara."

"Exactly. I hope to start with some information about your background."

A.J. leaned back. "As some of the guys might have already told you..." She paused. Marti waited. "I didn't go through traditional construction training and apprenticeship. My father worked construction and trained me at his side. I got vo-tech training and certification at Rose Creek University."

"I went to Rose Creek too. When'd you finish?"

"God. Twenty-one years ago. Which tells you my age, doesn't it?"

"Don't worry, I'm two years right behind you."

"I told Alex when he asked me that I didn't remember seeing you around campus."

"I was an English major."

"No wonder," A.J. laughed. "Still, RC's a great school with a high-quality liberal arts program. I let him know that too."

"Thanks." Marti moved in to catch A.J. off-guard. "I wanted to ask you about the status of women in traditional construction versus solar."

The project manager's smile disappeared. A.J. waved at her to stop the tape. Marti clicked it off then set it down so A.J. could see it wasn't recording.

"Green construction, particularly solar, is still a growth industry, a new technology. Everyone is still learning, both men and women. That's what makes it easier for women to compete on a relatively level playing field because there isn't an entrenched gender ownership of renewable energy. That means there's a window for women to develop themselves as experts in the field if that's what they want to do."

"How about here at Celara? I know Celara covers a lot of ground."

A.J. leaned in. Lowered her voice. Marti leaned forward in response.

"I would say there is some resentment by a few, not all, the project managers who came up the traditional way. They consider anyone who didn't follow the same path an outsider and an upstart, especially if she's female. And you do feel the unfriendly vibe. Other guys are lot more secure. They think it's great that I'm here. Usually the younger ones are okay. Even though they don't completely understand the project details, they do understand that any and all new projects bring financial security to Celara as a whole and get the word out that we're doing great work here. A rising tide lifts all boats, you know. The bigger picture is to always take care of the mother ship."

"So you're bringing in more business than Celara would have otherwise?"

A.J. smiled. "I don't brag on it, mind you. But yes I do. I design and install solar thermal as well as photovoltaic systems. As a matter of fact, solar thermal is more efficient, even though photovoltaic gets more press and more government funding. But whatever. We provide the client with what the client wants."

Marti nodded encouragement.

A.J. hesitated, "Sometimes that causes a little consternation. I happen to answer to the Vice-President. Do you know Nate?"

"No, I haven't met him yet."

"Well, I've been with Celara for almost three years. In order to get the idea across that we need to provide equal importance to solar thermal, I've had to prove the energy efficiency with systems I've installed with statistics, hard data, and customer satisfaction surveys. Nate absorbs those ideas and the usage data. Then he presents the results as his own." She looked square at Marti. "And I let him."

Marti raised her eyebrows.

A.J. shrugged. "I'm no pushover, Marti. But I know how to play my position." She shrugged again. "It's so easy to crash and burn here without knowing how to work the system."

"But I guess that's anywhere in Lake City."

"Lake City... Celara... it's all the same."

◆ ◆ ◆ ◆

Kate cornered Marti later that same afternoon when Marti passed Kate's desk.

"So are you here to stay?"

"I'm not sure. As far as I know, I'm here for this project only."

"Why are you really here?"

"I'm... here for the project."

"Well, why don't you apply for a permanent position? I'm surprised the firm hasn't asked you."

"I guess that's up to them. I'm not going to solicit."

"But what are you really here to do?"

Marti waited a beat. "Kate, I just told you. I'm here to research and write on Celara's solar construction activities. Other duties as assigned."

Kate stepped closer to her. Invaded her space.

"Other duties as assigned?"

Another person—nice, easy, friendly—might have taken a step back. But Marti knew this routine. You didn't grow up in Lake City's Central District without learning how to "maintain." Marti smiled, but squared her shoulders.

"Right."

"So they haven't said anything else? Evan didn't say anything to me."

"Anything like what?"

Kate searched Marti's eyes. Marti decided if Kate put hands on her, then damn the new job. She would not be handled by anyone, even if that person wore two-inch, salon-fresh, blood-red nails. Kate's pale green eyes didn't find whatever it was they looked for in Marti's expression. Kate returned Marti's smile, then pulled back.

Marti's shoulders relaxed. She was truly puzzled by what she didn't understand. That seemed just fine to Kate.

"Well, everyone's got their place around here."

"I suppose," Marti replied.

"I work very closely with Evan running the office."

Marti nodded. "Right. You're Evan's executive assistant."

"More than that, really."

Oh. So Kate wanted to mark her territory. *What the hell ever.*

"I realize I'm a guest here," she decided to go along to get along since she truly didn't give a shit. "I follow the rules."

That pleased Kate even more. "Some of the new girls just don't get it. Alex is well off and they get ideas about him."

"Really?" Marti allowed innocent eyes to go wide. "What kinds of ideas?"

"...Which is a mistake. He has a girlfriend anyway. Evan and Alex always rely on me to hold things together and if anyone interferes with the process, things fall apart. And if things fall apart, heads roll. I could tell you stories."

"I can imagine. But I'm not on staff here, you know. I'm here to do an in and out. I'm on contract. I get the job. I do the job. I finish the job. Then I leave."

"Research, right?"

Were they *still* going in circles?

"And writing." She smiled, "Other duties..."

"...As assigned. Hmm. I pretty much know everything that goes on in the office, Marti. So if you ever need anything or if anything confuses you, just let me know."

"I'll do that." *Like hell.*

Kate's claws, both physical and metaphorical, retracted slightly, but not all the way. "I've never seen an outfit like that. Where did you get it?"

"From a thrift store near where I live."

"Oh." Kate's eyes swept downward and up again. "Hmm." She smiled again. "So are you living in the city?"

"Yes, I'm renting a tiny little place." Marti decided it wasn't Kate's business that the tiny little place was Augie's couch and half bath.

"Well that's good." Kate laughed. She tossed red hair around, totally at ease now that they cleared the air. "I just try to look out for everyone around here."

*Yeah. Okay.*

"It's just a maternal instinct I have. Even Alex's daughter, she's such a sweetheart, just seems to gravitate towards me. We're very close."

"So you're like a mother figure?"

Kate's smile lessened a trifle, "Older sister, I'd say."

"Well doesn't Lexa have diabetes?"

"How do you know that?"

"She told me."

"So?"

"So you shouldn't allow her to eat candy, should you?"

The office cubicles nearby fell silent. Not a computer key clicked. Not a paper rustled. Not a throat cleared.

Marti credited Kate for holding her smile at forty-five percent. Green eyes focused directly on Marti's face. "Like I said, Marti, I look out for *everyone* here. I make sure things don't get confused and heads don't roll."

The cubicles held their collective breath waiting for Marti's response.

"That sounds like a job-and-a-half."

"I do it well."

"Great." Marti had enough of the bitch routine. "Okay then, I've got work waiting. I'll see you."

Marti pulled her mouth back Alex-style. She showed some teeth, turned her back, and walked away. She picked up her writing where she left off.

*Yeah, you started it.*

*But I ended it.*

*Think on that*

*For a minute.*

Love those Central District playground days.

Each of the few women in the office responded to the male-dominated environment in different ways. Whether it was a carefully displayed lingerie bag, clawing of other women into submission, subordinating intelligence, or the classic "keeping one's head down" technique, they did whatever it took to retain some levels of dignity and stability, if not upward-mobility.

Marti would have to figure out her own path. This would be a hard trick to play because she was acutely aware of her independent streak.

◆◆◆◆

April Fool's Day, she sat next to Evan in front of Alex's desk while they discussed the project. Actually, not yet. Alex made them wait while he looked up information on his computer. Small talk be damned. He would speak to his subordinates when he was damn good and ready.

He wasn't ready yet.

Bored, Marti took the opportunity to stare at him. He didn't mind that at all. In fact, he enjoyed female scrutiny. That annoyed *her* so she looked over his shoulder at the pictures on the wall behind him.

Here was Alex skiing downhill. Here was Alex wearing a wetsuit on a boat with friends. Here was Alex mid-handshake with the mayor and the governor. Here was Alex proudly displaying a shotgun in one hand and a murdered animal of some sort in the other. Here was a fluffy puppy playing with a tennis ball.

"Is that a retriever?"

Alex smiled at her. "It is. I used to have three—black, yellow, and chocolate. But Lady, the chocolate, is the only one still alive now. That's an early photo."

Marti forced herself to look away from his smile. She bent closer to the photo. "Oh, she's beautiful. I bet she's friendly."

"She's very friendly."

"Um, just so you know, Marti, Lexa isn't allowed to have candy." Evan wore a sly smirk on his face. "Kate told me that Lexa has been asking you for candy. You shouldn't give it to her."

Marti made a small sound of protest.

"Marti, its fine." He made a calming gesture. "Look, we're just making sure you know. Lexa is a very important person to us. That's all."

Kate and Evan somehow turned it around on her. Alex looked up from his computer with a glare.

"I thought you would take public transportation to the meeting."

"I had trouble making a connection. I wouldn't have got there in time without the taxi."

"Fine. Take care of it, Evan."

"I'm on it." Evan smirked again.

Marti glared back at Alex. *You're welcome.*

With that, Alex began the meeting.

"We need to convince our labor force that it is in their very best interest to adjust their skills for renewable energy. There are still a lot of people out there that have to be dragged kicking and screaming into a new way of thinking. We're working with a lot of stick-in-the-muds. Kind of like when a child grows older and oversteps a father's authority, it's an adjustment."

Marti nodded uncomfortably. *A child grows older and oversteps a father's authority?* The metaphor didn't quite jibe. She kept one side of her mind open to what Alex said about the project. The other reflected on her last conversation with Reverend March. Something just didn't feel right. She didn't know what. Something. *Fool me once...*

Still uneasy, Marti moved her pen as to keep up with Alex. She was here to do a job. Anything else was secondary to that.

◆ ◆ ◆ ◆

Evan's new pastime was to call her "dear" and "sweetie" after she completed any number of inane requests for him. Her stomach turned to hear the words because they implied an intimacy that she would never allow if he were the last man on Earth.

"I am not that fool's damn wife," Marti complained to Teresa on Augie's landline. "And that's not the worst. One day, I overheard him just outside my cubicle talking about a woman who annoyed him. He kept referring to her as a 'cunt' and a 'stupid bitch,' and one of 'the slowest women in the world.'"

"He might have been talking about you."

"He probably was."

"What kind of place are you working?"

"It's construction. I've never seen anything like it. I will say this, after he used that nasty language, the guy he was talking to kind of walked away. I didn't hear any agreement."

"So it's not all of them."

"It's enough of them."

"People like that love to see other people have meltdowns."

"The guy's pathetic. He spends more time acting a fool than getting actual work done. He blames other women in the office for things he forgets to do. I hear him throwing them under the bus all the time. Then he procrastinates on projects he doesn't like. Real lazy about details. He turns in sloppy work at the last minute. It's shocking to see what he gets away with."

"Maybe that's how he tells people that he's angry with them."

"Maybe. One day, I saw him cleaning out some shelves. He tossed a perfectly good briefcase into the trash. I almost said something to him about it. You know I don't like to see anything go to waste."

"I know."

"A few days later, one of the project managers asked him about it because it had important documents inside. He straight-up lied about knowing anything about it. I didn't say anything. But if I hadn't seen him throw it away myself, I would have totally believed him. He's very convincing with the bullshit. Now I know to get third-party verification for anything he tells me."

"Creepy."

"Tell me about it. I almost went home for the day when I saw him using an adding machine with spreadsheet software."

◆ ◆ ◆ ◆

Marti interviewed a few other project managers to learn how their traditional projects related to the solar side. She wanted to gauge their thoughts about the future of the industry.

She got pretty thorough discussions from a few of the men. Others were non-committal. Some, including Ronny, gave her an earful of information she would have to filter for sneering contempt.

One day, A.J. stopped in the break room with a client to get coffee while they discussed the progress of the client's project.

Ronny sat at a table with a man Marti didn't know. Both men smirked at A.J.'s entrance.

"Solar thermal is so gay," Ronny announced to the room.

Marti turned to get her lunch out of the refrigerator. *You're a guest, Marti. Watch and learn.*

Ronny's friend snorted and laughed with him. Marti moved to the microwave. A.J. continued with the coffee and threw a casual, "Oh hi, Ronny. I didn't see you sitting there," over her shoulder.

Marti pressed the buttons to cook her frozen meal.

"Uh oh. Blind spot," Ronny laughed with his friend again. "I guess that's why you're doing a change order." Ronny turned toward his friend in disbelief. "Is it next month already?" They snickered together.

Marti watched her food cook in silence. Even though she didn't work construction per se, she recognized the shot at A.J. for what it was—a question of A.J.'s ability to bring a job in on schedule and under budget.

Ronny told her in his interview that certain people lacked certain skills because certain people didn't put in the hours in certain apprenticeship schools getting certain training and didn't deserve certain positions, but still had those positions because certain other people were stuck on political correctness. It was a "goddamn shame" and it was "bringing down the whole industry."

She sensed A.J.'s dismay and embarrassment at the confrontation in front of her client.

What a shame that Marti set the microwave to nuclear. Her lunch exploded.

"God, that smells." Ronny announced his disgust around a mouthful of greasy barbecue pork sandwich and pickle. "What are you doing?"

He got up for a closer look. "Look at that. You don't have kids, do you?"

"No. Why?"

"Because the first thing you learn with kids is how to microwave a home-cooked meal the right way. My wife does it every night." Ronny enjoyed another good laugh at Marti's expense.

"Gimme that."

Marti took out her destroyed tray of lunch then put it in Ronny's meaty hand. Ronny flipped it into the trash.

"Now gimme that." She handed him the glass tray which he cleaned off. "Here." He handed her the dishcloth. "Rinse that out." She rinsed it.

After giving Marti a sidelong look, A.J. left with her client.

Marti smirked, shrugged, then got tomorrow's microwave dinner out of the freezer. She set the timer correctly under Ronny's mocking supervision.

Just another day at Celara.

❖ ❖ ❖ ❖

That evening she opened a letter from Chris that listed the classes and skills he learned—carpentry and metalwork. He sanitized tales of his life inside the system, she knew. Likely, he knew people on the outside couldn't or wouldn't imagine the truth. Was it always that way with him? She couldn't remember.

Could she have been a better sister to him? Somehow, when she hit the teen years, a gulf widened between her and her younger brother. He went off to do little boy things. She did teen girl things. They didn't have time for each other anymore. Did she listen to him? Did she take him seriously?

Did she really keep her eye on him? Did she pay attention to the things he didn't say?

She stopped smiling.

*Not always. No.*

In fact, she left him as soon as she turned eighteen. The streets took him. When she called her father's house from Rose Creek and asked to speak to her brother, Reverend March told her Chris was locked up in Lake City juvie.

◆ ◆ ◆ ◆

# 5  The Convention

**M**arti came through on relevant data for Alex. He told her that she had until the end of May to tell him about every solar installation project in the city, ongoing or recently finished.

She found last year's solar tour map produced by a community organization. She put a camera, voice recorder, and a notebook into her tote bag. She got on a bike the following weekend, and went to work snapping photos and taking notes.

"Why are you here again?"

"I'm working on a report about solar energy."

"What school do you go to?"

"Well, I attended RC, but this is a special project."

"Like an internship?"

Marti unzipped her hoodie. Removed it. It was hot outside. The building owner's eyes gravitated toward her tank top.

"Something like that. So this is great work. How long did it take to finish the retrofit?"

She spent Sunday evening on the lake shore writing up her reports. Monday morning, she typed them up then delivered them to Alex that afternoon.

"So they just told you all this?"

"Yes."

"Interesting."

She didn't like the look in his eyes. She decided to knock him off-balance.

"Well, no." She took a step closer to where he sat behind his desk. "The interesting part is when I thought I kept seeing the same guy in different places."

She enjoyed a quiet triumph when Alex's eyes dropped back to her report.

"But then I thought to myself, how can that be since I'm on my bike?"

Alex turned a few pages.

"It's not like someone was keeping track of my movements. I mean, what kind of weirdo has time for stupid things like that?"

Alex made a careful note on a page.

"Besides, I could easily lose the guy if I had to—twisting and turning through alleys, parking lots, one-way streets, and on the bike trail. Or I could lead him to an adult bookstore to give him something really interesting to report back to whomever."

Alex stopped writing.

"Or I could take his picture and license plate number, then run over to a cop to file a stalking complaint."

He put the pen down, sat back in his chair, narrowed his eyes at her.

"But why would I do that? My life is not that *interesting*. I probably imagined it."

"Probably." Alex shrugged.

"Actually, I'm sure that I did. So I decided to get the project over with and not worry about it."

"Good job, Marti."

Part of her wanted find a way to make him cry. But she couldn't help the other part of her that swelled with pride at his rare praise.

"I'm assigning you to Celara's booth at the convention center next week. We need the extra help."

"You may not believe it, but I can't wait."

"I believe it. That's why I asked you."

She didn't know what to say to that. He raised his eyebrows with an "anything else?" expression.

She walked back to her desk with a grin.

◆ ◆ ◆ ◆

"Alex and I are best friends."

"Me and Alex have never been apart this long."

"Nobody knows Alex better than me."

Evan bragged early and often to others in the office. Not about Celara. Not about his job assignment and position. Not about his wife. He bragged about Alex. Marti didn't get it. But then, she wasn't paid to get it. She was paid to get it done.

However, the look on Evan's face when he learned about Marti's assignments at the renewable energy convention was priceless. Marti chuckled at the memory as she strode through the main exhibit hall.

She gave Alex her schedule the day before. He returned it to her with the remaining slots filled in with tasks. She had three full days to cover.

She divided the hall into sections then calculated how much time to allot for information pick-up before and after workshops and general sessions.

Early the first day, Marti helped Evan and a few other Celara guys to finish setting up Celara's booth. That took about two hours.

"These days, you have to go green to get green. And that's what we're doing," Evan intoned to the first booth visitor, his face twisted to a sly smile.

On that creepy note, Marti made her rounds through the convention hall at competitor booths, picking up their information to consolidate into reports for Alex. She stopped at peripheral companies that offered new services, non-profits, advocacy groups, and the like.

Towards the end of the day, she ran into Alex. As always, he dressed to impress. His tailored charcoal gray suit fit close to an athletic frame. The snowy-white shirt dramatized his dark hair and brows and enhanced the brilliance of his eyes. The man was entirely too much. He knew it.

"So, Marti," he checked the schedule in her hand, "You should be on your way to the afternoon session, right?"

"Yes. Are you going?"

"Yeah. I decided I wanted to be like you."

"Yeah, okay," she snorted. "Fun times ahead."

He frowned at her. *Oops. A step too far.*

But no. He focused on her long dark hair that fell in a cascade of twists down her back instead of pulled back into the usual bun.

Maybe he didn't want her to wear her hair down? She wore a brown silk suit that nearly matched her skin tone over a darker brown shirt. He was her boss. She mirrored his image in feminine form. Unlike him, however, her suits weren't professionally tailored. They fit snug to her gym-toned body, yes, and she did what she could with a needle and thread. But... well... She did what she could.

She plucked at a few twists that swung forward. His eyes followed the motion. She cleared her throat.

"So, I'm going now." She edged away.

"I'll follow in a bit."

She halted. "Just so you know, Alex. Wherever I walked in the hall, people had good things to say about Celara's leadership position in solar."

"Really, did they?" His tone turned cool.

"Yes. You don't like that?"

Alex assessed her with a look cooler than his tone. What was his problem?

"Would you talk to me if I weren't the CEO?"

She gaped at him. Where the hell did that come from in the conversation? She took a step back, confused. Then she stepped forward again.

"Would you talk to me if I weren't the researcher?"

"I have a girlfriend."

"Are you sure?"

Her hair fanned outward as she whirled around then walked away from him. She made her way to a seat in the afternoon session, wondering what type of emotional abuse he endured in the past. But so what? It didn't give him an excuse to talk to her like a drunken frat boy. Was he drunk? Evan also bragged to the guys in the office about the partying he and Alex did together after work.

Perhaps someone used him for his resources in the past. He guarded against it happening again. She could understand that.

But she was also pretty sure he just called her shallow, or implied it. Granted, he was good-looking. Very obviously, he was well-off and well-maintained. Okay and he displayed a perceptive and intelligent sense of humor and all kinds of other things. But then there was the downside. For instance, this last conversation.

The afternoon session bored her. Or maybe she was distracted. Alex looked her way across the auditorium. She shifted in her seat to focus her attention on the speakers on stage. His eyes touched her profile now and then. He was desperately in need of a firm smack across the face. Too bad she couldn't reach that far to deliver it.

Alex found her again afterward. She decided to take the bull by his horns.

"Look Alex. It's just conversation. Once in a while, an employee will report the events of the day to her employer. So I'm not sure how our conversation went off-track..." *Unless Evan or Kate either said something or implied worse.*

"You know, Marti, instead of going all the way home, you can stay downtown in a hotel. We can set up a room for you. Or you can use mine. I'm not going to use it."

So he was trying to make up for being an ass by offering his hotel room. Great. The gossipers in the office would have a field day with that one.

"I can't. I have to take some things back to the office," she saw the frown before it formed on his face, "and run some errands in my neighborhood," she finished.

"Okay then. I'm going back to the office too. I'm all done here."

"Okay."

He might have offered a lift, but this time she was glad he didn't bother. The ride back through rush hour traffic would have been excruciating. Alex made his drive. Marti took three buses that ate a combined three hours of her life.

It was evening by the time she arrived to Celara. Almost everyone left for the day. He was still there. She snuck quietly past his door, dropped off the material from the exhibit hall then went home, exhausted.

Thankfully, she had her own place now. She smeared a large glob of peanut butter on a roll then gnawed at it without tasting it.

The next morning, Marti took her turn at Celara's booth. She greeted passersby, handed out information, and answered questions. Lexa joined her.

Marti wondered if Lexa spent most of her quality time with her father or *near* her father while he focused on work. Did Lexa and Alex ever talk about anything going on in her life?

For instance, she already knew Alex would spend most of today with the big boys in the executive meetings.

"There's Evan and Kate!" Lexa exclaimed. She waved. Evan and Kate wove between the exhibit booths in the distance. Marti politely waved too. Her favorite co-workers in the world waved back.

"Kate knows a lot of men."

Marti choked on the bottle of water she tilted back for a quick swallow.

"What?"

"Kate knows all the men at Celara."

"Well, of course she does. She works with them."

"I don't mean like that."

"Then like what?

Lexa didn't answer.

"What do you mean?"

Lexa answered that with a shrug.

Marti stared at her. "You... how old are you, Lexa?"

"I'm twelve," she shrugged, "but I'm not dumb though."

"No, of course not," Marti agreed not thinking quite fast enough to redirect the conversation.

"Kate's going to find more guys to come to Celara."

"More..."

"You know," she glanced sidelong at Marti.

"No. I don't know. Lexa, does this conversation have anything to do with the fact that Kate cut off your candy supply?"

"*Never mind.*" Lexa rolled her eyes at Marti's ignorance. She pulled out her cell phone to play a game on it.

Marti felt more stunned by the fact that Lexa knew what Kate did than by Kate actually doing it. That part didn't surprise her at all. In fact, it fully explained her and Kate's bizarre first conversation. The longer Marti thought about it, the more some other puzzling aspects of the office made sense.

Evan and Kate continued their purposeful stroll through the booths. Evan greeted various people, mostly men. He shook hands, and then guided Kate forward.

Kate's "skill," would go a long way to explain the unnatural power and access she enjoyed throughout Celara, particularly for an executive assistant. And if Evan was Kate's handler, then that increased his own power base at Celara, never mind his close proximity to Alex.

Kate pressed close to a man in a business suit. Evan wore a strange, small smile. How many favors did he reel in with his Kate-bait?

Marti shook it off because just then their booth's second shift arrived. She and Lexa took a walk around the exhibit hall. Lexa exclaimed over the pencils, and pens, and keychain giveaways. Thankfully, her chatter moved on to an upcoming dance recital.

They stopped at a booth for Save a Lake.

"Hello ma'am." A tall man with tan skin, hazel eyes, and brownish wavy hair smiled at her. "Do you like our lake?"

"I love our lake," Marti deadpanned.

"How much?"

"Very much."

"This much!" Lexa threw her arms wide. They all laughed.

"Enough to sign this petition preventing corporate energy interests from constructing wind installations in the middle of it?"

"More than that," Marti moved to pick literature from the table, "I love it enough to take whatever information you can give me on the issue so I can give it the proper consideration." She slipped a DVD, newsletter, brochure, and a few white papers into her tote bag. Lexa gathered up pencils and key chains.

The amount of information impressed Marti. "Wow. Someone came prepared today. Did you write all this yourself? I ask only because I'm a writer."

"Well, actually, I stapled the newsletters and folded the brochures. With love, of course."

"Of course," Marti laughed as she scanned a white paper. "But this looks like hardcore research."

"Well, here's the thing. The public increased its demand for renewable energy to reduce greenhouse gas emissions, to protect the economy, and for homeland security."

"Yes."

"We all want to do that."

"Right. We do."

"However, we don't necessarily want two to four hundred windmills with football field-sized blades slicing up migratory birds, interfering with property values and tourism on the edge of every major city that sits on the lake. No one wants that." He waited with expectation.

"I guess." Marti remained conscious that at this convention, she represented Alex's interests, not her own.

"Well, there's also an environmental impact in terms of fishing, water quality during construction, and the condition of the lake bottom to consider."

"That's quite a lot."

"So Save a Lake works to make the public and developers aware of the far-reaching impact of what might look good on paper, but not necessarily in practice."

"Wow," Marti deadpanned.

"Like that, do you?"

"This much!" Marti threw her arms wide and laughed. "Well, I'll read it, of course. But I actually prefer adventure novels. Does a great white shark figure into any of this?"

"Sure. It's a surprise on the very last page."

"I'll just bet."

"What kind of adventure novels do you read?"

"Oh, like H.G. Wells, Jules Verne, C.S. Lewis, and Emily Bronte."

"Emily Bronte's adventure?"

"Sure it is," Marti countered. "Thug-lovin' with Heathcliff."

"Please tell me you're kidding."

"I kid you not."

"Aren't all those authors dead?"

"Well, yes, they are. But I also like Dixon Elliot."

Her new friend looked incredulous. "You like Dixon Elliot?"

"Yeah! Do you read him too?"

"I can't stand that guy."

"What! Why do you say that?"

"Come on now."

"Come on what? You don't even know him." She gave in to the laughter. "What'd he ever do you?"

"Who ever heard of a Black Filipino cave-diver?"

Marti paused. "Well, I can't think of anyone in particular, but I'm sure they exist. I love the cave exploration series."

"Oh yeah, when he goes in the cave and then monsters chase him and then a shadowy military group comes through with guns blazing, the end?"

"So you do read him!" Marti exclaimed.

He shook his head, "Nah," and shrugged.

"Stop it." She couldn't stop laughing. "Just stop."

His hazel eyes flicked over her shoulder. The voice came from behind her. "Hi Marti. Where's Lexa?"

Evan stood too close. Marti refused to take a step back. She glanced around him. *Uh oh.* Lexa disappeared during the book club discussion.

Evan drew her aside.

"We'll have to pick this up later," she told the Save a Lake guy over her shoulder. He nodded.

"Alex is very careful about who he allows into his inner orbit, Marti. He's especially careful about who influences his daughter."

*Like Kate-bait?*

"You have to find her." Evan's voice increased in urgency. "Right now."

"I'll look for her."

"I can hold him off you for a little while, but not for very long." Evan gave her a nudge. She resisted the urge to deck him. Instead she leveled a stare that backed him away from her.

She sighed with relief less than a minute later when she spied Lexa two booths down picking candy out of a dish. She also saw Alex, a few booths the opposite direction talking with Kate. His arm was around the executive assistant's shoulders. Apparently, Alex wasn't as concerned as Evan thought.

"There's your father." She pointed him out to Lexa. "He's looking for you. I've got to get going though." She headed for the exit. "Thanks for your help today, Lexa."

"Bye, Marti!" Lexa had no idea she'd been lost.

Marti went home instead of returning to the office. She was pretty sure Alex wouldn't notice the difference. Not tonight anyway.

◆ ◆ ◆ ◆

Marti admitted three days was probably the limit for big conventions like this. On the last day, Alex didn't bother to show.

Most of the other staff at Celara took care of the day-to-day operations at the office. She was on her own at the booth until A.J. arrived at noon. A familiar voice broke into A.J.'s rundown of the presentation she delivered that morning on the specifics of Celara's past projects.

"Found you."

Marti turned. "Hello, uh..."

"Worth. Guess what, ah..."

"Marti."

"Marti, guess what?"

"I have no idea."

"I heard booth 43 is handing out free sandwiches with every DVD you buy."

"Well, there's not a lot I wouldn't do for a free sandwich."

A.J. broke in, "There's a lot I *would* do for a free sandwich."

"Fool that I am I came empty-handed." Worth snapped his fingers and they laughed at him.

"I gotta run guys. Sorry," Marti shrugged. "I've got my own presentation this afternoon. So, quick and dirty... Worth, this is A.J. A.J., this is Worth with the Save a Lake group. He's really an okay guy. Don't let him scare you."

She left them to it. At the room she went through her list. Alex instructed her to set up the room just right, to mention Celara Solar several times, to pass out marketing literature, to do a door raffle, to build a mailing list, and to have sufficient giveaways that featured Celara's brand.

◆ ◆ ◆ ◆

"We're talking about innovations in the solar and wind industries. We're talking geothermal heat pumps and radiant heating systems. However, it doesn't have to be expensive or exotic. Even simple things such as rain barrels, caulking guns, and insulation can make a difference.

In addition, materials reuse and recycling and home energy audits can bring down the costs associated with green building. In fact, Celara offers all these services."

Marti clicked. "Further, if you look at the next slide, there's an endless list of low-cost steps a homeowner can take including water conservation, insulation, and green landscaping. Let's throw in carpooling just for kicks and giggles."

Her audience groaned.

"All kidding aside," she cleared her throat, "back to real low-cost solutions: Plants, trees, rain gardens, gravel for parking lots instead of asphalt or concrete, and compost bins. It's all doable, reasonable, and pretty much what our parents and grandparents did in the good old days.

But let's not forget job growth. Building retrofits require roofers, insulators, and building inspectors. Mass transit and solar power projects require electricians. Solar power projects require electrical engineers. Both solar and wind power projects require electrical equipment assemblers. In fact, the renewable sector with the greatest need for electrical professionals, as well as helpers, assemblers, and laborers is solar power.

Overall, these projects keep in line with the Buckminster Fuller concept of 'doing more with less.' Those of you familiar with his work know that he was a genius in the areas of visual arts, design, architecture, engineering, mathematics, and sustainability.

So following his example, Celara aims to make its construction designs and installations more useful for people willing to solve the issues of homelessness, poverty, and correct administration of our natural resources. We have the manpower and expertise to handle large-scale projects and multiple small-scale projects."

Marti stepped away from the computer to deliver the close.

"Now. Whether or not you are religious, the first book of the Bible, Genesis, clearly outlines the human purpose on Earth as stewardship of the environment. That's also how we view our purpose at Celara.

One way to accomplish such stewardship is to 'build how nature builds.' In this way, we don't fight natural scientific design. We work with natural design to form efficient, fundamentally sound structures. Buckminster Fuller was ahead of his time, of course. Luckily, the world is finally catching up to his far-reaching vision to reverse and resolve the problems of Planet Earth, particularly those caused by human intervention."

Back at the office, Alex watched Marti's presentation as a live, streaming split-screen broadcast on his computer. She got the camera set-up correct.

He ticked off the number of times she mentioned Celara. Not too much to shill, but just enough to remind people of Celara's past performance. The religious reference did not have his prior approval, but he saw from the camera aimed towards the audience of about forty-five people that the point went home.

The audience applauded. She took questions. He hoped she wouldn't freeze up. Marti had the unfortunate tendency to shut down in front of crowds. He narrowed his eyes at her image on the other side of the computer screen. Earlier, when they discussed her presentation, he calmly reassured her that the only thing she had to fear was failing him.

"Make me proud," he ordered. Apparently, the pep talk worked.

"Alex, can we talk?" Kate walked in, interrupting the first question and its answer.

"What!" Alex looked up with a glare which Kate ignored. She stood beside his chair and gazed down at the computer screen.

"Well." She raised her brows. "Sorry to interrupt the show. Your little geisha girl's certainly putting on the charm."

"I'd be a fool not to take advantage of her intelligence. And I'm certainly no fool."

"Certainly not."

"What do you want, Kate?"

◆ ◆ ◆ ◆

"Fix these images, they're crooked," Alex told her. "They need to be right for the June conference."

"Will do," Marti answered.

It didn't take long for her to discover she needed graphic software to skew the images to the correct orientation.

"The only way to get this software is through me. And I'll tell you right now, only me and Alex have access to this software. It's expensive." Evan turned back to his computer.

Marti persuaded someone from IT to give her a disk of the older version of the software. The older version didn't have the function that skewed images to the correct orientation.

The next day, she overheard Evan offer the graphic software, the latest version, to another person in the office.

"Sure, buddy. I'll copy it for you and bring a disk right on over."

Marti felt the start of a pounding headache. She decided to take her lunch break early.

Later that afternoon, she explained to Alex why the images still tilted off-center.

"I'll take care of it," he said.

"Alex, on a different note, I had a question about something I noticed since I've been here."

"What!" he barked. "I don't understand you when you talk around in circles like that."

Marti sucked in her breath. Almost turned to leave. Instead, she stood in place.

"Why do you allow your staff to treat A.J. second-class in front of her clients?"

"Why do I allow..."

"What about loyalty and trust?"

"Wait a minute! What?"

"Isn't everyone at Celara on the same team? One big family working together for a common purpose. Right?"

"Right."

"How many female home and business owners do you lose when your staff acts and talks like pigs towards women? How many of their husbands pass you by because someone with a Celara business card disrespected their wife, or mother, or sister? How much money do you think you lose?"

"Did A.J. put you up to this?"

"Nobody put me up to anything. I don't carry water. I saw the whole thing in the break room myself and it made me sick to my stomach. How do you think your female clients would feel if they could have seen one of the male project managers deliberately humiliate and embarrass one of the female project managers in front of them? We have that conference coming up. I think we need to move to the front position in all arenas, not just some. Really think about the market share that goes to a Celara competitor when one of our own acts like a jerk, Alex."

"Okay. I believe I know what you're referring to. By the way, you do know how to use the microwave correctly now, right?"

"Funny."

"Look, a lot of these older guys are my father's hires. They have families. They go way back." He leaned back in his chair, challenging her with his eyes. "There is loyalty, whether or not you understand that."

"I just asked you the same thing."

"And I heard you. Anything else?"

Marti didn't know what to say to that, so she said nothing. Alex turned back to his computer.

◆ ◆ ◆ ◆

"How're the girls?"

"You'd know if you let me bring them."

"No, Terry. I keep telling you no. Not like this."

"They miss you."

"How can they? They barely remember me."

"Exactly my point."

Chris sighed at the same old song and dance he and Teresa went through every other visit. He looked away a moment from dark brown eyes that snapped and sparkled under glossy brown-black hair. Tried to think of something new to say.

"You know, Marti seemed invincible to me growing up."

Teresa blinked. Chris rarely spoke about his family.

"Marti was always different, Chris. I saw that myself. She's doing good in Lake City."

"Doing good, hunh?"

"Yeah. She got a job and a little place. She's doing all right."

"Seems that way, doesn't it?"

Teresa cocked her head. "Well, yeah."

"Marti doesn't like to ask for help when she needs it. In fact, she hates to do that even when she should."

"She always seems to have it together anyway."

"My sister is what I call..." He searched for the word. "Cautious. For years she was more like a mother to me than a big sister. My mother was gone almost all day earning our living. I always looked to Marti to make everything all right."

"You never really speak about your family, Chris."

"They've been on my mind a lot lately. Not my father. But Marti? Yeah." Chris cleared his throat. "When she left home to attend school, things didn't seem the same anymore. I couldn't believe how much I missed her. My father's family was... terrible. I felt by myself. I mean, don't get me wrong." Chris chuckled. "I was glad not to have her lurking over my shoulder. 'Where you been? Who you been with? Why are you wearing that shirt? It doesn't match your pants. It's time to eat this crappy food I made you.'"

Teresa laughed aloud with him. "Don't say that about her, Chris." She gave him a stern look. "That's your sister. I'm sure she tried her best."

"Yeah, she tried to cook. I tried to choke it down. But you know what? It still beats the slop in here. She used to make these little pizzas. You know those flour tortillas?"

"Of course I know flour tortillas!" She tossed glossy hair back from her shoulders. "Don't act like you don't know, baby."

"Well not like this. Marti spread on tomato paste and then she shredded government cheese over it and we'd bake them."

"Uhm," Teresa winced, "No, I don't know tortillas like that."

"I'm serious! A little oregano on top, if we had it. Boom! Little pizzas. We did what we could with what we had. Let's just say, I got it down with a lot of seasoning."

"I bet you did."

"I don't think I realized how much she protected me until she wasn't there to do it. Marti never could accept the 'whatever happens, happens' approach to life even when we were kids. She organized *everything*. She had me and herself on a clock all day long." He smiled at the memory. "If Marti didn't have a list, she got anxious. She didn't know what to do with herself."

"What did she protect you from?"

"Our parents." His voice disappeared. Teresa strained to hear him. "After she left, I got so angry. I took that anger to the streets. The streets loved me and every wicked deed I did."

"You weren't ever wicked, Chris. Not ever."

"Some people think so."

"Well, they're wrong. Don't let them tell you that."

Chris paused for a beat. "Those streets begged me for more and I gave them the best I had to give. But most of all, they taught me something." He leaned in closer to the glass partition. "Listen Teresa. Listen close. Even though I learned to fight and use weapons, I learned something else. It takes allies to stay above water. Man is a social creature. I always have somebody who has my back."

Teresa nodded, confused.

"Marti doesn't have anyone." He needed for her to understand.

◆ ◆ ◆ ◆

Later, in the yard, Chris sat around talking shit. "Fool me once, shame on me. Fool me twice... well, you really shouldn't try to fool me twice, now should you?"

"But you're laid back, dog."

"Yeah, you know. I do what I do. But here's the thing. Don't mistake my prison presence for unintelligence. Don't mistake my quietness for shyness. Don't mistake my kindness for weakness."

The men cut their eyes at each other. They knew the deal. Within the first week of his second bid for aggravated robbery, five men held him down

The second week, Chris recovered from the attack.

The third week, all five of his attackers died strange, unnatural, inhumane deaths. "Don't mistake my being under the radar for me not being there."

He made discreet inquiries through his network. He learned quite a lot about Celara's mission and philosophy. Their real mission and philosophy, not the bullshit listed in their brochures.

◆ ◆ ◆ ◆

# 6 The Party

Celara Solar Construction invites you to be a
guest at Metro Restaurant.
Cocktails 6:30pm, Dinner 7:30pm
Please RSVP by June 1

After Alex's rude implication and the warnings she got from the other women in the office, Marti didn't want to feed the stereotype of the gold-digging bimbo after the boss.

"Alex told me he wants to spend time with his real friends instead of dealing with people who don't mean anything to him at a party."

Marti related Evan's two cents that she overheard from her cubicle to Teresa.

"Do you know what they call me?"

"What?"

"The Boss's Girl. They whisper it and snicker just outside my cubicle."

"The guys?"

"Yeah."

"Maybe they're jealous because they're not the boss's girl."

"Maybe." Marti laughed. "So now there's this party coming up and already two people warned me to mind my own."

"Well, maybe you should listen. They might know something you don't know."

"Oh, I'm listening. I'm bringing someone with me."

"Who? I didn't even know you were dating. I've never really seen you in the mix, girl."

"I keep things low. And I'm selective, you know? Did Chris tell you how we grew up?"

"He told me some. But he doesn't talk about the past much."

"Two parents, a girl and a boy."

"Right."

"I was ten and Chris five when March and Christina divorced. I was thirteen and Chris eight when we moved in with March and his wife, Reba. I was eighteen and Chris thirteen when I graduated. I moved out of my father's home, and attended Rose Creek University downstate. That's where I did my thing. I saved my *adventures* for college. Just to play it low-key."

"I wish I played it low-key. That's about when Chris did his five-year bid downstate and Mari came along."

"Terry, don't trip."

"I'm not tripping. I'm just saying."

"I know. I always wanted Chris to join me downstate. But for school, not the other thing. Reverend March retired from teaching and launched his Internet ministry. I started teaching English and Creative Writing at Rose Creek Prep."

"And Chris finished his first stretch and came back to Lake City and we had Kina and then he went back in for the second stretch. That's how that story ends."

Marti remained silent. She pictured Teresa's face normally alight with laughter or argument saddened by the dreariness of family drama.

"Do you blame me, Marti?"

"For Chris?"

"Yeah."

"No, of course not."

"You sure?"

"Teresa, I'm sure. Why are you asking me that?"

"I don't know. I just always had this impression you and your family thought I should have kept him out of trouble."

"Are you kidding me? *We* couldn't keep him out of trouble. That was for Chris to do, Terry. Especially with two young ones. Do you know what? I used to blame myself."

"It's not your fault, Marti."

"I always wonder. I keep getting upset every time I think about it.

"Well, in that case, back to your sex life."

"Okay, now I'm really gonna get upset."

"Come on, Marti. You were always so conservative with the long sleeves and pants. Long skirts all the time."

"Lake City gets cold."

"You wore stuff like that even in the summertime."

"Okay, it's true. And sweaters and blazers in the winter."

"See!"

"In my defense, I do wear high-heeled boots. That's got to count for something."

"Okay. Two points. One for each foot. But don't change the subject. We're talking about boyfriends."

Marti let out a sigh. "I dated a couple of my colleagues at Rose Creek Prep."

"Aha! So you still kept things low. You went country! Were they teachers?"

"One teacher. One administrator."

"Two!" Teresa giggled. "Marti, Marti, Marti. Tell me this, girl. I have to know. Do they say hee haw, when, you know?"

"Stop it!"

"Come on! I won't tell *anyone*."

"Look, Terry." Marti lost control for a moment, laughing. "Look, I admit it. I did my thing here and there. But here's the deal. Would you believe that I've become even more selective as years go by? And I'm not getting any younger."

"Who are you seeing now?"

"Well, there's one guy I met. I thought about asking him to come with me to the party, but I don't have his contact information."

"Uh, Marti?"

"Yeah?"

"That means you're not seeing him."

"I know," Marti giggled.

"Okay, there is another guy."

"Did he tell you where he lived?"

"Terry!"

"I'm just saying to check all angles."

"I actually do know where he lives."

❖ ❖ ❖ ❖

For Celara's party, she wanted to make a good impression. She wanted to exhibit class. She wanted to show everyone that she felt beautiful. Most of all, she wanted to punish Alex.

So she wore a black cocktail dress that fit her like a glove and black pumps—perfect for a balmy Lake City evening wandering around an upscale restaurant patio.

On the way to Metro, she gave Augie strict instructions to pull her out of the party if she did or said anything out of hand—like curse out her boss.

She and Augie circulated the restaurant's banquet room. Alex stared at her from across the crowd. Or did he glare? His eyes glittered like diamonds.

She turned away.

Smooth as silk, he maneuvered into line behind her as she got something to eat. She maneuvered away with a plate of seafood and a glass of white wine.

Marti even caught Ronny's stares below her neck. *As if.*

She left Augie at their table a few times to greet the Lake City players at the party that she recognized from previous Celara meetings. She kept a watchful eye out for Alex.

Four glasses later, she looked up when Alex sat down at her and Augie's table. He left not only his girlfriend but also Evan to their own devices. Marti didn't know about the girlfriend, but she was surprised Evan allowed Alex to stray that far from his side.

Her head swam. A warm wind wound its way around her small group. She managed to rally her focus with Augie's help.

They got through a few minutes of polite chit chat about the weather, current events, and the food at the party.

Glancing about the room, Marti searched in vain for another topic. She didn't know how much longer she could last under Alex's microscopic scrutiny. She had nothing.

Evan smirked their direction. Something would come her way in the office. It usually did whenever Alex directed his attention towards her.

"What time is it?" she asked finally.

Alex glanced at his bare wrist.

"It's 9:30," Augie told her.

Marti felt, rather than saw, Alex's irritation radiate against the side of her face. It cut through the haze and killed her four-glass buzz.

They saw a few people head towards the door. Alex excused himself then took the host position to say goodbye to his departing guests.

"Whew!" Marti raised her glass. "I think we got through that okay." She drank to that.

"Is he married?"

"Why do you ask?"

"Just wondering."

"He has a girlfriend." Marti nodded her head towards Alex's companion. "See her?"

"You mean that Asian woman?"

"Yeah, you saw her?"

"Guys like him tend to make arrangements with women like that."

"Arrangements? You mean…"

"What money won't do, Marti."

"You think it's like that?"

Augie shrugged.

"So what about you? I mean, we never really talked while I stayed at your place."

"You never had time."

"I know. This job keeps me so busy. You see who I work for. So… do you have any kids? A significant other?"

"I have a teenage son and a daughter in college."

"I don't think I've ever seen them around."

"I'm estranged from both of them. Their mother—well, I'll just say, it didn't work out the best way it could have."

Marti nodded then changed the subject. Soon they made their own move to leave. Marti got their coats from coat check. Augie headed out the door in front of her. The door swung shut behind him before she could get through. She sighed then turned to find Alex right behind her.

"Good night, Alex. Thank you."

She held out her hand for him to shake. Feeling mischievous, she yanked him forward and laughed. He yanked her back towards him into a hug. Then he opened the door, guided him through. And it may be that her buzz returned because she could have sworn that he said, "See you tomorrow, my lady."

❖ ❖ ❖ ❖

Summer at Celara passed in a rush. The staff put forth a great effort to meet the onslaught of construction demands.

Marti mostly kept her mouth shut and allowed Evan his one-man dramas.

But she did shut down his attempt to take credit for a spreadsheet of data she created for the project. She simply raised her voice to speak over his at their meeting with Alex.

Evan paid her back with demands that she edit his usual last-minute rush jobs. Then he made alterations to work she already edited and got approved by the executive committee.

"Marti, where are the data sheets?"

"You have them. Remember, you asked me for my copy so you could use the numbers for your end?"

"Well," Evan lifted a couple of sheets of paper, "I don't see them here." He looked at Marti with expectation. "So maybe you should ask the executives for another copy."

Marti smiled sweetly. "I could do that."

Evan nodded at her with approval.

"Just about as well as you can since you're the one who misplaced them." *Payback!* Marti turned back to her computer.

Evan got on the phone to make the data request.

◆ ◆ ◆ ◆

"See, this is what happens. He creates chaos and confusion. Then he proposes a solution. Then he brands himself as 'Mr. Fix-It.'"

"Loser."

"Which is far more accurate. He put the wrong version of a document online and left it there for weeks. He claimed it was because I confused him even though the files were labeled. He even had the nerve to shout about it to me."

"You know what I think?"

"What?"

"You make it seem easy while he struggles to get his contribution done."

"But see, that's the thing. It's not easy. It's work. I work hard to get things done right and done on time. The thing is I don't go all around the office complaining to everyone who'll listen about how much work I do and how hard it is. I just do the work. They pay me. I do it."

"You make him look bad."

"He makes himself look bad."

"Other people might catch on, including your boss."

"I think the boss is catching on."

"Wouldn't it be about time?"

"Just about."

"Hang in there."

"I'm trying but that freak show is really making my job harder than it has to be."

◆ ◆ ◆ ◆

"Marti," Evan approached her with the same solemn urgency she recognized from the convention when he ordered her to look for Lexa. "The office is going to close fifteen minutes earlier than usual. Everyone's leaving. I'm leaving too. Trust me."

He shouldn't have said that. The last sentence activated Marti's sixth sense. Something out of the ordinary, even for Celara, would happen. Earlier in the day, she noticed a box of hard liquor in the hallway.

She overheard Ronny say, "The pizza's ready," a few minutes ago.

If the office was closing any minute, why order a pizza?

Despite the urgent rush of Celara's staff from the building, Marti allowed curiosity to override caution. She drifted towards the warehouse. Lingered.

She really should have left.

The lights flicked off. A far door closed. She was alone. Clean, industrial works of art lined the shelves. Sculptured sections of copper and steel pipe bent and curved. Silvery metallic machines glistened in the twilight that crept through small windows near the ceiling. Tools with jagged-edged teeth waited for tomorrow's exploits. Careful not to make a sound, she re-entered the main building.

All was quiet. But she saw the light in Alex's office. Alex's door was at the front of the building. She couldn't leave without him seeing her. Why did she play with fire?

She stopped at his doorway. "Were you bored on Christmas Eve?"

"No I just needed to get some work done." He looked pissed.

She stared at him a moment longer. Paid close attention to the expression on his face. Earlier in the week, Marti walked into Alex's office and saw a side table piled high with stacks of gifts. What he did he do to obligate himself to that extreme? She wondered whether he had a gift for her and how he would make her earn it. He stared back at her.

"Merry Christmas, Alex."

"Merry Christmas."

She turned to leave through the front entry. Evan rushed in with the pizza.

"I guess I can't trust you," she smirked.

She waited for the bus at the stop in front of Celara. She wondered what she would hear on the voice recorder she dropped into the planter by Alex's doorway.

◆ ◆ ◆ ◆

"Close the door."

Alex and Evan went through their list of companies in search of the next project.

"By the way, Alex, I've been meaning to tell you. We have a connection inside Lakeside Power."

"Who do we know?"

"Marti's friend from the party."

"Him?" Alex looked annoyed. "How can that guy help us win the bid?"

"It can be done."

"Evan, stop fucking around. We're behind schedule."

"Trust me."

◆ ◆ ◆ ◆

As soon as she walked in the door, Marti received a call from Reba, Reverend March's second wife.

"He kept it quiet. I guess he didn't want anyone to know. But then, he is a man of God and he knows all about Holy Ghost power."

"Why didn't he say anything? I mean, after all we're his..." Marti trailed off.

"Children." Reba took a breath. "Look, I know things have never been quite right between us, Martina. Every day and every night, I pray for you and Christian. I pray for all of us that the healing will come down and cover us with the blood. But even though I've asked a blessing, I think that's also part of the reason he didn't say anything."

"Come again?" Marti wished she had the foresight to snag a bottle of hard liquor from Celara when she had the chance.

"Look, he doesn't even know I called you and told you this, but it's looking like your father's going to need a transplant soon."

"A transplant? What kind?"

"He needs a kidney. The dialysis has been going on for years and its wearing him down. The sufferings of Job have always been his cross to bear."

"Reba, does he have... diabetes?"

"You already knew?"

"No. I mean, I guessed from some things he told me earlier."

"Adult onset."

"So, he needs a transplant. How soon?"

"As soon as possible. There's a long waiting list. Lord, help us!"

◆ ◆ ◆ ◆

# 7 The Conference

**M**arti enjoyed an intense round-robin in the gym and around her neighborhood on Saturdays. She did the post office, grocery store, and public library circuit. She ran other small errands on her list as she biked around North Central like a mad woman.

Sometimes she saw an afternoon movie or did some light housekeeping. Today, she wasn't sure whether to stare into space at a coffee shop or on the lake shore. She did neither. Instead, she re-read a letter from Chris.

Apparently, Chris knew some homeboys who'd just seen a movie. In it, an employer of a vague corporation surveilled his employees. The employer collected damaging information as leverage to force cooperation in shady projects. The employer also used the information as a pre-emptive strike in case an employee ever decided to sue him for any reason.

◆ ◆ ◆ ◆

"I need more data."
"Okay."
"Data we're not supposed to have."
"Okay."
"From a man with a, let's say, controversial past."
"I guess I'll sit."

She listened to Alex's list of directives and his deadline. "That's what you'll be doing." He shifted papers on his desk. That's why he missed the open-mouthed expression of horror on Marti's face. He took up a pencil. He wrote something on a piece of paper.     That was his second hint of their conversation's conclusion.

Ten silent seconds passed.

"I can't do it." For the first time, she refused him.

"Why not?" He knifed her with his eyes from across the desk.

Marti stared at Alex in silence. Did he not just hear the things he told her? Did he not care about her safety? *No, he doesn't care.* Well if he didn't, she did. She stood up.

"I can't fulfill this assignment based on what you've told me and the concerns I have about what you've told me." She took a step back from his glare of outraged disbelief.

"That guy you're *concerned* about has the key to move Celara's market position forward. You need to be *concerned* about that. That's why you're here, after all."

She took another step back.

"I can't do it." She walked out of his office. She sat at her desk. She picked up her purse. Waited to be fired.

Evan took the assignment. How did she know? He told Ronny all about it just outside her cubicle.

"The reason Alex counts on me is because I do exactly what he says needs to be done. Some people have every reason ready not to. Then they wonder why they're on the outside looking in."

Alex ignored Marti's existence for a full three days.

❖ ❖ ❖ ❖

She learned two things in martial arts class at her gym. Attack or defend. The best defense was an offense. So maybe it was time for her to be offensive.

On her landline, she verbally abused Evan and sometimes Alex. Sometimes she made leading statements. Sometimes she withheld information. Sometimes she flattered them. Sometimes she reported the behavior of one or the other that she knew would piss the other off. She had to know if what Chris implied was true.

In the office, she observed... anger, defensiveness, smugness, and resentment. Men with egos love to talk shit. They love to brag. They love the idea of knowing something you don't know. So she ramped up her verbal abuse to goad either of them into admitting their knowledge of what she said.

"He comes out with his usual bullshit excuses about why his end of the project didn't work, why he left typos, why he lost computer files. Either he doesn't give a good goddamn or... he actually is that stupid. I'm still not sure. I can't believe Alex allows it."

"How do you deal, girl?"

"Redundancy. I keep multiple backups in multiple locations."

Alex's demeanor became colder. He drove her to get information ready to present to Celara's executives, including last-minute changes and adjustments to the presentation they would proof together.

"What!" He barked at her from behind his desk "Why are you still here? Shouldn't you be writing something for me that's due at 9 a.m. tomorrow?"

Marti turned away from the cold grey stones that occupied the spaces where Alex's eyes used to be. She walked from his doorway back to her desk. Sat stunned a moment. Then she put her head down on her folded arms.

*Don't you dare cry.*

She didn't cry. Instead, she dragged herself to the bus stop, wading through snow that rose to hip level. That same snow delayed her bus and train. She didn't get home until ten o'clock the night before the presentation. Payback was a mother.

"I don't take abuse lying down," she told Teresa. "It's not my nature. Either stand and fight or walk away."

"So what are you going to do?"

"I'm going to stay."

"Why, Marti?"

"Because it's not over until *I* say it's over."

◆ ◆ ◆ ◆

Nine o'clock the next morning, Marti stood in the hallway outside the conference room. She watched Evan, Kenneth, Nate, and Alex stroll into Alex's office. The door closed.

Strange. They scheduled the nine o'clock meeting for the conference room and to also include her. She walked back to her desk. Fifteen minutes later, she heard the directive over the intercom. "Marti to the conference room."

She arrived with her paperwork in hand. Silver-haired Kenneth; six-foot, four-inch Nate; and watchful Evan sat on one side of the table. Marti sat opposite. Evan had the typical smirk on his face.

In walked Alex with, "Sorry. I had to take a call. Let's get started."

He sat next to her then asked for the press releases she wrote to announce new ideas and techniques at Celara.

"What is all this?" Alex frowned at the stack she placed before him.

"It's what you asked me to work on. I sent copies to everyone by email."

"Do you guys have copies?" Alex quizzed the room.

"No, I don't have anything," Evan responded through his smirk.

"I didn't bring mine either," Nate chimed in.

Kenneth bumped a stack of paper on the table. "I've got mine."

"Make some copies," Alex ordered.

Marti gathered her own stack then went to work on the copy machine. She collated. She stapled. She stacked. Ten minutes later, she walked back to the conference room. Alex stood in the hallway on another call. Back inside, she passed stacks to Nate and Evan. She put a stack at Alex's place. They reviewed the first press release.

"What am I looking at?" Alex frowned. He sat down with a puzzled look.

"These are all the press releases."

"Okay, but what has already been discussed? I mean where the hell are we?"

Marti opened her mouth to speak. Evan's cheshire grin grew wider.

"Just a second." Alex stalked out to use his phone again. Half of his stack of paperwork fell to the floor. He didn't bother to pick it up. The other men looked at her.

*My mother collected rain water for us to bathe in and then we used that bath water to flush the toilet.*

Kenneth went through three more press releases with her. They made the corrections together. Neither Nate nor Evan contributed. *Probably waiting for more drama.*

Cue Alex, stage left.

Alex paused by his chair. He looked at the papers on the floor. He looked at Marti, as though she were the reason that the press releases lay scattered at his feet. He launched into a story about his past sports injuries and the fact that he was scheduled for an MRI later that afternoon. He might need surgery. The doctors didn't know.

Marti didn't move.

Alex sighed. "Good help is so hard to find." He bent to pick up his papers.

At the last second, Marti decided to notice. "Oh, did you need help with those?" She picked up the very last sheet of paper then dropped it on the table in front of Alex with a sugar-sweet smile.

*When the gas company and the electric company double-teamed us, Christina gave us flashlights and sleeping bags. She told us we were camping in the middle of Lake City in the dead of winter.*

They started the fifth press release. This time, Alex appeared totally lost. "You know what, I'm going to step out and take care of some things. You guys do whatever needs to be done here."

Marti, "Well, I guess we can continue and then just let you know..."

Alex turned his back then walked out the conference room.

Marti sat surprised at the ultimate show of disrespect. Nate laughed.

*Damned if we didn't roast marshmallows over that fucking barbecue grill, Alex!*

She wouldn't let him get away with it.

"Don't go away mad, Alex," she called. "Just go away."

He looked back at her from the hallway. Kept going. This time, Kenneth laughed. Evan followed Alex out of the conference room with a stern look.

*There's nothing you can do to me, Alex. You're way too late. It's already been done worse by better... my own father.*

Nate shrugged his massive shoulders then wandered out after the others. Marti and Kenneth were the only two who remained. Kenneth grinned across the table. "Now, let's get some actual work done, shall we?"

They finished the press releases. Then Marti recited her research. She and A.J. had an unspoken deal. A.J. provided background. Marti showcased A.J.'s projects to the executive committee.

"New solar homes sell twice as fast as new homes without solar. Even classic Victorian homes retrofitted with solar sell approximately three times those without. This is because buyers like the classic look upgraded with modern technology. So that is another client incentive.

The trick is that, in Lake City, builders have to follow LEED standards. So contractors who want to green build should join USGBC and get LEED certified. Field workers should be trained too.

Finally, Celara would do well to expand its solar thermal division to balance the photovoltaic, diversifying its options and expanding its existing client base."

Well, if no one else gave a damn, she impressed Kenneth. He took her research seriously enough to at least comment, "That would mean hiring new staff. We can't afford that expense in this economy."

Alex returned to the room in time to overhear Kenneth's assertion. Marti could see Alex was annoyed that the meeting continued without him.

*One monkey don't stop no show, Alex.*

Evan, as always, followed close behind. They both stood, arms crossed, waiting for Marti's response. Nate flopped down on a chair, obviously wanting to be elsewhere, but not wanting to be left out either.

"But you can afford to hire unskilled labor and train them to do assembly and any other tasks that don't require licenses or certifications—transport, unpacking, stocking, job-site inventory. Worksite clean-up."

Kenneth shook his head, "But what are you saying, exactly? Sick leave, vacations, pensions? That's too much."

Alex jumped in, "Well yeah. I mean, we have to treat them like human beings." He indicated Marti. "Marti's not full-time though. We don't have to worry about her. Haaaa! Ha! Ha!"

Marti sat expressionless. True enough, she didn't have benefits. But she took what she could get and did the most with what she had.

Bored with her, Alex focused Kenneth's attention on another topic. Marti waited to see if they needed any more information from her. They didn't, thank God.

Alex concluded the meeting with a bang. "I didn't tell Marti I was gonna throw her under the bus. If this blows up in our faces, I'll just tell everyone it was all her idea. She's in charge!"

Marti unclenched her teeth. "Well, at least let it be the #128 bus since that's the one I take home."

Nate weighed in, "If you've got something to hide, you better take care of it now, Marti!"

"Welcome to your world, right Nate?"

"Yeah, we're gonna send someone to your house," Alex announced with glee.

Marti smiled, "Yeah right, razz the researcher."

"You're not the researcher, Marti. You're the consultant."

Marti frowned. When did that happen? And what did it mean?

She provided evidence and support for their agendas. And a paper trail?

He wouldn't. He wasn't that low down. He wouldn't.

*I didn't tell Marti I was gonna throw her under a bus.*

*We're gonna send someone to your house.*

*If you have something to hide, you better take care of it now.*

Actually, Alex could do plenty if he chose to do so.

◆ ◆ ◆ ◆

The next week, she, Evan, and Alex each made a trip to Malden for the conference. They were to meet with other executives in the building industry. Not together. She did her usual three-leg commute, staying aware of her surroundings so she didn't miss her connections.

"Change, is a business reality. Any business who denies that reality will collapse. Believe it. You can change for better. Or you can change for worse. Those are the only two options. Get on board. Or get out of the way. In fact, get out of Celara's way. I mean that. Celara's not a mom and pop store. Not any longer. We're growing."

Alex paced back and forth, center stage. All eyes on him, just the way he liked it, the way he needed it.

"People want to get inside Celara's head. It's not hard. It's easy. Very easy. And I'll tell you." He stopped pacing, drew out the anticipation. "Celara's a big company that thinks like a small company. We're lean. Agile. Hungry. We don't forget where we came from. And we don't sleep. We turn on a dime at Celara."

Alex worked stage left. "So back in the days of our one company pickup truck with the hand-painted logo, we didn't have the power and resources and the market reach that we do now. But we had spirit." He moved stage right. All heads in the audience swiveled back and forth, as if they refereed a fierce tennis match between Alex and his opponent—100-proof ignorance.

"We're sleek and swift with our decision-making. You want to be where I am? You want to take Celara's place? Then follow the leader. Be swift. Be confident. Keep it simple. Don't serve the bureaucracy. Serve the people."

Marti felt relieved she wouldn't have to talk at the gathering. In this way, she and Alex complemented each other with perfection. After the endless executive back-slaps and handshakes, "Marti, here, take these," he loaded her with the presentation materials. In other ways, they did not complement each other at all.

Alex drove himself back to the office. Marti sighed, not looking forward to the two-bus, one-train commute back into the city then north to the suburbs in the heat of summer.

She reluctantly rode back with Evan, who at least offered her a lift. During the ride, which seemed to take forever, Evan informed her that Alex fired anybody he felt was disloyal to him or to Celara. He provided several ominous examples.

"I keep telling them, they should feel lucky to even have a job in this economy."

Marti could not suppress the rebellious spirit that rose inside her.

"Oh really?" Marti snorted. "So how does he find out? Are there hidden cameras in the women's restroom?"

"No, of course not."

"God, that's so perverted and disgusting."

"No, no."

She laughed extra loud at his consternation. She found her triumphs wherever she could.

One positive result of her conducting so many interviews in the office was that she established relationships with the other staff. Whenever she felt out of sorts, she stopped by someone's desk or office for a quick chat to normalize the day.

She and her lunch crew met every day at noon in the break room.

"So what did you bring, Marti?"

"A can of soup. What did you bring?"

"My wife made me dumplings with chicken and broccoli."

"Mine's organic." Marti scraped clam chowder into a bowl for the microwave.

"Mine's homemade."

"Come *on*, Alan. You didn't make that."

"My wife did. That counts."

"Okay, Alan. You win today. Tomorrow, look out. I'm going to watch that cooking show where everyone yells tonight. And then, you'll all be surprised."

"We'll be surprised if it doesn't come vacuum-packed in plastic."

"They give you a choice these days. Paper or plastic."

"Or fries with that."

"No fast food. No way."

"We'll see, Marti. We'll see."

Wallace walked in with a whoop. "They're talking about the super grid again." He picked up the remote and changed the television to the economic news channel.

Alan wasn't impressed. "They're always talking about that. I think they like the way it sounds when they say the words. Super grid. See? Super grid. They keep saying it, but they don't even know what it means. See? Look at her." He pointed to the television. They waited for it. "...super grid..." They laughed at the blank stare in the news anchor's eyes.

"Come on," Marti tried to defend her. "It's twenty-four hour news. She's probably been up all night."

"Or maybe she's just as depressed telling us about the economy as we are listening to her talk about it." Wallace took his turn at the microwave.

"Ugh, change the channel," Marti ordered. Alan obliged. No one really wanted to listen to the dreary economic news of the day.

She never discussed her job. Strangely enough, they didn't ask. They must have known better. Or maybe, they didn't want to know.

❖ ❖ ❖ ❖

Anita, the account clerk, stopped by her cubicle while Evan was at lunch. Marti saw Anita around the office, from time to time. But her vibe seemed so angry that Marti kept clear.

"Even though I've been here fifteen years and I have an accounting degree, they passed me up and brought in a new guy." Anita pressed her lips together hard enough to pull the frown lines around her mouth into sharper focus.

"That doesn't make sense."

"No, it doesn't."

"Why would they recruit someone new when you're right here?"

Anita leaned forward. Marti leaned back.

"Because it's a boys club. You don't know? Promoting me would mean increasing my salary to their level and a lot of them can't take that."

"That's too bad."

"I'm just letting you know how it is," she whispered, eyes fierce.

"So why do you stay?"

"I need the check. That's why most of us stay."

Marti wondered if someone told Anita to be happy she even had a job.

❖ ❖ ❖ ❖

Whenever Alex and Evan behaved towards Marti like animals, that was how she chose to think of them. Alex was the alpha and Evan was the beta. At least it seemed that way most of the time. Something wasn't quite right with that scenario. Something a little more complex was going on. Something she couldn't see. She got on the landline to see if she could flush it out into the open.

"One day, Evan acted completely out-the-box. Insufferable. An off-the-charts loon. He walked, or stalked, more like it, back and forth behind me while I sat at my desk. He could see that I was writing something.

So just to calm him down, I left my notebook on my desk for him to go through after I went home for the day. Because he goes through my computer, cabinets, desk top, and maybe even my purse regularly."

"Seriously?"

"Oh yeah, shit's in different places from where I leave it. Not just from vacuuming or cleaning either. Once I saw Ronny coming out of my cubicle when there was no reason for him to be in there. We don't work on any projects together."

"That's overstepping."

"Well, at least Evan doesn't call me sweetie anymore. I acted like I couldn't hear him whenever he did. So, eventually, he stopped."

"Well, good."

"And he's married. You'd think his wife would set him straight on women since his mother obviously didn't, but it seems like that's not happening. He's not been socialized correctly."

Teresa laughed. "Well, since you know who you are and what you will and won't do, that makes it easier to teach him."

"He's a real slow learner, Terry."

"It's never too late. But back to your desk area, you keep track of what's where?"

"Oh yeah. Every night I memorize what my desk looks like. Then I see what it looks like the next day."

"Gotcha."

"So anyway, I knew if Evan didn't see the writing, he would go further berserk than he already had and make life in the office even more difficult for me. So I left my notebook out for him to go through. But not before I tore out the pages with my notes on his idiocy."

"Oh, Marti."

"I only left the notes on the research articles I planned to write for the website. That's no big deal. He'll see the finished product anyway. Then I went home."

"What happened?"

"Well... when I arrived to work the next morning, Evan was NICE, for a change."

"Rope-a-dope."

"Yeah. Game-playing's not my nature though. I go home with a pounding headache. That's blood pressure."

"Watch your health, girl."

"I try. The hour I do at the gym every morning is the only reason why I lasted this long. But now it's at the point where I'm just breaking even. Breaking even is not a life."

"No, it's not."

"Anyway, my latest assignment is to attend an environmental organization's meeting to take notes for Alex. He doesn't want to be seen there, so he's sending me."

"Take care of yourself."

"I will."

Marti ended the call, feeling better that she'd gotten things off her chest. She didn't know what really happened.

❖ ❖ ❖ ❖

Overnight, Evan took copies of Marti's writing back to the graphologist. The earlier sample from her interview turned out to be inconclusive.

"She has an independent streak," the guy told Evan.

"No kidding."

"No. I'm not kidding. You can count on her to fulfill her duties without supervision. But..."

"But what?"

"She may break away or cease work if something doesn't make sense or it violates her ethics."

❖ ❖ ❖ ❖

"So you really, absolutely can't come?"

"No, sweetheart. Daddy's busy with an important project."

"Everyone else's parents are gonna be there."

"Lexa, look. We talked about this. I'm a single parent and that means we need Mr. and Mrs. Dallas to help us out. They're going to record your performance for me like they always do and I can watch it when I get home."

"Sure you will, Dad." Nothing beat pre-teen sarcasm. "I'll ask you if you liked my solo. You'll say yes. Then I'll tell you I didn't have a solo. Then you'll get mad..."

"Lexa, stop it! I'm keeping a roof over our heads and trying to take care of business."

"But Daddy..."

"You're going to have to be a big girl and grow up and realize that people have to do the things they have to do. Celara doesn't run itself any more than your homework does itself. For instance, did your homework do itself tonight?"

Lexa remained silent.

"I didn't think so. We're not having this conversation again. Understood?"

She still didn't speak.

He raised his voice. "Understood?"

"Yes."

"Be good to Mr. and Mrs. Dallas." Alex hung up the phone. He dialed the elderly couple who managed his home affairs.

"Make sure to give her the flowers while she's still on stage so everyone can see how important she is to me. I want her to feel good about her hard work."

"Yes, I understand, Mr. King. We'll follow your instructions to the letter."

"I know, Mr. Dallas. You always do."

"We handshake the dance instructor and offer her your regrets. Then we take Lexa out to a nice restaurant."

"With dessert."

"With dessert. Of course."

"She deserves that."

"She does, indeed, Mr. King. And we'll make sure she gets to bed on time."

"That's all I ask."

"All very reasonable."

Alex stared into space.

Mr. Dallas cleared his throat. "Sir?"

"I keep Lexa fed and clothed, don't I?"

"Yes, you do."

"She has her immunizations and regular doctor visits, doesn't she?"

"She does, sir."

"Her teeth get cleaned on schedule, right?"

"They do, sir." Mr. Dallas knew for a fact that Mrs. Dallas cared for Lexa as if she were their own.

"Lexa attends the best accelerated programs in the best suburban schools and gets the best ballet training my money can afford. I mean, I'm not rolling, filthy rich, but I do my best as a single parent in a broken home."

Mr. Dallas waited a beat to see if Alex had anything to add to the tale of woe. "The missus and I know you do, sir."

"Sure, I could have used some support from her mother, but the family court said otherwise. But I'm keeping her out of trouble while other people's kids are running wild in the streets."

"And family court is the last word, in these matters, I suppose."

"I..." Alex frowned at the uncertainty he heard in his voice. "Yes!" He ended the call.

He sighed, looked at the reports on his desk. He didn't like the way his voice sounded when he spoke to Lexa. It reminded him of someone he used to know. He liked the way her voice sounded when she spoke to him even less. It reminded him of someone else he used to know... a long, long time ago.

❖ ❖ ❖ ❖

"Ms. Aland is out sick today," the student behind the museum's front desk told Marti.

"That's okay. I'll just browse around." She saw a familiar face in the stacks. "Worth? The convention, right?"

"Marti, hi!" He waved her over. "Have a seat. I could really use a break. I need to clear my head before tonight's meeting."

"Save a Lake at the library, right?"

"Are you going? We could use the support."

"Actually, I'm attending for Celara."

"Oh." After a long pause, he cleared the table. Then he took her arm. "Let's go."

The meeting got underway. She sat in the back. The voice recorder sat on the chair beside her. She also took notes, just in case.

Worth stood at the podium, "The proposals off Cape Cod and other parts of the East Coast stalled. However, Ohio and Wisconsin developers floated plans recently."

"What about Lake City?"

Marti's ears pricked.

"I'm told that an unnamed developer has, indeed, approached state officials with plans to build at least two hundred, possibly as many as four hundred turbines about five to seven miles offshore..."

The meeting collapsed for a full five minutes under angry and outraged remarks before Worth regained control.

"People. People, please. Everyone just please calm down and listen for a minute. The developer's plans are in the initial stage. For all we know, its just talk to test the waters."

"Or someone's already in bed with the state and the feds and they're about to ram it down our throats while we're not looking."

"Just a second..."

The speaker's voice escalated, "Look here. I run a boating business. My family's been here for years! What, am I gonna sell those windmills as some sort of new-style Olympic obstacle course for tourists? You think they're gonna go for that? No way!"

He got up, made an exasperated sound, shouted, "No way!" again, and then stomped out.

The heat of the meeting ebbed and flowed until the librarians shooed everyone out.

She and Worth sat down to dinner at the café in her neighborhood. Marti felt annoyed and uneasy about the position Alex put her in. What could she say in conversation? What couldn't she say?

"Rule number one, Worth. Let's not talk about Save a Lake, windmills, or boating businesses. Okay?"

Worth laughed. "I got nothing left anyway, Marti."

That out of the way, the conversation deepened. She revealed to him her father's need for a kidney transplant.

"Do you have children?" she asked him.

He sighed. Waited a beat. "I'd give anything to have them back. I had a girl and twin boys. They died with their mother in a car accident."

"I'm so sorry, Worth."

"My heart breaks everyday. It heals up. Then it breaks again whenever I think of them."

"I can't begin to imagine."

"I know. I would never want anyone to imagine. My mother still cries if I happen to mention their names so I've tried to move on from it. But pain like that, you never do forget."

"No, I guess not. Do I know your mother?"

"Yes, you know her." Worth looked at her strangely. "Beryl Aland."

"Beryl? I don't remember Beryl having a... oh, wait. I think I do remember seeing you around when I was younger. I didn't realize...

"Because I'm Black and she's..."

"Not Black." Marti filled in. His eyes were hazel like Beryl's and his hair was golden-brown. But the year-round tan on his skin revealed a mixed-race heritage.

He laughed. "Right. Not Black."

"How old are you, Worth?"

"Thirty-five. And you?"

"Thirty-nine. I guess I thought you were her nephew or a f..."

"Foster child?"

"Friend," she improvised lamely. "No." Marti shook her head. "My God, I'm really wrecking things tonight. I'm sorry, Worth. Really, I am."

"Well, forgiveness seems to be on the menu tonight. I forgive you, Marti," he intoned.

She obliged him with a smile. "Seriously. Beryl never mentioned anything. And I never made the connection because your last name is Rizal instead of Aland."

"She didn't marry my father, but she met someone who treated her well and married him. He was Filipino. She kept her own name for her own reasons. Independence, I think. I took his name because he actually was a father to me. A good one. He's since passed on."

"Sorry to hear that, Worth. I can't believe I never knew. I guess I never asked. But, look. If he was good to you, it sounds like you're the lucky one."

"At least at this table." He squeezed her hand.

Marti laughed. "I don't have any children myself. Issues, you know. The Reverend was not a good father to me and my brother. He was a worse husband to my mother."

"And so he should die?"

Marti looked away.

"Would you feel better if he died? Or would you feel worse?"

"It's not fair, Worth." Marti's eyes filled with tears. "It really isn't. He treated us like trash. Now he needs us and he can't even come down from on high to ask for help. It was his holy-roller wife who called me about it."

"Then maybe you shouldn't do it for him." Worth slowly shook his head. "Actually, that's a very bad idea, now that I think about it."

Marti gave him a quick look. "You mean... just let him die."

"No. That's not what I mean. Besides, it wouldn't work. You have a conscience. It always comes back to how you feel about yourself."

Marti sank back into her seat then closed her eyes. But he kept talking.

"Maybe you should do it for you. To prove to yourself, if no one else, that you're not like him. That you're actually *more* than what he made you."

Marti looked down at her plate and nodded. Tears got in the way of any reply she might have made.

◆ ◆ ◆ ◆

# 8 The Test

- Gossip, Politics, Head games _hrs
- Hissy Fit, Whine & Cheese lunch _hrs
- Cigarette Break _hrs
- Actual Work _hrs

*You want to sneak behind my back? I'll see to it that you won't like what you find, sweetie.*
Marti left Evan's Daily Work Schedule in the top drawer of her desk where she knew *someone* would look. She also left a copy in the document file of her laptop. Again where someone would look.

For her own entertainment, she filled out the form week after week. She took her fun where she could find it in the dog days of August. You want to listen to my phone conversations? I'll make sure you won't like what you hear, *dear*.

"Alex told me to review the website. He wants it to be perfect, he says. Okay, so fine. It takes two-and-a-half to three hours to review the entire site. Evan decides to make it more interesting by refusing to do edits. Or, if he decides to make the edits, he adds in more mistakes. Passive resistance, head games, and made-up technical gobbley-gook... anything but fixing it. I truly don't know if it's stupidity or spite. But whatever. I get paid by the hour. Those games he plays cost Celara money, not me."

"Well, I'll be."

"I'm supposed to get frantic because Alex is pushing me one way and Evan's pulling the other. But, you know, even if I'm working with infants, it's still a job. If they want to pay me by the hour to clean up Evan's bullshit, oh well. I put his bullshit on my time sheet and keep it moving.

But anyway, Evan's back to his classic game. He asks me to review his work for mistakes. Over and over. One morning, I hadn't even put my purse down yet and he's like, 'I made some changes, can you review the website again first thing this morning?'

I told him, 'I can't do that since I have other work to finish.' Then I did my work. After I finished, I viewed the website. He hadn't done a single thing. He said he had problems publishing the files.

I told him, 'Well, when it's done, then let me know.' Then I went to lunch. But not before I sent Alex an email to let him know the reason for the delay."

"He's a bully, Marti."

"I know. I've noticed kind of hostile behavior directed my way. Real subtle, but it adds up."

"Like what?"

"Well, last Friday, no one knew where my check was. I needed it to buy my lunch because I was flat broke. I'd just paid rent and some other things. I called around the office and looked different places. No one had a clue. I didn't get my check until I was walking out the door. By then I was wondering about bus fare for next week."

"Where was it?"

"Ronny was holding it."

"Holding your money?"

"Holding my money."

"That's crazy!"

"Okay? I've never had to deal with shit like that on any job before."

"Actually, that's kind of serious."

"I know! No one's ever messed with my money before. I've worked for all sorts, but the money was always right. But anyway, he gave me this weird smile like he wanted to make me angry about it."

"What an ass."

"I know. He's always like that. I say good morning to him. He just looks through me as though I'm not there."

"Geez. At least he can say good morning back."

"The very least. Anyway, I'm in the break room. I'm making myself a cup of tea. In flies Kate on her witchy, bitchy broomstick and by that time, I'm washing out my cup in the sink. She snarls at me, 'We have a dishwasher!' And then she's giving me this dirty look. And I told her, 'I'm washing it by hand because I'm going to use it again.' And she's just standing there staring at me in this crazy way while I finish drying it with a paper towel like she's trying to think of something else shitty to say."

"Sounds like you're working with a bunch of crazies."

"Would you believe she stopped me in the hall later the same day and informed me that she moved my lunch back into the freezer because that's where it belonged?"

"What?"

"First of all, I could not believe she actually put her hands on my food."

"I know!"

"I told her I was defrosting it for lunch. Then I waited to see if she would actually make a big soap opera about a frozen dinner. I mean, how petty are you going to get?"

"What'd she do?"

"She walked away."

"Whatever."

"So by then, I was actually tired of the break room. I ate my lunch at my desk. Anyway, *someone* complained and I was reprimanded for eating cooked food at my desk. Only uncooked food is allowed at the desk because, otherwise, the smell might disturb my neighbors. They showed me that in the employee manual."

"What were you eating, fish and garlic?"

"No! Broccoli, cheese, and rice."

"Sometimes broccoli smells."

Martina laughed, "My broccoli smells like roses!"

"Yeah right."

"Okay, so the next day, I carried my lunch to the park and then someone made a comment about *that*. I can't even remember who. But anyway, I took two days off just to rest. That's why I'm calling you from home now. I know it sounds small, but small shit adds up. Lots of little cuts."

"Well, it kinda sounds like you're never allowed any peace to actually get work done."

"Oh, I keep to my deadlines. A good writer does. But they make the job harder. I think they want to let me know I don't belong. Anyway, Alex sent me an email asking why I'm taking two days. I didn't have an answer for him."

"Uh oh."

"Guess whose paycheck's going to be delayed again."

"Yours!"

"That's Celara."

◆ ◆ ◆ ◆

Marti's wisdom teeth attacked her entire face. She pulled back the corner of her mouth to see that they impacted the others and changed from white to ivory to brown to black in a hideous rainbow. It would take several hundred dollars for the surgery. She waited for payday so she could pay a dentist to yank them out.

Only... payday came and went with no check. She waited another day. No check. Being a contract employee, as Alex pointed out with such glee, she had no dental insurance. Her teeth radiated disgusted anger and scorn through the nerves from the top of her skull to the base of her neck.

Over the weekend, she slept sitting up, propped by pillows. She felt ridiculous, but any time her head brushed against anything, her nerve endings knifed and clawed unnatural rage from her head down to her shoulders. It got worse and worse. Sunday night, she called a nearby hospital's emergency room to see if they could help her.

"We don't do dental work, ma'am."

Do you do anesthesia? Any brand. *Dear Lord in Heaven, please send me a drug dealer to help me. Let him be called Big Dookie and have gold teeth. Amen.*

She tried to muffle her screams, but she couldn't touch her face. She kept it down to loud whimpers and groans. Who knew what her neighbors thought was happening to her.

◆ ◆ ◆ ◆

"Alex, its Monday. What happened to my check?"

"Where are you? Are you calling me from the office?"

"No. I'm at home because I didn't get paid."

90    Lee McQueen

"Look. Just come in. There'll be a check here for you."

"I'll come tomorrow."

She arrived to Celara the next day to find... Evan waiting to speak with her.

"So... Evan. Alex told you the deal?"

"Alex is out today."

"Did he leave my check?"

"No. I can't find him."

"What do you mean you can't find him?"

"He didn't say where he was going."

"He just left?"

"He just left."

"Like right before I got here?"

"About half an hour ago."

"You have his cell number, don't you?"

"He turns it off when he's in meetings."

*Like hell he turns it off.* "Well, should I wait?"

"Yeah, okay."

Marti sat hopefully at her desk. Unfortunately, she made the mistake of resting her head in her palm, her typical thinking position.

The pain grew intolerable. She took shallow gasps of air. She tried not to move her head when she stumbled to the women's bathroom. She shook out two more extra-strength aspirin. She crossed the overdose limit hours ago but she didn't know what else to do. She applied a numbing gel that morning which dulled the pain somewhat. But she was too far gone for it to have any real effect.

What else could she do? Buy crack? That's it! How much does crack cost these days? Or maybe some crystal meth. The real good quality kind. Right now. *Are you there, ecstasy? It's me Marti.*

Marti tilted her head to the side, yawned her mouth open, applied more gel to her back teeth. Kate walked into the bathroom. Marti was in too much pain to worry about her and Kate's past encounters or how she must look. Pride did not go before a fall. Pride went before pain!

Kate used a stall. She stared at Marti's reflection in the mirror as she washed her hands.

"You know what? Once it hits the nerve, there's nothing you can do without a dentist."

"I know," Marti whispered. "If I thought I had enough money, I'd pay a Central District gangbanger to shoot me in the face. I really would."

"Honey, you could probably find one to do it for free," Kate laughed.

Despite herself, Marti laughed too. "I don't think I'm gonna make it through the day, Kate. I can't even think."

"Let me see." Kate peered into her mouth. "Ew! Yuck! They're infected, Marti! You need to get them out right away. I had a root canal once. I hate dentists. But I couldn't do anything at all until he took care of it."

"You're right." Marti spoke almost without moving her lips. "This isn't working anymore. I'm outta here."

Kate washed her hands, "See ya. Good luck."

"See ya," Marti mumbled back.

"Marti, wait."

Marti turned back, braced for it.

"I've been meaning to talk to you about something important. Something you should know."

Marti felt at low ebb. "About what?" The pain killed her softly.

Kate hesitated. "Look, I'll get back to you on it, okay? I can see now's not the best time."

Marti nodded, relieved. She gathered her things from her desk. She didn't know what to do once she got home though. For sure, she couldn't lie down. Maybe she could knock her teeth out with an ice skate like the Tom Hank's character on *Cast Away*. Bang her head into the wall. Jump off a bridge. She'd do anything and anyone to stop the horrible hot wire that sliced through her. *God, somebody help me.*

She reached the front entry. Evan met her there with a check. "Get well."

Every rattle of the train and bus made her wince. She leaned against the window almost passed out from the pain. Other passengers looked away. Marti realized she was one of the drooling, crazy people most commuters avoided on public transportation.

She told Teresa the rest of it. "The dentist took one look at me and put me on antibiotics immediately. The infection was pretty severe and would have poisoned me, he said. He yanked all four in the back the next day."

"Ouch! So do you think Kate took care of it?"

"Likely. Nice to know she's human. She wanted to talk to me about something but I have a lot of work piled on my desk to work through. Speaking of that, Alex asked me to transcribe the notes of the meeting that I missed. I actually heard him on the tape ridiculing me for being out those days. He goes, 'We've been having trouble with absenteeism around here too.'"

"What! On tape?"

"Yeah, like he didn't give a damn if I heard what he said."

"Or maybe, he wanted you to hear."

"That's my boss. Anyway, my neighbors won't have to wonder why I'm screaming all by myself anymore."

Teresa laughed.

◆ ◆ ◆ ◆

"A wise man once said, 'The truth is incontrovertible; malice may attack it, ignorance may deride it, but in the end, there it is.'"

"Abraham Lincoln?"

"Winston Churchill."

"I know what the truth is, Beryl, but how can I fight for it?"

"Marti, look. You're dealing with a pillar of the community with a lot of resources at his disposal—people and money in endless supply. You cannot beat him at his own game. He's been playing it for too long and the referee probably owes him a favor. Get it?"

"Yes, but..."

"But what?"

"There's this woman there named Alice Janson. We call her A.J. She works in the field as a project manager which means she's under a lot pressure. I see them try to get at her too and mess her up. But she's been there three years. I really don't know how she's been able to last."

"Alice Janson? I know that name. Wait." Beryl pulled a newsletter from a file in the business section of the museum. "See? Here. She belongs to a group that meets every month to discuss women in construction and how to succeed."

"So that's how she deals."

"She must be tough."

"I guess. She holds her own."

"What does your boss say about the behavior?

"I don't think he knows."

"Honey, he knows. From what I've heard and what you've told me about the man, he knows everything. He may even be the cause."

"Maybe. I don't know."

"Look, management always sets the tone for what is allowed and what isn't. In a toxic workplace, with abusive management, bullies thrive. A healthy work environment doesn't tolerate a bully. Their negativity and unproductive behavior would stand out and be reprimanded."

"You may be right," Marti replied slowly. "Evan couldn't get away with so much if it weren't allowed."

"Sometimes, it's best to move on, but if you want to stay or need to stay because of the money, you're going to have to figure out a way to work around their ugly behavior."

"Well, what do you suggest?"

"First, don't portray yourself as your boss's equal. Whatever he brags about, look completely awed by it. Whenever he trips the light fantastic, don't bring him back to Earth. Let him have his fantasies. And if he's forgotten something, misplaced something, made mistakes, or missed crucial information, don't blame him. Blame the something for being missed or misplaced. Blame the information for not being known."

"Wow," Marti nodded her head. "That just might work. Even though it sounds like dealing with an overgrown child, I'm going to try it."

"He is a child, Marti. But he has an adult's ability to cause you lasting harm so be careful."

"Beryl, I'm pretty sure that I've already broken every rule."

"Well, still give it a try."

Marti told Beryl about Reverend March's diabetes and need for a kidney transplant. "Chris is in prison, you know."

"I know."

"They moved him back to low max here in Lake City, but that still leaves me as the best match. Otherwise, Reverend March would get stuck at the end of a long waiting list. I just feel so angry when I think of what I'd have to give up for this man who threw me away like trash and then gave the best years of his life to another woman's children."

Beryl winced.

"Marti, when we, meaning me and your parents were younger, I could tell something wasn't quite right in the way your father treated your mother. Like he would forget to do things or not think to do things that needed to get done. And that continued after they married, when Christina was expecting you. Sometimes I saw her walking around the neighborhood and I'd give her a lift. She would need things from the store. Once I saw her carrying something heavy back when it was snowing outside. I gave her a ride home. When we got there, I saw his car parked out front. I didn't ask any questions, but it just seemed strange he didn't give her the keys or take her himself."

Marti didn't reply because what could she say? *My father would never do something like that!* Her shoulders slumped. Reverend March did things like that as naturally as he breathed air.

"There were other things, but I'm not going to get into it right now. Just in general, people on that higher plane, in that particular dimension, view themselves as God's gift to the world. They consider themselves excused from the rules and morals the rest of us regular folks follow. Anyone who disagrees just doesn't know. Because how could anyone inferior know anything?"

"Are we talking about my father or my boss?"

"I don't know. Are we talking about your father or your boss?"

Marti didn't have an answer.

"Live and learn. Just thank him for keeping you humble. You can't change him."

"So, nothing can be done?" Marti asked slowly.

Beryl shrugged.

For some reason, Marti felt sad.

◆ ◆ ◆ ◆

The next day, Marti saw Nate and José, one of the two minority male project managers on A.J.'s team, talking in the hallway. She couldn't make out Nate's words, but she did make out the tone—disrespectful. José glanced at her. She could see in his eyes that he was under siege. Nate's large frame towered over the smaller man.

Nate followed the object of José's brief focus. Marti glanced away when she drew parallel to show she wasn't trying to eavesdrop. She felt Nate's gaze narrow on her. He waited until she rounded the corner before he resumed speaking to José.

Later, Nate crowded his large frame into her while she used the copy machine.

"You're so hard to get along with."

"Nice. Real nice, Nate."

"I'm just kidding. I really am a nice guy."

"It shows."

"That's what's called a sense of humor, Marti.'

"Oh really? Okay, say something funny so I can see for myself."

"Come on," Nate rolled his eyes.

"Wow, I asked for a job with challenge and got you, Nate. Thank you, universe!" Marti laughed and walked away.

◆ ◆ ◆ ◆

"Lily, I can't keep covering for you. She's starting to ask questions."

"I need at least a year to get back on my feet, Alex."

"A year?" He couldn't hide his exasperation. "You're going to be in a year this time, Lily? Twelve months?"

"Alex, I'm trying my best."

"She needs a mother."

"I can't right now. I'm not well enough. You know I'm not well enough. And you know why."

Silence.

"Alex, you agreed to take full custody while I got better. You promised me you would. It's the least you can do."

"Lily."

"Seeing how you treated me when we were married."

"Fine."

"Alex..."

"I said fine! Its fine, Lily. I'll take care of it. Do what you have to do."

◆ ◆ ◆ ◆

Marti spoke on the phone with Teresa.

"No way would I ever let someone be a father to my child if they behave like an animal towards me or they allowed others to behave like animals towards me. If that's the kind of people you have in your life, we sure aren't ever going to get together in that way because accidents do happen."

"Oh, I know," Teresa laughed.

"Terry. You know I'm not talking about you. I'm just saying I can't trust someone to raise my children if they bring them around people who hate them because of how they look or their gender. And if someone's friends and family are crazy and have problems with minorities and women, for damn sure, you are not going to raise a child of mine. The world is hard enough."

"I know."

"What really scared me is Evan was especially stressed out a couple of days ago. The boss yelled at him."

"For good reason?"

"With them, who knows? It's always one thing or another."

"Anyway, Evan made a joke about bringing a gun to work and shooting everyone."

"Oh."

"Yeah. *Oh*."

◆ ◆ ◆ ◆

One night, Marti had a terrible dream. A shark chased her while she ran around a sinking boat. The shark leaped from the water at her over and over.

Marti knew the shark would surely devour her. She yanked herself out of the dream. She woke up full of fear, alone in a dark room.

◆ ◆ ◆ ◆

Because of the dream, she was extra alert when she got the call from Augie. Augie never called. They usually just happened to see each other around North Central. Theirs was a no-sweat, low-pressure, every now and then kind of companionship. Movie here. Movie there. Lunch, dinner, walk on the beach. What have you.

"Back in the day, I worked on a project for Celara."

"Celara. You mean the place I work now?"

"That's right. Alex supervised me."

"Wait a minute. Why didn't you say anything when I asked you to Celara's party?"

"It was some years ago. Thirteen, fifteen. Something like that. It wasn't a pleasant experience."

"Oh really? Do tell."

"I think they didn't like the way I looked, if you know what I mean. Or they didn't like my style. It took me a long time to find work after dealing with them. Someone hooked me up at Lakeside, but if they hadn't, I might have starved to death. Construction shops are some of the most racist organizations in the nation."

"Maybe that explains it. I've never experienced the weird vibe I have at Celara on any other job."

"Here's the thing. A construction firm with enough juice can prevent people they don't like from working on their projects or on the projects of their friends."

"Like a blacklist?"

"A list of Blacks, more like it. But more than that, they can also squeeze out minority and female contractors from bidding and refuse to sub-contract them. In Lake City, as I'm sure you've seen, the population demographic does not match the jobsite demographic."

"I guess it depends on the contractor."

"See, these contractors underbid and then come back later for the necessary funds for a change order because they have that kind of juice."

"I see."

"And if they do work with a minority contractor, they use him as a front for their own gain. But they still exclude minorities and women from positions of power. You know what I mean? They use the 'there aren't any qualified' excuse. Not like they're looking real hard."

"That's horrible."

"That's your employer."

"No, that's my contractor. I'm not an actual employee."

"Whatever. But certain of these construction firms make it difficult for minority workers and minority construction firms to get ahead. You have to know somebody. And they know everybody. Even though there's plenty of work to go around, they don't like to share. They want it all."

Marti remembered Alex's goals for Celara's future. After all, he stated them clearly during her interview. She thought about her treatment in his office, A.J., A.J.'s staff, the other women.

What was supposed to happen? They would harass A.J. until she made a major mistake then take over the solar division she built up? Squeeze out the few women and ethnic minorities she hired on her crew? Augie's insights corroborated everything she learned so far about Celara.

"Well, I think it's possible that some people do carry the capitalist ideal too far," she replied carefully.

"They want that fresh, clean, crisp, new, *green* money, Marti. You know, you're in a perfect position to do something about this."

"About what?"

"Celara's gangster behavior."

He shocked her into silence.

Then she finally said, "What exactly are you talking about, Augie?" *I need more data.*

"Marti, they're trying to take it all. That means the green energy industry too which is a pretty open field—for now. But who knows for how long? They don't want to leave anything for anyone else. These days, you have to go green to get green. And that's what they're doing."

Marti held her breath, waited to hear more.

"It's not right," he concluded. "Marti? Marti, why'd you go quiet?"

*These days, you have to go green to get green. And that's what we're doing. These days, you have to go green to get green. And that's what we're doing. These days...*

"Oh Augie, that reminds me, I actually have to get started on a report."

He tried to interrupt her, but she disconnected. Thirteen or fifteen years ago, when Augie worked for Celara, Celara was still under the leadership of Alex's father. Celara wasn't green yet. Though Alex might have supervised Augie, if they spoke then, it wasn't about anything green. Green wasn't a notion until Alex assumed leadership of the firm four years ago. The solar focus was a recent development with A.J.'s arrival about three years ago. That meant Alex and Augie spoke recently.

*I need more data.*

Her mind whirled like a microfilm machine. Page by page, she visualized the research she acquired.

She sped forward. Backward. She visualized the words—Lakeside Power Plant. Augie's employer. Not on a white background. On a grey background. Newsprint. But not an article. She remembered now. A classified ad. The kind she usually skipped because, frankly, they were boring.

The local weekly paper lay on the side table where she tossed it. She turned the classified ad pages one by one until she got to the Legal Notices.

**LEGAL NOTICES**
Advertisement for Bids
Lakeside Power Plant

Sealed proposals for the upgrade of Lakeside Power Plant will be received at 987 Smith St. until 10am, one month from the date of this notice. At that time, the bids will be publicly opened and read aloud.
1. Description of work for bid: The proposed construction consists of: efficient lighting-fixture upgrades, new electrical control-system schemes, installation of products and device for heat and power systems, solar photovoltaics, energy-storage devices, energy-monitoring and management systems
2. The procurement will be subject to federal and state regulations.
3. This procurement strongly encourages increased use of disadvantaged businesses and entrepreneurs.
4. All pertinent documents are available at 987 Smith St.

5. All bids must be accompanied by a Bidder's bond, certified check, bank cashier's check or bank draft payable to Lakeside Power Plant for ten percent (10%) of the total amount of the Bid as provided in the Bidder instructions.

6. A mandatory Pre-Bid conference of all prospective Bidders and/or their representatives will be held at 987 Smith St. All Bidders are required to attend and participate in the conference.

7. Rejection of Bids: Lakeside Power Plant reserves the right to reject any or all bids and to waive technicalities. Unless the Bids are rejected for good cause, award of contract shall be made to the lowest responsible and responsive Bidder.

In the next column, she saw the other notice dated one day later.

**LEGAL NOTICES**
Notice to Disadvantaged Businesses

Celara Solar Construction is seeking qualified disadvantaged businesses for various upgrades for the Lakeside Power Plant project. All disadvantaged businesses should contact, in writing, (certified letter return receipt requested), Alexander King at Celara Solar Construction to discuss the subcontracting opportunities. All negotiations must be completed prior to the bid opening date.

*I need more data.*

At Celara's party, it didn't seem as if Alex and Augie knew each other. But Lake City was a little big town. Everyone knew everyone else or knew *of* someone else.

So what was the civil rights speech about, really? What was her role? *Close the door.*

Marti's unease grew. A.J. would run this job. A.J.? She couldn't believe A.J. was part of the club. At least no more than she she was part of the club.

A.J.'s boss, Nate, and then, of course her own boss, Alex, pulled the strings. She and A.J. danced.

The next morning, she carried the weekly to the office. Evan and Alex held a whispered conversation outside her cubicle for about half an hour. Because it sounded so creepy, she walked away for about ten minutes. That's what she usually did whenever Evan went into orbit. She made copies of the bid notices.

When she came back to her cubicle, Alex and Evan were still at it with the loud whispers.

"What are you doing?" She shouted—jokingly, she hoped.

"We're just talking about confidential matters," Evan answered.

"You guys sound like serial killers." She laughed.

The air that circulated over the office cubicles constricted. Everyone in the vicinity gasped aloud. She felt prickles on her skin. How *dare* she speak to Alexander, the King like that!

Half an hour later, she felt a presence behind her. Alex loomed over her. He didn't meet her eyes. Instead, flat, crystalline discs of silicon stared over her shoulder at her computer screen which revealed her latest report. Supportive research lay scattered across her desk.

He walked away. She turned back to her desk to see what he found so interesting. The bid notices and their copies lay amongst her research. The print was small she reassured herself. But she recognized her denial for what it was.

Hyper-alert, vigilant, and aware, Alex noticed *everything*. Marti closed her eyes.

◆ ◆ ◆ ◆

Alone in her apartment, Marti composed a letter to Chris. She would see the movie after she finished her latest project.

Why did she stay? What did she have to prove and to whom? She couldn't change Alex any more than he could change her.

Chris wrote her back urging her to see the movie now. It was just that good, his homeboys told him. If she waited too long, she may not have a chance.

Days passed.

Marti yanked back the veil from her childhood. She forced herself to remember Christina's slow, destructive descent. Her mother became another person before her eyes.

Christina allowed her husband to ruin her better nature and destroy her happiness. What could her mother have done differently?

Marti shook herself.

If she had nothing, she had self-respect. That is what it came down to. Alex could take many things away from her because, face it, he's rich, connected, and powerful. But he could not take away the love she had for herself. It was not her responsibility to change him or to save him. But it was her responsibility to save herself.

She had a choice.

Marti gave it one more day of careful thought. She walked through a typical day in the life at Celara. She examined her thoughts, feelings, and emotions since she joined the project. She didn't sleep enough hours. She suffered stress headaches. She alternated between fear and anger at the spy games and malicious immaturity.

"Dude, you are so acting worse than a girl," Evan told Ronny when Ronny urged him to hurry along some reports.

Evan sent out a notice for an all-staff meeting, to which Marti was not invited.

But that wasn't all.

Alex excluded her from the executive meetings too. Instead, he assigned her to interview one of the executives prior to the meeting. As always, she had her voice recorder.

"Why not biodiesel?"

"Iowa's stronger in that arena."

"But they're also stronger in wind, right?"

"Well, yes."

"So why does Celara trend towards wind and not biodiesel?"

"Because while Iowa dominates biodiesel and wind usage as a percentage of total energy output, Lake City has a stronger manufacturing base."

"And?"

"That means we can build turbines more efficiently here than they can there. Celara gets in line behind no one."

"But not biodiesel?"

"Of no interest."

"And hydro?"

"Not cost effective. Too many uncertainties. It would be a nightmare to build that kind of industry on the lake."

She wrote up the interview. Then she went back through the write-up line-by-line because the executive disputed everything he told her.

Her paycheck was delayed again.

She was tough. She was! Wasn't she? She wasn't a quitter. She wasn't! Was she?

She dealt with everything they threw at her. Still, the violation of her privacy remained the ultimate deal breaker.

Marti quietly arranged her exit.

"The majority of the work for the project is complete." She inched her resignation across his desk. He didn't change expression. He didn't bother to look down—her interview all over again. He waited.

"I can telecommute. You know, work from home to finish the next two weeks and whatever else remains from my end of the project."

"We'd be happy to consider you for any freelance assignments as they become available."

"Great."

She shook hands around the office. Made vague remarks. Packed up her desk. Left.

◆ ◆ ◆ ◆

That night, she called Reverend March. The conversation, as their conversations always did, went quickly downhill.

"Why did Reba have to be the one to tell me about it? We've spoken several times and you never mentioned that you needed a transplant or that you were diabetic. Even though you can't bring yourself to acknowledge me as your biological child and inform me of something I need to know..."

"When you take that ugly tone, you sound just like your mother."

"Don't you fucking talk about my mother, Reverend!"

"Language, Martina! I am *still* your father!"

Marti didn't reply.

"Why are you even arguing about something that happened thirty years ago?"

"You're arguing too."

"That's enough! Look, Martina, it's about time you grew up and learned some truth about how things really were back then. How many times do you think she showed up at my home drunk? How many times do you think I stopped by in the middle of the afternoon and found her laid out with whiskey and cigarette butts everywhere? How many times did she approach me with her hand out for food and then I come to the house with groceries and some strange man's got his head stuck in the refrigerator eating whatever's left? I gave her money to finish the remodeling. Who knows where that went? But what kinds of things do you think she offered to do for me if I gave her some extra cash?"

"You're a liar!"

"It happened, Martina."

"You drove her to desperation. She did what she had to do for us since you didn't give a damn. She knew you didn't care about her. And she knew you didn't care about us either."

"She's the one who bailed, Martina. She's the one who took the easy way out."

"Easy? You made her life a living hell. I saw it all the way up until the last moment. And if you saw all of those men in our house, then why didn't you do something like a father should?"

"Martina..."

"And Chris knows that you hate him. Your own son. Why do you hate him so much? He was a little boy. He didn't do anything to you."

"He's not a little boy now, is he? No. He's a grown man and responsible for himself and how he feels. Speaking of Christian, what about you, Martina? Where were you when he started that fire? That's what sent her over the edge."

A sick feeling developed in Marti's stomach. "You told her to do it!" She couldn't hold back a sob.

"My life was worth five times more than that of a drunken alcoholic slut who couldn't even feed her own children or clean her own house."

"I can't believe you!" Marti gasped. After all these years, he finally said again what she hoped was just a nightmarish creation of her mind—his last words to Christina.

"Get off that high horse, Martina. Where were you? What kind of sister were you? What kind of daughter? Ask yourself the same questions you're asking me for once."

"Stop it!" She wouldn't reward him with her tears. At last, she saw him for what he was, a selfish, selfish man who devoured everyone and everything that threatened his supremacy. Christina... Chris... her.

"You know, I hate to say it, but you and your mother are just alike."

As soon as they started, her tears stopped. That was supposed to be the show-stopper. That was her usual cue to fly off the handle. That statement was to bring down the curtain in their long-running off-Broadway drama. Scream. Defend her personal worth. Beg for approval and forgiveness from a judgmental audience of one.

Not anymore.

For thirty-nine years she wondered what was so wrong with her, that Reverend March could be so disappointed. All along, it was him. *Him!*

Marti summoned her coldest tone. "I'd rather be like her than you. At least she loved us."

"Martina."

"You have disappointed me, Reverend March."

She hung up the phone.

*Fuck your kidney!*

♦ ♦ ♦ ♦

Her job hunt did not go well.

*Lake City Tribune* HR Recruiter: "Ma'am, if you want to be a copyeditor for *Lake City Tribune,* you have to come through me. Maybe start with an unpaid internship in the Central District. Eventually, you'll be able to work from North Central after you put in a few years."

Marti: "The Central District? Isn't that where those five women were thrown into garbage dumpsters and set on fire?

Recruiter: "Yes."

Marti: "And the police have no leads?"
Recruiter: "Well, maybe you can help with that."
Marti: Dead silence.
Recruiter: "It's a competitive market. You have to prove yourself."

Agent at Staffing Agency: "You do realize that we do background checks and pull credit reports?
Marti: "Yes."
Agent: "Well, we'll also need you to take a medical exam, drug test, lie detector test, and personality test. Just wanted you to know that."
Marti: "The job ad didn't mention those requirements."
Agent: Shrugs.
Marti: "All that just to write web content?"
Agent: "Afraid so."

Non-profit executive: "See, the thing is... I mean, you know. I could get a work-study student from one of the colleges to report on community events for $2.50 an hour."
Marti: Feels dismayed.
Executive: "Tell you what. Let's just talk back and forth about it a little more. I'll get back to you in a few days."

Small independent press owner: "Okay, I thought you said you had an English degree."
Marti: "Yes."
Owner: "It says here that it's a graduate degree, *not* a PhD."
Marti: "Right."
Owner: "Okay, I'm pretty sure you said you had a PhD."
Marti: Knows for a fact that she did not.
Marti: "I said I had a degree in English. My resume defines the degree that I said I have as an M.A. Masters level."
Owner: Indicates her portfolio.
Owner: "So, you really wrote all this?"
Marti: Incredulous.
Marti: "Yes, I really did."
Owner: Long pause.
Owner: "You're on public transportation, aren't you?"
Marti: Silence.

Owner: "Miss, I'm very sorry. I just don't feel comfortable with your application."
Marti: Silently stands up. Shakes hands.
Owner: "...the confusion... my obligation to this firm..."
Marti: Turns her back and walks out.
Owner: "...that everyone fit in and be upfront and feel comfortable with one another."
Marti: Is already on the sidewalk.

◆ ◆ ◆ ◆

Marti walked into her apartment. She turned on a lamp. She sank down on her sofa. Sat still for a long time.

Amid mass lay-offs and hiring freezes in a bad economy, most people would consider it an extremely bad time to walk away.

Most people, according to Evan, would consider themselves lucky to have a job. In fact, her own father would call her a fool.

She would pay a big price for leaving Celara.

◆ ◆ ◆ ◆

# 9 The Separation

Autumn in Lake City was like no place else on Earth. The temperature dropped just a few degrees. Most leaves still remained green. An early morning lake wind urged her and Worth forward.

She felt so relaxed around Worth, or was it the bike? They pedaled along the lake trail together. Like Worth, she had a lot more time on her hands. Unlike Worth, she had serious concerns about paying her bills.

But not today, she reminded herself. Today, the sun overpowered the morning chill that blew off the lake. Marti smiled when the cool breeze turned into a warm embrace.

"I just like to get my mind off things," she told Worth. Worth knew only that she took a break from work. She decided to leave the gory details of her situation for another time.

"So it's kind of rough on women there?"

"It's all in how you play the game."

"Play to win. Is that the secret?"

"I wish I knew—then I'd be winning."

"What about the woman who was with you at the booth?"

"The little girl?"

"No. The big girl. A.J., I think her name was."

"Oh yeah."

"I spoke to her a little after you left."

"She's doing all right as far as I know."

"I got the impression of a pit bull."

"What? A pit bull?" Marti laughed into the wind.

"She chewed my head off."

"That doesn't sound like A.J. What did you do, Worth? What did you say to her?"

"Come on, Marti."

"You, come on, Worth." Marti teased. "Look, her bark is worse than her bite. She has to be tough because she leads a crew of men. But I've never seen her go on attack for no reason."

"Okay, well it's not like I dropped a box of nails off the roof."

"Oh Worth." Marti laughed hard enough to nearly fall off her bike. "Stop it. Stop! I was trying to feel sorry for myself today. You messed up my plan."

He grinned back at her. "All in the charm." The wind ruffled his light brown hair, blonde in places from the sun.

"Of course it is."

She and Worth turned their bikes around to head back to the museum. Worth disappeared to continue research on the lake. Marti helped Beryl at the front desk.

"I've found myself weeded out a few times. Overqualified. Underqualified. It's really rough out there this year."

"It's a rough time for everyone," Beryl reminded her. "Do you regret walking away?"

"Not at all. I mean, I miss the money, of course. But it had to be done. In the meantime, I did learn quite a bit about life while I was there."

"Winning doesn't always mean staying in a bad situation. But it does mean standing up for yourself."

"Let's just say, I have a lot more insight than I did before."

"Then it sounds like you won."

"I've been doing volunteer work. And I've been taking community classes between job interviews."

"Good, good."

"Best of all, I'm keeping up my gym routine. I'm still hoping for good things in life. Beryl, I want to thank you for helping me to see it through."

"Of course, dear. You never know. Someday I might need you to see me through something."

"Well, I'd like to. But you always seem to have it so together."

Beryl chuckled. Marti dove in.

"Worth's a good friend for me, Beryl." She hesitated. "We've never really spoken about him, but you know what? I didn't realize he was your son when we were younger."

"He told you?"

"He did."

"Well, Marti, I can say with completely unbiased authority that Worth is a very good man."

"That he is." Marti waited for Beryl to elaborate. But instead, Beryl turned just a tad away. Her white and gold mane of hair covered part of her face.

"So, does he do research every day, or does he hang out with anyone in particular?" Marti couldn't stop her curiosity on how Worth earned a living because she knew his work with Save a Lake was as a volunteer.

"He keeps to himself, Marti." Beryl's voice flattened, grew cooler. Like her son, Beryl was polite, but not forthcoming.

"Oh." Marti didn't dare to ask about the loss of Beryl's grandchildren.

"He's not looking for anything more than what he has right now." Marti sensed the warning underneath the words. *Stay away from my son.*

◆ ◆ ◆ ◆

After March gave his doctor permission, Marti listened to a thorough explanation of the surgical procedure. It would have to be done sometime within the next year.

She crossed that task off her list with a sigh. Time to return to the task at hand—her job search.

"Because of the economy, we decided to cancel this position. Good luck in your endeavors," the email stated. It went pretty much like that the third week.

◆ ◆ ◆ ◆

"It's life experience, Teresita."

Teresa allowed a wistful smile at Chris's use of the Spanish diminutive.

"The school of hard knocks. State Pen, rather than Penn State."

Teresa's smile disappeared.

"Baby, its gallows humor," he told her. "I have to laugh sometimes. Dwelling on things I missed out on in life would drive me insane if I let it. It's driven a lot of people here over the edge. They scream about it every night."

"You are not crazy, Chris."

"I've seen... every horrible thing that could be done to a human being here. You have no idea."

"I know, Chris."

"I learned that a dark heart beats inside every single human God created. People, no matter who they are or where they are, will do very bad things to protect what they consider most important—money, pride, possessions, reputation."

"Not me." Teresa shook her head.

"Oh really?" Chris raised his eyebrows. "What if someone tried to hurt Mari or Kina? Then what?"

"Then I would kill them!"

"See? Remember that movie I told my sister about..."

"Where the employer considered the woman a threat?"

"And they would do anything, which is everything, to shut her down."

"I don't want anything to happen to her."

"Just keep me informed."

"She talks to me."

"That's all I'm saying. Marti is my sister. That's my family. Anybody who messes with her messes with me. I can't let that happen."

"Are you afraid for her?"

"I can't afford to feel afraid for her."

"Maybe she could move in with me and the girls."

"No."

"But..."

"No." His tone signaled finality. "I don't want Mari and Kina involved."

Teresa nodded.

"Time's up." The guard walked towards Chris with purpose. Teresa sat still. He walked away.

Back on the yard, his boys recognized the arctic cold burn in his eyes. They averted their own. When he was ready, he would ask them for what he wanted. Eventually, they provided him with more information on Celara.

Alex sent her an email. "Give me a jingle."

That one line filled her with dread. What more did he want from her? Another job. Though she carefully deposited each check, she still needed a source of income. She could ride things out maybe a couple more months, but she needed the money. What choice did she have?

*Call. Don't call.*

*Call. Don't call.*

After she called him back, Marti met Alex downtown outside his early morning business meeting. Pride went not only before pain, but also before the rent and student loan bills.

It was as if she never left.

"I need your help to market and promote a forthcoming retail division for Celara Solar Construction."

He handed her a package.

"But first, you need to modify this business plan to fit Celara's needs."

Marti opened the package and took out a thick binder. Alex watched her flip through it. His cell phone rang. He turned away to take the call. Same old Alex.

She scanned quickly. Noted a lot of information gone through with thick, black marker. Censored. She frowned. Where did this information come from?

Alex finished his call.

Marti pointed to the blackened parts "Why is all this…"

"I need it done in three weeks." Alex wheeled around, stepped back into the meeting, shut the door in her face.

Some things never changed.

"Good morning and how are you, Alex? Been getting your fiber? No? Pity."

◆ ◆ ◆ ◆

Augie completed the deal in the dark hours before the sun came up that morning. He handed them a package. Tonight, any minute now, they would hand him a package. He waited for the guy in the evening shadows of late September. He checked the glow on his watch.

A car door slammed in the distance. Augie straightened his shoulders. He would show no sign of weakness. Monsters like these fed on weakness. A few minutes later, a man emerged from the shadows. Augie walked forward. He met the man in a patch of moonlight that filtered through the exhaust towers. The conversation didn't last long. There wasn't much to say.

"See this? This starts the clock. You have sixty seconds to clear the area. You already know where to put it?"

"Yeah, I know."

"Okay. See ya." The man shrugged then walked swiftly back to his car. He drove away with the headlights off.

Actually Augie had *six* seconds to clear the area. Needless to say, he wasn't fast enough. When Lakeside Power exploded, his life joined the fiery red tornado that raged upward to the stars over Lake City's clear, black sky.

◆ ◆ ◆ ◆

*Lake City Tribune's* morning edition reported news of the explosion. Breathtaking photographs and video of the blaze dominated local news outlets. Then regional news seized the story on an endless cycle complete with wailing fire trucks, sinister plumes of smoke, frantic shouts, and expressions of horrified glee from onlookers pushed back by Lake City's finest. Internet reports created a national melee. The whole disaster merited its own theme music and logo.

"At this time, Laura, we are unaware of casualties. The company is conducting an ongoing roll call of its employees through various means of communication. We do know from unnamed sources that Lakeside Power was in the midst of complicated and drawn out contract negotiations with its workforce as well as contemplating strategic upgrades to its operating technology. This is in light of its impending sale..."

Marti sat stunned for hours in front of her television. She called Augie's cell phone with dread. Heard only a buzzing noise. She called his landline, hung up on his recorded greeting over and over.

Evening news reported the failure of one employee to check in with Lakeside—August Daniels, Project Manager.

◆ ◆ ◆ ◆

Chris watched the story unfold in the recreation room. By then, the media described August Daniels as a "person of interest." A U.S. Marshal, the Lake City police chief, the Lake City fire chief, and a Lake City search and rescue representative provided analyses of How Such A Tragedy Could Have Happened.

Statements changed from "no comment" and "not enough information at this time," and "too early to judge" to tentative speculation on various hypothetical worst case scenarios. The sympathetic tone grew darker.

Local and national news media developed a sinister psychological profile on August Daniels. They uncovered every unfortunate deed from grade school forward. They camped outside his family's home. They interviewed his friends and co-workers.

"She's keeping a low profile," Teresa reported. "I haven't seen her out. I know she's home, but I can't keep her on the phone long enough to ask her what's going on."

"Celara's keeping a low profile too, even though they're one of the major bidders for Lakeside's contract."

"How do you know?"

"How do I know anything?" Chris shrugged. "Look people who worked on Celara's crews years ago still make the sign of the cross when they talk about it."

"My God."

"Thuggish intimidation and bullying always starts at the top. You have a puppet master who makes a little twitch of the strings. Next thing you know, a chain of fools starts dancing, making a big show in front of everyone." He paused. "Nobody bothers to look up to see what's really going on."

"What's really going on?"

Chris laughed. "Baby, you don't want to know."

"Yes, I do. So I can walk the other direction."

"How can I explain this?" He steepled his hands to assume the role of lecturer. "Celara is the special type of concern that gives to charity. That makes speeches. That wears suits. That attends conferences. That wins awards. That shakes hands with the mayor, the governor, the congressmen, the senators. That goes skin diving in the Caribbean. That skis in

Switzerland. That drinks wine in France. That plays golf with the big boys."

"That hired Marti?"

"Yes."

♦ ♦ ♦ ♦

Marti flipped through the retail business plan, Alex's baby that he ordered her to nurture and develop to market. Her unease heightened to suspicion then full-out horror.

It couldn't be.

Fear fluttered in her stomach, tried to escape her body in a scream. *Don't give in to panic, Marti. Panic will not help you. You need a clear head to figure this out. Think, girl.*

She went back to the Christmas party. All of them were there that night. She replayed a mental film of the evening.

Alex sat to her left. Augie sat to her right. She was pretty sure neither of them acknowledged the other in a familiar way. They were pleasant. They talked about nothing important.

But... she glanced up... to see Evan smirk her direction. At the time, she thought it was because she sat between two men and that he planned to relay some salacious type of gossip about her reputation in the office the next day. It would be just like him. She told herself to brush it off as a perversion of Evan's own sick mind if anyone in the office said anything about it to her. But no one did.

If Augie worked for Alex, as Augie said, and if Alex chose to blacklist him, as Augie claimed, then Evan would know that. Everyone knew that Evan handled Alex's delicate work. Maybe, for once, the smirk was not for her. Maybe... it was for Augie?

Her stomach rolled over.

Despite Alex's acting ability, she didn't pick up anything false that night. Maybe irritation with her at one point, but then that was normal for him.

*Close the door.*

Alex might not recognize Augie or remember a disagreement from years ago. But Evan would if he maintained Alex's status quo. Marti sat back on her sofa. She blew out a breath. *Wait.*

The next morning, search and rescue found the body of one August Daniels fifteen feet away from an incendiary device.

◆ ◆ ◆ ◆

"Well, you asked me about power plant accidents in the Midwest. We've got news clippings that go back several decades." Beryl handed her four boxes of documents.

Marti chose the box that held papers for the last twenty years. She ignored the waves of nausea in her stomach. She compared her list of recent Celara project acquisitions. Eight of the ten projects matched. A friendly firm that she remembered subcontracted Celara and participated in one of their meetings won the other two. Ten for ten then.

Going back five years, small accidents, acts of sabotage, break-ins, equipment and supply thefts, labor disruptions, even a chemical spill preceded each explosion. Each explosion preceded a project takeover. Of all the firms in the vicinity, only Celara maintained the logistical capacity to finish the necessary work on schedule, usually with emergency government funding.

Beryl found Marti with her head in her hands. Marti straightened up, careful to mention "how tired she'd been lately, from all the research she'd been doing." Beryl said nothing.

◆ ◆ ◆ ◆

He had observers high and low. While his employees zigzagged frantically around the office, he already knew where they would go, what they would say, how they would feel, how they would react. He heard their whispers as desperate screams through clenched teeth. He absorbed their energy then smiled with delighted triumph. He watched them raise and lower eyelids that acknowledged secret plans and alliances.

All of them open books that he turned page by page. Buttons he pushed. Cards he shuffled. Games he played. Channels he tuned. Puppets. Dolls. Action figures. *Pets*. The ringmaster of the circus the world knew as Celara Solar Construction called forth each of his performers to amuse him and thus, earn their slice off his cake.

He gave them so much of himself. He sliced off pieces of his wealth and power then doled them out as treats to the select few who proved themselves worthy by taking care of his dirty work. All the risks he took to acquire greatness and to make their lives better didn't matter. No. Nobody cared about that. They made him angry with their lack of gratitude, their shitty attitudes.

Where was the support? Where was the loyalty? Where was the part when they gave back to him? *When the fuck did that happen?*

And what the fuck was Marti's problem? Where was his fucking business plan!

Alex got up with a ferocious grin then quick-stalked his way through Celara's divisions kicking cubicle ass.

"So the underachievers, nincompoops, and the incompetent feel taken for granted? You want some thank yous? Is that what you want?"

Work or its closest imitation ceased. Alex held everyone's undivided attention. *Let it begin.*

"Thank you, Evan! Thank you for billing hours of overtime writing one fucking, fucked-up-ass misspelled letter!"

Alex walked four steps forward to hit his next mark.

"Thank you, Ms. Neglectful! Oh yes! Thank you, Leslie for forgetting to messenger the construction permit applications downtown yesterday. Goddamn, thank you!"

He projected his voice all the way back to the warehouse, a thunderous warning of the approaching storm.

"For the love of God, don't everyone jump up and thank *me* for leading this ship of fools out of the Dark Ages. Heaven forbid anyone should thank me for anything!"

*Here I come!*

"Ronny, don't let me interrupt a two-hour business lunch complete with a three-glass martini minimum. Fucking loser."

His head swiveled stage right.

"It's three o'clock, A.J.! Does anyone know where Celara's clients are? Hello? What the fuck? Echoooo!"

Finished with the engineers and project managers, he found the estimators. He hit the button that stopped the blueprint press.

"How about I buy lunch? How about I fucking play bartender too and mix the drinks my-goddamn-fucking-self! Would you finish the estimates on schedule then? Would you? Could you, goddammit? Could any of you be my goddamn neighbor and get your shit together and get some shit done around here?"

White-hot bolts of power ricocheted around the cubicle maze and scorched the glass windows of the corner offices.

"Are you entertained? *Are you fucking entertained?*"

Alex stomped back to his office. His employees picked up the pieces of their self-esteem tornadoed all over Celara's walls and ceiling.

*Fuck! I need another vacation.*

"This is fucking ridiculous," he said aloud. "Evan to see Alex," he summoned over the intercom.

Evan entered then moved towards a chair.

"No, don't sit. This won't take long." Alex waved him back. "We have to get Marti back here fulltime."

"I agree."

"She'll report directly to me. Not you. You can't handle her."

"That's probably for the best." Evan knew Alex wasn't in the mood for a debate. The entire office knew that. "But I'd like to offer a suggestion."

"What!"

"Just in case Marti refuses to come back, we should attempt to recruit someone like her."

"Evan." Alex closed his eyes for a brief moment as if to find the strength to deal with a dull two-year-old child. "There isn't anyone like her. Which means Marti absolutely cannot refuse."

Evan remained silent.

"I'll have to encourage her to make the right decision for herself and Celara. I'll certainly do my best to explain it to her as nicely as I can. Because if I can't have her, I'll be damned if anyone else will and that's a fact. And don't fuck it up for me next time"

Evan gripped the back of the chair he wasn't allowed to sit in.

"That's all." His boss waved him away.

❖ ❖ ❖ ❖

"Look Terry, I've been looking at my options all this month. Guess what?"

"What?"

"It didn't take me that long. You know why?"

"Why?"

"Because I don't have any."

"There's always an option, Marti."

"Terry, I'm trying to tell you. My economic outlook is growing grimmer every day. Utility bills, student loan, rent. It never stops."

"But your father..."

"Terry, no. Surely you must realize by now that our family is not like your family. It's not the same."

"Okay, I have a little extra I set aside."

"You mean take money out of the mouths of two little girls? My own nieces? Absolutely not. And let me tell you this. If I thought for a minute you were depriving Mari and Kina to help anyone who could help themselves that would absolutely piss me off. I would definitely have to tell you about that."

"I wouldn't."

"Good. Don't."

"So what're going to do?"

"What I have to do."

"Chris won't like it."

"Then don't tell him."

Teresa blew out a breath. "I'm not going to keep secrets from him."

"I'm sorry. You're right. I'm not gonna ask you to do that. Just..."

"Just what?"

"I've looked at it from every angle. The economy is dying in the gutter like, like its throat got slashed and bled dry by a broken bottle. I mean, you see the news."

"Of course. We had to let three more people go at our restaurant. You know we'd hire you in a minute, but we're barely getting by now."

"I know, girl. That's what I'm saying. High unemployment. High taxes. High prices. More people than jobs. And guess what? Alex can and likely will, hell, probably already has, destroyed my career. I can only see one way out."

Teresa shook her head. "There has to be another way."

"Teresa, I've tried everything. Only one door's open. And yes, it leads to the darkest, dankest basement of my nightmares."

"What does your gut tell you?"

"My gut says," Marti couldn't stop the sigh, "Well, actually, it's more like a warning klaxon from the deepest part of my soul."

"You should listen."

"I am. I hear it. But I've got to do what I've got to do. I'm going to finish his job. I'm going to give him what he wants."

"Marti, don't."

"I'm going to throw heaps of it into his face until he throws his hands up."

"Think about it for a while longer."

"I'm out of time, Teresa. I've been running on fumes since I left Celara." Marti blew out a sigh. "Look. I'm going to hook him to an intravenous tube and fill his veins with it until he overdoses. I'm going to open his mouth and force-feed him until he's absolutely sick of it and vomits at the sight of me. Then he'll want me to go. That's when I'll get out."

"That's your big plan?"

"I got nothing else."

"Chris is not going to like this."

"You already said that."

"I'm just saying."

"I know. I hear you."

"Then why would you do something you know is a mistake?"

"Okay, Terry. I'll tell you."

"Tell me something that makes sense."

"I'm trying! It's like this. I always remember my and Chris's mother from a child's perspective. Because I only knew her as a child. You see?"

"Right."

"A couple of days ago, I went back to the Central District for the first time since me and Chris went to live with the Reverend. It's been over twenty-five years. I took a bus to the stop by our old house. The new owners finally finished it. They planted a couple of trees. Or someone did. It actually looks like a home now instead of an urban survivalist camp- the way it used to look when we lived there."

"What did you do when you got there, Marti?"

"I thought about things for a while. Really thought things through. Then I turned around and walked away from all the things that should have happened but did not. I left the things that could have happened, but did not. Those things did not exist. That life did not exist. Those people did not exist and they never will. Yesterday is gone."

"Marti, Marti..."

"But even with foresight and hindsight, here I am." A little sob escaped her despite her best efforts to push it down. "I'm on the ropes, Terry, just like my mother. I said I would never let myself get to this place."

"You're being too hard. A lot of people are in trouble these days, Marti."

"But unlike my mother, I don't have children. I don't have responsibility to anyone but myself. And still I messed it all up. I used to judge her for the way she brought us up, but I'm starting to understand it a little better know. Christina did the best she could with the cards she'd been dealt by life, by God, and by Reverend March. Me and Chris ate every day, you know. We had a roof over our heads. We had an education. It could have been better, yes. But then again, it could have been so much worse."

Teresa remained silent.

"I waited for the return bus and by the time it arrived I decided that no matter what circumstances threw at me, I would survive."

"You're sure want to go through with it?"

"I owe Christina that, at the very least. I'm not a quitter."

◆ ◆ ◆ ◆

As the first order of business, she returned the security key assigned to her by Celara back to Leslie at the reception desk. She knew she could not deal with both Alex and Evan on a full-time basis. Small doses only. Very, very small doses.

For too long, Alex set the agenda and assigned Marti's role in his dramas. She was not helpless. She was not without power. She was a writer, no? Then *she* would lay out the scene. She would do as he asked. But she would do it *her* way.

She had all the information she needed to complete Alex's assignment from previous research. She would still meet her deadlines. A writer did that.

"Leslie, do you mind giving them that message for me since they're not here?"

Leslie made a dramatic show of glancing left and right. Marti did the same from instinct. She leaned closer to hear Leslie's lowered drawl.

"I passed by Alex's door yesterday afternoon while he was shouting at Evan."

"Again?"

"Oh you know those two." Leslie smiled. "I didn't linger or anything, but I kind of heard things. You know Evan worked hand-in-hand with Kate to run the office?"

Marti nodded.

"Well, Kate, being Kate, reached too high. She tried to, you know, cut out the middle man to get to the big guy directly."

"Alex?"

"Um hm. He wasn't having it because there was some kind of problem with Lexa."

"What happened to Lexa?"

"I don't know. She got sick at school and Alex was furious."

"Oh, because of the candy?"

"Something like that." Leslie drew back. Turned her head aside.

Marti waited.

"Anyway, Alex confronted Evan about Kate's behavior, or that's what it sounded like. He goes, 'Evan you need to keep Kate in line and see to it she doesn't hurt Celara, and especially not my daughter.' Then a lot of cursing that could peel paint off the walls."

"That sounds about right."

"Then Evan goes, 'I'm on it, Alex.' Next morning, we saw Kate's office space had been swept completely clean overnight. No computer. Nothing but a letter of resignation taped on her cabinet for all who passed by to see. I looked at it. It was just a standard letter of resignation with a signature."

"Really?"

"Somebody said she left town."

"Must have been serious, whatever it was. Wait a minute. Les, I almost forgot. Kate told me she wanted to talk to me about something, right before I saw the dentist. I never got back to her because things got so hectic. Do you know what was on her mind?"

Leslie shook her head.

"Maybe she knew she was in trouble with Alex or Evan and wanted to tell somebody?"

"I have no idea, Marti. She didn't say anything to me."

"Hm. Look, do you have her home phone number or her cell phone number? I kind of feel like I need to figure this out."

"I'm not supposed to give out employee phone numbers," Leslie told her. "But then," she paused, "Kate's not an employee anymore, is she?"

"No, she isn't."

"Neither are you, are you?"

Marti smiled. "No, I'm not."

Leslie winked then wrote Kate's contact information for her on a piece of paper.

"Thanks, Leslie."

"Don't mention it."

"Okay."

"Seriously. Don't mention it to anyone. Honey, you probably did the right thing by working from home. He thought you were after his job."

Marti frowned. "He who?"

"Evan."

"Evan? You're kidding me. Who would want his job? My talents lie elsewhere, thank God."

"What I mean is he could see that Alex really needed you and how hard you worked on the project. It had been stalled for a year and a half before you came."

"I couldn't possibly do what Evan does."

"No, you couldn't." Leslie glanced at her sidelong. "Not many could. But you could've replaced him as the boss's favorite."

Just then, a visitor entered the front lobby. Leslie smiled and nodded as Marti headed for the door.

"Good luck, honey."

"Thanks, Les."

Marti nodded, then left Celara. With two children in college and a chronic back condition that required medical insurance, Leslie kept her head down. But she had a good idea of the obstacle course Marti ran; the same course she, Helen, A.J., and the other women navigated every single damn day.

That night, Marti left Kate a message. "Kate, I'm not sure what's going on or what happened at Celara, but a while ago you said you wanted to talk to me about something. I'm concerned because I never got back to you, so I'm checking in, okay? I don't want to bug you. Get back to me if you need to." Marti left her phone number then disconnected.

◆ ◆ ◆ ◆

In the far north suburbs, Alex sat with his psychologist friend in his home office.

"Everyone's looking at me like I'm some kind of monster."

"Are you a monster?"

"I don't know. I might be." Alex paused. "Yeah, I probably am. But that doesn't matter. I can't understand why passion still flows below the surface of my skin even when I try to force her from my mind. I can't shake her off. She's important to me. I need to get her back. You need to figure out how I can do it."

They watched the tape of Marti's interview again. This time, the psychologist pointed out something they missed the first time.

"If you notice, she never takes her eyes off you the whole time you're in the room."

"What? Did she think I was going to steal her purse?"

"Watch again. When you get up to walk out of the room, where is she looking?"

Alex chuckled to himself. "Sweet, sweet, secret little Marti."

"A thorough review of Ms. Butler's history, attitude, demeanor, and writing reveals that major psychological motivating factors to her character originate from a need for career fulfillment, maintenance of professional reputation in the business arena, as well as a strong need to compensate for a lack of development in the personal arena of her social life."

"English please, Doc."

"Specifically, Ms. Butler's adherence to business ethics and social morality can be subjugated to and exploited by a combination of incentives—sexual attachment and career advancement."

"Get to the point."

"I conclude..."

"Small words this time."

"Careful consideration of all factors submitted indicates Ms. Butler will ably serve you as a right and left hand on an executive level. But you have to bind her to you in order to gain her loyalty. Give her a reason to come back to you. You say she isn't with anyone right now, right?"

"I saw her with some jerk. But I couldn't tell what it was with them. It didn't look serious to me."

"Then you know what you have to do."

Alex's eyes glittered. He smiled. "Well, there are worse things."

◆ ◆ ◆ ◆

Alex referred to the methods he used to get what he wanted from people as "strategic resource management." His targets, if they knew it was happening, would call it gaslighting. Hard to detect. Hard to identify. Even harder to prove, Alex's special talents took incredible personal strength and self-awareness to resist.

Alex spent the rest of that afternoon constructing an email that he sent with the subject line, "Business Plan! And the Next Presentation!"

> "I never would have thought that such an independent free spirit like you would be so afraid to take a risk.
>
> I sense that you're feeling kind of sad about how things haven't been working out. I don't blame you. I know you are a special person, kind and sensitive.
>
> I don't know what's caused the vulnerability and mistrust inside of you. I just feel this wall rising up and making it hard for us to move forward together.
>
> We want the same things, Marti. But we keep disappointing each other.

Don't run away and hide now, Marti. Stay with me, and let's work it out so we can both grow stronger together and understand each other better. We should open up to each other and try to see from each other's point of view. Tell me what you want and need from me in order to be happy again. I'll do whatever it takes to make you feel better about things. I'll do anything to get you back where you belong.

Think about what you really want and need from me and from life. Think of what you've been lacking. Think of a way that I can make it happen, then tell me, so we can get started on whatever it is right away and you can meet your responsibilities.

Sometimes I might have seemed kind of abrupt and distant. All I can say is sometimes, I've had my feelings hurt in ways you probably didn't realize at the time. I react poorly to things like that. But my heart is completely open to you. I'm ready to take the next step to bring some productive integrity back into this process..."

It went on and on like that. Marti finished Alex's pleading demand. Dark shadows circled her eyes from a lack of sleep. She lost weight.

"Alex, the deadline you gave me to complete the business plan is impossible."

Silence answered her over the phone.

"Okay?"

"I just extended it by one week, Marti. It'll take them that long to wrap their minds around it anyway. Besides, there's a second part."

"What?"

"I need you to create a presentation for Celara's executive committee on a hypothetical power plant. Not just photovoltaic, solar thermal too."

"A power plant."

"That's right." He hung up on any opinion she intended to offer.

Her gut twisted and rolled which reminded her of the transplant surgery that still hung over her.

Though Reverend March didn't deserve her help, she deserved to feel peace. She made up her mind to do it, even considering the ramifications of how the surgery would affect her own health. However, she put off the call to her father's doctor. Right now, she had to get her own life under control.

Locked inside a tight box, life squeezed her on all sides.

◆ ◆ ◆ ◆

She sat with Teresa while Teresa took a break during a slow period at her family's restaurant.

"Marti, why are you telling me all this?" Teresa held up a hand. "I mean, despite what you discovered at the museum, despite what Chris told you over and over, despite your intuition telling you to run the other direction, you're going to do it?"

"Terry, where could I turn? Alex is friends with Lake City Police. He sponsors their charities. He knows defenders and prosecutors who know judges. He plays golf with everyone who's anyone in Lake City on the weekends."

"You're gonna let them keep pushing you around?"

"According to Evan, and Evan would know, the threat of retaliation is real. If Alex is capable of what I think he is, then it would be in my best interest to cooperate."

"Okay, I'm on the record as saying 'no.'"

"Maybe I can go back to teaching. Or something like that."

"Marti, the public school system just had massive lay-offs."

Marti's mind raced to find a solution. Her fear made her angry. She especially didn't like Alex's slithering beneath her skin like that.

Fear was the reason she called him back and agreed to both deadlines. *She had no choice.* Then she decided pride was the motivation. She did it to finish what she started. She wasn't a quitter. She felt compelled to push back against his implication of cowardice.

What she didn't admit, because it was sick, was that... a part of her simply wanted to see him again.

◆ ◆ ◆ ◆

She called A.J. who answered from the field. Celara's lone female project manager made a heroic effort to bring her project in on schedule and under budget. Late fall in Lake City was notoriously dicey weather-wise. Marti gathered that Alex went especially hard on A.J. in the office.

"Good luck with it, A.J."

"Good luck, yourself, Marti."

On A.J.'s recommendation, Marti arranged to work with Kace from engineering to prove the case for expansion of existing processes to Celara's executives.

◆ ◆ ◆ ◆

"Gentlemen. You want to create new markets? You can do that. You can do three projects concurrently within a six-week schedule. A project manager, a superintendent, and eighteen electricians can do that. But as extra insurance, you can add extra helpers to the labor mix. More on that later." Marti clicked to the next slide.

"These projects would include roof-mounted, ground-mounted, building-integrated, and tracking arrays. Both NEC standards of safety and improved installation practices for photovoltaic energy systems mean a decreased likelihood of shocks and fires..."

Her voice caught. She made sure not to look Alex's direction. "...or personal injury. For instance, on a power plant..." her voice wavered again.

This time she saw Alex narrow his eyes at her. She recovered then pressed on. "... a tracker system that tilts towards the sun maximizes exposure. Moving parts create maintenance issues. We all know that. But it may be good business to have Celara return to provide maintenance. There's money in the comeback. Finally, we can assure the client of maximum sun exposure with multiple mounting orientations."

The executives leaned forward. She clicked the money slide.

"At this time, Celara has the capacity to create the largest ground-mounted solar energy system with tracking in the Midwest. From the ground up, it would take two years for initial operation and five to become fully operational. To retrofit an existing power plant would also take two years."

Kace took over with the specifics of heat pumps and solar heat gain coefficients. Marti stacked her papers. She formed a vague plan to snatch up her belongings and race for the door.

Alex's eyes burned on her again. She looked away from the door, down at her notepad. She scratched unnecessary notes on Kace's discussion of thin-film versus polycrystalline silicon products.

"This would be a substantial system. At least six separate solar systems, approximately one megawatt in size, which would require thousands of photovoltaic modules utilizing multiple large string inverters."

Kace concluded, glanced briefly at Marti, then sat down. Her turn again.

"This hypothetical power plant depends upon engineering and design. Of course, that means building information modeling which we already use to test procedures and processes, to calculate loads and, to customize the system's design. Additionally, Celara's proprietary installation systems and techniques would bring cost down considerably for both new structures and the retrofit allowing for minor engineering on the roof rafters.

Okay, back to labor. Eight non-skilled helpers supervised by the professionals would complete the installations in fewer than six weeks. Celara's mounting hardware doesn't penetrate the roof. That means no leaks and shorter installation time. Happy clients. Return business and referrals. Good times."

She sat down.

Alex delivered the close. She had no doubt he would get what he wanted. The man could sell a pocket full of rain in the middle of a thunderstorm.

"Gentlemen, we have not colonized Mars. We have not cured AIDS or cancer. We have not solved world hunger. Why?" He shrugged. "Because Celara's not working in those industries." A master of timing, he paused for the laugh. Familiar with Alex's performances, his audience delivered.

"We work in power and energy right now, my friends. What we want is to take the future of new and emerging technology. We research it, develop it, design it, install it, and maintain it. As leaders and experts, we keep 'em coming back, as Marti said." He flicked his eyes over her then back to the room.

"Because of Celara's hard work to research, refine, and patent its proprietary installation techniques, we can control and outbid most of the market in Lake City. Even better, we have global patents pending. We have just enough time to get our solar thermal processes streamlined. Policy support for our photovoltaic technology is strong and growing stronger in Lake City.

While Japan, South Korea, Germany, Italy, Spain, China. California and New Jersey have the strongest support from their governments, Lake City is coming to recognize the inevitability of photovoltaic and solar thermal technology dominance over traditional methods."

The executives in the room shifted. Some nodded. Again, Marti struggled not to look towards the exit. She dared not to betray the slightest hint that she knew how Celara brought about policy support.

"Celara is recognized as the Midwest go-to for solar systems. We can do it all. Still, we want to strengthen and increase our ties to our trusted mechanical, water, heating, and lighting sub-contractors and partners. We want new markets in surrounding municipalities—industrial, military, and agricultural."

She didn't want to hear any more. She didn't want to carry another list back to Lake City History Museum to discover future truths.

"Now is not the time to hesitate or shy away from progress. All indications and research determine that the future belongs to Celara. We have the technology. We have the talent."

*Thank you, Kate.* She felt guilty for the mean thought. Her and Kate's relationship neutralized to tolerance, if not friendship, after Marti's dental emergency.

"What we need is to continue to build the industry and the demand."

She wanted to get up and run from the room. Every corner and crevice filled with Alex's wide-eyed wonder at the limitless possibilities. She watched, fascinated. It was a performance geared to electrify.

*Sell it, Alex! Sell it!*

His face flushed with the power of knowing all eyes were on him, including Marti's

He turned to her. "Okay, that's all Marti. Thank you, Kace." Alex indicated the door.

Dismissed, she and Kace gathered their notes and visual aids then wheeled the audio-visual equipment out of the room so the star chamber could continue its closed-door deliberations.

Kace returned to research. She headed towards the front exit. *Nearly there.* But no. Alex quick-stepped past her, waved her towards his office.

"Marti, I just need to follow up with you on one detail."

"Sure." *No! No!*

She followed him into his office. He closed the door behind her and she hesitated. He waved her to a chair.

"Is everyone taking a break?"

"I'm giving them time to mull over the possibilities and talk it over. I don't want to push too hard too fast. But we need to get this show on the road for next year. A few naysayers will speak up. The others will reason them out. I'll come back and hit them with some hard market numbers. If we don't take the industry, someone else will. You and I already know that."

*Nod, Marti.* She nodded.

"They know that too. They just need the courage to take the first step. We'll probably finish up in an hour."

Marti knew her own performance must have pleased Alex. She knew this because he actually looked directly at his pet, Marti, instead of ignoring it when it pissed him off.

"Did it go as you wanted?"

"Ah, you know, we've got some fraidy cats on board."

"Most of them seem responsive."

"It's hard to light a fire under them sometimes. They won't jump on board until its safe."

"Well, a couple of them are worried about the old school workers and how they'll react to new trainees coming in. Jenner mentioned he'd gotten death threats. He's got a family to think about."

Alex waved all that away. "There's always someone dragging his feet. Look, Marti, we're alike in that we put fun on the back burner too often."

*Wasn't he just in Paris on a trip to stock his wine cellar?*

"Long days in the office. A lot of whoopty-do and drama to get work done. But you know, sometimes, when I need a break, I think about all that weird stuff you used to come in here and say to me."

"Like the ordinances that work against lake installations?"

"Sarcasm. There you go again." He chuckled. "It gets my mind off things. No one else talks to me that way."

"They don't dare."

"But you do."

"I guess I'm not as smart as I look."

"Or are you?" Alex looked pleased with their little razzamatazz. "I meant everything I said in my email. Every single word. I feel a lot more inspired, more alive with you on my team. Like things can finally get done around here."

Marti stared at him wondering where the conversation would go.

"You're very special to me, Marti. I don't know if you know that."

He stared at her. She stared back at him. Much as she wanted to, probably needed to, she couldn't get in front of his head game.

"Lexa is spending this weekend with her best friend since I'm so busy. I'd like you to have dinner with me tonight."

"Dinner tonight. Together?"

"Yes, together." He smiled slightly.

"What for?"

The smile disappeared. An awkward silence stretched.

"I mean... by ourselves?"

He sat back in his chair. Challenge. The flint rose up and dared her to try again. Without razzamatazz.

"You... you know that I've got to finish the business plan, right? You said..." she cleared her throat nervously.

"I said..." he encouraged.

"We're... coming up on deadline. I'm almost done, Alex." she finished in a rush, anxious to throw a slab of fresh meat for Alex to gnaw while she made her escape.

The flint subsided.

"Right, the business plan. How's that coming along? Finding everything okay?"

Marti swallowed. "I'll be finished next week."

"Next week then."

Alex shifted papers around on his desk, not looking at her. After a brief moment, she recognized her usual dismissal. She stood up. Backed out of the room. She didn't turn around until she was completely through the doorway.

Then she ran to the bus stop.

He would not forget or forgive. She leaned her forehead against the bus window and closed her eyes.

◆ ◆ ◆ ◆

"That fucker asked you out?"

"Something like that. When I turned him down, he got chilly."

"But he's chilly that anyway, isn't he?"

"He doesn't like to be told 'no.' He doesn't take it very well."

"What do you think will happen?"

"Oh, I'll be left out of the loop. My check will be delayed."

"So, more of the usual."

"Okay, right? He'll delegate Evan for malicious gossip or 'jokes' about my job status."

"So what else is new?"

"Right. Here's the thing. I met every deadline and double-checked my copy. But much as I tried to stay even-keel, to stay professional, and to focus on performance, they do have ammunition."

"What ammunition?"

"I missed days at work, remember? I stayed home some days to get my head straight after Alex and Evan played two-on-one. I overheard Evan tell Ronny that it took me too long to write my reports. I was a waste everyone's time and money."

"What do other people say?"

"I got along fine with my lunch crew, A.J., Leslie, Kenneth, and a few others. But some on Evan's side of things really seemed to go out of their way to try to get at me with 'Gotcha!'"

"Suddenly I don't mind that my mother is my boss."

"Miss Analicia is so sweet."

"You haven't seen her mad."

"And I don't want to. Miss Analicia doesn't play."

"No, she doesn't. But she loves me like an only daughter. You know what I mean?"

"She kept you around the house."

"Until Chris."

"I know." Marti laughed. "Chris is the reason she went so nuts on you. Let me tell you, Terry. You don't want to leave the restaurant. It's rough out here."

◆ ◆ ◆ ◆

On her way back from the restaurant, she ran into a group of construction workers that milled about the alley behind her apartment building. They waited for something. She made to pass by. Two of them moved aside.

"Hope we're not blocking your way."

"Hi." She kept walking.

"Do you know why we're here?"

She stopped to read a picket sign, but kept a slight distance from the crowd of men.

"We're protesting a contractor who uses foul business practices. Not holding to the integrity of the construction trade."

"On this building?" She looked up and around. Nothing indicated construction. No trucks. No signage. No equipment.

"Yeah, they're not paying the workers a living wage or providing benefits. It makes it bad for the rest of us."

"Oh, that's unfortunate." She paused. "Good luck with it then." She took a few steps forward. "I've got to get going."

"Tell anyone you think should know that we're here and what we're doing."

Marti smiled, nodded, and waved at them over her shoulder. She felt prickles under her arms. Multiple sets of eyes crawled across her back.

The next time she left her building, she used the front exit. She checked for a construction permit. She didn't see one in the windows or on the doors. Wait. *Wait.*

◆ ◆ ◆ ◆

# 10  The Anniversary

"Look, since 2007, the Renewable Future Fund invested $40 million in competitive projects. That's about $190 million total leveraged in energy research and development. Together, we'd be able to create at least 2300 jobs the first year."

"Alex, tell me this. Where are these numbers coming from?"

"It's all in the research for anyone who takes the time to do it. Celara took the time."

"You got any specifics? I mean, what exactly are you planning to do?"

"We're going to implement research and training for large-scale gearbox testing facilities."

"For what?"

"To support turbine component manufacturing."

The Lake City player snorted.

"It's a wind blade manufacturing initiative to foster mass production of wind turbines. Right here in the Lake City region. No outsourcing."

"Who can afford that? Alex, let me tell you honestly. You're dreaming, son."

"It's the future, my friend. If we want to live in a healthy place with clean air and water, with rewarding jobs and careers for friends and family, we have to take advantage of opportunities like this as they present themselves."

"Look, fuck that feel-good crap. It would take monumental logistics and infrastructure to set this up, Alex. We're not talking about building a tree house here."

"No, we're not. And we need training and education to do it."

"I just don't see it. I really don't. I want to see it. I know you see it. But I don't see it."

"I know. I realize that. It's all true. Energy efficiency, retrofitting, and then new manufacturing... it all takes time to set up."

"Time is money." He sat forward. "Time is *my* money."

"The Renewable Future Fund is money. That includes utility rebates on one end and then community college curriculum on the other. We're covered."

"No. We're not covered. There's a risk for everyone who puts their company on the line. I can't believe what you're thinking about doing to Celara. Your father wouldn't have taken a chance like that."

Alex's voice grew quiet. "My father is no longer here."

"He was a good man."

"He's dead."

"I'm sorry."

After a long pause, Alex rallied. "We'd have to coordinate anything we do with the state and involve all sorts of organizations."

"Like?"

Alex ticked them off. "Utilities Board, Energy Center, Utility Association, Electric Cooperatives, Energy Coalition, the Group of Cities, Economic Development Office, Chambers of Commerce."

The Lake City player whistled. "Why don't you just win the lottery while you're at it? Or herd a bunch of cats?"

"I just might do both. Look. No question we have to deal with these guys."

"All of them?"

"All of them. Every single one. Even some two-bit environmental groups who've brainwashed a lot of the lakeside developers. It's the only way to ensure that we have adequate capacity to transmit large quantities of wind energy within the state and regional load centers."

"Everybody's gotta have a dream."

"We don't have to dream it. We can be it. One way to do it is to go for the super grid. We could coordinate our efforts with the East Coast guys and amplify from the Midwest to the East Coast. If we collaborate with industry, the associations, and state agencies, we can guide the certification process for the workforce."

"Maybe."

"But if we go in like cowboys, operating outside the system," Alex shook his head, "it'll be a long row to hoe. Now *that* would be herding cats."

The Lake City player remained silent.

"I don't feel like I'm getting through to you on this today."

"No, not today, Alex." He put money down on the table and got his coat. "My recommendation is that you stick to the special projects. That's what's keeping us on top. Don't mess up our thing, Alex. The way it's been is the way it ought to be. People might get upset."

Alex pushed the Lake City player's money back. Put his own money on the table then stood up with his father's friend.

"Just consider it. People come to Lake City for the quality of life. Adding good-paying, long-term manufacturing and construction jobs to the mix makes us heroes."

"I'll just say good night for now."

An icy rain stabbed into the heart of Lake City, harsh and unceasing.

◆ ◆ ◆ ◆

People in the city liked to pretend that they had no idea how to drive on ice though they did it every year. After a tortuous drive back to the far north suburbs, Alex sat at the desk in his home office for a long moment.

Finally he exploded with volcanic rage.

"Get your shit together! Get your ass in gear, and get the fuck on the phone!"

He launched the voice-recognition software on his computer then busied himself with other work while the tape played back.

The tape stopped. He tried to maneuver the software to clear the files from the recorder since he already loaded them on his desktop computer. Evan or Marti usually took care of those details at Celara. *Thanks for nothing!* Alex reviewed his work.

He frowned.

He went back to add some additional punctuation, italics, and self-righteous CAPS. He printed the pages, sealed them, and mailed them with instructions for Harlan to clear the copy. He would take out an anonymous full-page ad in the weekly he'd seen spread across Marti's desk when she should have been working on his projects instead of slacking off. She owed him big-time.

◆ ◆ ◆ ◆

Harlan read the document, once, twice, three times. Not in complete disbelief, this was Alexander King, after all. He provided over twenty year's worth of legal counsel to the King family. It wouldn't be the first time he dealt with an *unfortunate episode.*

Still, he sighed when he pushed the intercom button on his phone.

"Harriet, I need to schedule an immediate telephone conference with Alex King."

"Under what heading should I bill?"

"Uhm," the lawyer flipped through the pages again, "Bill for one hour." He shook his head. "No, bill for two hours. I'll tell you the heading later."

Something told him Martina Butler was more than what she appeared to be when he watched her interview tape. He didn't know why he chose not to warn Alex about her. Now, he knew. Even when Alex pushed button after button, she kept her cool. She decided her own destiny then and now and that set Alex on edge. Harlan admired that ability in her. Indeed, it was a character trait to which to aspire. He filed that thought away.

He pulled out a legal pad to outline an agenda for his and Alex's conference—defamation, libel, slander, sexual harassment, gender discrimination, race discrimination, stalking, etc. He camped out in the law library and spoke with Alex from there for two hours. He repeated himself several times and flipped through the pages of more than one law book.

◆ ◆ ◆ ◆

Celara Solar Corporation invites you
to help celebrate 10 years of success!
Cocktails 7:00pm, Reception 8:00pm
RSVP for directions.

Underneath the announcement, Alex wrote cryptic instructions for Marti to drop off her deliverables. The words marched with bold force across the invitation, followed by several exclamation points as if to dare her not to first read then obey.

"Yeah. Okay. You asked for it, you got it," she muttered under her breath. She pushed into the very back of her closet to find a slinky, dark red sheath dress. She found an even slinkier black coat to cover it. Snow covered the ground. Her breath blew out in puffs of cold mist. Sure, it was freezing, but she didn't care. Alex needed and very much deserved to be punished. "I'll bet he's already drunk," she bitched in the cab on her way to Alex's large suburban home.

She left her coat in the foyer then looked across the party. A beautiful chocolate Labrador retriever ran amongst the guests—Lady. A group of men she recognized as high flyers in real estate surrounded Alex. "Well, look who's sailing without a boat." She headed his direction.

All-eyes-on-me excitement turned Alex's face red—or maybe it was the liquor. "And then he said, he said... listen, he goes, 'Its cooler by the lake!'" The men around him threw their heads back and roared. "Cooler by the lake!"

*Please.*

With an, "Excuse me, this is business," Alex gripped her elbow, wheeled around, then marched her outside towards his greenhouse.

She showed him her reports and the business plans. She started the voice recorder he lent her because her own recorder went to small electronics heaven. She set it on a heated table filled with starter plants.

"The wave of the future is to diversify solar services, offering customization of both solar thermal heating as well as photovoltaic electrical systems for the client. Retail of simple solar devices would add to the bottom line. However, it is still advised that qualified technicians do all the installation and maintenance of complicated systems."

"Marti," he raised his voice over the tape, "I need you to begin research on the possibilities of Celara Wind."

"Celara what?"

"Celara *Wind*," he repeated, already irritated with her. "So adjust the Celara Solar business plan for wind turbine manufacture, construction, installation, and retail. Give me a timeline and a budget. I need it rough in two weeks. Presentation-ready in a month."

Marti shuddered. She would never be free of him. It would never end. The more she gave him, the more he wanted from her.

"Also, I've been talking to some people downtown. I need a speculation on windmill construction and related installations in the lake."

*Fuck me. Really?* She couldn't refuse him because to do so would invite further retaliation.

"I can't do it."

"Look," he gestured impatiently, "I've got a stack of research from other wind energy companies around the world. There's a list of people from Iowa you can talk to. You know how to find anything else you need."

"You can't afford me, Alex."

"Excuse me?" He raised his eyebrows. "I can't afford you?"

"I raised my price."

"Did you? Really?" The eyebrows drew down and nearly met in the middle.

Marti took a step backward from the bladed flint slicing at her.

"I... yes. The economy..."

"Yes, the economy's bad, I know. Celara's gone through some tough times, lately too. We actually tightened the operations budget in order to cover additional markets and plan for this new initiative. Don't you think you're being selfish?"

"No?" She heard the uncertainty in her voice. He heard it too. He took her hand in his.

"I think you are, Marti. Think about everyone else on staff that's got kids in college, mortgages to pay off. A few of them have medical bills." *Leslie.* "Don't you have any compassion for them? Any consideration?" *What would he do? Fire her?*

"Alex! You're forgetting you're talking to the researcher. Celara's doing better than nearly every construction firm in the city. And there's a reason why."

Alex raised his eyebrows again. "Oh?"

Marti pulled her hand away. "I know how Celara acquired those jobs."

"Do you?"

"Yes. I do. You know too."

"Do I?"

"Yes. You do. All those accidents going back seven years." She pointed her finger. "You do know what I'm talking about. It's not just coincidence. Alex, you have to stop. You have to! I don't want to be part of it."

"Okay Marti. Okay. Calm down."

"Alex, I am calm. I know you told me you took over from your father when he became too ill to run the shop. I know you had big shoes to fill and a lot to prove. But you don't have to do things like that anymore. You're perfectly capable..."

"Marti, Marti."

"You don't have to..."

"Shhh."

"You can find a better way. I know you can. You can!"

Alex drew closer to her, put his hands on her shoulders. He stared into her eyes.

"Look, maybe you're frustrated with how you've been treated in the office. I'm taking steps for that. But don't make something out to be what it's not."

Twin moon-like orbs glowed down on her, inescapable spotlights that pinned her into place like a mesmerized deer about to be overrun by a semi.

"Alex, it's not going to work." She heard the scorn in her voice. She hoped Alex heard it.

"Marti, I know that I've been riding you hard lately. And maybe stress has turned coincidence into paranoia. But if I'm hard on you, it's because I count on you so much. I need you. There's no one else I trust to be able to do what you do for Celara. I need you, Martina. I simply can't let you go. Especially now. We're on the brink of something truly wonderful. Don't you realize it? In a few years, the entire U.S.

electrical grid will be upgraded and synchronized for renewable energy. The super grid is revolutionary. And in the Midwest, we'll be right in the middle of everything. You can be part of it. You should be part of it."

"Alex, listen to me. Please listen. Something is very wrong at Celara and it cannot last forever. I have to leave. I *am* leaving."

"But we have an arrangement."

"No freelance. No contract. No consulting. Nothing. I can't do it."

"Can't or won't?"

Marti broke eye contact. He released his grip on her. He picked up the stack of paper she gave him and looked it over. He set each sheet down on the table, one by one.

"Marti, I guess I've got to tell you the real reason I can't let you go."

Marti frowned, her guard up.

"Tonight, before you got here, I walked around greeting everyone. But all my thoughts were of you. They're always of you. I wondered where you were and whether you'd bother to show up. And if you didn't, whether I could join you wherever you chose to be. You should know that I feel so helpless with you sometimes. I simply don't know what to do or what to say to you anymore. Some days I dream of you and me falling asleep together and letting the world go around by itself."

Marti released a long, misty breath. She glanced at the door. It was *way* past time for her to leave. The heater couldn't break through the chill that surrounded her. She edged away. Alex turned to face her.

"Marti, give me what I want and I will give you everything you need. You won't ever want for anything. Whatever those other guys give you, I can give you better."

What other guys? She frowned. She couldn't figure out what the hell he was talking about. Was it a metaphor?

Her recording continued, "Use of lower-skilled labor, college interns, career-changers, youth programs, and possibly, prison labor to assemble equipment and do non-expert tasks on the jobsite..."

She found his humble admission then submission to her extraordinary. She never thought she'd see the day. He waited for her response. The tape of her voice droned on.

"Open hiring and training further to women, particularly in sales and marketing in order to connect to female entrepreneurs, non-profit directors, homeowners, heads of households, and wives of undecided male clients..."

She knew his performance for what it was—a performance. And yet, as she already came to realize, he was a genius performer. In fact, she was likely his biggest fan. How many times did she sit amazed to see the variety of people who rolled over for him? Often, she herself didn't realize that Alex worked her until the deed was done.

He knew how to push every button. Falling under his spell was like being embraced by quicksand.

She knew the type of man who stood before her. She knew better than to take what he said at face value. She knew better than to give him the benefit of the doubt. She was an adult. She wasn't naïve. She wasn't some star-struck, love-sick groupie. He didn't love her so much as he loved what she could do for him. He wanted to own her intelligence, her gifts and talents, her skills.

He wanted to set the agenda for her life and future to serve his. And yet... the more time she spent with him, the harder it became not to give him what he wanted. Because not to give him what he wanted invited the usual criticisms, the indifferent withdrawals, the arrogant demands that threw her off-balance.

She knew all this. But, by God, she didn't walk out of the greenhouse.

"...minority subcontractors and trainees as well as bilingual workers to reach across cultural divides since Lake City remains one of the most culturally diverse cities in the Midwest. For this reason, cross-skill and cross-cultural training is the key to a stronger workforce."

Marti realized that though she feared Alex, she also desired him. She wanted to be angry. She wanted to hate him. She did hate him. She did! *Hate him, Marti!*

He took from her and demanded more.

*Well wasn't it about time he gave her what she wanted for once?* The small, questioning voice inside her increased in strength and confidence. She didn't fight it. After all, she and Alex were both adults.

He appealed to her. He appalled her. He drew her. He repelled her. The phantom menace frightened her. *Slap him, Marti!* She raised her hand to do it. But she couldn't get her hand to work right. Her body responded to his nearness the wrong way.

Instead, her arms slid around his shoulders because she needed to hold onto something solid to keep from falling, falling.

Strong hands gripped her in return. His voice and the sweet, subtle smell of expensive cologne surrounded her. He pulled her fully against him. His hard warmth permeated through her. She couldn't stop her body's trembles wherever he touched her, many places. She clung to the nearest heat source she could find in a cold world.

Her mind detached, watched, and understood the mistake she was about to make. But the blue-silver vortex of his charisma swirled higher. It pulled her under. She tugged his head down to hers.

They sank back together onto the heated table. With the sweep of one arm, he knocked everything to the floor. All the anger she held inside during her tenure at Celara she took out on him in the greenhouse. Though she bore his full weight, thanks to her daily gym workouts, she managed to punish him for at least an hour.

He kept his promise. He accepted and absorbed all of it. He gave her everything she wanted and needed from him, everything she demanded until they pulled away from each, exhausted.

"You do realize you can't go back inside like this?"

Her dress hiked up over her hips and off her shoulders in a torn, crumpled mass. Alex yanked out the hair clip that held back her twists. He used them to pin her into place on the table. Now the long ropes flowed freely down her back. Her makeup streaked across her face as though she were a music video extra.

Alex tucked in his shirt then zipped up. Without further ado, he looked as though he just finished a leisurely midnight stroll. *That's our Alex.*

She smiled with a shrug. "I know."

"Wait for me here, Marti. I'll get our coats then take you home."

"Before you go, Alex, would you pull up my hose?"

He complied stroking her legs all the way up.

"And pull down my hem?"

He did that too squeezing her backside.

"And straighten this out?"

Marti pointed to the top of the dark red dress he tugged down then tore in a frantic attempt to get at her breasts. He smoothed his hands over her breasts now, taking his sweet time to pull the torn sides together.

"Thank you, Alex."

She smiled, lifted her head for his kiss. He grinned and placed his hand on the back of her neck. He yanked her towards him, smeared her makeup further. She laughed, and then sighed. He completed his possession of her mouth stroking his tongue over hers in a slow kiss.

"I'm going to take you home, Marti." He kissed her neck. "We'll continue this where we left off until we're both comatose under a blanket," he whispered to the secret place behind her ear. She groaned.

Satisfied with the night's work, Alex smiled and whispered, "You won't want for anything ever." Then he left for their coats.

The cold chill of the night air made her shiver.

Oh no. No, no. No, no, no, no, no!

What the complete bloody hell did she just do? She wasn't even drunk! Why did she do it? Why? *Marti, Marti. You're not gonna win this one, girl.*

Her voice squawked from the floor where Alex knocked the recorder. "Rather than aggressive bid techniques, focus on research, development, integrity, and community service to win the hearts, dollars, and policy support of Lake City."

She sighed. Trust Alex to miss the best part.

"...Those pdfs are in the same file folder as your spreadsheet. So maybe you could just go ahead and do research on the issues I've outlined and analyze the data I've provided you with to improve your efforts and change yourself for the better."

Marti frowned. She didn't realize this was on Alex's recorder.

"Some good has come out of our time together. I've definitely grown and matured as a well-rounded human being from appreciating your "differences" from other normal people I know."

She stiffened. She heard something in the darkness beyond the greenhouse windows.

"I want to dance to your beat. And that is why I need you to contact me. I'm pretty sure that I have some more improving to do and you are the one person who can supply enough raw materials for me to work with."

She peered through the window panes. Was it Alex out there with their coats?

"Look, I'll just cut this short. I need you. I love you. I want you. Get your shit together. Get your ass in gear, and get the fuck on the phone!"

Marti jumped. *What on Earth?* She wondered if the message was for her, his ex-wife, or his girlfriend from the Metro party. Maybe some bizarre performance piece?

❖ ❖ ❖ ❖

Evan watched Alex leave the greenhouse. Then he waited to see what Marti would do. Earlier in the evening, the Boss's Girl entered Alex's home then made a beeline for Alex. Of course, Evan followed them outside. In the darkness, he listened to their back-and-forth about Celara.

Too bad Kate wasn't here to monitor this situation for him. But then Kate forgot the rules of the game and tried to play a player. Oh well.

As usual, Marti yapped and cried and complained about everything under the sun. Since her arrival to Celara, Evan made regular additions to Marti's portfolio. He waited for Alex to reel her back in line with the information he helpfully provided.

What he got instead was an unbelievably animalistic coupling that, rather than excited his lust disgusted him and made him seethe with anger.

The lying little slutbag. He knew it! He *knew* Marti was a whore all along, just like every other woman he knew. Every single one. It never failed.

Always. Always! They resorted to the backstroke to advance their careers.

And from what he heard on the tape, Alex had doubts about Marti too. Evan slunk away into the night.

◆ ◆ ◆ ◆

# 11 The Exit

"**D**id anyone say anything about you leaving your own party early?"

"I told them I got lucky."

Marti gasped. Alex laughed. He turned on the car's heater. She would ride in elegant style tonight.

"No, Marti. No. I just told them I had to take care of something at the office. They know I work around the clock. Besides, after I shook hands all around and told them to liquor up, nobody gave a shit where I was going. My home staff will keep it flowing from the wine cellar then wrap things up."

Marti laughed. "Brilliant, as always, Alex."

"Buckle up for safety." He smiled back at her. "So where do we go from here, Marti?"

"At the light, hang a right. Right here."

Alex turned the corner.

"Down this road about ten miles, over the channel bridge and then I'm two more blocks down on the left at Day and Carter Road. I'll tell you when to stop."

"God, I love having you around. I actually meant 'where do we go from here' about you and me. But thanks for the directions too."

"Oh that." She laughed with him. "Well, where do you want to go?"

The voice came from the back seat. "Good question, Marti."
Marti shrieked. Alex swore, "Fuck!" then pulled over to the
side of the road, piled high with snow.

"Evan, what the fuck?"

They noticed the gun at the same time. Marti looked to Alex
for direction. "Sit still," he told her.

"No Alex. Keep going. We've got to get our little Marti safely
home. It's over the channel bridge and then two more blocks
on the left. Day and Carter Road. I'll tell you when to stop."

With another glance toward the gun, Alex pulled back onto
the road.

"Marti, you know, I hate to see you deluded. It really, really,
really... really, really causes me actual pain to see you walking
around with your head in the clouds. Maybe the time you
spent in that ivory tower being all prissy made you think shit
doesn't stink. Well, it does, you know. Shit stinks to high
heaven. Especially when you wallow in it. Right Alex?"

"Sure," Alex replied tonelessly with a flick of his eyes to the
rear view mirror.

"There's a way to get things done in Lake City. It just doesn't
happen by thinking about it, or dreaming about it, or *writing*
about it, sister. It takes way more than that, I can tell you."

Marti waited for more information. She didn't have to wait
long.

"Palms get greased, favors owed, threats made, bids rigged,
projects sabotaged, inspections forced, code violations
overlooked. And that, *little girl*, is how it works. *That's* how
things get done in the city. Right, Alex?"

Alex sighed. "Right, Evan."

"Tell her about Lakeside."

"You know that's confidential."

"Tell her, Alex. She needs to get things straight in her head.
She needs to learn how we do things at Celara. Go ahead. Tell
her everything."

Alex kept his eyes focused forward.

"Celara would take over the Lakeside contract and retro-
convert it not only to photovoltaic, but also to solar thermal.
Then purchase majority ownership. We had our guy keep
track of the bidding. After we approached him, he requested a
commitment, a show of confidence in his own plan for a small
solar retail business. I agreed to review the business plan.

Marti closed her eyes. "The plan that you gave me to adapt for Celara."

"But wait. There's more! Tell her the rest of it, Alex."

"You tell her. I'm driving."

Evan picked up the story. "We gave him half up front. He'd get the other half after you decided the plan was workable and after he completed a job for us as a show of faith."

"The explosion," she said weakly.

"Exactly." Evan giggled.

"Augie died in that blast," Marti whispered.

"Accidents happen, Marti," Evan replied. He burst into full laughter this time.

"Augie was your guy?" Marti glanced at Alex who tightened his lips.

"Circle gets the square! Do you know, he actually threatened me?" Evan sounded incredulous. "Your *Augie* told me that he was going to tell you the full truth about Alex. Let me tell you, he settled back down after we promised him the extra funds. Hell of a guy, he is. Was. A true friend, hunh Marti?" Evan's voice hardened. "The guy had no honor at all and he deserved what he got."

Marti stared straight ahead. Whatever began to grow and flourish between her and Alex in the greenhouse just withered into something twisted, dead, and dark.

"So based on that, Marti needs to understand what it takes to really be part of the team. Am I right, Alex?"

Alex glanced at the rear view mirror. "Right."

"She needs to know there's nothing that she won't do to prove herself loyal to us."

Alex hesitated. "Loyalty is important."

Marti stared at Alex, stunned.

"You heard him, Marti. I've already proven myself time and time again. Right, Alex?"

"You know I count on you to hold it all together, Evan. I've told you that."

"That's right! And anyone not on the team gets dealt with and that's the way it is."

Marti cringed. Evan sneered. "See? I told you. She doesn't get it. You women are all the same. Useless. All of you."

Chris warned her. He told her to exit the situation immediately. So did Terry. She made a half-assed effort. But then in the greenhouse... she cringed again. Now the two of them dragged her even deeper into their bizarro underworld where up was down, left was right, and right was wrong. But she still recognized sarcasm when she heard it.

"Marti, Marti, Marti. I'm so sorry the big, bad world hurt you." He didn't wait for a response. "There's a war going on out there, little girl. Don't you know? Not just overseas. I'm talking about right here in the city. I'm on the battlefield *everyday*. And in a war, sometimes there's friendly fire. Sometimes, there's collateral damage. Sometimes, there is sacrifice. Do you get it now? Some things cannot be helped. We all have our positions to maintain and our roles to play. You do know your role now, don't you? No?"

"What is my role?" she asked.

"Marti, if Alex wanted something done, I made it happen. If he wanted something undone, I made *that* happen. The best way I knew how. I told you life was a battlefield. And I am a soldier. I walk through the fire for Celara and for Alex. Don't I, Alex! I do what I have to do. I do what needs to be done and when I do it, it stays done. While the whiners and complainers talk about it, I *am* about it. While you're lecturing and shaking that prissy little finger of yours in all directions, I'm about it, Marti! I'm getting the information and I'm getting it done."

"What information?"

"Marti, oh my God!" Evan shook his head in disbelief. "Come on! We were telecommunications and electronic surveillance before we were solar. It was all right there in your research. *Jesus!* Where've you been? Hello?" He snapped his fingers by her head. She flinched away. He sniggered.

"Look honey. Quit looking at the details and see the big picture. You put on a hardhat and a tool belt, and you can get into just about anywhere you want. But take the receptionist for a whirl and you can return as often as you like. But that's not all. Money and power provide the means to follow people wherever they go. Key loggers at work, video at home, GPS on their cars and cell phones. Did he really take the day off for sick leave, or did he spend the day at the strip club? Oh, I just wonder. *But not anymore!*

They go to the pharmacy, grocery store, doctor's office, post office, and library. They visit prostitutes, girlfriends, mistresses, and yeah, sometimes boyfriends too. Amazing what people will tell you, show you, *give* you for, oh, one hundred to a thousand dollars. Simply amazing. But maybe not surprising in this economy.

Surprising is what you find in their trash cans. Oh God, *the humanity!* Surprising is what they'll confess to their priests and therapists. And not everyone locks up their credit card bills. Sometimes, they just leave them lying out and you can just... go down the list of pervert tendencies. It's called leverage, honey. Get to know it."

"It's thuggish intimidation."

"Alex, how can you stand it?" Evan demanded. "Marti, will you please wake up the fuck up already? You're making me goddamn tired. Look, there's good and there's bad. Someone's either for us or against us. It's their choice. And by the way, you still haven't decided what side you're on. You need to decide right now."

If she died, her death would be on Chris's conscience too. What would it do to him? *Chris, Chris. I'm so sorry.*

"No, I understand now, Evan. I do. I had to do it. You see, I had to know."

Evan narrowed his eyes. "Know fucking what?"

"What you were made of, of course. I need to know what I'm dealing with and that you're a stand-up guy. I took it to the limit because I don't like weak links."

"Really?"

"Yes. Really. I pushed you to see if you were all I thought... that I sensed you could be. That's why I've always pushed you."

"Oh yeah?" She felt his intent stare. "And what did you decide?"

"That nobody does it better. Do you know what it does to me to see you do your thing? It inspires me, Evan. I suspected all along that you had what it took to take the entire world along for a ride and then kick it off once the ride was over. That's hardcore, baby."

"Do you like it hardcore, Marti?"

"You mean you didn't know?" Why, all of a sudden, did she feel like she was in the middle of a Pam Grier movie? "That's how I get it. That's how I give it."

"You sure fooled me."

"That's why I'm so good."

"Join us, Marti. You're so focused. We need you to help keep us on track. Together, we'd be unstoppable. Alex, you, me... Between us, we have all angles covered in Lake City. Because let's face it," she felt his breath crawl along her neck, "with Kate gone, we're missing a soft touch."

He leaned in closer. "Of course, Marti, me and Alex would have to take you for a test run first. Make sure that we know what we're getting." Evan stroked Marti's soft hair and cheek with the gun. "But then... looks like Alex started without me. I guess that's why he's the Boss. But Marti, ohhh Marti," he groaned aloud, "I can't wait until it's my turn to touch you on the inside too."

Marti shuddered. She choked back the horrible scream that pushed against the back of her throat. The car's heater smothered her.

"Teach you the ropes. Show you how to make a man beg for mercy. Mmmm." He groaned as his lips touched her ear. She didn't want to think of what he did with the hand not holding the gun.

She knew from past research that rape was an act of violence. It had nothing to do with sex and attraction. Evan didn't even like her. He liked power and control. It was the idea of her subjugation that excited him.

"Oh, my God. A body like yours was just built for industrial espionage, babe. Oh, wait. No. Corporate Research... *Director*. That's your new title, sweetie. Director of Corporate Research and Business Intelligence. It'll look good on your resume. And I just know you could do it."

So he intended for her to take Kate's place.

Evan's voice went back to normal. "Alex already knows it. Don't you, Alex? Because once Marti starts, she never stops. You get the gold star for perseverance, honey."

Alex's fingers whitened on the steering wheel.

"Tell her what you told me. Tell her what you used to say about her."

"Those were just jokes, Evan."

Evan snickered. "No they weren't."

Marti decided she didn't want to hear what Alex used to say about her, particularly when she made him angry, which was often. She could just imagine.

"I'm in. I'm on the team, Evan. Let's get it started."

Evan's voice roughened with anger. "Don't fuck with us, Marti. Don't you do it, babe. Don't do it!"

She stared forward into the black night that swallowed the road. Eyes wide open, she was too scared to blink.

"Kate was the last woman who fucked with us. Now where is she? *Nowhere.* Think about that, Marti. Think real long and hard about that. She actually said that I could never be the man Alex was. I told her to shut the fuck up over and over. But she kept talking shit. I tell you what, she didn't mock me so much after I slapped her around and then fucked her to death."

Marti couldn't shut out his hateful voice.

"Oh yeah. Over and over and over I did it to her hard and held her by the neck until she stopped breathing. I didn't even know I had that much endurance. Marti, how long would you bet I could make you happy?"

*Please let it not be true.* No one deserved to die in such a horrific manner, not even Kate. Marti felt her stomach churn. The back of her throat clutched. A sick feeling bubbled up her esophagus. She struggled to keep her composure, to keep him calm.

Alex looked shocked. "My God, Evan."

"I took care of it, Alex. Don't worry. She tried to play us off each other. She had to go." Evan turned toward Marti. "And no one's ever going to find out." He gave a hard stare to Marti's profile. "Are they?"

Marti stared through the windshield into the dark nothingness of her future. Evan meant for her to die tonight. And maybe after he had his way with her while Alex either watched or joined in, she would actually beg Evan to shoot her.

Alex closed his eyes a brief moment then refocused on the icy road. "Evan, there was never anything between me and Kate, you know. Look, she tried with me, sure. I held her off because I knew you two had something going on. She was just fucking with your head trying to get you to react." Alex hit the steering wheel with his fist. "And you let her!"

"Alex. You know... its fine. Kate was a bitch." He turned back to Marti.

"She was a *bitch*, Marti. She was a warm piece of moist ass. She was a cunt. Fuck her. That's all women are, Marti. Cunts.

Even *you*, special as you are. You do know that's all you'll ever be to him... and to me?"

Evan giggled.

Marti felt disgusted by Alex's silence. What did it say about Alex that he allowed it? He was the father of a young girl and yet he tolerated this hateful, vicious, violent misogynist as his right hand. Evan learned the alpha lessons Alex taught him well.

She leaned her head against the passenger window. She looked out into the black night that covered the road like a shroud. If she saw another car, she couldn't possibly flag it down with a gun to her head. But it didn't matter. There was no one in front or behind on the dark emptiness of the road. They were alone. The trees and fields covered in white, fluffy blankets never looked so beautiful under moonlight.

The three of them contemplated Evan's horrible confession in silence. Marti almost wanted Evan to shoot her. Let it be over soon. She wanted to die right now. Right this second. *Shoot me, Evan. Shoot me. Shoot me!*

Evan smirked at Marti's humiliation. He glanced at Alex. The frozen, sick expression on Alex's face didn't serve to validate Evan. He frowned, confused.

She wanted to jump from the moving car then throw herself headlong into the ditch. Let the snow comfort her in its downy softness. Let her sleep in peace tonight.

She wanted to love Alex. Correction. She still loved him. But not knowing where Alex ended and Evan began made it hard to believe that she could pull Alex back towards the light. She wouldn't join him in the dark. With every word of Evan's that Alex didn't deny, she lost more hope, felt greater despair. Augie... Kate...

Who next?

Who's left?

*Me.*

The strength it took to pull Alex back from the precipice would kill her. Tonight. Not much longer. Any minute now.

Chris told her everything she needed to know. Why didn't she listen and get out? It was pride. Pride made her ignore every warning God provided. Christina was her mother for a reason. Chris was her brother for a reason. Did all of that happen just for Marti to throw her life away?

*Mother, I love you. I miss you so much. But I want to live.*
*Then live!*

Marti took a deep breath. She held back revulsion. She had to convince him.

"She deserved it."

"The fuck you talking about?"

"Kate. She obviously asked for it, Evan."

"Right, Marti. Right." Evan paused. He allowed his voice to go silky soft. "Just like your mother asked for it?"

Marti felt cold prickles on her skin. "What?"

"Evan, don't. Don't do it."

Evan laughed. "Come on, Alex. She's tough. You keep telling me that."

"Don't, Evan. Just stop."

"Aren't you, Marti? You're tough. You sit there just like you always do. So cool, calm, and collected. So... calculating. Rolling over every single little detail in your little, teeny, tiny head." He snorted. "Meanwhile, nothing ever rattles that icicle cage of yours. Or does it, you lovely little ice queen?"

Marti turned her head to look at him. Evan stared cold, beady, black eyes into hers. Angry eyes. Alien eyes. Spider eyes. She looked towards Alex's profile. He frowned, shook his head, but didn't meet her eyes. Marti faced forward again.

Evan's quiet voice spun cobwebs that filled the car with sticky strands. "Why do you think she did it, Marti? Hmmm?" He held them paralyzed within a hot, smothering cocoon. She couldn't breathe. They approached closer to the channel bridge on the way to her apartment building.

"Do you think she slooowly reasoned out the details the same way you do and slooowly came to the conclusion that your father's life was worth five times more than that of *a drunken alcoholic slut who couldn't even feed her own children or clean her own house?*"

"Marti no! No!"

Even as Marti screamed, angry tears started in her eyes. She twisted as far as the seatbelt allowed. She reached to claw Evan's face. To gouge his eyes. To shut his mouth. To make him pay. To make *someone* pay. To kill him. *To kill him.*

Evan batted her hands away with a hearty laugh. Then he backhanded her across the left temple with the gun.

Her head ricocheted right. Stunned, Marti didn't feel the pain at first. She took a deep breath. The dull ache radiated a red mist in front of her eyes. Tears rolled down. Trapped within Evan's cocoon, she couldn't move. He raised the gun again.

"I've had just about enough out of you, Martina Butler. Me and Alex have completely had it! You think you can do my job? You think you can do what I do? It's me and him in it together. You'll never mean more to him than I do. I walked through fire!" His voice escalated to a scream. *"Never! Do you get it you bitch? Never! Do you get it? Do you? Do you?"*

She was sure she would feel the bullet impact her skull. But she wouldn't feel the path of splintered bone when it ripped through her brain. Alex yanked the wheel hard to the right. Evan's gunshot broke her passenger window.

The car spun on the ice. It hit the guardrail on the left. Then it whipped across the road head on towards the right guardrail. Evan flew into the windshield on impact. He crumpled face down between Marti and Alex.

Marti screamed. The car tipped over the rail.

"No! No!"

She screamed and screamed again. Somehow they landed right-side up on the icy embankment. Alex pushed pedals but he couldn't see around his driver's side airbag.

The car skidded sideways down the ice-covered concrete towards the water.

"Marti, get out!"

"No! No!"

"Jump! Do it, Marti! Do it now!"

"No!" Marti, completely done in by the shock of Evan's revelations, the gunshot by her ear, and the vision of her forthcoming death froze in total disbelief. The channel rushed closer.

It wasn't happening. This wasn't Evan's bloody forehead flopped over the seat. This wasn't her boss trapped behind the airbag shouting at her. The car didn't hit the water. It didn't break through the ice. It happened to someone else.

But this was ice-cold water and broken glass that poured onto her. It shocked her back to life.

"God, no!" She undid her seat belt. More water gushed over them. The car sank. She tried to reach Alex's belt. But her hands were too cold. She couldn't make her fingers work. Alex's own hands, blocked by the airbag, tangled in the belt. He couldn't reach down.

Marti cried from frustration.

"Go Marti. Go!"

"No," she whimpered.

"Marti," he whispered. "I want you to leave me here. Just go."

She shook her head.

"Get out!" he yelled, his face red and furious.

The water rose to chest level. The car sank lower. Terror drove her. She shoved her way past the torrent coming through her window. She thanked God for her cardio routine. She kicked her way back to the hole that showed black in a patch of white. She burst through gasping and crying.

She wanted Alex. She wouldn't leave the channel without him. She didn't know why she loved him, but she did. She took two deep breaths then dove back down. *Alex*.

This time, she freed him from the seatbelt, but she couldn't pull him from behind the airbag. He took shallow breaths from the narrowest sliver of air left. Marti took a quick breath.

She tugged at him again. Something struck her on the side. The cold water revived Evan. He still held the gun. He tried to raise it above the water. The cold made his hand shake. He swung the barrel first towards her then towards Alex. His eyes looked like empty black holes in a face gone deadly pale. Icy water slowed the bleeding from his forehead.

Marti chopped hard at Evan's hand. Evan dropped the gun. Alex retrieved it. He and Evan struggled for possession below the water. Alex shot his air bag, deflated it.

Evan's hands reached above the water to claw at him. Demented glee twisted his face to a hideous expression. Marti understood his intent. At this point, Evan didn't care if he lived or died. But if he did die, he would take Alex with him.

Marti tried again to reach Alex, to pull him away from the spider that grasped and clutched. She felt her body shake and jerk. The cold water bit through her all the way to the bone. She knew she'd never make the surface again, not against the current. The car shifted again. The air space disappeared.

Just before she blacked out, Alex kicked Evan's head away then surged past her out the car window.

♦ ♦ ♦ ♦

She woke with a cough and a choke in her throat. Alex bent over her. She retched and cried. Alex hugged her to his chest.

"Marti, Marti. Oh my God, Marti."

"Alex?"

"He won't hurt you anymore," he kissed her.

Still exhausted, Alex and Marti lay in each other's arms on the cement barrier of the lake. She heard gurgles from the water. She felt no sense of comfort from solid ground. The ordeal had only just begun.

"Alex, is it true what he said about Kate?"

"Marti, my father told me every day that he saw me, which wasn't often, that I was special. Since I was better than everyone I had to *be* better than everyone. Every single damn day. Every single damn time. He kicked my ass every chance he got to make sure I understood that second place was never good enough. He ground me under his heel to make sure I always knew that it was my duty to protect of the family name. I had to earn the privilege of being his son. I had to prove myself worthy. I don't know if I managed to do that before he died. I would have done anything to earn his respect because it didn't come easy. Nothing from him ever came easy."

Marti closed her eyes. She felt the same despair she felt in the car.

"I know that doesn't compare to the heartache you experienced growing up. But things can always get better. They can for both of us. They will."

"Alex..."

"Stay with me, Marti. It's going to get better, I promise you. I'll see to it."

"What about Kate?"

"What *about* Kate?"

*I've been meaning to talk to you about something important.*

Alex loosened his arms and rolled onto his back "I needed her help to keep Evan in line."

"Well, that worked."

"It really didn't work the way I thought it would."

"What happened?"

"She knew exactly what she was getting into. I told her the deal."

"But you didn't tell her how sick he really was."

"I don't think even I knew how crazy in the head he was."

"I wish I never met him."

"Or me?"

She didn't answer.

"Marti, I couldn't go against him when he had a gun to your head!"

Marti ignored that and pushed forward. "How did you get Augie get involved?"

"What?"

Marti looked him in the eye. "You wanted me to work him, didn't you?"

"I just needed the data. That's all."

"Did you know what would happen to him?"

Alex sighed.

"Did you?"

He didn't answer.

*He gave her the business plan... with Augie's information... already blackened out... Prior to Augie's death in the explosion...*

Marti closed her eyes. She shivered in her wet dress. She choked back her tears. She would not cry in front of him.

*He knew Augie would never use the plan again...*

The strangest thing was that she didn't mourn Augie. She never loved Augie. It was Alex, she mourned—the man Alex might have been if he tried, but now could never be. That man would never exist.

"Alex, your daughter needs you."

"What's Lexa got to do with this?"

"You don't pay attention to her."

"Marti, Lexa's not even here. This doesn't have anything to do with her. She's safe."

"Do you even know where she is?"

"She's safe, I said!"

"Back at that drunken grown-up party with people getting liquored up?"

"Marti, look. I have someone watching her. Will you focus, please? I told you about going in circles."

"Fine."

"Marti, listen. I've been crazy without you close to me. I don't know if you missed me, but I missed you. You made me feel so alive. Like I could do anything in life. Even though you acted kind of shitty to me sometimes."

Marti snorted.

"I know you've got your own issues to deal with and whatever I've contributed to the pain, I'm sorry for. But the way you tossed me aside like I didn't matter... it made me angry and sad. Do you know that I listen to your tapes just because I love the sound of your voice and that they help me pretend you're still with me? How pathetic is that?"

"Very."

"Look, I know things are complicated, but you're important to me. I want you in my life."

Just then, Marti noticed the broken bloody trail in the ice. She stared at Alex's bleeding hands and the blood that oozed through cuts in his shirt. He must have fought like an ox to pull them both through the ice and up the embankment. How did he drag her dead weight from below and keep her afloat?

Alex continued his soliloquy staring up at the stars, lost in the fantasy. Evan slipped further towards sleep everlasting.

"I dream about you, Marti. Intense dreams. I didn't want to tell you all this because I wanted to allow you your peace. But I am not ashamed of how I feel for you. I would tell even the entire Earth."

How desperate and lonely Christina must have felt to actually pull a gun on Reverend March only to be faced with the magnitude and force of the indifference of her husband, the father of her two children, towards her. In her last moments, Christina comprehended his enduring contempt for her.

Marti looked ten years into her own future. She saw herself in the same position. She clutched at Alex. She begged him to show any sign that he realized that she was an actual human being, not a tool to take out of a box and put back in once he finished with her. How many more bodies would he bury? How many secrets would she keep for him? What kinds of lies would she tell herself to make everything seem all right?

She pulled out one of his well-oiled guns. Alex stood before her full of scorn for her show of weakness. The flint glittered in his eyes. Hand shaking, she pointed the gun, made her demands. He laughed. She cried.

As she lay beside him on the shore of Evan's grave, she realized that he would never change. He was incapable. He simply could not and would not. It was what it was.

Marti rose to her knees. She pulled herself upright to her bare feet. She walked away in small jerks and drags. Mental and physical exhaustion slowed her steps.

"Marti... Marti..."

She took two more jerky steps away from him.

*"Martina!"*

She paused.

"We're not done!"

Marti took another step. She just could not handle any more of his shit tonight.

He sat up. "So this is how you deal with it? Are you fucking kidding me? This is what I hired? When the going gets tough, Marti runs away. Is that it? That's how Marti deals?" He raised his voice to an outraged shout. "Goddamnit, Martina Butler!"

She stopped.

"You are still on the clock, Martina. *Get back here!*"

Marti turned to stare at him in disbelief.

"I'm fucking talking to you, Martina. Don't you damn well turn your back on me!"

"What Alex? What!" She shrieked back. "What!" And yet another, "What!" for good measure when he took a breath to speak.

Now that he had her attention, he lowered his voice, "Marti, you explained to me that things would end up with you leaving several times. But I thought you would change your mind. Or maybe it was just a test. I thought if I played things right, I could pass it. Look, we had something great going. And I felt that you sensed the same thing as well. And... I know it was my own actions that made things go downhill. If I could go back, I would definitely change some things."

"*Some* things? Alex, you are unbelievable. What is that noise that keeps escaping from your face all the time?"

"Okay, I'd change lots of things. I'm just not sure what to do any more because it seems like lately, I make all the wrong choices when it comes to you. I tried my best to block you out.

But then I would dream about you and when I woke up, I remembered you weren't there. Not only that, but that you couldn't stand me. But I'm not mad at you. Even when it seems like I am. And even when it seemed like I wasn't paying attention to you, I really was."

He stood up.

"I'm just so glad you don't hide your feelings from me anymore. You took the time to really look at me, past all the bullshit and see me for who I am. Our time together tonight was so beautiful. It's never been that good for me before. I know I can make you happy. We can make each other happy."

"I'm cold and I'm tired, Alex... and you're crazy."

"I know I am the man who could be a good father to your children."

She stiffened. The loathing and contempt she felt for him came from a place that she didn't know existed inside her. *Good father to your children.* How many times did he need to do it in order for her to get it? How many ways could a person violate another? The physical body was one way—his dead assistant's way. But to actually steal her private thoughts, dreams, secrets, and desires from her? To take without asking what she would have given him freely once she trusted him? What kind of man did that?

The man who "lied" next to her on the embankment.

Marti remembered the various side comments, snickers, and knowing glances from Alex and some members of his goon squad—the sly insinuations that added to her unease in the office. Never anything she could put her finger on. But Evan confirmed what she always suspected.

"Alex, do you understand what just happened here?"

"Do you really expect me to sit here and try to figure out what you're referring to?"

"No. My expectations of you are pretty low by now."

That pissed him off. "Fuck! So why don't you save us both some time and tell me." He paused. "Well?" he demanded.

She plunged right in. "You acquired a great deal of personal information about me, Alex. You shared it. You raped me psychologically and tried to humiliate me with what you learned."

She waited. He didn't speak.

"The only way any of them could have done it is if you allowed it. Encouraged it. Ordered it. Rewarded it. Hell, participated in it. My entire tenure with Celara was one big mind fuck. Wasn't it?"

"Don't say that."

"I already said it. And you haven't denied it."

He shook his head.

"Even on the brink of death, even after the life-altering moment we shared not more than *ten minutes ago*, even after," she couldn't say Evan's name out loud, so she gestured to the channel, "all that, you're still the same. Always wanting the upper hand in order to win any interaction with me or anyone else."

He tried to protest. She overrode him with a voice that sliced like a switchblade.

"On paper, you seem like everything I could possibly want in a man—wealth, charm, success, vision, athletic good looks, vision, power, leadership. But the deepest, darkest, most primitive instinct within my soul says to run fast and run far."

"Come on, Marti. Run fast? Aren't you being a just little melodramatic?"

"Alex! Somebody died tonight! We," she jerked her finger back and forth, "you and me, almost died tonight. What the fuck is wrong with you? Do you realize that this happened to us in the real world?"

"Of course I realize it. What do you take me for?"

"I just told you what I take you for. I'm not going to tell you again."

"Yeah, like I believe that."

"Shut. Up." She made a dismissive gesture. "Shut the fuck up. I cannot handle these Jekyll and Hyde personality changes from you anymore."

"Jekyll and Hyde? So now I'm a monster? Is that it? Then why don't you just say I'm a monster, Marti, instead of making this Joan of Arc martyr speech? I have to listen to this?"

"You don't have to do a damn thing more than you've already done, okay?" Marti smiled. "I always did admire your confidence, Alex. Hell, face it. The swagger totally turned me on. And then those moments when I wanted to hold you so close to me."

"Like in the greenhouse?"

"Who are you really?"

As always, she looked into his eyes for the truth. She waited for the moonlight to reveal it to her. The dreamy lapis lazuli shredded into silver shards of broken glass. She turned away in fright.

"Don't let him win, Marti. Not now."

"He hasn't won. Neither have I. And you certainly haven't."

She turned her back, then walked away. Soon, she no longer heard the water gurgle as it swallowed secrets and lies. She heard only the slide and jerk of her footsteps. She zombie-walked away.

Her tears froze into icicles when they rolled off her face.

◆ ◆ ◆ ◆

## 12 The Offer

If only she walked out of the interview and never turned back. Getting lost on the wrong bus was the desperate effort of the universe to protect her.

Marti bent cold fingers to knock on Beryl's front door barefoot, bedraggled, and freezing in a soiled, torn dress. The dark red color hid the blood stains.

"Marti!" Beryl looked up and down the street. "Oh my God." She pulled Marti inside. "What happened to you?"

"Beryl," Marti couldn't stop shivering, "I need your shower."

Beryl's voice sharpened. "Wait a minute. What happened to you, Marti?"

"Please, I'm freezing. Help me, Beryl."

Beryl held her by one arm and searched her eyes. "Marti, we can call the police. I'll call right now. If we do, you shouldn't shower yet."

Marti pulled away. "It's not what you're thinking Beryl."

Beryl stepped in front of her, arms crossed. "Then what is it, Marti? What happened to you? Who did this?"

"Beryl, please don't make it worse." Marti put up her hands. "Please."

Beryl's eyes glistened. She shook her head in surrender. "Okay." She swallowed and took a breath. "Okay."

Beryl gathered soap and towels. She left them for Marti in the guest bathroom.

"Here's a nightgown and bathrobe."

"Thanks. I might be a while."

Beryl, an old school Lake City player, pressed her lips together. She retreated to her living room to wait.

Marti couldn't remove the dress stiffened by ice. She got into the blazing heat of Beryl's shower with it on then cried for at least fifteen minutes. When she emerged, freshly scrubbed, Beryl showed her the guest bedroom. Marti slept until noon.

Back from lunch, Beryl provided Marti a change of clothing and a white, plastic bag. Marti held out her arms to take the bundles. Beryl noted the scratches. From the ice. But Beryl didn't know that.

"Marti, your dress is completely beyond repair. I don't know what happened to you..." She looked at Marti's arms again. "Did someone..."

Marti shook her head. Looked away. Beryl exhaled. She drove Marti back to her apartment. Marti stared out the window the entire time. She didn't want to talk about it. In fact, she wanted to pretend it never happened.

"Marti, you don't have to face whatever happened alone. Whoever did this to you should not get away with it." Beryl got out to walk her to the building's front door. The building manager opened the door to Marti's apartment.

Marti waited until the elevator doors closed behind the building manager. She turned to Beryl who still stood in her apartment doorway. "That's just it, Beryl. He didn't get away."

She shut the door on Beryl's look of shock.

◆ ◆ ◆ ◆

For the next three weeks, Marti didn't leave her apartment. Outside, was the holiday season. Inside, time stood still.

If the cops came for her, she wanted her arrest to be at home, her removal from mainstream society, dignified. Not some common back alley, crack house, or parking lot takedown.

She unplugged her landline. Every once in a while, Beryl or Worth buzzed her intercom. They buzzed and buzzed until she answered. She thanked them for stopping by, but she didn't invite them in. She told them she was tired which was the truth. Sometimes, she didn't answer. They gave whatever they brought with them to a resident who dropped it on her welcome mat without ceremony.

She opened her apartment door to find a basket of fruit or bread and cheese from the deli. None of her neighbors asked questions. That was the kind of building in which she lived.

She roused herself just once to make a visit to the pharmacy. Then she roused herself a second time to take a bus to the next state over.

"Name?"

"Janet."

"Last name?"

Marti searched the room. Her eyes landed on the floor.

"Carpet... Carpenter."

The receptionist followed Marti's eyes.

"Okay, Janet *Carpenter*. Please have a seat and fill this out. We'll need identification."

"I... my purse was stolen. So..."

The receptionist rolled her eyes as if to say 'Is that the best you could do?'

Marti waited her out.

"The doctor will be with you soon." The receptionist sounded resigned. Marti's was likely not the shakiest story she would hear in a clinic on the interesting side of town.

The doctor snapped Marti's file folder shut. "First of all, I can confirm that you are pregnant, Janet."

*Merry Christmas to me.*

"Do you have any medical information you wish to share about the baby's father?"

*Other than the fact he's insane?*

The doctor read the expression on Marti's face. Moved on to nutrition. On the way out, the receptionist handed her a package of supplies and information about prenatal care for low-income women.

Marti waited at the bus station. Her shoulders slumped forward. Even though she had an education and thirty-nine years of life experience, in the space of seven months, she royally screwed things up for herself. She felt such a sense of failure, her greatest fears realized. Who could she tell? Who would believe her? She barely believed it herself. Where could she turn?

The bus rolled down the interstate back to Lake City. She reviewed her circumstances again and again. The facts did not change.

Let's see. Single. Pregnant by a loon. No job. Brother in prison. Religious fanatic of a father who was dying. Her own unintended contributions to a criminal enterprise.

Was that everything? Did she leave anything out? No? Then congratulations! She actually topped Christina. Back where she started, she took a moment to recover in the bus station bathroom. She could almost hear the indignant rattle of the janitor's mop handle reprimanding her yet again.

But she also remembered the promise she made outside her childhood home and once again in Alex's car. She would not give up. The way wasn't clear right this moment, but she would get through it. The one thing she did know was that she would not kill this baby. At thirty-nine, the baby was a long time coming. It was hers and it was the very least Alex could do. She washed her face, straightened her spine, then returned home.

She read through the information package the clinic gave her. She signed up for social services that offered free food and vitamins to pregnant women and mothers of small children. She cleaned her apartment. She sold an accumulation of books and other odds and ends to have extra money on hand. She paid what bills she could from her savings, made deals on others, and continued to seek work. She shopped for groceries, dragged her laundry cart behind her. She stretched a dollar as far as she could take it. Then she took it further.

She would have to call Reba to tell her that she couldn't do the kidney transplant. But she wasn't ready yet to explain the reason why. That invited the complaints, the judgments, and the triumphant religious condemnation—all of which would send Marti screaming over the edge. One day soon, she would make the call. Not today. Not tomorrow either. Soon.

She went back over every painful step of her relationship with Alex. She reviewed the laughing threats and indignant complaints. His moody eruptions and vengeful attitude. Whenever he said, "love me, want me, watch me, pay attention to me, depend on me," his audience knew their participatory role was to admire, agree, approve, cheer, then beg for more.

She played her part. At first. But constant maintenance on Alex's happiness drained her energy. She got to the point where she no longer gave a damn. Perhaps for brief moments, when she stood up to him or when she tried to save his life, he respected her. But then it became more of the same.

Her careful review of the situation from every angle always ended with her leaving him to save herself.

◆ ◆ ◆ ◆

A new year meant new beginnings. Beyond the safety of her front door, a steep cliff dropped to jagged rocks that craved nothing more than to devour her whole then swallow her into the darkest pit on Earth.

Two additional weeks passed before *he* knocked on her apartment door. He didn't bother with the intercom. A resident must have let him in.

"Marti. Marti!" *knock, knock,* "Marti, open up!" *knock, knock,* "Marti, I'm not leaving. I know you're in there," *knock, knock,* "I can see your lights from the street," *knock, knock,* "Open the door, Marti. Marti!" *knock, knock, knock.* "Marti!"

She woke, at last, from auto-pilot. Other than Ronny, Alex's main accomplices at Celara—Evan and Kate—were dead. Augie was dead, vaporized into the atmosphere. There remained only Marti. But if he wanted her dead, then she would be. Like the rest. After all, Alex still had his goon squad. Someone would be promoted to lieutenant status. Who would take Evan's place? Ronny? Time to get it over with. She opened the door.

"Why are you here?"

She took him by surprise. He didn't speak.

"Have you come to finish what Evan started, Alex? Are you going to break me down further or rape me into the Celara way? Because I'm ready to be on the team now. I've earned it, don't you think? Who shall I service next, Alex? Or will you just kill me and get it over with now?"

Alex gave her his flinty look. "Marti, it wasn't rape between us. You know it and I *certainly* know it."

Marti lowered her eyes, moved away from the door. He entered. Too late she realized he didn't deny an intention to kill her. She crossed her arms over her body in protection.

"Lexa just recovered from a diabetic coma."

"Oh my God!"

"That's why it took me this long to get back to you."

"How is she? Oh, the little girl!"

"It was a setback, obviously. She went on this... sugar binge and..." he swallowed. "They think it was deliberate."

"Deliberate. Deliberate?"

"She knew what would happen. The doctor questioned her and apparently, she told him enough to make him think she wasn't really trying to... kill herself. She just wanted... her father's attention."

Tears started in Marti's eyes. She shook her head.

Alex blew out a long breath. He lost color from the skin that he usually kept carefully tan. It looked as though he didn't sleep or eat well. Perhaps he stayed by Lexa's side for once. Perhaps he gave his daughter the attention she was willing to die for.

"But before that, the school nurse called to tell me my twelve-year-old girl was pregnant."

"What!"

"Apparently, she had a reputation at school for... making friends the wrong way."

Alex figured out the negative impact Kate's influence too late. Marti bit her lip. She had no idea of what to say.

"We took care of it. I said some bad things to her and that's when," he swallowed, "she tried to hurt herself. But now her mother has temporary full custody. They looked at me. Then they looked at the alcoholic. They decided that the alcoholic was the better choice."

*Lexa's mother. His ex-wife.*

Wearily, Alex moved the conversation along, "Police investigated the accident, Marti. They found Evan's body in the car."

"I know."

"They concluded he was alone in the car." Marti legs felt weak. She sank into a nearby chair. "Here's your coat and purse by the way." Marti flicked her eyes toward her belongings. She didn't move to take them. Alex dropped them without ceremony on another chair. She noted that his cuts healed.

"Why is it so hot in here?"

Marti didn't bother to answer.

"They found he had a history of reckless driving documented by an accumulation of numerous moving violations. And, of course, he always spoke of his rock climbing and bungee jumping in the office. Classic adrenaline junkie. However, what they didn't discover were records of sexual harassment accusations at Celara Solar Construction."

"Of course not."

"But they did find a juvenile record of sexual assaults and two restraining orders against him as an adult processed by Lake City."

Marti gasped in disbelief. "So, the asylum let him out on a day pass and that impressed you so much you decided to hand him the keys to Celara? Why would you hire someone like that and expose other people, like *me* for instance, to him?"

"I didn't have access to his juvie record."

"But everything else, Alex? Or did you hire him specifically for those reasons?"

Alex made no reply.

"I can't work for you anymore. Never again. So don't ask."

"Yeah, I figured." Alex, ever arrogant, set his coat down on the same chair but didn't sit. To have the psychological advantage, Marti noted. "I also figure you could have kept going once you got out of the car the first time. Instead you came back."

Marti turned her head aside. Stared at the floor.

"Why did you come back?"

Marti remained silent. She wasn't sure herself why she risked her life to save his.

"Why did you come back for me, Marti? I need to know. It's important."

Alex walked over. He lifted her chin with a gentle touch. His brilliant eyes softened to a quiet clarity. Marti looked into them, mesmerized.

"You know, for the longest time I wondered what lay under that hard candy shell of yours. I got a small look the other night it all happened. And it was the most beautiful torture," he leaned in closer, "I've ever endured."

Her body responded. Her body always responded to him. That was how he would destroy her.

"A layer of soft gooey warmth insulating a blood pressure cuff that gripped me and wouldn't let me go."

Marti glared at him.

Alex used the flaw, the hurt, the vulnerability, the mistake as levers to break down anyone who threatened his supremacy. She watched him do it to others many times. He drove his first wife to drink the same way the Reverend drove her own mother, Christina.

"Even when I begged you for mercy. Oh Marti, Marti." He nearly touched his lips to hers. "I can't think of anything else."

Disgusted, Marti slapped his hand away. Turned her head aside.

Alex sighed. He retreated back to the chair. "There must be something I can do for you."

*Did he know? Did he follow her to the clinic? Did he pay someone to tell him?*

"You already saved my life," she answered.

He glanced at her hands. They crossed her middle. Those glittery flecks of crystal never missed anything.

"After you saved mine."

"Well, then that makes us even."

"No. There's everything else I didn't help you with earlier." He took a step closer. "And now."

Marti felt the familiar force of his will envelope her. This time, a blue-black vortex rose to smother and drown her like the channel tried to do that horrible night. She stepped away.

She remembered someone who looked familiar on the way to and from the clinic. At the time, she denied the thought as paranoia. Her life was not that interesting she told herself.

"Even when you're nice, you're still yourself, Alex."

"Excuse me?"

"All this" she gestured with her arm, "whatever you keep coming out with..."

"All this what?" He scowled.

She took a step towards him. "You can't control me."

"I'm not trying to control you."

"It would do you no good to try anyway. You cannot."

"I don't know what you're talking about, Marti. I come here telling you that I'm here for you and you blow me off with 'whatever you keep coming out with.'"

"It's never going to be enough for you."

"What isn't?"

"Any answer I could give."

"Any answer..."

"How much do you love me? How many different ways can I make you prove it? How can I control you? How much can I get away with before you leave me?"

"Where are you getting this?"

"I would have to hurdle for you again and again. And Alex, you raise that bar impossibly high for anyone but yourself."

"Look, you've been reading those magazines and those he-said, she-said books..."

"I'm reading that look on your face."

"Okay, so now you're a mind reader? You have ESP? I didn't see that on your resume."

"It's all there right in front of me to see."

"See what!" His voice rose to a shout. "What are you going on about?"

Marti shrank away. Turned her back. Retreated to a shelf that held photos and knick knacks.

"Marti, I'm sorry, but I told you I don't understand you when you talk like that."

She gave a small laugh. "No matter where you start, Alex, you always revert to your default setting—swagger, ego, arrogance, selfishness, and shame games."

"You really need to stop, Marti."

"No. *You need to stop.* You don't have any sense of fairness or understanding, Alex. None."

"You're wrong, Marti. Very wrong."

She contemplated her family photos a moment. "There is something, Alex. Something you could do that would mean everything to me."

Alex smiled with quiet triumph. Finally, the conversation made sense—a business negotiation. And a wily contender Marti was. That body, those lips, those eyes. He couldn't resist her. They lay in each others arms while Evan's life slipped away. Neither Alex nor Marti made the slightest attempt to save him.

Marti shuddered at the gleam in Alex's eyes and the memory of that dark, black night. Evan's psychotic glee and Alex's inability to defend against it thoroughly destroyed whatever might have developed between them. Maybe the next lifetime. Certainly not this one. Evan's ghost still shimmered between them like a phantasmal, poison cloud.

"I can take care of you, Marti. You'll never want for anything. I'll give you everything you've ever desired. I'll *be* everything you ever desired. You don't have to face life alone anymore."

She looked up to see that Alex watched her every movement and expression. Again the blue wave of his charisma sweep over and through her. It sought to drag her down to the undertow.

"Don't just think of yourself. And don't just think of me. We're grown-ups, aren't we, Marti? Think of," he hesitated, "*the future* and what you'd like it be. For instance, I do think you'd be good in Lexa's life. She really likes you." Marti trembled. Lexa. Poor lonely, Lexa really did need two parents.

Marti ached to put her arms around Alex again. She longed to feel his body support hers.

She wanted to be part of him again. She wanted to feel his heat spread through her. She wanted to breathe with him, inhale him, taste him until she became dizzy, lost in the whirlwind with Alex. The attraction between them remained. She felt so lost without his touch.

This was the moment to tell him. This was the moment to say it aloud. The words strained to escape the knot of her vocal cords. It would be so much easier to give in, to give him what he wanted.

But at the back of her mind, she saw the goonish face that looked so much like another face she knew... Without the dirt, sweat, and facial hair and the blue-gray pit bull on a chain he could have been... Ronny. Holding a cell phone. Taking a picture. For Alex?

That was the way it would always be with him.

Watched. Stalked. Hunted.

How long before Alex drove her past the point of no return? How long before she shouted at anyone who tried to intervene, "You just don't understand him like I do! He's had a rough life! He had a bad childhood! His father never gave him the praise he deserved! He needs me to help him be better a better person!" How long, indeed, before she lost her mind and then her soul?

She and Chris smiled at the camera as babies. As small school-age children, they waved in a happier moment. Christina snapped that photo. Trips and vacations here and there. Then none. Then Marti in her graduation gown when she grasped for the freedom to live a normal life.

"All you have to do is say it, Marti. Tell me what you want. Tell me what you need from me. I will give it to you. I will do anything."

*All you have to do is say it, Marti.* She opened her mouth.

But he wasn't done. "I take care of my responsibilities. You know that I can. You know that I will."

She thought of Lexa's lonely disappointment and heartache, second fiddle to her father's multiple agendas. Always last on his list.

Marti knew Lexa's driven feelings stemmed from the desire for any sign of positive parental attention. If Lexa didn't receive the positive, she'd campaign just as hard for the negative. She'd continue to rebel and wind up damaged, bruised. Marti shivered. Would Alex inflict the same frantic desperation onto a daughter of hers? A son, he would mold into his own image—like Evan. But a daughter?

She couldn't push the words through her lips. While she might gamble with her own life, she would not gamble with the life that grew inside her. The baby represented her greatest hope and inspiration, her best opportunity for a new start.

"You do know that, Marti?"

She formed sounds into words.

"I... yes, Alex. I know."

She told him what she wanted. She saw the triumph in his eyes. Then she saw the shock and anger when she continued.

"I want you to leave. Don't come back. No!" She raised his voice when he tried to interrupt. "Don't you ever darken my doorstep again. I don't want you, Alex. After you do what you say you'll do, our business is done."

She sat as still as a statue long after he left. Her arms wrapped around her knees. Even underneath a blanket and a bathrobe, she never felt so cold.

"Because we treated you like a child even though you were an adult, we cut off your ability to be accountable for your actions and to make your own decisions. It wasn't your fault, Chris. I should have told you everything years ago. But I don't think I realized how much it drove you until I read your letters. But I think I just tried to forget."

Chris sat motionless across the dingy glass partition. His eyes never left his sister's face.

"That day, I decided to visit the mall with some girls from school. I thought they were my friends because I really needed friends then. But they weren't. They boosted clothes so I left them at the mall. I didn't want to get in trouble if they got caught stealing. And besides, I was supposed to be home waiting for you. But by the time I got back, well, you know."

"I set that fire. Then she killed herself."

"You didn't set a fire, Chris," she answered with a flat voice.

"I set the fire, Marti."

"You didn't set a fire."

"Yes, I did."

"No, you didn't."

"Yes..."

"No, *you did not*." Marti raised her voice, overrode him with her own as only an older sister could. "You tried to cook for yourself the way you saw me do it."

Chris bowed his head.

Her eyes glistened. "Because I wasn't there to do it for you."

"Marti... I..."

"Didn't you?"

He met that with silence.

"Christian!" She startled him.

"Wow." He blinked, then leaned back. The smallest hint of a smile softened the square line of his jaw. "Good to have you back, Sis."

"Didn't you?" she persisted.

"Yeah."

Her face crumpled. "Chris... what're you doing in here? I never understood it. You don't belong here. Why did you let them think you did it on purpose?"

"Because that's what *he* told them."

"The Reverend?"

Chris nodded. "I was too young to argue for myself. And by the time I got older, everyone believed what they wanted. I believed it too. I could always see people looking at me funny because of it. Like I was crazy. Then it seemed like after that, I couldn't do anything right. I *felt* crazy."

Marti closed her eyes. "I wasn't sure what to believe either. It didn't seem like you, but when you didn't say anything... and then the Reverend..."

"It was an accident, Marti. I swear it was an accident."

"I believe you. But there's more you might not know."

He looked at her with surprise.

"After the fire, Reverend March mocked Christina. He was relentless with it. I mean, he was always like that anyway. But he stepped it up. He called her a bad mother who couldn't care for her own children. It crushed her. She started drinking and basically, she became alcoholic. That was how she coped with all the stress he put on her. You remember how she was always sleeping and always in a bad mood?"

Chris nodded.

"It was the alcohol. Remember how we used to collect her empties and redeem them for candy money in that little wagon?"

Chris chuckled. "We made the best of things."

"I guess." Marti smiled back.

Her smile faded. "One night, he stopped by really late. For what, I don't know. He usually didn't come that late. But anyway, you were already asleep. I wanted to spend time with her so I waited up until she got home. He must have waited for her too outside because they walked in together arguing like usual. He really laid into her and... Christina pulled the gun out on him—the one he left her for protection since he knew he wouldn't be around. Reverend March dared her to shoot him with it. He called her weak. He told her..."

Marti swallowed. She fought back the tears. Visitors that cried made the guards nervous.

"He told her that his life was worth five times that of a drunken, alcoholic slut who couldn't even care for her children or clean her own home."

Chris tightened his lips. He squared his jaw again. His eyes hardened. He looked away from Marti. He knew if she saw the cold, raw hatred in his eyes that she would likely get up then run away. That's what the other inmates did.

"And that's when she... pointed the gun at her, her... head."

Marti breathed in and out. She tried to hold the sobs at bay. "She pulled the trigger and... it didn't go off at first. It just clicked. And I screamed at her 'No! No!' But then the gun fired and..."

Marti paused a moment. She swallowed down the sick feeling that rose up whenever she remembered the aftermath. How Christina looked laying there on the floor with the smallest memories from the corners of her mind scattered against the walls, the floor, the ceiling. She couldn't stop the tremble in her voice.

"Even after the first click, he had a chance to stop her. He could have said anything because he knew she was serious the first time she pulled the trigger. But he just stood there and laughed at her. Like it was yet another one of her epic failures. He could have stopped her. I tried to. But... she didn't listen. Or maybe she didn't hear me. I'm pretty sure he wanted her to die. He drove her to it. And then the police came and he told them what he wanted them to hear.

I truly hated him after that. But I kept quiet. I tried to forget. I never really talked about it to anyone, including you. It was too much to remember. But, you see, he never really let me forget. He said that what happened was partly my fault for not being there with you when the fire broke out. That upset her. He held it over me and would just insert the implication into our conversations. That's how he kept me in line whenever I challenged him about how we were treated by his new family and Holy Ghost Reba, or when I told him that I remembered what he did to Christina. I kept quiet, Chris."

Chris looked down. "You know, he always did act like caring for his own children, us, was some kind of chivalrous act of charity. Like he was doing us a favor. I never understood that about him."

Marti looked up in surprise. Chris rarely shared his feelings. Encouraged that she finally got through to him, she pressed on.

"He's not the hero he makes himself out to be, Chris. Without those delusions of moral superiority, he has nothing. He *is* nothing. And Chris, you're not the villain he makes you out to be. You never were. And neither was I. At least I hope I'm not to you. Do you believe me?"

"Yes."

"Can you forgive me for not being there?"

"Yeah. I mean, I never held that against you."

"No?"

"Sounds like Righteous March was the one who put you down for that."

Martina nodded.

"And not telling you everything?"

"You probably should have told me, Sis."

"I know. I should have said something. I'm so sorry. I wish I'd been stronger for you, Chris. I really do. But you know the truth now." She paused. "Look. By the end of January, you're going to be contacted about your probation by someone who will have the ability to assist you in ways me and the Reverend haven't been able to."

Chris narrowed his eyes. "Who?"

"I... can't say right now. Just watch for it. Be ready to do what has to be done. You won't have a second chance. This is it, Chris. It's all I have. The only way it will work, is if you rise up and believe that you actually deserve the very best out of life instead of the worst. You'll have to stop destroying yourself for something you never did. You're going to have to make up your mind to grow beyond the circumstances and be better to yourself than you've been before."

Marti paused. "I want you to know... Chris, I'm not coming back to visit you in this prison or any other prison." She looked around the low max facility they'd moved him to from downstate a couple of months ago. "I *hate* it here. I always hate it here."

"So do I."

They laughed together. For a moment, it felt like she was eleven and he was six and they watched Saturday morning cartoons together with big bowls of cereal at the ready until Christina came home from the restaurant.

At last she admitted, "I'm going to have a child, Chris. You'll be an uncle in about seven months."

His eyes lit up with questions. She shook her head.

"One other thing. Reverend March is diabetic. He needs a kidney transplant. Reba told me. I confirmed it with the doctor."

"Diabetic?"

She nodded. "Within the year, he's going to need a transplant because the dialysis is wearing him down."

"I didn't know."

"Of course not. That would mean he'd have to admit to being a human being. You know he's never been able to do that, especially with us."

Chris waited for the rest.

"I was going to, but now... with the baby..."

Marti stood up. She didn't take it further.

"Look. Make the most of what will happen for you the next few days. I'm going now, Chris. I meant what I said. We do want to see you again. Me and the baby. But not here."

Chris nodded.

"Another time, another place, Sis."

Marti hurried away.

◆ ◆ ◆ ◆

"Reba, leave us alone a moment, please."

Reba hesitated. Her husband put up a good front, but after a round of dialysis, he usually needed a few hours to recover. She looked towards their visitor. They already exchanged pleasantries.

Reverend March waved her off. "It's okay. We'll be fine."

The two men sat across from each other. Both their shoulders straight and square. Reverend March waited to hear what a man he never met had to say.

Alex broke the silence, which gave the first round to Marti's father.

"Your daughter, Martina Butler, and I have a relationship."

"Interesting. She's never spoken your name to me."

Alex ignored the dismissal. "I care about Martina, very deeply. I want to marry her."

Reverend March said nothing. A quick study, this time Alex waited.

The Reverend scowled. "Who are you?" His voice drifted from irritation to scorn.

Alex did his homework. He knew all about the Reverend's Internet ventures. "I own Celara Solar Construction. Martina joined my staff..."

"And you decided to give her a hand up the ranks?"

Alex paused to allow the remark to sit in the atmosphere by itself a moment. Then, "No. I decided that she was the best thing that ever happened to me."

"What has she decided about you? I mean, you *are* here by yourself."

"She hasn't decided yet."

"And why do you think that is?"

Alex didn't answer.

Reverend March leaned forward, spread his hands wide. "Sir, my daughter doesn't love you."

"I'm not convinced that's the case."

"Not convinced? Or don't know?"

Having made an incision, the older man circled closer for the kill.

"Why are you here? Shouldn't you be *there*? With her?"

"I'm thinking that another voice might provide her a different perspective. And that if we met and we spoke together, you could provide that perspective."

"Sir, you are making a terrible mistake."

"A mistake, sir?"

"Listen carefully." Reverend March enunciated each word. "My daughter, Martina Marie Butler, does not love you."

"Respectfully, sir. How can you possibly know that?"

The older man leaned back, satisfied. His work here was done.

"Reba!"

She materialized instantly. "Yes, March?" A little too instantly. He indicated for her to help him to his feet.

"Mr. King needs to be on his way."

Alex stood. The three of them walked towards the front door of the older man's retirement condo. Marti's father opened the door. He leaned against his wife. Alex passed through then turned in the doorway.

"How can you know that, sir?" he repeated.

Exasperated, Reverend March dropped the hammer.

"She doesn't love you because she doesn't love anyone, including herself. Especially herself. I'm very sorry."

Reverend March shut the door on Alex who faced solid wood in absolute astonishment. A few moments later, he sat, still stunned, in his car in the parking lot.

He remembered the alert from Lexa's school. Normally, he deleted those text messages as soon as he received them. Mrs. Dallas took care of all that. Not this time, he thought grimly.

Family court allowed Lexa to come back to him on weekends ever since he reassured the judge by taking a weekly parenting class. That and the fact that it was pretty obvious to everyone, including Lexa, that Lily's "treatment" for her "illness" was far from over. He dialed Lexa at home.

"Lexa, Monday's the parent-teacher conference, isn't it?"

"Yes, Mrs. Dallas is taking me." The flat tone of low expectations filled the long silence between them. Alex closed his eyes in the face of the self-loathing reflected in his rearview mirror. Now was not the time to wallow. He had a child to raise.

"I'm taking you," he replied in a firm voice. "We'll need to talk about getting you caught up to the rest of the class."

"Do you remember where my school is?"

"Lexa!" Parenting class kicked in. He adjusted his tone. "We'll have dinner afterward and you can choose the restaurant."

"What?" A pause. "Okay."

He smiled because he could tell he caught his daughter by surprise. "So I'll tell Mrs. Dallas the new plan. Did she already cook dinner for tonight?"

"No, but she's about to start. She's in the kitchen now."

"Tell her not to. I'm going to cook dinner tonight."

"Uhm... what did you say?"

"Come on, kid. That the best you can do?"

"Oh. I mean, hooray!"

"Yeah, right." Alex started the ignition. "Depending on what I find out at your school, I may have to cook dinner Monday night too for your own good. That'll learn ya." He hung up on Lexa's giggling protest. It relieved him to know the kid still had a sense of humor, especially with the father she put up with all these years. He felt pretty proud of himself.

"But if any provide not for his own, and especially for those of his own house, he hath denied the faith, and is worse than an infidel. First Timothy, fifth chapter, eighth verse. Look it up, *Reverend*."

Chris leaned into the glass. He matched Reverend March's quiet voice of fury and tight jaw measure for measure.

"You're a fraud and a phony and the worst father God ever inflicted upon a brother and sister. Because unlike a lot of deadbeat dads, you actually had the means to care for us and provide for us, but you chose not to out of pure spite. So what does that make *you*?

Let me tell you what's been happening in Lake City while you've been stroking your own ego and believing your own hype. Oh yeah, Reverend. They let us use computers in low max. I've seen the Internet channel. You're pathetic and delusional.

Your only daughter has been brutalized by predators. She won't talk much about it. Certainly not to you, because she knows you don't give a damn. But she's been done very wrong by very bad men. I know where I was. Where the *fuck* were you?"

Reverend March narrowed his eyes, opened his mouth.

"Don't even worry about it, Rev. I've got her now. No one's gonna hurt her any more, including you. Especially not you. Not on my watch."

"What happened to Martina, Christian? Some guy out of nowhere came to see me..."

Chris snarled his top lip. "You happened."

He regarded his father with the full blast of cold, arctic hatred he didn't allow Martina to see.

"And by the way, what kind of man, what kind of *Christian* man goads a disturbed woman into pulling the trigger and then blames his own daughter and son for their mother's death? That fire," he leaned in close staring death into the Reverend's eyes, "was an accident! It was an accident by a hungry little boy in the house alone who didn't know any better who tried to cook himself a meal. But why would you bother to ask me about it instead of going around telling everyone you knew and who knew me that I tried to burn the house down on purpose? Who throws their own son under the bus?"

Chris sat back in mock curiosity. "I wanna know, Reverend. Why don't you explain that one to me? Why don't you put that on your Internet show and explain it to all your followers?"

Reverend March's face slackened. All of a sudden, he looked like a man worn down from dialysis—old and unwell.

"You sad, old, sick, twisted motherfucker. You are an abomination in God's eyes and a complete failure in mine. That's what you are. Me and Marti don't need you in our lives anymore. You've caused enough ruin and harm to us both and we're still recovering from it. And by the way, thank you for all the help you didn't give Teresa or Mari and Kina. I thank God for that indifference, because that means out of all of us, *they're the lucky ones.*"

It was over, or so the Reverend thought. But Christian picked up the telephone again.

"Oh, and by the way, the way you took care of yourself before is what got you here." Chris indicated the Reverend's torso. "Too bad about that kidney transplant, *Reverend.*"

He set down the phone receiver. Stood up straight. Turned his back to his father. Walked back to the guard.

◆ ◆ ◆ ◆

## 13 The Dialogue

Alexander King, "Evan Lewis provided a vital service to Celara Solar Construction. His contributions will be missed."

**W**inter no longer looked beautiful. The sweet, fluffy marshmallow and confectioner's sugar top layer covered a dirty, gray, salty, sandy base that showed itself with dreary persistence. Police investigators concluded that icy road conditions and reckless driving claimed the life of Evan Lewis.

Not until then did Marti remember Alex's trips to the Caribbean. He was scuba-certified. His training as a swimmer was how he saved her that night. He owned a wet suit and other underwater equipment. That was how he retrieved her belongings and his from the submerged car, Evan's tomb.

Marti shut down questions of her own responsibility. She had neither the physical strength nor the endurance needed to save Evan that night. Period. As for Alex, he made his own choice... her. She didn't want to dwell on that night anymore and neither did the *Lake City Tribune* judging by how deep they buried the small blurb.

Steady as the snow falling, the wind blowing, the clock ticking, the sun and the moon rising and setting, Worth stopped by every few days with stacks of newspapers and magazines that he said he finished reading.

She pushed the intercom button. "Worth, did Beryl send you here?"

"You live on my way to the museum." He spoke over the intercom. "My research is ongoing so it's not a problem."

"Okay, I can buzz you up, but I can't let you in. I'm not dressed."

They went through that song and dance for a couple of weeks. He knocked, waited for her to buzz him up, listened to her excuses, dropped off whatever he brought, and then walked away from her door and let himself out of the building.

One day, she buzzed him up as usual, ready to tell him she was cleaning out her closets and there was a lot of dust floating around her apartment. He ignored that and knocked and knocked and knocked, much like Alex, until she opened the door.

"Well, I'm glad to confirm that I haven't been speaking to a recording."

She laughed at him. "Of course not."

She invited him inside. He didn't mention the lack of dust in the air, which was kind. They chatted about this and that. Marti knew he would report back to Beryl. She put on her game face. She tried not to look like how she felt—defeated.

"Now and then I travel to do research," Worth took a casual glance around the room. For empty liquor bottles or drug paraphernalia probably, Marti thought. That's what she used to do to Christina. If not for the baby, Worth might find pharmaceuticals lying about.

"For Save a Lake?"

"Well, that and other things."

"Things like..."

"Too much to go into. But I'll be going on a short trip soon."

Marti smiled. "I appreciate the heads up, Worth. Look. I know things seem weird around here. I'm just not myself lately. I realize that. I know I'll have to face the world again on my own."

"You'll be just fine, Marti."

"Thanks. I appreciate your confidence."

"You should appreciate *your* confidence."

Mystified, she wondered why she didn't feel the passion for Worth that she still felt for her loon of a former boss.

❖ ❖ ❖ ❖

"Fishermen found the body of a woman identified by Lake City Police, who used dental records, as Katherine Winterset.

The former Celara Solar Construction employee's body washed up in a tangle of weeds, half-buried in snow and ice in the channel just a few miles downstream from another Celara employee, Evan Lewis. Alexander King, head of the renewable energy construction company, provided police investigators with background information. According to Mr. King, Evan Lewis and Katherine Winterset maintained an intimate relationship outside the office. Police investigators have the understanding that a lover's quarrel led first to murder, which Lewis allegedly tried to cover up, then to suicide. According to other unnamed sources, Evan Lewis was a disturbed young man who needed help. Jason, back to you in the studio."

◆ ◆ ◆ ◆

"Unnamed sources, hunh?"

"That's what they say."

"They say things around here too, Terry."

"Like what?"

"Word around the way is that Evan Lewis was into foul shit. Celara's working double-time clean the pile he left behind. Payoffs, bribes, settlements, firings, transfers, relocations, new hirings, employee counseling... that just about covers it. They say sometimes you reach too high, you fall. You play with fire, you get burned. Stomp with the big dogs, they go rabid and turn on you. That's what they say around here."

"I'm so glad Marti's out of it. She shouldn't be involved with those people anymore."

◆ ◆ ◆ ◆

"Ms. Butler, its Lake City Police. Please open your door."

Marti opened the door. She already decided not to fight her arrest. She would hold her head up high. Two officers stood in her doorway. She waited for the Miranda warning.

"Ms. Butler, we'd like to talk to you about Katherine Winterset."

That didn't sound like a list of her civil rights.

"Do I need a lawyer?"

Keen eyes squinted. "Why would you think you needed lawyer?"

Marti concentrated on the ceiling. She paged through past research to figure out why she needed a lawyer. Nothing came to mind.

"Well, on those cop shows, people always lawyer up."

The officers exchanged a look. The younger of the two cleared his throat. "Ah, miss, you aren't under arrest. If we wanted you, you'd already be in cuffs."

"Oh." Marti waited. They stared at her.

"May we come in?" the older officer asked her. *You slow-witted idiot*, he didn't say, but his face did.

"Um," again Marti looked at the ceiling. "Okay." She didn't offer a seat. The three of them stood inside her tiny foyer.

The younger officer gave it a go. "Ms. Butler, you left a voice mail message for Ms. Winterset?"

Marti thought for a moment. "Yes."

He waited for her to explain. She waited for the next question.

"Apparently, you thought Ms. Winterset had something to tell you?"

"Yes."

"Do you have any idea what she had to tell you?"

"No. That's why I called her. To find out. You see, I didn't know, so I had to call to find out because I didn't know and I had no idea, really," she took a breath, "so I called her..."

"Did Ms. Winterset call you back?"

"No."

"Did you speak to Ms. Winterset at all after you left that message?"

"No."

"Did she speak to you?"

"No."

"Did you receive any communication such as an email or a letter or a note from Ms. Winterset?"

"No."

"Did you see her or meet her anywhere?"

"No."

The older officer lost patience. "Are you even aware that Ms. Winterset died a couple of months ago?"

Marti met that with silence. The silky spider threads that crawled across her neck distracted her.

"Miss?"

The web closed off her throat. She couldn't breathe.

"Miss?" The older officer snapped his fingers by her face. Like Evan did that night. She flinched away.

His voice became louder, slower. "Ms. Butler, you seem completely unaware of what we're talking about. You did know Katherine Winterset."

"I thought I did." Marti shrugged. "But not really."

"Then why would she want to speak to you?"

"I never did figure that out."

Both officers studied her expression—blank, confused, weary, exhausted.

She used scissors to slice through red cloth. She burned the pieces one by one in her bathtub. She flushed the ashes down her toilet with bleach.

◆ ◆ ◆ ◆

The next day, Harlan visited Marti to gather necessary details. She appeared numb, almost catatonic. Much as he wanted to ask her if she were okay, he chose not to. He wasn't there to see her to fall apart. He had a task to fulfill and a job to do. She seemed relieved by his indifference. She barely noticed when he left. Pretty much how Alex's police friends described her to Alex. But she definitely wasn't the "mental retard" the older officer insisted she was.

As always, he followed his client's orders. Yet another bizarre Alexander King situation to put to rights. One of many.

"We can arrange to reduce your probation from ten years to six months."

Though he no longer trusted the motivations of others, Chris acknowledged and understood their existence. His remarkable gifts of stoic calm and acceptance complemented his street smarts.

"You already know that one condition of your probation is immediate, full-time employment."

Chris nodded.

"That's the court's condition. My client's condition is that you provide a particular service for a particular business venture. A show of your faith towards the success of this endeavor would result in satisfying the court and guarantee a show of gratitude from my client at the appropriate time."

"I guess a lot can be accomplished on the golf course."

Harlan measured Marti's brother, noted the strong familial characteristic in sheer will power. Marti may be down, but she wasn't out. Not by a long shot. Alex still did not understand what he was up against.

"Indeed."

Both men recognized the clear difference between business and personal. Neither of them mentioned Marti.

◆ ◆ ◆ ◆

"Your father wants to celebrate Chris's return with a dinner party next week. Praise God!"

"My father?" The mist and smoke cleared from her mind.

"Yes. It's so wonderful. The Lord is a way-maker."

"The Reverend March Butler?"

Reba laughed. "Yes, Marti. The one and same. He wants to make sure Christian knows he's an important part of the family and to welcome him back home."

"Home? He's staying with you all?"

"No. That's not a part of God's plan."

"So it's more like a welcome back, not a welcome home."

"He'll stay with Teresa."

"Oh. That makes sense." In fact, it made perfect sense. Teresa seemed determined to reunite her daughters with their father. Marti agreed that Teresa and Chris belonged together.

"So, I need to call Teresa to let her know what time to bring Christian and the kids. Do you have her number?"

"Actually, is it okay if I have her call you, Reba? I'm about to talk to her anyway."

Marti disconnected before Reba answered. She dialed Teresa. Got her up-to-speed.

"My mother's coming with us," Teresa insisted.

"Miss Analicia? Does Reba know?"

"She will. My mother's very protective of Mari and Kina. She knows Chris is their father, of course. But she hasn't seen him in years. And she doesn't know the Reverend or Reba at all."

"That's probably for the best. Just let Reba know so she'll have time to pray about it."

"Praise God! We'll bring something extra with us."

Marti giggled. "That should help. Actually, I'm thinking of asking two friends of mine to come too. I'll bring a couple of dishes with me."

"You're going to cook something?"

"I... well... I'm going to get something."

Teresa giggled.

"Terry! Girl, whatever. It's all part of the plan."

"What plan?"

"I figure if I bring guests, he'll behave."

"The Reverend? Hmmm."

"I'm sure it'll be fine. You don't think so?"

Teresa decided on diplomacy. "I'm just thrilled to have Chris home with us. So are the girls."

"That's the important thing."

"Right."

"Tell those sweeties their Aunt Marti said hello."

Marti waited fifteen minutes for Teresa to make her own arrangements then called Reba back.

"What are you cooking?" Reba sounded suspicious.

Marti bit back a retort. "I'm picking up potato salad and red velvet cake from the bakery."

"Oh." Reba sounded relieved. "That's okay then."

Teresa's mother, Analicia, arrived with Chris and Teresa. She took firm charge of Mari and Kina. Reba gathered that Analicia didn't speak English, which Marti knew wasn't true, but Teresa went through the motions of translating anyway.

"She says these are beef tamales. They just need to be heated for one minute in the microwave. These are chicken fajitas. Maybe heat for thirty seconds only."

Reba beamed at Analicia who inclined her head in regal silence. Marti was pretty sure Analicia would be the one person allowed to remain sane tonight.

The Reverend made his own efforts to be magnanimous. After more introductions and greetings and endless hugs and thumps on the back for Chris, they sat around the table.

"Beryl, it's been a long time," the Reverend said.

"Yes, it has," Beryl replied. She turned to Reba. "Thank you for having us over. We love Marti and we're so happy for Chris's return home."

The Reverend answered for Reba. "Yeah, fancy that. I really don't keep up with my daughter like I should, I suppose. I had no idea she'd gone and reacquainted with old... friends."

Marti's hackles rose, but Beryl had her own method for handling the Reverend.

"She's been assisting me at the museum." Beryl smiled smoothly Marti's direction. "Her help is invaluable."

"So, Martina, it seems you've been keeping pretty busy," the Reverend observed.

Reba broke in. "Worth, now don't be shy. We're just God's regular folks around here. Help yourself to whatever you see."

"Thank you, Mrs. Butler," he smiled. "I always appreciate the opportunity to take a break from research."

Reverend March persisted. "Speaking of work, about your job, Martina..."

This time Chris broke in with, "Reba, can you pass that potato salad down to me? I can guarantee that you won't have any leftovers to put away. And I don't mind helping with dishes after either."

"Why thank you, Christian," Reba beamed.

"As I was saying," Reverend March raised his voice. "What is going on with you and..."

"I don't work there anymore," Marti broke in.

"Yeah, well, something's going on. Your *boss* came by here to see me. Spent the whole afternoon talking about you."

Marti's mouth hung open. "He came..."

"What on God's good earth have you been doing, Martina?"

Chris gripped his fork, but kept a light tone, "Hey, this is a party. We're not talking business at a party, *my* party, are we?"

Reba turned to Teresa in desperation. "Are Kina and Mari getting enough?"

"Yes," Teresa nodded until she saw the stricken look on Reba's face. "I mean, I think they could have more salad."

The table watched Teresa fussily pile more salad on her children's plates ignoring their murmurs of protest. "Kina and Mari, this is good salad," she insisted. "Let me get the dressing."

"We're talking family business now, Christian," the Reverend replied, fed up with the numerous attempts to interrupt his train of thought. "You need to catch up."

"What did you and he talk about?" Marti asked.

An uncomfortable pall settled over the table. Everyone seemed to realize that no matter how the dinner celebration started, it would not end well. Reba stared at the black eyed peas. Beryl and Worth comprehended the beginnings of a family drama about to launch. They seemed resigned to wait it out. Without a word, Teresa's mother picked up Mari and Kina's plates and walked to the next room. The girls trailed behind her.

"The fact that a relationship between the two of you would never work."

Sheer, white hot anger created a ringing noise in Marti's ears. She saw her father's mouth continue to move, but she couldn't understand his words.

"How dare you?"

"I am your father. That's how. Are you pregnant?"

That did it. Marti closed her eyes. Her forehead into her hands. Silence filled the room for exactly fifty-three seconds.

"Marti. Marti." She felt Beryl's arm around her shoulders.

"The boss got you pregnant then fired you. I can't believe this." The Reverend threw his napkin on the table in disgust. "I simply cannot believe it."

"Stop right now." Chris stared at his father with loathing. "Martina's the only one in this family who ever gave a damn about me. I won't hear anything about her from *you* of all people."

Reverend March shot his son a look as if to remind him whose house he was in and at whose table he sat.

"Well, it's all out in the open now." Beryl made an exasperated noise. "Marti, look. The behavior from the folks at Celara is not an indication of your worth. It's an indication of their twisted state of mind. That lack of awareness of the rights of others and fragile ego you encountered are character weaknesses."

"Excuse *me*!" Reverend March put up a hand. "I will handle my household, Beryl."

Beryl contemplated the Reverend a long moment. She turned back to Marti.

"Marti," she glanced at Chris, "and Chris," she looked back at Marti. "I didn't want to tell you this before, but I feel that I should because it's time. I'm not sure how much you knew back when you were younger."

Keeping her arm around Marti's shoulders, she stood and faced Reverend March.

"While Christina was pregnant with Chris, your father and I... we..."

Marti's eyes grew wider.

"We had an affair. We tried to be careful but Christina did discover the affair. She didn't know it was me. At least, I don't think she did."

The entire table sat shocked and confused.

"I believe it was self-defense, but March challenged Christina's fidelity and Chris's paternity."

"What!" Teresa shrieked. "That's crazy! Chris looks just like him."

"Like I said, it was a defensive move from March."

Chris laughed. "Of course it was."

Marti started to protest again. "But," then she remembered. "We used to see you around. Then we never saw you until I visited the museum in junior high."

"I know, Marti," Beryl replied.

Marti turned to her father. "You and Christina divorced. And then all of a sudden, you got religion. You always used religion as a weapon against Christina. And us too."

"But that's why he was so hard on her, Marti—and you and Chris. Because of his own guilt about what he and I did."

Chris swore. Teresa muttered what could have been either a prayer or a curse in Spanish. Reba mentioned something helpful about the Holy Ghost.

Reverend March broke in. "Beryl, you've done enough, don't you think?"

"He hammered Christina until she broke and became everything he said she was." Marti paused. "My mother didn't deserve that from you, Beryl. She didn't deserve that from *him* either. But still, you were supposed to be her friend."

"I saw the result of what I'd done. I've felt terribly ashamed about it ever since."

Marti spared a quick glance to Worth. He sat frozen to his chair. She spoke quietly. "You know Beryl, it would be easy for me to blame you for the destruction of my family, but I can't.

My father is to blame. It always comes back to him. All of us, I think were afraid of him at some point."

"Including me, Marti," Beryl replied. "He threatened to reveal the affair to Christina unless I stayed away."

Beryl took a deep breath. "Christina actually had to fight your father for custody of you two."

"What?"

"Beryl, I'm warning you. Stop this now."

"Oh my God," Reba moaned. "Oh my God."

"He tried to take you away from her. She wouldn't give you up. He even tried to bargain for either you or Chris. She wouldn't allow him to split you up. The divorce was hard enough, but the custody battle wore her down. He was always looking for an edge. Some mistake that he could run to the judge with. It drained all of her resources and her energy. When he saw me helping her, he threatened me about the affair, and so I..." Beryl shrugged helplessly, unable to hold back her tears.

"You are not going to stand here in my house, Beryl..."

"Quiet!" Chris shouted.

Marti felt a stab of disappointment shoot through her. She thought about never again speaking to the woman betrayed her mother." She looked again at Worth, then reconsidered.

"I'm familiar with the threats he makes, Beryl. He's done the same thing to me and to Chris all our lives."

That was why the fire and the Reverend's jibes affected Christina so badly. Soon to be a mother herself, Marti couldn't begin to imagine the depths of Christina's pain and despair.

The Reverend stood with considerable effort. "Get out of my house, Beryl. Get out! You are out of order and you are way out of line." He pointed to Marti. "Look what you've done to my daughter. Look at her!"

"You started this, Reverend," Chris told him.

"You are not going to bring this vindictive trash talk to my son's welcome home celebration."

"Welcome home for which son?" Beryl asked.

A long silence passed. One by one, every head in the room turned to Worth. He sat to the Reverend's left. Marti felt relieved when they first sat down, because it meant neither she nor Chris would have to be near their father.

However, Worth's proximity also meant the resemblance to Reverend March Butler became more pronounced. He saw through Beryl's hazel eyes, but the Reverend's strong jaw line shaped his face into the distinctive square. The same square that shaped Chris's face. Worth's tall height cemented the ancestry. In fact, Worth and Chris were virtually the same size and build. Marti couldn't believe she missed it. Worth's lighter skin and feathery brown hair threw her off.

Their ages backed Beryl's claim. Worth was less than a year younger than Chris.

"I'm so sorry, Worth," Beryl said sadly. "But it's time you knew. It's time everyone knew. I'm sorry, Marti."

Marti felt anger, and yes, revulsion at the possibility that eventually she and Worth might have... *oh my Holy God*. In that instant, Marti understood Beryl's pushing her away from Worth. Beryl, alone, knew her son was Marti's half-brother. Marti mistook it for latent racism and actually felt a little disappointed with Beryl at the time. She shook her head in complete disbelief.

The dinner party could not get worse if a group of terrorists ran in, lined them all up against a wall, and shot them where they stood—then spat on them. Good thing her father didn't know about her visit by Lake City's finest. She still couldn't bring herself to confide in Chris or Teresa.

Reverend March wheezed, coughed, sat back down. Reba jumped up to help him drink a glass of water. Marti saw a movement from the corner of her eye. Analicia leaned in the doorway with a look of concern. Marti noticed with relief that she kept Mari and Kina from coming back into the room. Teresa waved her mother back.

Reba tried to pat the Reverend on the back. "Please March, remember your health. You have to be careful." He shoved her hands away with an impatient growl.

Reba turned to the group, "Everyone, I'm sorry. I think it's time to cut this short."

*No kidding*. General agreement murmured across the table.

"One moment, Mrs. Butler." Worth spoke, his voice wooden and toneless. His hazel eyes focused on the wall behind Reba. Marti was certain he was in shock. "I just want to say one thing. If what my mother claims is true," Beryl made a small movement, "and Reverend March Butler is my father, then I hereby present myself as a candidate to donate a kidney."

He turned to Reba who sat back down after her husband rejected her attempt to comfort him.

"I understand he is in dire need of assistance with not many candidates willing or able to step forward. Judging by what I've just seen and heard today, that comes as no surprise."

Reba suddenly looked sad as if she just realized the unimaginable possibilities of for better or for worse. Either that or the sheer amount of prayer it would take to resolve tonight's disaster overwhelmed her.

Worth spoke at last to Reverend Butler. "Even wolves raise their young."

He put down his napkin, stood, then reached to shake Reba's hand. "Thank you." He nodded towards his newly-discovered father. "Reverend."

"You all can take a plate home, if you like." Reba's voice sounded hopeful. No one bothered. Her eyes glistened.

Everyone stood. They gathered their belongings in silence. Outside Reverend March and Reba's door, Marti, Worth, and Chris shared an impulsive hug. But still, it seemed as if everyone were afraid to speak because who knew what other secrets would jump out to attack them all.

A cold wind blew them separate directions.

Because of the wind, they missed the sound of Reba's sharp slap across her husband's face. He retreated to the bedroom. She scraped the unfinished food into the garbage disposal and ground it to a thick, chunky, brown liquid.

◆ ◆ ◆ ◆

# 14 The Negotiation

"**I**'m okay."

She said it over and over whenever Chris, Teresa, or Worth stopped by to see her. "I'm okay." She also said it to Beryl whenever she called. "I'm okay." But for the moment, Beryl and Marti kept a polite distance from each other.

Two nights after the aborted celebration for Chris, she and her two brothers along with Teresa and the girls tried another dinner together.

By then, Chris visited a dentist from around the way who replaced his gold caps with white veneers. An old friend cut his long hair close to the scalp. He hid his tattoos under long sleeves. Those that he couldn't hide under clothing, he covered with make-up that Marti bought for him, two shades darker than her own. She told him he looked great.

After Teresa retreated to put the girls to bed, Marti, Chris, and Worth cleaned the kitchen together.

Chris cleared the table and scraped plates. Marti washed and rinsed dishes for Worth to dry.

"I remember you from camp that year." Marti frowned before she realized Worth spoke to Chris.

"I remember you too."

"Funny, wasn't it?"

Martina's eyes moved from Worth to Chris, back to Worth. They forgot about her. She decided to let them say whatever it was they needed to say to each other.

"Sick, more like it. That place..." Chris shook his head. "They shut it down the next year, you know."

"I know."

"What place?" Marti broke in.

Chris answered after he exchanged another look with Worth. "Summer camp on the North Shore. You never knew about it, did you, Marti?"

"Knew what? I know the Reverend sent you there because he didn't feel like being a father that year, or any year, but that's all. That was my first year away at school."

"What happened?"

He didn't answer.

"Christian!" she demanded in the big sister tone Worth figured he better get used to. Since Chris remained silent, Worth took the plunge.

"The counselors took advantage, Marti. Especially the lower income kids."

Marti covered her mouth.

"The middle class kids like me and the rich ones, they left alone. But the kids from Central District got treated real bad."

"Oh no, Chris."

Worth made a calming gesture. "He fought them off, Marti. I saw it."

"That's why I got sent to juvie. I broke someone's nose. I'd do it again."

"Next time, I'll help," Worth put in.

"It was enough that you walked in when you did. Otherwise..." Chris shook his head.

"God, what a horrible place. I told my mother I never wanted to go back. I didn't tell her the reason why, but I never returned."

"Neither did I, of course. I got locked up."

"Chris, I..."

"It's not your fault, Marti."

"I know. I just can't believe I didn't even know and you never said."

"It was a long time ago."

"But..."

"I handled it. It's over. Shut up about it."

Marti left it alone. They continued with the kitchen clean-up in silence for a few minutes.

"But I tell you this, Mari and Kina spend their summers at home with me and Terry. No question."

The rest of that night, she and Chris regaled Worth with tales of the silly things they used to do together as latchkey kids. Worth laughed in all the right places, though he appeared wistful, at times. His kids would have been about the same ages as Chris's girls.

Marti felt herself come back to life. She decided to start another exercise routine that included yoga, walking, and swimming.

◆ ◆ ◆ ◆

"I want to use this small window the court allowed me to figure out how to be a father. I want to reacquaint myself with my children and my family—you and Worth, at least. I need to re-integrate myself back into society."

"We got your back, Chris." Marti got on the phone to arrange for Chris to spend blocks of time with her and Worth during the next four days before he started work on A.J.'s crew the following week. They took him shopping for clothes and other bits and pieces to help get his life back on track.

When Alex stopped by to check on Chris at the jobsite, A.J., ever the diplomat, walked off to take care of things elsewhere. Chris assembled solar panel mounting gear for installation by the older members of the crew. He kept his voice even and low. To anyone that watched, he and Alex discussed the job at hand, or maybe the weather.

"I love my sister, Alex. Every criminal and thug on the block and on the street knows how much I love my sister. They have her back. They look out for her. So do I."

Chris took a step forward, invaded Alex's space. He reached past his boss to get more parts out of the box to assemble. He watched Alex's eyes to make sure that the communication was clear.

"They watch for people watching her in neighborhoods they don't belong. They take down driver's licenses and find out that people live at 12202 N. Benson and leave their house at seven and come back at 6:30. You know what I mean? They get architectural floor plans to figure out the who, the what, the where, the when, and the how. The why is already understood."

Chris fit more metal pieces together. He used a tool to twist them tight. "That's what the street can do."

The two men looked at each other.

"My sister's moving on with her life." Chris placed the finished part into a box. "I believe she mentioned that. That needs to be clearly understood, you know what I mean? She's not looking back at anything or anyone from the past. I appreciate the opportunity I have here. But it's time other people start moving on with their lives too."

Alex gave the slightest nod. "You're doing good work here, Chris." He allowed his voice to carry. "I'm hearing good things from A.J." He paused, shook Chris's hand, then lowered his voice. "Maybe I can check back in with you from time to time. See how things are going."

Chris shrugged. "Yeah, you can check on my *work*, sure." He held Alex's gaze with hard eyes. "Doesn't mean there's gonna be anything for you to know about anything else."

Alex nodded again, turned around, spoke to A.J. on the way out, then left the power plant.

Chris took out his cell phone. "You see him?"

The man sitting a block away in a non-descript pickup truck gave a quick glance Chris's direction. "Yeah."

"You know what to do."

"Yeah." The man followed Alex's car. He didn't bother to conceal the fact. After all, he had clear instructions to see and be seen.

Later in the week, word spread among the crew that Alex took an extended leave of absence.

"I'm going to run both the Lakeside Power and the Lake City Correctional projects," A.J. told Chris.

"Cool." Chris nodded but kept his hands moving. His latest task was to count out parts to box up.

"Good." A.J. hesitated. "Chris. I need you to pass on a message."

"Yeah?" Chris gathered a pile of parts.

"To Marti."

His hands stilled.

"I'll make it short." A.J. cleared her throat. She pretended to examine Chris's work. They both knew the rest of the crew kept a close eye and ear on everything management said and did. "As far as I know, nothing will come Marti's way. Nothing ever will. Marti still has a friend who believes in her. That friend will try to see her soon."

A.J. turned, then walked away, her face impassive. She made casual stops at everyone else's section for appearance sake. It didn't pay to play favorites on the job.

Chris continued with the hustle. The boss lady's message checked out because his boys already told him the same thing.

◆ ◆ ◆ ◆

Six months later, thoughts of Alex still came to mind. It was as if Marti were haunted. And because his baby grew inside her, perhaps, she always would be. Silver strands decorated her hair that she never noticed before Celara. Like Alex told her father, their relationship would never work.

"Beryl, I guess I understand why you discouraged me from Worth. By the way, we never... you know."

"I know, Marti. He's preoccupied with someone else actually."

"Really? Who?"

Beryl shook her head and smiled slightly. Like mother, like son.

"That's fine. Look, I know we haven't spoken a lot about things lately, but Worth's been spending time with me and Chris and Chris's family. We've been making up for the lost years."

"I'm glad." Beryl nodded though she looked as if she might cry any second.

Marti changed the subject. "Well, as we all know, I've got some free time on my hands lately. The job hunt is not going well, but I still like to keep busy. So if I can help out more at the museum..."

Beryl needed a few articles written for the museum's newsletter right away since the files were due at the printer next week. Marti agreed to write two articles.

"The museum doesn't have the budget to pay for them though. It's all volunteer."

"I know. I don't mind. I mean, of course, I need an income, but I also have to keep my research and writing skills up-to-date. I never know where my next job is going to come from, but I want to be ready for it."

"Sure, honey. Sure."

"Beryl, while I'm here, can you tell me more about Christina?"

"What do you want to know?"

"She never said much to me and Chris about anything. All this time, I thought she'd be better off without us. Sometimes, she looked so depressed and sad. And the drinking. I always thought she wished she didn't have to take care of us."

"No, no, no. Never, Marti. You two were all she had in the world. You kept her going. She loved coming home to you. Before I had to stay away, she always told me about how smart you were and how she didn't even have to ask you to help her. You just did. And how happy Chris was. Always smiling, no matter what. She needed you both to get through the hard times."

"Sometimes, I even thought she must not have cared about us." Marti pressed her lips together to keep her composure. "That maybe she hated us for making her life harder."

"You were greatly loved, Marti. She didn't want to leave you. Not really. Her death wasn't your fault. And it wasn't Chris's fault either. I think she just got hit one time too many. And..."

"I loved her," Marti choked out. "I did."

"I know you did, Marti. She knew too. She knew you loved her. She couldn't have made it that far without you and Chris. She just... got tired of fighting. But honey, she's not tired any more. She doesn't have to fight because she's already won. I know she's so pleased with what you and Chris are doing with your lives. Marti, can you ever forgive me for what I did?"

"I'm not angry, Beryl. I just... need some time. Okay?"

Marti splashed her face with cold water in the museum's bathroom. She looked at herself in the mirror. She saw Christina, the younger, beautiful Christina she remembered before all of their lives changed, reflected back to her. For the first time, she felt truly grateful. Christina, indeed, was her mother for a reason.

She hugged Beryl on the way out, "Thank you, Beryl. You helped me more than you know today. I'll get on those articles right away."

"Good luck, honey."

◆ ◆ ◆ ◆

Marti and Teresa still met for lunch once in a while. These days, Chris, instead of Analicia, kept the girls on his days off. Everyone, especially Mari and Kina, were thrilled to have him back.

"Terry, I owe you an apology."

"Girl, for what? What the hell have you done now?"

"I'm serious."

"Okay. What?"

"When you first started with Chris, I..."

"You wondered why he was with me and if I was using him because his father was well off and how could I be so stupid as to get pregnant... twice... by a man who did two bids?"

"You knew?"

"Well, I wasn't sure until now."

"I never said..."

"You didn't have to."

Marti looked away a moment, ashamed. "Terry, I'm so sorry."

"Marti, forget it. You're my girl. You've become my best friend. Your family is my family. We're practically sisters." Teresa reached out to hug her. "Besides, you didn't hear all things my own family said about you guys."

"Still, we Butlers have a lot to learn from the Garcias."

"Honey, you don't want to be like us. We're crazy!"

"Well, yes, but you're also very loving. I'm just glad everyone accepts Chris now."

"Not the way they used to be towards him. Look, I told them. I said this man is the father of my children and I love him. That's the way it's going to be. Case closed, okay?"

"And now?"

"Now they can't get enough of him. And they're trying to turn Mari and Kina into little princesses. You know I don't play that."

"Yes, you do."

"Okay, I do." Teresa laughed.

"They're so lovable. They're great girls, Teresa."

"Just like their Aunt Marti."

"Don't... you're gonna make me cry." Marti sniffled

"Marti, are you..."

"Don't say it. Don't ask me if I'm okay. Everyone's been asking me that. I'm fine. I'm fine. I'm fine."

"Okay, okay." Teresa held up her hands in surrender. "So, is it over? All that chaos with Celara?"

"Chris thinks so. He said that Alex went to ground in Michigan on an extended leave. No one's supposed to know where he is, but Chris found out. Some little island up north." Marti waved her hand in dismissal. "They say he's hunting game and chopping wood all day. Living off the land."

"Money's nice to have when you want to pretend to be poor."

"Yeah. Pretend. Anyway, A.J.'s handling his projects. You know the female project manager."

"Yeah, Chris's boss. Do you think they'll keep doing the same old stuff?"

"Honestly? I don't know. That culture of greed and power runs deep. I don't know if they can stop."

"Look, Marti, I'm glad you're okay. I wouldn't wish what you went through on anyone. But I will say this. Me and Chris are closer now. I mean, I always loved him, of course. But when I saw how much he cared for you, it made me realize that he would be like that for me and our daughters. He would stand up and fight for us against anything or anyone. Even against his father if he had to. We need someone like that in our lives."

"I know. My little brother grew up on me while I wasn't watching. I'm so proud of him. You know he doesn't brag on himself."

"Maybe he should brag," Teresa sighed. "Then people would know."

"What's probably most important to him is that you know. I don't know if you already have, but maybe you should make sure tell him that. He needs to hear it now because he never got it when he was younger. We didn't always acknowledge the good things that he did and that was all of our mistake. I'll have to remember to do my part too."

"Are you going to talk to the Reverend?"

"No." Marti shook her head. "Our conversations tend to not end well."

"No kidding."

Marti smiled. "I've wasted enough time and energy on things that don't matter. I don't feel obligated to him as a daughter. He doesn't need to feel obligated to me as a father. We're free of each other."

Teresa nodded, troubled.

"But you know," Marti continued. "I did stop by his Internet channel. Would you believe that I saw this video labeled 'Alexander the Great' of all things."

"Girl, no."

"Girl, yes. So I clicked on it. He goes on and on about an ancient king who bit off more than he could chew and was defeated. He had this big scowl on his face doing the fire and brimstone thing."

"And you're still not going to talk to him about all of it?"

"No," Marti was decisive.

"But the video..."

"If it makes Reverend March feel better, then good. It doesn't make me feel anything. I don't want to deal with him or Holy Ghost Reba while I'm carrying."

Marti changed the subject back to her brother. "Terry, I know you and Chris have your ups and downs. I've known him all my life and I can tell you that he's had some bad breaks. But underneath it all, he's a good man. He'll love you for the rest of your life and give you the world. He won't ever leave you."

"I want him to be back for good."

"I think he is back for good. I think he finally realizes how much he's needed by all of us. He's putting in serious time on the Lakeside project. Just a couple more months and he'll be done."

"What about you?"

"What about me?"

Teresa nodded towards Marti's expanding middle. "Marti, you still haven't said. Is Alex King the father?"

"Teresa..." Marti shook her head wearily. "Please. Don't."

"Okay, okay. Cool."

"I just..."

"Girl, don't say anything," Teresa hugged Marti. "Look, we came out here to shop! We'll just buy some basics and you can have what I kept after Mari and Kina got older."

❖ ❖ ❖ ❖

Late April, Alex returned to Lake City for a progress report on A.J.'s projects. He picked an outside table in a small, out-of-the-way café frequented by college students.

"They just found out about a brother they didn't know they had," A.J. told him. "He's about the same age as Chris, five or six years younger than Marti."

"By their father?" Alex raised his eyebrows.

A.J. nodded the affirmative.

He frowned. "Wait a minute. Their brother, is he that..." He interrupted himself. "I thought she was dating that Save a Lake guy."

"No," A.J. responded. "Worth Rizal is her brother. They weren't dating."

"How do you know?"

"I know."

"How?"

Alex waited for an answer. "I see," he said comprehending the defiance in A.J.'s expression.

"Do you?"

"I believe I do now."

"So anyway, she isn't seeing anyone, but she's expecting."

"Expecting what?"

A.J. shot her boss another look that spoke volumes. Alex stilled. "She told you this herself?"

"Chris did. I... thought you should know. He also said she's living off her savings. He's helping her out as much as she'll allow."

"Marti's a top-notch wordsmith." Alex picked up his cell phone. Checked for messages. None. "Anyone would be glad to have her on their team." He checked for his favorite team's score. They lost.

"Don't do it, Alex."

He checked the time. "Don't do what?" Same as the time on his watch.

"Whatever you're thinking of doing. Chris said any interference would only upset her. She wants to be left alone. They all want her left alone."

Alex and A.J. ate in silence. He looked up. "A.J., if Chris is performing on the job as well as you say he is, then we should probably increase his compensation." Alex took another bite. "You know, positive reinforcement," he decided.

A.J. leaned back, relieved. "I can do that."

Alex tipped up a bottle of water, took a casual swig. "And so she's having a pretty healthy pregnancy?"

"From what I hear, yes. I haven't spoken with her." A.J. took a casual bite of food. "You haven't run into her yourself, lately, have you?"

"Nope. Been busy." Alex switched back to the construction projects. He asked A.J. to recommend a project manager to accelerate development of Celara Wind.

"We need someone good to take a leadership stance. We need someone to make inroads on the lake scenario." He paused to allow those words to sink in. "Time's wasting."

A.J. didn't respond. No matter. He planted the seed firmly into her head. There it would remain to grow and flower into his vision for the future.

She and Alex, actually Alex, made a choice on the project manager. The meeting concluded.

◆ ◆ ◆ ◆

Two older adults leaned their heads together in intimate conversation. Marti spotted them from across the street when she and Teresa came out of a discount store. In their business suits, Alex and A.J. stood out from the college crowd.

Marti kept pace with Teresa even though she could not believe her eyes. A.J. replaced her.

They got into Teresa's car. She decided not to say anything to Teresa

*You ought to be glad. While he's with her, he's not thinking about you. Isn't that what you wanted?*

"So, Teresa, it's real good of you to help me shop for all this stuff." Marti held up the list of baby supplies that Teresa wrote up for her.

"Girl, that's nothing. That's only the first part of the list. We're coming back this weekend."

"Tell Chris thanks for me, okay?"

Teresa started the ignition. "You're not supposed to know."

"I know. He would never throw that in my face or expect me to crawl on my knees for it."

"Look, Marti. Chris says you always used to take care of him. Now he wants to take care of you. And frankly, when you're pregnant, you're allowed to accept help." She backed out of the parking space. "You didn't know? They didn't put that in the manuals you're always reading?" Teresa laughed at her.

"I know, but you have two children of your own."

"Marti, I *swear to God*, I'm warning you. Not another word." Teresa held up one hand and manipulated the steering wheel with the other. "Step back and let him do it. It's important to him and because it's important him it's important to me."

"As long as he doesn't feel taken for granted."

"He thinks it's time for a reversal of roles. So do I." Teresa drove out of the discount store's parking lot. "It's good for you both."

"I give up."

"About time, Big Mama!"

Teresa's car passed the table where her baby's father and her former work colleague huddled together. Marti turned her head away.

"I'm tired of the past." She fiddled with the seatbelt. "I want to leave it behind. Way, way behind."

"Can you?"

Marti sighed. She still didn't want to think about her role or her level of complicity.

"Chris said I'd be okay."

"If Chris said it, then it's true. Now stop worrying so much. It's not good for the baby."

"I know."

Teresa turned up the music in the car. "See? I told you. It's a party in here!"

Marti laughed. But deep inside, she probed her soul. Did she know on any subconscious level what Alex would do with her research? Not at first. But eventually... yes, she did. Harlan could establish the paper trail without breaking a sweat.

Alex was always so careful to create several degrees of separation from any wrong-doing.

Not she. Who knew? Her mind didn't work that way. The fact that Marti and Kate argued publicly... the fact that she lived with Augie for a short period and had been seen in public with him... the fact that she was in the car with Evan that night... Alex could buy a witness to say just about anything. She didn't know how much evidence linked her to the deaths, but she did know that she was on the radar of Lake City police. Not only that, she hindered their investigation. And thus, Alex ensured her silence.

◆ ◆ ◆ ◆

BUSINESS WRITER<br>Martina meets your deadlines!

Following a cold, cleansing rain, spring arrived at last to Lake City. Marti entered the same café where she held her first meeting with Augie what seemed like ages ago. Someone answered her online ad.

Even though she ate for two these days, she requested no reference from Celara Solar—not A.J., not Kenneth, nor her lunch crew. She wanted to leave the past far behind. No job leads. No contacts. Nothing. She traded all her leverage to assist the negotiation of Chris's parole terms.

What would happen when whoever she was supposed to meet today got a look at her gigantic pregnant belly?

Worth waved to her from a table. She smiled and waved back. He stood and she gave him a hug.

"Worth, hi!"

"How are you, Marti?"

"I'm fine. Great, actually. I'm meeting someone here for a job interview."

"Have a seat," he indicated the chair across from him.

"Oh, I can't right now, Worth. Next time, okay? I have to make sure I'm ready for..."

"The person wanting a business writer."

"How did you..."

Worth waited with a wide smile.

"Worth?" Marti sat down. "What's going on here?"

"Well, see there's this guy, an only child, or so he thought, who didn't really have a lot of friends, but he always liked science and exploration. His mother sent him off to summer camp one year. He never went back because the counselors were weird. But anyway, he got into the whole great outdoors thing. Blah, blah. So now he goofs around writing stories about a Black Filipino cave-diver of all things..."

Marti sank back in her chair. "My Holy God."

"... who joins a shadowy military organization that goes underground, gets chased by scary monsters, saves the day, and gets the girl."

"It cannot be you."

"I know."

"Worth, it can't be."

Worth watched her track back through their past discussions all the way from their first meeting at the convention, to their discussions about family, to the times she probed how he earned a living.

"It *is* you. Worth!" She actually teared up. Gotta love these pregnant hormones. "I don't even know what to say. I'm so proud of you, *Dixon Elliot*."

"Shhh." He smiled back at her. "I'm low profile, remember?"

He ordered their lunch. Marti's interview with her youngest brother began.

"I need a research assistant, fact-checker, and an editor. Someone to crack the whip and keep Dixon Elliot organized and on schedule because he can get distracted."

"I can do that."

"According to Chris, no one does it better."

Marti laughed. "And Chris would know."

"Ah, the stories he's told me."

"All true."

"So okay. For the first time, the hero of this series is going to be matched by a female opponent. Each has their own agenda, but they join forces now and then to save the world. So we, me and Dixon, need a female perspective to get the feel of this new character just right. So far so good?"

"So far so good. But, really, how did you get into cave diving?"

"The challenge. The possibility of seeing things no one has seen before. It's kind of mystical."

"Is there anything left in North America that no one has seen before?"

"There's a least one thing. People forget there are extensive cave systems in the Midwest."

"Where?"

Worth held up his hands. "The location's need-to-know for now. We had to dig for access, but we found it. Fresh, uncharted territory, underground."

"Wow. It sounds like one of those extreme sports."

"No more than mountain climbing or scuba diving."

"I guess someone has to do it. Otherwise we'd never know what's down there."

"Well, the equipment is a lot more sophisticated now. Plus, there's protective gear and training to make climbing or crawling to get through the tight squeezes easier."

Marti shivered then changed the subject.

"So you already know I have an English degree and I taught Creative Writing for fifteen years." She pulled out her portfolio. "Some letters from Rose Creek administration and from former students." She pulled out additional documents.

"These are writing samples from Lake City History Museum's newsletter and a reference from a woman you might know, Beryl Aland."

"Nice lady." If Marti caught the smallest nuance in his voice, she declined to comment. He and Beryl would work out their pain in their own way.

With hesitation, she showed him the published news releases from Celara that she wrote. The work spoke for itself. She had nothing to say.

He shuffled through the papers. She didn't know if Worth knew the entire story. The hurt, confusion, fear, and humiliation she experienced was too hard to speak of aloud and in detail. She could only hope Beryl wouldn't say anything about the night Marti showed up on her doorstep in a shredded red dress. Besides, Worth being a writer and a world traveler, probably already imagined the unimaginable. He restacked the papers then passed them back to her.

"It's a three-book contract," Worth told her. "You would be employed for the next three years through my publisher. Full-time, flexible schedule, benefits. The works. You'll be forced to travel to exotic places, see the world, and experience new things. Put up with that prima donna Dick all the time."

"*Dixon* sounds pretty feisty."

"You cleared the first hurdle," Worth laughed. "You can handle him. You still have two additional interviews with the editorial team and head publisher. You up for it?"

"I say I'm lacing up my track shoes."

"You're good?"

"I'm ready to burn rubber and go for the gold." And she was. "Let's hurdle some deadlines."

"All right then."

"Deal?"

"Deal."

They shook on it. Their food arrived. That kept them occupied for a few minutes. Marti put her fork down.

"Worth, are you okay being a part of who we are? You're so good for me and Chris."

He squeezed her hand. "The only thing I regret is not getting to know you and Chris sooner. I'll never get those years back. I mean, here I thought I was all alone, but instead, I have an older sister and a younger brother."

"And two nieces."

"And two, beautiful nieces. It's lovely and I'm so thankful."

"And you have a father."

"I do have a father... who is not perfect. He is who he is."

"Worth, I'm glad you're going through with the surgery."

"I'm sure he's glad too even though he might not say it."

"And," she hesitated. "Beryl?"

He looked down at his plate. "Not now, Marti." Shook his head. "Please."

"Well, you came into all our lives just in time."

"Come here."

He hugged her as tight as he dared around the expanse of her middle.

"Not only two nieces, but maybe three. Or a nephew, hunh?"

"I don't know which."

"Come on." He punched her shoulder lightly. "How about a nephew?"

"Soon, very soon. Worth," Marti held his hands. "Worth?"

"Yeah?"

She searched his eyes. "You're aware who's pressing for wind construction in the lake?"

"I am aware."

"You understand my dilemma?"

"I do understand." He squeezed her hands. "I'm keeping myself informed of all the players and all the agendas. Don't worry, Marti," he hugged her again. "I'm not going to let anything happen to you. It'll work out the way it's supposed to."

◆ ◆ ◆ ◆

She still suffered from dreams. Not the shark dream anymore. Alex piloted a space ship that spiraled out of control. Doors blew open. Passengers and crew vanished through an open hatch. The ship crash-landed.

"Why did you do this, Alex?"

"I did it to wake them up. Look at them, Marti." He pointed. "They're complacent. I stimulated them. I made them appreciate life and my ability to shepherd them through."

"You're a destroyer."

She woke up. Realized that she hated him.

◆ ◆ ◆ ◆

"Where's Lexa?"

Alex glanced towards the speaker phone and smiled. "Mrs. Dallas is due to bring her back from shopping in about half an hour."

"So you have the whole house to yourself, hunh?"

"Yeah. If I were twenty years younger I might throw a party. Get into some trouble."

"Those were the days."

"You ought to know, Kenneth."

"Yeah right."

"Well, now my daughter's the cool one in this house. I'm just fuddy duddy old Dad getting in her way, taking the entire cool out of the room."

Kenneth guffawed. "So the custody thing's all good?"

Alex let out a hissing breath. "The way things are shaping up, it might become permanent soon. We'll see. I'm gonna surprise her with some horseback riding this afternoon."

"Oh, she'll love that."

"So, anyway. I've got a little time to work something out, but only just a little. Today is actually Lexa's day to be my full focus, not work. That's what my counselor said."

"Gotcha."

"I still need your feedback on an idea."

"I'll do what I can."

"I've been back over the research again and again. But it's not enough."

"Okay."

"I still believe you have to go green to get green. But I also want to leave a positive legacy for Lexa and..." Alex halted. "I want whatever children I have to hold their heads up and not have to apologize to anyone for anything they have or anything I did to get it for them. I don't want them to feel shame."

"You've been doing a lot of thinking, my friend."

"Well, with you on operations and A.J. in the field, I had time to get some things figured out. Kenneth, you know it's always been my goal to push Celara to lead, not follow. I'm looking for new ideas and new methods. It's time to release Celara from the old way of doing things."

"Actually, I couldn't agree with you more."

"Okay, so there's that. Landing the super grid contract to construct, install and, maintain the Midwest region would be the best leverage to get the other contractors off our backs. Lakeside should be the last "special" project we do."

Kenneth remained quiet.

"Can't hear you, Kenneth."

"I'll tell you, Alex. I don't know what brought this on, but I'm glad for it, whatever it was. We were rapidly approaching diminishing returns on that level. You must have reached that conclusion too.

"So anyway, the super grid is the brass ring. That's the mother of all jobs."

"Well, yeah. That would provide years of work for the old school employees and the new trainees without a bloodbath on the jobsites."

"We could dare to dream about it. But here's the thing. Even though the super grid is a nationwide endeavor, it's not a sure thing. Not without federal funding and the extra incentives that go with it."

"Right."

"However... windmills and other installations in the lake are doable."

"Uh..."

"Denmark and Great Britain have wind farms in the North and Baltic seas. Other developers formed plans for wind turbines in the Gulf of Mexico."

"Yes. All true."

"If it were to be done in Lake City, Celara and no other should do it."

"Key word is 'if.'"

"Yeah, well. Look. Yes, there are critics and naysayers, but it's not like that ever stopped me before."

"No."

"It certainly never stopped my father."

"Alex, you do realize that your father—and I'm only telling you this because I've worked with you both..."

"Kenneth."

"Just a second, Alex." The interruption surprised Alex because it was so uncharacteristic of Kenneth.

"I'll make it quick because I know you have pressing family concerns to address. Your father was a great man, Alex. Yes. I respected him. He took me under his wing and taught me everything they didn't know in school. I'm forever grateful. But..."

"But..."

"Your father subscribed to a philosophy that I did not agree with entirely. The ends justifying the means. Paving the road to hell with good intentions."

"But you worked with him for decades, Kenneth."

"He had great leadership abilities and vision."

"What're you really saying?"

"I'm just saying there's different ways to achieve those ends. We win, the other guy loses. We lose, the other guy wins. Or, we both win."

"You lost me."

"Transmission lines are the only real obstacle, at this point. We can focus on that. Maybe do an end run."

"I like an end run. What's the play, then?"

"Unskilled labor for assembly, transportation, and clean-up. All but actual installation. The second part is forgoing turbines in the lake using surrounding farmland instead."

"Yes to unskilled labor. No to farmland. I want the lake."

Kenneth sighed. "That's doing things the hard way, Alex."

"The hard way is the way I like it. Forget the regulators. The strongest and most organized and most vocal opposition to the wind project comes from Save a Lake. They've united everyone from property owners, tourism boards, fishermen, and sports enthusiasts, to bird watchers against progress. Even the heads of environmentalists explode because they can't decide between clean energy verses a clean shoreline."

"Kind of like chopping down trees to make way for solar panels?"

"Yeah, I still remember two years ago, Kenneth. No need to remind me. Live and learn, right? Look, I've got to go. Thanks for your input on this. I'm going to consider all sides. But Lexa's on her way."

"Give her my best."

Alex hung up the phone. The night Marti changed the game, he dove underwater. Then he instructed his detective to break and enter. His college friend recovered a series of portfolios from Evan's condominium before making an anonymous phone call to police about seeing a car go over the rail of the channel bridge.

Alex pulled out the portfolio Evan compiled on Worth Rizal, the main driver behind Save a Lake. He looked up only when Mrs. Dallas announced Lexa's return.

Despite their years of work together, he didn't find a portfolio on himself amongst Evan's greatest hits collection.

Regardless, he had a plan now. He just needed to set it into motion. He got up with a smile to greet Lexa.

❖ ❖ ❖ ❖

A.J. emailed her. Marti agreed to meet her old acquaintance for coffee. She couldn't hide from the real world forever no matter how much it hurt to face it.

Marti walked into the neighborhood coffee shop which seemed to be her home away from home these days. She liked the idea of home field advantage.

The café was pretty full. A.J. waved. Marti headed her direction to a window booth in the corner. A.J. smiled then stood up. Marti managed a cautious smile back.

They hugged. Marti suddenly realized she was glad to see a familiar face even though she still wasn't sure what direction their get-together would take. If A.J. was the Boss's Girl, then what did that make Marti?

She appreciated, at least, that A.J. didn't stare too obviously at her expanded abdomen. She pushed the memory of A.J. and Alex leaning towards each other in the restaurant across town from her mind. What Alex did and with whom he did it was not her business. She was the one who walked away.

They ordered lunch. Marti decided to set the tone.

"A.J., Chris kept me up-to-date with things. I wanted to thank you for taking him on. It meant a lot to all of us."

"How is he?"

"He's good. Real good. He's doing the youth counselor thing now. Thanks to your reference and a few others, he's Assistant Director. They love him there."

Marti never asked Chris about Celara's work at his former prison. She didn't want to know any more than what she already did—that Alex played to win.

Always.

Every time.

"He's a leader. The men listened to him. I know his circumstances. I know his background. And I know you too. So there was nothing to hide or be concerned about. As long as he does what needs to be done, he'll always have a place on my crew whenever he wants or needs one, no matter the project. And believe you me, he did great. Lakeside Power's on track."

Marti flinched at the mention of the power plant. A.J. noticed. She leaned in, lowered her voice.

"Marti," she hesitated, "I realize things were, *unusual*, at Celara in terms of how some things were done."

"So you know... you knew how Celara accelerated its market position?"

"Let's just say, I became aware. And by the time I did become aware, I was part of the problem."

"I think I became part of the problem for a while too. What about now?"

"Many things have changed."

"But what about Lakeside? You don't mind?"

"I'm choosing to look towards the future, not the past. I'm choosing to be part of the solution."

"What solution?"

"You know Nate isn't Vice-President anymore?"

Marti shook her head. "I didn't know. I haven't kept up."

"He's gone elsewhere." A.J. smiled faintly. "I'm Vice-President now."

*I know how to play my position.*

"Congratulations, A.J." Marti gave her hands a squeeze. "That's wonderful." She swallowed. "And well-deserved, I might add."

"Alex has been on sabbatical. He... had some reflecting to do." This time, Marti did catch the slightest flick of A.J.'s eyes downward. Though Marti's face burned, she decided she still wasn't ready to talk about it to anyone at Celara. She didn't want to add another branch to the office grapevine, though it was way too late to be concerned.

"Anyway," A.J. moved the conversation smoothly forward, "while he was gone, Alex cleared the way for me to make decisions and I've been producing results. The first order of business was a seriously overdue change in personnel. Anyone not on board with the new direction and new philosophy was invited, well okay, *encouraged* to leave." A.J. shrugged. "And they did."

"Good."

"Old problems don't belong in a new economy. The hiring's more inclusive. There's less nepotism. People have to prove they can produce results instead relying on mommy and daddy to get them in. Work is rewarded based on merit, not so much favor-mongering and back-scratching. Or back-stabbing. That forces everyone to compete on an equal playing field. It's done wonders for morale. But this is the kicker, and I'm pleased to say it openly. That covert, malicious misogyny I've always dealt with and always hated is gone."

"Our friend, Ronny?"

A.J. leaned in. "Gone, Marti."

"Harlan must have billed overtime."

"And then some."

Marti nodded for her to go on.

"It is absolutely not allowed. Of course, we still have women in administration. Leslie's still there. Helena's still there. We offered them a chance to move up. Neither of them seems to want to, but that's okay. The important thing is that the choice is there."

"Anita?"

"She left by her own choice." A.J. shrugged. "Celara's hiring women for professional positions now. Women with training in the renewable energy arena. Word has gone out that Celara won't tolerate anything that affects the bottom line. We can't afford to lose jobs from women who own businesses and homes, or even women married to men in real estate. And we can't afford to lose business and referrals from minority clients, either. When staff quit, we lose the money that we invested in training and continuing education. Those are things *I* won't tolerate. I do not like to lose money, Marti. Not at all. Especially not in this economy."

Their food arrived. Both women held the discussion until they got about halfway through their meals.

"Celara Solar's stronger now. Alex hasn't fought me on a single thing and because of that, we're finding more customers."

Marti felt the pang of jealousy draw a ragged line across her heart with a dull knife. She covered by pushing the rest of her food around her plate.

*It's over.*

A.J. continued. "He already said that he plans to preoccupy himself with Celara Wind."

"Celara Wind? So he's actually going forward with it?"

"Full speed ahead."

Marti didn't respond. She no longer had an appetite, but she forced herself to take a few bites.

"He managed to come up with solutions for the new division based on your business plan for Celara Solar."

Marti dropped her fork. "And that includes wind installations in the lake?"

"That's undergoing feasibility," A.J. replied. "There are a lot of elements to consider—federal and state permits, cost estimates. It could take years."

Marti sat back. "Alex's greatest strength has always been creating visions for the future."

"I agree. But we still have Kenneth to keep the numbers in the right columns. So an alternative he and I are worked out is to build wind farms on rural land."

"Kenneth's good."

"Marti," A.J. took a sudden interest in the café's other patrons. "We're pretty sure not so many accidents will occur in the Lake City region anymore."

Marti sucked in her breath and cleared her throat. She took her own survey of the room.

A.J. continued. "That's the past." She faced Marti again. "There's nothing for anyone to be afraid of anymore."

"Good to know."

A.J. squeezed her hand again.

"I haven't forgotten you, Marti. You have a friend. Here's my card."

Marti took it, noted aloud, "Alice 'A.J.' Janson, Vice-President, Celara Solar Construction. Wow. So it's official." In a "go sister" kind of way, she felt genuinely proud of her former coworker's accomplishments. "Congratulations, again, A.J."

"If you need me, just call or email. Okay?"

They stood up and hugged.

"And I'll say congratulations to you too, Marti." This time, A.J. acknowledged Marti's pregnancy with a warm smile. She didn't catch any hint of pity in A.J.'s demeanor. That was a good thing because any show of pity would end the conversation on an entirely different note.

A.J. gave Marti a secretive smile. "I'm actually seeing someone myself. I have no idea where it will lead but life is good." She waited for Marti's reaction.

Marti nodded without comment. She didn't want to talk about Alex—not to A.J., not to anyone. Even Chris knew better than to ask her to confirm the identity of her baby's father. If Chris agreed with the Reverend that it must be Alex's, he didn't say.

"In fact, I may follow down the same road." She looked again at Marti's stomach. "We may be family soon."

Marti's calm exterior provided only a thin shell for the pain and despair inside her.

"Take good care of yourself, Marti," A.J. ended with a parting smile.

"Thanks, A.J. I will."

Marti sat alone at the table, stunned by A.J.'s revelations both about Celara and her personal life.

Alex gave Marti's off-the-cuff remarks about Celara more consideration than she realized. One-by-one, down the list, he got everyone on board, pulled the trigger, and executed.

Still, he didn't have the courage to face her. Instead, he gave the kiss-off message to her father.

*That's the man I loved?*

She realized then that she lost him. Alex moved on with his life. Apparently, A.J.'s child would be a brother or sister to her own.

◆◆◆◆

## 15 The Mediation

Marti drank from the bottle of water she kept close at hand in the heat of July. The train dropped her close enough to waddle in for another visit with Chris at the youth center. Her brother sat at his desk. Alex sat across from him finishing a thought.

"We need to have a sizeable labor force trained and up-to-speed at least a year before work begins to show them that we're serious and that we can make things happen."

"It can be done, Alex. I know people who know people who need jobs."

"They have to make a commitment to the project."

"They will."

Marti hesitated then entered. "Wow, so I guess you guys are best buddies now or something." She did not disguise the accusation in her voice, especially since the two men looked guilty. She aimed a significant glance Chris's direction.

Her brother cleared his throat. "I'll see how Lexa's doing with the other kids." He spoke over his shoulder, "I'm just outside here if you need me, Marti. Just yell."

Marti stared at him through the office doorway until he slid out of view.

"What are you doing here?" she asked Alex, deliberately rude.

"We're two men who have something in common," Alex answered. "Why don't you sit down?"

"Chris has me in common because he's my brother." She felt bitchy, hot, and tired. "What do you have?"

Alex dropped his eyes to the swollen mid-section that poked him in the face.

"Perhaps you'd like to get off your feet?"

Marti's face heated. She eased herself into the chair beside him. "Like I just said, what do you have?"

"I have Lexa and a new outlook on life. I have hope for the future." His eyes remained a clear, still blue. He never looked more vulnerable. "Marti..."

"Yes, it's yours," she snapped.

"I know. I wasn't going to ask that."

"So you knew all this time?"

"I... Why didn't you tell me when I talked to you?"

Good one. In fact, she *loved* the way he turned it around on her. Let the games begin!

"Marti. Look, I know I'm flawed. I know this. I've thought of nothing else these past few months. When I saw what Lexa did to herself, it killed me inside. I wanted to trade places with her in the hospital bed. Then when I saw you that day, you looked as though you wished I were dead."

"I never wished you dead. I wished you normal." Marti sighed. "How is she?"

"She's good. She's having fun out there. She promised her mother and me that she would never do anything like that again. Lexa's forgiven me. Family court made it official. My daughter's back where she belongs—with me."

"Don't push it too far."

"No, no. Lexa's one of the best things I've done with my life. I'm not taking her or anybody else for granted." He glanced at Marti's middle again.

Marti got up to look through the window of the office door into the gymnasium where Lexa kept time with the other girls in a pretty vigorous hip hop routine.

"Look at her go." Alex stood close to watch Lexa's performance with her.

"She's good."

"Yes, she is. She loves to dance. She's really talented. I went to one of her recitals the other night. I was so proud of her. I can't believe I missed out on so much. She's happier now. That means a lot to me."

Distracted by his nearness, Marti sat back down.

He took a breath. Sat down next to her. "Marti, I don't know where to begin."

"Alex, did you know what Evan planned for Augie and Kate?"

His shoulders slumped. "I told Evan to take care of things. I didn't tell him how and I didn't ask. Here in Lake City, things get rough on the construction front, you know? Only the strong survive. My father taught me that. I explained it to Evan, but something got twisted in translation."

"You think?"

"I didn't think he'd take it to that level. I thought, maybe strongly-worded phrases or you know, sabotage. A favor for a favor and I'd look the other way. That kind of thing."

"Mmm."

"That's just the price of doing business, Marti. It's like that."

"Yeah, Alex. Evan told me all about the way it is in the car. Remember?"

"All I wanted Evan to do was tell Kate to stay in line. That's it. She caused unnecessary chaos in the office. I wanted Evan to redirect her energy to something else."

"Like recruiting new talent?"

Alex glanced at her, tightened his lips. Marti remembered the frozen, sick expression on his face when he learned of Kate's death and the horrific way she died. No, he didn't know.

"Lake City police came to see me about Kate."

"I know."

"Well?"

"Well what?"

"Aren't you going to ask me what I told them?" She waited a beat. "No. You aren't going to ask. Because you know that too. Don't you?"

"Yes," he replied in a soft voice.

"Why would you do that to me?"

"I wanted to protect you, Marti. We erased the tape, but I wanted to make sure that you understood to do what was best."

"Best for you?"

"No, for you. You handled it well."

"I stonewalled the cops well? Thanks. That's why you sent Harlan?"

"No. He was coming anyway. I held up my end."

"Fine. I believe you about Kate. But what about Augie?"

"Evan told you."

"Tell me again."

"I was jealous of him, okay? I admit it. When I saw him all over you at the party and in your face and you sitting there laughing it up while he leaned in..."

"Excuse me? Laughing it up?"

"Well, it didn't look like you minded. Were you and he..."

"Oh, get off it! You came with someone else too."

"I know!" he snapped.

"See there? Exactly. What about A.J.?"

"What are you talking about? She wasn't even there."

Marti snorted. Alex shook his head, waved her question away.

"It's just, I imagined him and you together and it pissed me off."

"So you told Evan..."

"To teach him a lesson. That's it."

"You had no idea?"

"Marti, I didn't arrange for him to die, I promise you, I didn't know. Evan went too far. Too, too, way too far."

"Augie and I didn't have that kind of relationship."

"But you lived with him. Spent time with him."

"Alex," she said it slowly just for him, "Augie and I did not have that type of relationship. Ever. I rented his sofa. Get it?"

"Then he must have been an idiot."

"Oh. My. God." She snapped her fingers at him. "Will you focus? What about the people who helped Evan? It wasn't just him."

"Laid-off. Replaced. Retired. Pretty much glad not to go down for what he did."

"I heard Harlan's been cleaning house for you. Things have been changing for the better. Did you do it to cover it all up?"

"Marti, Celara employs hundreds of people. You do realize what would happen if the company went under? Where would they go in this economy? I have to move Celara forward."

"Yes, I know, Alex. Chronic medical conditions and college tuition and mortgages. You already told me all that."

He closed his eyes and shook his head. "Marti, it's different now. Circumstances have changed. If you'd only stayed around..."

"If I stayed, we'd be right back where we started. I had to go. Besides, you moved on anyway."

He frowned at her. She ignored the question in his eyes.

"Alex, you set Augie on me, didn't you? After I outright refused to do what you wanted, you set me up to see if I'd go along with his crap."

"It was Evan's idea..."

"Alex." She closed her eyes and reminded herself to stay calm. "Alex."

"Okay. It's true."

"Why did you allow Evan to do so many terrible things? Why did you let him get away with so much and hurt so many people?"

Alex dropped his eyes. He slumped forward with his elbows on his knees. Marti felt a small measure of fear.

"Alex!"

He exhaled. "Marti, you probably learned that my father had a debilitating illness that killed him slowly, piece by piece."

She nodded.

"He was hooked up to so much equipment in the hospital that it looked like a science fiction movie whenever I visited him. Every once in a while the hospital staff stuck something new in him to keep him alive. They were constantly taking tests and drawing blood and experimenting. Poking holes in him all the time. He was in so much pain. He hated it. He wanted to rest."

Marti held her breath, sure now where the confession headed.

"One day, Evan came with me. He greeted my father. Then he left to wait for me in the lobby. My father asked me to free him. He was tired of this life. He wanted to start the next one. That's what he said."

Marti felt her eyes water. She pressed her lips together in order not make a sound.

"I wouldn't do it at first. He cursed me. I made sure he really meant it. Then I did it. I freed him. I put the dosage button in his hand. I told him that I loved him. I said goodbye. Then I left."

Alex cleared his throat, coughed, gathered himself. "There was no autopsy. They listed his illness as the cause of death. He was cremated."

Alex paused. Marti waited. She didn't dare to speak.

"But every once in a while, I caught some look on Evan's face or a subtle turn of phrase that made me suspect that he didn't go to the lobby, but that he stayed and listened at the door and saw everything. It would have ruined me and my reputation. And my ability to lead Celara and work with my father's hires. It's no secret that my father and I didn't have the best relationship. Everyone knew that I wanted to move the company forward in a different direction. We argued now and then. People could easily make what happened in that hospital room into something it wasn't. I just felt under so much pressure not to lose ground."

"Alex," Marti put her arms around him. "Evan used everything you taught him to turn on you. You know this, don't you?"

He nodded. "He left his cell phone in the room and aimed it to record what I did."

"Do you have the video?"

"I found it. I destroyed it. It's gone."

Marti tightened her hold around him. "Then it's over now. It's all over. It's the past."

How many people in Lake City, breathed a sigh of relief when Lake City police found Evan's body?

"Marti, I came close to losing everything. Lexa, you, Celara. And the little one. I had to take time away to look at everything I ever said and did up close. I had to take responsibility for bringing a viper so deep into my life. No more bullshit excuses. It wasn't a pretty sight, I tell you. I've been a complete jerk with just about everything and everyone I know. Including you. Especially you. Marti, I'm trying. I hope you can acknowledge where I am now instead of where I was."

They heard a quick knock at the door. Chris walked back in his office. He looked from one to the other, then back again.

"So, we're about to close up here for the evening. Marti, you cool?"

"Yes."

"You need a ride home or..."

Alex tensed. "I've got to take Lexa to her mother's for an overnight visit, but I was wondering," he cleared his throat and spoke to Chris, "if Marti would like to ride along," he turned to face Marti, "and maybe I can take you to dinner afterward?"

Chris looked for something he couldn't find in his desk drawer. The men waited for her answer.

"We can do that, Alex. We need to talk some more anyway."

"I'll go get Lexa." Alex walked out the door. Chris and Marti looked at each other.

"You sure you want to open that door again after all you went through?"

"I love him, Chris. I just can't help it. I've tried my best not to. Believe me, I'd actually rather not, but it turns out I do. I think he loves me."

"He risked a total beat down the first time he came here," Chris growled. "I couldn't believe it myself until he started talking."

"The first time?"

Too late, Chris realized his slip. "Celara's doing some installations here. I made arrangements for some of the boys to help him. If it goes well, we're going to start a solar and wind training program through the youth center. If *that* goes well, we may or may not start training folks from around the way. Baby steps."

Marti's mouth hung open. "Around the way?" Chris braced himself for a lecture that did not come. "It's a wonderful idea, Chris."

They smiled at each other.

Alex walked back in the office with Lexa.

"Marti!" She threw her arms cautiously around Marti's pregnant middle. "You're so big!"

"I know."

"Ready?" Alex led them outside.

"So Marti, be sure to call me when you get home to let me know you made it okay." Chris didn't look at her. Instead he stared past her at Alex.

"Real subtle," Alex muttered under his breath.

"Okay, I will," she reassured her brother.

"Be sure to call."

"I will."

"Cause otherwise..."

"Chris, I'll call."

They stepped outside. Teresa pulled up to the curb with Mari and Kina. Alex watched Chris's children jump out of the family car and strike up a cacophony of greetings.

From the corner of her eye, Marti saw Alex's start when he heard Teresa's voice. She winked at him. No more secrets. No hidden agendas. No more games. Not with her family.

Chris made the introductions. Teresa whispered behind Chris's back. "It's him, isn't it?"

Marti nodded.

Chris got a box of baby clothes, toys, and supplies out of the back of their car. Marti held out her arms to take the box. To her surprise, Chris brushed past her to shove the box hard into Alex's chest. Marti didn't miss the smug challenge between the two men. She rolled her eyes.

Teresa pushed her girls and Chris towards the youth center. "Have a good time!" she called.

Alex herded too. He nudged Lexa and gestured Marti towards his car. Thankfully, it was a four-door sedan so Marti settled herself inside without strain. Alex put the box down. He buckled her in, closed the door, then put the box in the trunk. Marti wondered just how long the solicitous behavior would last. Maybe until A.J. started to show?

Lexa asked the obvious. "Is that my father's baby?"

Silence.

Alex started the engine. He checked all the mirrors. His fingers tightened on the steering wheel. They waited for Marti's answer.

"Yes."

Alex gave her a quick look, then put the car in gear.

"Finally! I always wanted a little brother or sister."

"Oh, really?"

"Yeah! Which is it?"

"Which is what?"

Lexa rolled her eyes. "Is it a little brother or sister?"

"We'll find out any day now."

"Really?"

"Really. Very soon as a matter of fact."

Alex looked at her again. He gripped the steering wheel tighter then pulled away from the curb.

◆ ◆ ◆ ◆

They dropped Lexa off at Lily's. Alex called ahead to a restaurant where they picked up a Thai meal, Marti's favorite, then took it to Alex's large house. He showed her the rooms she didn't have time to see the night of the party. Marti wondered what one man did with all that square footage. *Threw parties, obviously.* Alex gestured outside.

"You remember the greenhouse."

"Good times."

Later, Alex discovered that Marti would tolerate him next to her on the sofa better if he rubbed the pain from her back and shoulders. After a long session, he pulled her against him.

"I dreamed of moments like this with you while I was away."

"Now, apparently, it's real."

"Is it real?"

"Is it?" She turned to look at him.

"I want it to be, Marti," he said, his voice humble. "I need you. I know we can make a relationship and a family together."

"Hold on just a second." Marti put her hand up. "Why are you saying this to me when you're with A.J.?"

"Why do you keep bringing her up?" he asked exasperated.

"I saw you together."

"We work together."

"You eat lunch together."

"So *what*?"

"I saw you sitting there all secretive where you thought no one would see. Well, I saw you," she jabbed a finger his direction.

Alex stared at her. He closed his eyes. Then he laughed. Marti muttered her disgust. Alex laughed louder.

"Marti, A.J. and I work together. That's it."

"You already said that. Besides, you and I worked together," she reminded him.

"Look, I promoted her because she proved herself."

"Oh, and I didn't?"

"You left, remember?"

"Are you sure her promotion wasn't for another reason?"

"Oh my God. I can't believe this. Marti, no. No."

"Alex!"

"Marti, you saw a business meeting. Well, actually, you saw me trying to pump A.J. for information about *you*. We met at that restaurant because I didn't want anyone else to overhear."

"You..." Marti started then stopped. So..." She looked confused.

"A.J. is seeing someone, but it certainly isn't me."

"But she..." *Met with you after she met with Alex to reassure you.*

Marti's shoulders relaxed. Alex, perceptive of the moral advantage, moved in for the close.

"There's only one woman I want, the only woman I've ever wanted since the day we met. And I think that woman cares about me too. Doesn't she?"

"What about that woman you were with at the party??"

"Her? What about her?" He shrugged. "I haven't seen her since we..."

"Since we what?"

"That night."

Marti looked into his eyes. "Alex," she spoke quietly. "I know you met with my father. Why did you tell him a relationship between us could never work?"

"I never said that." Alex's eyes sharpened to crystals. "I told your father that I cared for you deeply and wanted to take care of you." His mouth thinned. "Your father said you couldn't possibly love me."

"He was way out of line. What he said was untrue."

"So you do love me?"

Marti lowered her eyes. "I just meant..."

"Meant what?"

"That he doesn't speak for me."

After a skeptical look, he laughed. "I'm surprised he dared."

"Oh Alex," Marti laughed with him.

"My sweet girl." He embraced her. "I've missed you. But you didn't answer my question."

"Don't fuck me, Alex."

"Only with your permission," he pulled her against him.

It became harder for her to concentrate. "One last thing. I need to know at least three things you wouldn't do for money or power."

Alex tensed, hurt.

"I need to know *now*, Alex. Right now." She waited for his response.

"Marti, about my father..."

"I believe you about him. You don't have to explain anything else to me about it ever again. I believe you, Alex, and I believe you made the right decision. It is your story to tell, if you choose to. I won't."

Alex's tension eased. "I would not murder or arrange a murder. I would not allow Lexa to suffer. And Marti," he tightened his arms around her, "I would never allow you to suffer. Hopefully, I would never, ever be the cause of your suffering."

"Well, you caused this baby I'm about to give birth to," she teased.

"Well then, that's very different. We both caused that. Tell you what," he pulled her tighter to him, "I'll get you the best drugs money can buy."

"Don't try to make me fall in love with you, Alex. I don't want to. I won't."

Alex blinked.

"Tell me this. Are you willing to give up power for happiness? For love?"

"I will love you forever," he continued. "If that's what you want."

"Alex, what I want..." she stiffened.

"The hell was that?" He pushed her forward.

"Did you feel that? My water just broke."

"Uh. *Oh my God*. What should we do?"

"Uhm." Marti looked uncertain herself. She read all the books. She made a detailed to-do list. She packed an overnight bag with all the necessities. But her list and overnight bag were at home.

Alex noted her blank expression. He jumped up and waved his hands like a rapper at a comeback concert.

"Come on! We've got to get going." He pulled her arm.

"Stop!" She pushed him away. Then she grabbed his wrist. The contraction hit before she could say anything else. Alex dialed 911. He threw the phone away when Marti groaned through clenched teeth. She barely took two breaths before another contraction rolled across her abdomen.

"Alex, help me! I think its coming!"

"Don't you know?"

"Shit! It's coming! Help me, Alex! Please help me!"

"Okay, uh..." He looked around.

"Do something!"

He took a step away.

"Where are you going? Don't leave me! Don't leave!"

"I'm not going anywhere. I'm just trying to see what kind of supplies I have on hand."

Another contraction hit Marti. She groaned then panted through it. She gripped Alex's hand.

He winced. But he still seemed puzzled. "Doesn't it usually take longer than this?"

"Quit criticizing me!"

Fast-forwarding through all the shrieking (Marti) and the cursing (Alex), the professionals arrived just as a stressed-out Alex pulled his newborn son into his arms. He made a desperate run to the front door, let the emergency team in, then raced back to his new family. They rushed to clean up the baby and took care of Marti.

Still shaken, Alex followed everyone to the hospital. Marti finally remembered to call Chris who shouted that Alex 'better not have hurt you' through the telephone before she broke in with news about his nephew. Rather than wake the girls and pack them into the car, he and Teresa would meet them at the hospital in the morning. Marti decided to contact Beryl and Worth the next morning as well and Alex would call Lexa to come meet her new brother.

What little remained of the dark just before dawn still belonged to them.

Alex almost said something about his Christian Alexander King's first name, but backed down from the ugly look Marti shot him behind the nurse's back. That was about an hour earlier. Now, Alex held her hand. He leaned in to kiss her and Christian, then rested his head next to hers on the hospital bed.

"Alex, I forgot to ask you, where's Lady?"

"Lady?"

"The chocolate lab, where is she? I didn't see her."

A long moment passed before he answered. "She passed away while I was gone, Marti. Mr. Dallas told me that she went to sleep one night and never woke up."

"Alex, I'm so sorry. I know you loved her." Her eyes filled with tears.

Five minutes passed before they felt like talking again.

"It's not a romance, Alex."

"Well, I happen to remember heaving bosoms..."

"Stop it."

"Somewhat exotic adventures and a purple passionate..."

"Please don't do that."

"Burning, blazing splendor."

"That's enough!"

"For a moment, at least."

Marti sighed, "Please God, make it stop."

"Look Marti, we don't know the future. But we both know this baby is the greatest gift we could ever have given each other. Maybe it's forgiveness."

She looked away.

"Alex, neither of us is a threat to the other anymore. Can we call a truce?"

"A truce?"

"Look, you'll always have a place in Christian's life. I promise you that you will. But not necessarily in mine."

She saw the scowl, but she told herself it would be all right once he got used to the idea. She forgot that Alex's will was just as strong as hers.

He helped her back to her apartment. Christian's baby bed, stroller, and toys made the small rooms seem smaller. He knew to wait until her guard was down before he launched the first shot across the bow.

"Marti, I think you and Christian should move in with me."

"I want my son raised with honor and decency, Alex."

"*Our* son should have the best of care. By the way, I thought we called a truce?"

"Excuse me? You don't think I can raise a child?"

"You don't think I can be honorable and decent?"

Marti met his gaze with calm. No answer was the only answer that question deserved.

"Fine. Fine, Marti. Fine!" Alex ran a hand through his dark hair. "Look. Like I said, you do want the very best of care for Christian, right?" he asked her.

"You know that I do. How can you even ask me that?"

"Can you explain to me precisely how you plan to give our son the very best of care all by yourself?"

Somehow, despite her best efforts, he took control again and put her on defense. Alex held up a hand.

"Marti, look, I'm sorry. I'm doing it again, I know."

Marti narrowed her eyes and crossed her arms. "Don't waste any more of my time."

"Marti, my mother and father were not happy together. He focused on business. She focused on... other men."

Marti sat in a chair. "Which of them focused on you?"

He stared back at her in silence. Marti nodded her head. "Got it."

"My mother remarried a guy in Paris who paid attention to her. I was young. I didn't understand everything. So when my father ran her name into the dirt, I agreed with him that she was as low class and disloyal as he said she was. He discouraged me from contacting her. She tried to reach me through our household staff. I turned away from her. Told my dad what she tried to do. He fired the staff. She didn't try to contact me anymore. I thought that proved that she didn't care. Later, my father told me that he intercepted communications. She had no leg to stand on in court because he had proof of her affairs."

"She's still in Paris?"

"She is."

"But you've been to Paris."

"I have."

"Well, did you see her?"

"I've seen her each trip."

"What? But you tell people..."

"That I'm buying wine to stock my cellar. And I do. But I also show my mother pictures of Lexa and give her copies of Lexa's performances."

"Oh." Once again, Marti adjusted the kaleidoscope of Alex's complicated persona. "Does Lexa know?"

He shook his head.

"Does she ask about her grandmother?"

"She thinks her grandmother is dead."

"Alex."

"She also doesn't know about her aunt, my younger sister."

"What on God's Holy Earth are you," Marti paused to find the words, "thinking about? I mean... *are* you thinking? Are thoughts actually processing through to your nerve endings?"

"For the last time, I'm asking you to help me create the family that we all need and deserve to have."

"Alex, listen to what you're telling me. Listen to what you just said." Marti shook her head slowly. The kaleidoscope shifted minute-to-minute. "What do the words you say sound like when they hit your ears?"

"Marti..."

"Our children have relatives they don't know and have never met. Your daughter has a grandmother and an aunt she doesn't even know are alive. Why would you do the same thing to her that your father did to you?"

Alex pressed ahead with typical, single-minded focus. "Marti, even though you've started work with Worth's publisher and can bring money home, you can't do everything. How are you going to work full time, run your own household, and care for a newborn *effectively* all by yourself?"

"I know all this, Alex. I know. But other women manage. Just a second. Wait!" She stopped his interruption. "By the way, Lexa needs positive female role models. You should know this by now."

"Think about it. Chris and Teresa have their hands full."

"I know that."

"Worth is completely absorbed with his research, right? And he's never even raised a child. I have, by the way."

"Don't you say another word about Worth, Alex."

Alex raised his voice. "Beryl has the museum. Reverend March and Reba..." he shrugged.

"Absolutely not!"

"Right! That's all I'm saying."

"Listen to me, Alex. Listen! Lexa will never forgive you for concealing her grandmother and aunt from her."

Alex continued. "You don't have time for childcare and healthcare for Christian." His stubbornness wore on her. "Who's going to take him to his doctor visits? Who's going to do the grocery shopping?"

"All right!" she screamed. No need to engage further. Neither of them wanted to hear what the other had to say. Christian wailed from his crib.

"Great. You hear that? Real good, Alex."

"I've got to get going." Alex headed for the door.

"Oh, *hell* no."

"While you're getting packed, I can set up a nursery for Christian, a home office for you, and then... uh... your bedroom."

"Wait!"

Christian's wails escalated to full-bodied screams.

"Alex, get back here!"

It was all too confusing. Disoriented, Marti couldn't think fast enough to stop Alex's man-handling. The next evening, Mrs. Dallas helped to get her settled in a room on the second floor of Alex's huge home. Christian's room was next to hers. On the other side, her new home office. Summer into fall, she worked on Worth's latest book. She exchanged files with him by computer.

◆ ◆ ◆ ◆

"I'm leaving your father."

"Okay." That was all Marti could think to say when Reba called her at Alex's home. Life moved forward, after all.

"It's just been too much for me to deal with lately. He's been impossible to live with ever since we had that dinner. But I know for a fact that God never gives us more than we can bear."

Marti felt no sympathy for the woman who stood by while her two step-children lived a miserable, neglected existence in her household. In fact, Reba bored her. Christian held her total focus these days.

"I understand you have to do what's right for you, Reba."

"But there's something I've wanted to tell you for a while now and it never seemed to be the right time. There's something you should know about Alexander King."

Marti braced herself for the worst.

"When he was here he told your father that he wanted to marry you. Your father told him you couldn't love him because... you didn't love yourself."

Marti's mouth fell open. It took her a few extra seconds to form a thought. "You were there?"

"I was there. I heard the whole thing. He came here hat in hand and let his intentions be known. You didn't know?"

"I... not quite."

"I know you're living with him, Marti... in sin."

Marti fought to keep herself from cursing Reba out. *Deep breath. Deep breath. Wait for more information.*

"I don't know if he changed his mind or if you changed yours, but I thought you should know where his head *used* to be."

◆ ◆ ◆ ◆

# 16 The Arbitration

**B**right red, purple, orange, and yellow leaves spiced the air with an earthy scent. It was a beautiful day in the neighborhood. A wondrous day for a confrontation three decades in the making.

By the time Marti arranged for Christian's care and made it across town on the train, the Reverend's condo, normally neat as a pin, was strewn with random piles of junk.

Reba did as she said she would. She uprooted herself from a twenty-eight-year marriage then headed for the hills. She would live with one of her children, the Reverend said. The other bedroom that he converted into a mini-studio remained dark and still.

He sat in the midst of the failure of his life. Marti sat across from him.

"Where's your son?"

"He's with Terry."

"I guess his grandfather will get to see him one of these days."

"Why? Do you want his kidney too?"

He stared at her a moment. "You know if you ever need help taking care of him..."

Marti shook her head in derision. "My child is cared for, Reverend. Terry's always been there to help me with him. So have Chris and Alex. Every step of the way. Christian will never lack for love. He will never go hungry. He will never feel unworthy. I will never put another person's child over him. I take care of my child. He is the most wonderful person you never showed the slightest interest in knowing until you found yourself in trouble. But I love him. Everyone who has a heart loves him."

Reverend March sat silently.

"And because of Alex and Worth, I can save for Christian's college education. You see, I don't want him to take out loans, or work himself into a walking coma, or have to call home to beg for grocery money. I wouldn't do that to him. I actually don't know what kind of parent would."

Her father winced.

"Because unlike a certain person we both know, I won't leave my son with no resources for his future. Unlike a certain person who allowed his second wife and her adult children to accumulate his wealth, everything that I'm worth, all of that goes to my son. Remember when I called you senior year terrified that I wouldn't be able to pay my final tuition bill in time to graduate? Well, guess who did day labor to scrounge up just enough? It was me and the ex-convicts out there picking up trash out of the gutter for three weeks!"

Reverend March bowed his head.

"Oh yes. My professors gave me the emotional support that you withheld. How many nights do you think I cried alone in the dark because they disconnected my lights and phone? If the restaurant didn't allow me a meal per shift I don't know what I would have done. I carried twenty-one hours that last semester. I worked those gutter jobs and kept up with class work while you sneered from a distance. All those snide remarks I took from your wife's family and you said not one word in my defense. Why didn't you, Reverend? Is it because you agreed with them?"

"No, Martina... I... just wanted everyone to get along."

"Which meant me and Chris got thrown under the Holy Roller Express in your and your phony wife's happy parade. Reba's children brutalized him on your watch, you know. And when you sent him away that summer, he was attacked!"

Reverend March flinched. "You mean you knew?"

"You knew too?"

"He told me a few months ago. Something about Deacon Thompson."

"It was Deacon Thompson? That sick fucking freak! How could you let it happen? Why didn't you protect him instead of letting them send him to juvie? How could you?"

"How was I to know, Martina? He didn't say a single word about it to me until last year."

"Why didn't you ask Chris what happened?"

The Reverend March didn't answer.

"Right." She never felt more disgusted. "Well, Worth knew. He was there the same summer, he told us. It's all true. Why didn't you ask Chris what happened?"

He still didn't answer.

"Because you didn't want to know. Because you didn't want to care." She jabbed an accusatory finger towards him. "Doing nothing's always been easier for you than giving a damn, hasn't it, Reverend?"

"Martina."

"You didn't do right by me or Chris and you know it."

"I know," he sighed.

"But at least you bothered to acknowledge our existence. What you did to Worth was unbelievably cowardly and selfish."

"I'm no coward and I am not selfish, Martina. I'll not have that from you. I had no idea!"

"Then what are you? He was right here in Lake City the entire time, Reverend."

"I honestly didn't know Marti. You saw him. He looked to me like he could have been Filipino."

"Are you kidding me?"

"I thought the other guy was his father."

"You mean Beryl's husband? The man who took care of your responsibilities and gave him his name? Come on, Reverend. You can count to nine months just as well as anyone else." Marti snorted. "Fancy that. Worth, the one you denied, is the one who's stepping up to save your life."

She waited for him to answer. He said nothing. She got up to pace the room.

"You know, on my way over here, I actually thought about moving you in with me and Alex. But it's his house, not mine. And that would have required retro-fitting the stairs and doorways. Installing all this equipment." She waved towards the hardware in the living room. "Besides, you don't like him."

Marti stopped pacing.

"You know what? I can't even secure the funds to buy you a cheaper place or pay for home care. You remember the woman you left with a mortgage and a car to pay off, don't you? *Christina.* Your first wife and my mother. I had the nerve to attend college so no one could ever do to me what you did to her. And," she shrugged, "well, now I have student loans to pay off. I sold my future to the federal government, Reverend. There's nothing left for you."

Reverend March met her eyes. "Daughter, I don't disagree with you. Not at all. In fact, you're right about everything. But I can tell you this."

"I'm not finished." Marti raised her chin. "Every time I asked you why things were like they were, you always said, 'They need a father figure in their lives.' Guess what, March? Me and Chris needed you. We needed the father figure! Holidays and birthdays, where were you? Always with them. You gave the best years of your life to *her* children. They didn't even give a damn whether you lived or died as long as you paid for their house and their food and their light bills and their phone bills and their cars and their bail and all the rest for their friends and cousins and boyfriends and girlfriends. And now that they've screwed you over and Holy Ghost Reba's left you, now you want to look to us?"

Reverend March Butler didn't answer for a long time. Then he smiled. "I've noticed something about you, lately. You're more confident. I wonder why that is?"

"I'm no longer afraid of you."

"No, it's obvious that you're not," he replied quietly. "The young girl I knew was quiet and reserved. Always suspicious. Very guarded."

He waited to see if she disagreed. "She hid behind lists and schedules. Facts and figures."

Marti flinched, but didn't bother to dispute what she knew to be true. "Yes, she did." She sat down again.

"Probably to keep her life under control because the two authority figures she needed to guide her through life failed to finish the job."

That did it. Marti choked out the tears she could no longer hold in.

"Martina, I'm so sorry. For everything wrong thing I said and did. I'm sorry for every right thing I didn't say and didn't do."

"I waited thirty years for you to say something. That's all I ever wanted to hear from you. That's all you ever had to say, Reverend. I don't know what took you so long." She went to his bathroom to splash cold water on her face.

"Martina," he continued in a stern voice when she came back. "If any man does not recognize your value and appreciate everything you have to offer him, then he doesn't deserve you. You're a lovely, intelligent, caring woman. Walk away from the man who doesn't know how to handle that Walk away from the man who tries to destroy you. Walk away."

"You needed to tell me that twenty years ago."

"I'm your father no matter how old you are."

"Why did you put Alex off? And why did you allow me to believe he didn't think our relationship would work?"

"Look what foolish pride got me, Martina." He gestured at the clutter. "Look around. What do you see?"

She looked around.

"Rooms full of broken dreams, children that can't stand me, grandchildren I never see, diabetes, and a dialysis machine that barely keeps me alive. My ministry's on hiatus. You wouldn't believe the angry messages I got after Reba told people she was divorcing me. She's taking half, you know."

"I can just about imagine what she told them. The same things she used to tell you about me, probably. Reverend, look. About the surgery..."

"Wait, Martina. Wait," he held his hand. Marti sat back on the sofa.

"Alexander King might have disappointed you. I might have disappointed you. But if you see your way towards forgiveness, you'll find yourself surprised."

She nodded, rose, and walked towards the door. Put her hand on the knob.

"We've seen the road behind, Martina. We know what's back there. There's nothing back there for any of us anymore. *Nothing*. It's time to look at what's ahead and to expect the very best, no matter what. You're almost there. I know you'll make it the rest of the way. I promise you, you will."

Marti bowed her head and whispered, "I'll bring Christian by." She lifted her head and looked at him. "We'll stay as long as you behave."

"I'm behaving now, aren't I?"

"Well, keep doing that." Marti laughed, closed the door behind her, and went to meet Worth.

◆ ◆ ◆ ◆

Chris pulled a brush across Mari's tangled curls. Kina tried to explain her doll family to Alex who had a hard time with the genealogy. Christian slept in his arms.

"Teresa's family used to look down on me—those two stretches, you know. Some days, it looked to me like her father wanted to kill me. Like he was just waiting for a reason to blow my head off." Chris blew out a breath at the memories. "Her mother thought I was dirt." Chris tried to snap on a hair clip to hold the mass of glossy ringlets back from Mari's face.

"Are you almost done?" Mari turned her head.

"Wait, Mari."

"What about now?"

Chris grimaced at Alex. He brushed her hair back again piece by piece the way Teresa showed him. "Well, her father passed away, I'm sorry to say. I mean, I never had anything against him. Teresa's an only child so they were very protective of her. But she loved me. And I loved her. There was nothing anybody could do to stop that. Not even her or me could stop that. Then Mari and Kina came along." He smiled. "Analicia came around somewhat. She knows we're a package deal."

Chris gave Alex a sidelong look.

"But really, it wasn't until recently, not until I got out and turned it all around that Analicia actually looked me in the eye like she was glad to see me. I had a good-paying job." He winked. "Thanks for that, by the way."

Alex grunted his response. Kina decided to take her dolls to a dance party. She shook them like maracas. Alex burst into laughter.

"Kina, are they dancing or did they get caught in a tornado?"

"Dancing!"

"Okay." Alex got another doll to shake at the one in Kina's hand.

"No! Like this!"

"Like this?"

Mari twisted with a giggle to see for herself.

Chris sighed. "Back to the drawing board." He started Mari's ponytail a third time. "This time, sit still, Mari, or we'll never get this done."

"Daddy..."

"Mari, we're not leaving the house until your hair's put together. You know Mommy's rule."

She sighed and settled back.

Chris picked up his and Alex's conversation without skipping a beat. "I came home every night and brought my pay with me. Analicia *really* liked that."

He and Alex shared a quiet laugh.

"I took over care for the girls while Teresa went to work at the restaurant. So Analicia had more time to herself and could enjoy her own life. It took some adjustments for all of us. But it worked out."

"Yeah. I can see you've got things handled around here."

Kina took her doll back from Alex. She would carry on the dance herself.

"I'm sorry, Kina," Alex told her. "I'll try better next time."

She handed him another "Try this one."

"I'll practice a little over here, okay? Then I'll be ready for the party too."

"Okay," she approved.

Alex beamed back, already wrapped around her finger.

"That's my girl. She's very forgiving, Alex. You should have been here the first time I tried to brush Kina's hair." He shivered. "I still get the shakes when I think about all that screaming."

He tugged Mari's ponytail, finished at last. "But I'm good now, Mari, hunh?"

She jumped up. "Yes!" Hugged him. "I love you, Daddy!" Turned to Alex. Held out her hand. "Can I have that?"

Alex handed her the doll. Mari jumped right into Kina's dance party without missing a beat.

"Now that I proved myself as a father, they always have my back. I mean, Teresa's family has strong love. They call me for help, I go right over and bring a toolkit to fix whatever. I need someone to look after Mari and Kina, they come right on over or I drop them off, no questions asked. They can't get enough of the girls." Chris smiled at his daughters. "Everyone loves them. Especially Analicia." He winked at Alex.

"I get invited to all their family stuff. There's always something going on. Teresa's happy. I'm happy. It's working out."

Alex cleared his throat. "Yeah, I kind of wondered where I fit in with the Butlers. Or if I did."

"Oh, you're in, my friend. You're here to stay, as a matter of fact."

"That so?"

"No one told you? Once in, always in. Look, Alex. I don't speak for anyone else but myself. Not Terry. Not Marti. Not our father."

Alex braced himself.

"I got no problem. As long as you do right by Marti, I got no problem. Just don't have her come to me saying you raised your hand to her or caused her pain. Or my nephew. Because then I will have a problem. And, of course, my two girls and my lady are my life. That's family. There's no negotiation on that, my friend. That needs to be clearly understood."

"Right. Of course. I can't imagine anyone trying anything like that."

"Glad to hear it." Chris cleared away his daughter's hair accessories. "Other than that, I don't know what to say other than we all have to do the best we can to be the best we can be."

"I agree."

The two men watched Mari and Kina's frantic doll game that made no sense to anyone but themselves.

"I love my home," Chris admitted.

Alex didn't answer. After a long pause, Chris asked the obvious. "What about you?"

Alex shrugged. "Sometimes it's good."

"Sometimes?"

Alex shifted. "A couple of days ago, I passed by Christian's room. I heard Marti on the phone. She was trying to call Teresa."

"Why?"

"Because Christian had his first smile and she wanted to share a picture of it."

"Oh yeah. She sent me that too. It's a beautiful thing. I didn't get back to her yet."

"Well. Yeah, I know. Then she tried to call Worth. Didn't get him on the line either. I think she sent it to him too."

Chris waited.

"Then she sat there with Christian a long time."

"Did she know you were home?"

"She knew."

"So what did you do?"

"I went back to my office. I figured, if there was something she wanted me to know, she would come tell me."

"Uh hunh."

"It took her a few hours, but she finally got around to me. It was a good moment. But I'm pretty clear now where I stand on her list of priorities."

"Look Alex. I'll tell you this and you can decide what it means for you." He shrugged. "Or you can pretend you didn't hear it. And then it'll be whatever."

Alex waited.

"Marti likes things to be under control. She does. She likes things to be certain, not uncertain. If things get out of control or she doesn't know what's going to happen next, she gets..." Chris searched for the words.

"Unhappy?" Alex offered.

Chris nodded. "Unhappy. It's a trust issue. I mean, our father left us. So she didn't trust him to do what he said. Our mother had problems so she didn't trust her to take care of things either. Then I started running the streets, and well," he shrugged, "she didn't trust me. She never relaxed. She was always on guard against chaos."

"That sounds about right."

"Now that I think about it, she didn't really calm down until I started to handle things the right way. Come to think of it, I did have to come right out and tell her to mind her own business. And then she did. I told her in a way that was respectful, of course. That's my *older* sister, you know."

"I know."

"But she understood that I meant what I said. And then she found out that she could count on me to take care of her whenever she needed me."

Alex winced. Chris let Alex's acknowledgement of his own failures to pass without comment.

"What about Worth?"

"Worth? Our brother from another mother. What about him?"

"Well, where does he fit?"

"He's our brother." He gave Alex a strange look. "That's where he fits."

"I ask only because he's part of this organization."

"Save a Lake." Chris got it. "Oh. Now I see."

"Right. I'm trying to figure out how to negotiate around the fact that he and I..." Alex tried to find the words.

"See the same thing a different way."

"Right." Relieved that Chris understood the nuance, Alex continued. "I'm here. Marti's there. Worth's way over there. They're working together on this book."

"And it's awkward."

"On top of everything else," Alex muttered.

"I'm not going to interfere in Worth's thing. So you have to find your own way through to an answer on all that."

"But you don't mind?"

"Mind what? That you've got a business to run? Do your thing, man. You have to keep a roof over my sister's head don't you?"

"That's right."

Chris nudged Christian. "Got to feed my nephew, right?"

"I certainly do."

"I hear he eats a lot."

"He certainly does." Alex beamed down at his son. "Look at him. He's smiling right now."

"You're right, he is. Mari, Kina, come look at your cousin's smile!"

The girls squealed and gathered round.

"Takes after his mama, hunh? She smiles too when it's time to eat, right Alex?"

"Don't even try it, Chris."

"See? You're learning already. You'll be all right."

"I'm certainly trying."

Mari tried to tug Christian out of Alex's arms liking this new doll much better than the others. Christian whimpered softly in his sleep. The two men stood up.

"By the way, Alex, they want to go green at Analicia's restaurant. Asked me if I knew anyone who could handle a small job without breaking the bank."

"So do you?"

"I don't know. Do I?"

Someone fumbled at the front door. The pure joy of Chris and the girls to see Teresa back from the restaurant cut through Alex's heart. He never greeted Marti with arms wide open. He couldn't remember the last time she held him so tight that he couldn't catch his breath.

He had to look away.

◆ ◆ ◆ ◆

"We'll return to Lake City with additional research that I'll need you to incorporate into the story."

"What's your basic outline of the sequence?"

"A clandestine underground operation in an undiscovered Midwestern cave system."

"The Midwest? Not some far-off island with a raging volcano and waving palm fronds?"

"Things happen in the Midwest too, Marti."

"Yes, they do."

Worth's phone rang. Marti flipped through pages of maps and photographs and drawings. Worth's voice took first an urgent then a resigned tone. He disconnected.

"What's going on?"

"Two snags. Normally, I take two men I trust with me on trips like this—Quint and Brian. In case anyone has an accident, one  man stays with him. Then the other one goes for help."

"Makes sense."

"Brian had a family emergency. Couldn't be helped."

"Oh no. That's too bad."

"Yeah. Quint didn't get into it. I don't think he knew exactly what Brian's deal was. But anyway..."

"That leaves you one man short."

"Right."

"I'm in shape. Maybe I could go."

"What?" Worth looked at her, incredulous.

"What?" she demanded.

"You have to be trained, Marti. Cave-diving's too dangerous without training."

"You can show me."

"There's not enough time. We can only keep the location secret for so long until others stumble on it and ruin everything."

"I'm not going to tell anyone, Worth."

"Marti, that's not it. I'm just saying, we have to go now while we have the equipment and the time in my and Quint's schedule to do it. And then there's another thing." He sighed and raked a hand through his feathery hair.

"The water table's higher than we planned. October's usually okay, but we're almost to November and that's always a rough ride. There's been some flooding due to the weather out west."

"So that means..."

"That means underwater exploration. I mean, we can do it. We're all trained for that, but it's still too dangerous for just two people. We could get away with four underwater, but five is better. So really, we're two or three men short."

Worth pounded his fist into his palm. "Dammit!"

Marti was sure that was the first time she'd ever heard Worth swear.

"Worth, I may know someone who can help."

◆ ◆ ◆ ◆

Worth faced the speaker phone. "We're under the gun, Alex. I'm coming up on deadline and eventually word will get out about the location. I can't keep it secret forever."

They hammered out more logistics and parameters around the expedition.

"Okay. I'm in. I can bring two scuba guys with me so we'll have five. We all know how to navigate and maneuver in tight spaces. Send me the details."

"Marti will bring everything to you. I don't trust it online. I'll bring my equipment over in a few hours. That should give you enough time to look things over and make your own arrangements."

Marti knew Alex by now. He never lost focus on the bottom line. Ever. He played to win, always. Every time. He needed Worth's assistance to swing key public support Celara's way. Alex would use the trip as leverage for Celara Wind.

◆ ◆ ◆ ◆

"Me, Roger, and Dylan will get everything loaded while you and Marti talk. Quint's almost here. We're rolling in ten minutes, okay?" Worth left them alone in Alex's home office.

Alex smiled at her. "Ten minutes, Marti."

The boy's club wouldn't wait much longer than that to get the party started.

"How long will it take again?"

"It's looking like four to five days."

"What about Lexa?"

"I told you, Marti. Lexa's leaving tomorrow on her own camping trip for the week with some of her school friends. They're picking her up this afternoon."

"Right."

"If you could, would you see that Mrs. Dallas has everything put together for her?"

"Sure."

"You'll have the whole house to yourself." He searched her eyes for something.

"I know."

Alex came closer, which made her nervous.

"I... I could get a lot done on Worth's book while everyone's away."

Alex approached so close she could feel the heat from his skin. He kissed her cheek. "Kiss Christian for me."

Marti caught a whiff of the soap he used, the same subtle scent as his cologne.

"Sure, I..."

He brushed his cheek in a whisper against hers. She trembled against him before he pulled away.

She drew a sharp breath. "I'll do that." His skin felt warm. And now, so did hers where he touched her.

He smiled, satisfied with her reaction.

◆ ◆ ◆ ◆

The men set out.

They wore hard hats with LED lights. Each man backed those up with an independent light source. Clothes, boots, wetsuits, ropes, first-aid kits, various containers of food and water.

Evan walked point to note specific details of the cave. Alex walked second in order to aim his digital camera wherever Evan pointed. His scuba buddies, Roger and Dylan, walked in the middle. Dylan took back-up photographs. Roger carried video equipment that also recorded audio.

Evan called to the rear. "You got it, Quint?"

"Yeah, we're all good back here." Every few yards, Quint looked back to memorize the cave's details. He marked their trail the old-fashioned way with small stacks of rocks. The men worked well together. They made their way further into the cave system.

Evan and Alex walked further ahead of the group.

"Here's the thing, Alex. The super grid would be a long distance transmission network."

"Yeah, I already know that."

"You've also got to know that problems with the scale would result in transmission congestion. That requires rapid diagnostics and coordinated control systems because the transmission capacity would have to be higher in order to keep the power output consistent."

"The technology's improving every day."

"Not fast enough to meet your timetable."

"Actually, it is. It already has."

"So there must be something else holding you up. Otherwise, I'm sure you wouldn't be here with me and Quint. Am I right?"

Alex smiled. "Well, you're no slouch."

"Neither are you. Look, I'm sure you've thought it all through. Never mind the property owners, environmentalists, and Lake City's tourism industry all waiting for your head on a platter. How are you going to cover the cost for the transmission lines? You're going to need extra connections in order to get the power from the turbines all the way to the power grid."

"Like I said, we can cover the cost with a strategic labor mix, Worth. I've been doing projects for years. It can be done."

"Fine. I'll give you labor. You would know more about that than me. But you're still under-estimating the opposition and the overall cost. Counties in other states have enacted ordinances against wind power development. You'd have to have state approval and you know they'll stall the legislation as long as possible. Even with labor, the cost is astronomical. You can't do it alone."

"We're actually working on that as I'm sure you've gathered."

"Look, I get it. Obviously, you're a player in Lake City. I know that. Everybody knows that. You don't have to prove to me what I already know. You might be able to roll over at the municipal and state level, but are you really prepared to take on the feds? By yourself? You'll take Celara under just to prove a point?"

Alex started to speak. Worth held up a hand.

"Yeah, okay, you know people who know people. But the lead reviewers on an offshore project of that scale are federal. Plus, you'll need multi-state cooperation to cover the initial cost and federal cooperation for logistical support and permitting." He shrugged. "You're King of the City, Alex, sure. But you're not King of the United States. You're a big fish in a little pond. If you go out into that ocean alone, with that big chip on your shoulder," he shrugged again, "I can't speak for your chances."

Alex shook his head with a laugh. "Worth, the future is here. You can't stop renewable from taking over. Sure as the sun goes up and down and the wind blows left to right, tomorrow's gonna wipe out yesterday. It always has. It always will. That's the way of the world. It's time to get on board or get out of the way."

Worth snorted and lowered his voice. "I'm not as easy to intimidate as you might think, Alex. This isn't Marti you're talking to."

"Leave Marti out of it," Alex snapped.

Though their voices lowered further, the ugly tone from both men came through loud and clear. The three men in the rear fell back from the tense exchange.

"Oh really?" Evan pointed a finger at Alex. "You're the one who put her in the middle of it and tried to use her like a crowbar."

"The fuck are you talking about?"

"Don't tell me you didn't know we knew each other, however you found that out. You've had people on me and Save a Lake for a while now. We've always known that. But after I met Marti at the convention and stopped by your booth, all of a sudden she's at our meeting. Fancy that."

"If you say so." Alex laughed. "But doesn't it sound just a little paranoid?"

Worth ignored the jeer. "Just so you know, you didn't learn anything that we didn't intend to be public information."

"Whatever you say." Alex snorted.

"You used Marti, Alex. You've always used her. You're using her right now. The worst part of it is she knows it."

"Hey Worth? Fuck you."

"Isn't it obvious to you that she doesn't trust you?"

"None of your business, friend."

"You're damn straight it's my business. That's my sister you don't give a flying fuck about."

"Fuck *you*, Worth." Alex thumped his chest. "I'm the one who delivered our son! I paid for everything! I moved her into *my goddamn house!* I'm taking care of Marti and I'm taking care of my responsibilities. No one can tell me I'm not."

"Yeah. That's a lot of money you're throwing around. What more do you think you can buy from her? What more do you think she can do for you?"

"She could love me, for once. How about that?"

"Ah." Worth halted. "The way you love her?"

Alex paused, raked his lips back into an ugly grin, then strode forward. "Speaking about trust, let's talk about you and A.J."

Worth kept pace. "What about me and A.J.?"

"You just *happened* to get close to my VP. That it?"

"Yeah," Worth replied. "That's exactly it."

"Just how do you think *she's* gonna help *you*?"

"My suggestion is that you change the subject. Right now."

Instead Alex gave another ugly laugh. "So, how does it work? You pump her when you pump her?"

Worth froze. He faced Alex. The two men stared each other down. The three who walked behind halted.

Ten seconds into the stand-off, Worth socked Alex in the jaw. Alex shoved him back. They shouted and swore at each other. The other three men ran to separate them.

But it was too late.

Worth screamed as he fell backward into darkness.

◆ ◆ ◆ ◆

# 17  The Investigation

"He fell, Marti."

Chills ran up then down her arms. What did he do? What did he do to Worth? What happened to her brother?

"It took about eight hours, but we found him."

The whimper began in the back of her throat.

"Marti," Alex paused and spoke carefully, "He was pretty broken and bruised. He was delirious from pain by the time we reached him. By the time we got him back up to the main passage, he went into shock."

Marti measured her breaths. Forced back the hysteria.

"We transported him back down the corridor and up the main shaft. Then we called for a chopper to airlift him to a hospital."

"He's alive?"

"Of course he's alive. What'd you think?"

Silence stretched out long between them. Dead air crumbled to dust.

"So, that's what you thought." Alex answered his own question.

"What... about you?" Marti asked him.

"What about me?" Alex ground out.

"Are you okay?"

"I'm fine," he snapped.

"When are you coming home?"

"We're driving back so I'll make it in later tonight after I drop everyone off. I'm bringing all of Worth's stuff with me." He tried to sound upbeat. "We have video of the trip. We mapped everything we saw down there. I photographed the formations and Quint installed safety equipment on the way back. By the way, how does the name, The Rizal Caverns, strike you?"

"I don't know how it strikes me, Alex. My brother's lying broken in a helicopter. I can't really think about the cavern's name right now."

Too late, Alex realized he screwed up again. He disconnected the call. He knew from her voice she was about to cry. He couldn't deal with that.

Icy remembrance of three ghosts slid down the side of Marti's neck. Or... was it four, including his father?

He had an explanation. *Doesn't he always?* She would face that when she faced him.

"Beryl, you know about Worth?"

"Yes, he's on that research trip. I thought he told you."

"To the caverns, yes. I... There's been... an accident."

Beryl sucked in a breath.

"He's fine for the most part," Marti added. "He's on his way to the hospital."

"Which hospital?"

"They're airlifting him back to the city hospital."

"Airlift?"

"Yes. I'm waiting for Alex. He's driving back and then we can meet you there."

"No. That's fine. I'm on my way now, Marti. I'll go to the hospital and call you." Beryl's tone held a sharp edge that Marti recognized. Suspicion.

"Okay."

"I don't think he needs to be overwhelmed by a bunch of people while he's getting medical care."

"Okay."

All of a sudden, Marti became 'a bunch of people.' Not Worth's sister. Not Beryl's friend. Add Alex to the mix and the wall rose higher. Just great.

She wanted the house quiet to work on Worth's book. So earlier that day, Marti dismissed Mr. and Mrs. Dallas for the week. When Chris and his family stopped by Alex's mansion, she cooked the evening meal herself. She left extra for Alex for whenever he got back. From the living room, she and Chris could hear Teresa feeding the girls in the kitchen.

"Chris, Teresa already told me you're going to donate the kidney."

Chris nodded. Marti got back up to hug him a long time. He pulled away gently.

"Obviously, Worth can't now. Also, I don't want my girls to look at me one day like I used to look at him. Like a stranger. I'm doing it for Kina and Mari."

"I understand." Marti smiled.

Chris stilled. He shifted his gaze away.

"What happened to Worth, Marti?"

"I don't know exactly. Alex said he fell."

"Is that right?"

Marti didn't answer.

"I'm sure we'll hear from Worth soon," Chris searched her eyes.

She nodded, determined to push back the nauseating roil in her stomach. The churning brought back the memory of Evan's hideous death.

"Chris." She moved around the room, restless. "No one completely understands my and Alex's relationship. I don't think either of us could explain it to ourselves let alone anyone else."

"Marti, think very carefully about this situation. I've withheld comment, because I usually trust your judgment."

"Usually?"

"A lot has happened around this man."

"I know. I was there, remember?"

"So you know there's a pattern."

"I don't think we can say for sure until we hear from Worth."

"Are you okay in the house alone with him?"

"Chris!"

"Marti." Her brother's frustration came through loud and clear. "You know, I want to give him a chance to explain, but look. Things aren't right here. You can't hide from that and you can't hide from me. You told me he crosses the line like he doesn't even know a line is there. *You* told me that." He pointed at her. "You."

Marti froze.

"You're right. I did." She sat in a nearby chair. Put her head in her hands. "Chris, I never told you about the night Evan Lewis died," she whispered.

"No, you didn't." He sat down.

"Chris, are you ready to go?" Teresa entered the living room with Mari and Kina.

"Almost." Chris didn't take his eyes of Marti as if he thought she'd try to escape the room with the truth. "I have to work something out real quick. Give us about ten minutes, Teresita."

"Its fine, Terry." Marti tried, but failed to reassure her friend.

"Okay." With obvious reluctance, Teresa returned to the kitchen with the girls.

"Evan confessed to everything. He arranged for Augie Daniels to die in the explosion. And he," Marti swallowed back something sour, "assaulted Kate Winterset then threw her body into the channel."

"He confessed to you?"

"Me and Alex."

"You and Alex were with Evan the night he..."

Marti looked away in the face of Chris's shock. For the first time, she rendered her brother speechless.

"We were... nearby."

"Marti." Chris shook his head as if to clear it. "Marti."

"No, Chris. It was an accident. Alex... saved me from him."

"Saved you?"

"Yes."

"And left him?"

"The car sank too fast," she whispered.

Chris looked at his sister as if he never saw her before in his life. "Evan said he did... what exactly?"

"Augie Daniels. Kate Winterset. Among other things."

"For Alex?"

"What do you mean 'for Alex?'"

"Was Evan acting under orders?"

"Orders from Alex?"

"You *know* what I'm talking about, Marti."

"Alex said he didn't know what Evan would do."

"Marti." Chris raised his eyes to the ceiling, exasperated. "Of course he'd say that. And Evan's not around to say otherwise is he? No. Because Alex left Evan in the car to die."

"I almost died too. I just told you Alex saved me."

"I wonder why?"

Marti stared at her brother in silence.

"Actually," Chris counted on his fingers, "I think I already know."

Marti's face burned. She gave birth nine months, almost to the day, after that night. "Alex is a hero, Chris. Not a villain."

"It's funny how a lot of people don't seem to be around to say otherwise."

"Evan confessed, Chris. I heard it."

"Then he died."

"Chris, I love you but you're wrong about this."

"It never occurred to you, Marti? Really?"

"Chris... give him a chance. Please."

"Worth is family, Marti."

"Tomorrow. Please wait until tomorrow, Chris. We'll hear from Alex and we'll hear from Worth and we'll work it all out."

"The thing of it is, I actually want to believe in him myself. I mean, I like the guy. He and I talked just the other day..." Chris's voice faded. "About Worth..." A charged silence took over the room. Marti slowly shook her head.

"I need to hear something by tomorrow, Marti. *Tomorrow*. Otherwise, this has gone far enough and the behavior needs to be addressed. We've seen too much."

Chris called over his shoulder. "Terry! We're leaving *now*." Chris lowered his voice. "Marti, you might be so bold as to embrace the sun, but you won't burn anyone else up with you."

"Chris!"

He didn't look at her. "Tomorrow, Marti."

Tears filled her eyes. She turned away from Teresa and the girls. Teresa knew better than to ask questions. She lowered her eyes as Marti walked them to the front door. Alone, Marti stood in the doorway of the huge, dark house. She watched her brother's family drive away into the night. Silence swallowed the echo when she closed the front door.

She ran like the wind to Alex's office. Alex would arrive within the next hour. Tomorrow, Chris would kill him, or make arrangements for something to happen. Then Chris would go back to prison. The aftermath would tear her family to pieces.

She turned on Alex's desktop computer. Typed in the password she saw him use. She scanned files.

She spotted an audio file titled, "Marti." She listened to the entire nutty diatribe in near disbelief. If she knew now what she knew then, her son, very likely, would not exist. She read the accompanying written manifesto, especially the parts she missed the night of the greenhouse. She went through the charts and graphs of slights and insults he documented with detailed examples.

He would be back soon. She needed to shut down the computer. After she did that, she went through his desk drawers and found... another copy of Augie's business plan.

Her hands shook when she paged through it. This copy included Augie's identifying information plus cryptic notes written to Augie in Alex's hand.

Marti frowned. She tried to figure it out. Alex gave her the censored copy to adapt for Celara. But he kept the clean copy to work on himself. He wrote notes to Augie on it. Which meant... that he intended to return it to Augie, after he got what he needed for Celara. Which meant... that he didn't know that Evan intended for Augie to die. It was all she had to stop the madness.

She left his office for the second floor to look in on Christian. She heard the sound of heavy feet downstairs. Alex stowed the equipment and research in his office.

Marti felt the need to wash a gritty residue off her skin. She stepped into her shower. Stayed there a long time. Alex knew she was home. Did he wonder why she didn't greet him? She stepped out of the shower. Moisturized. Brushed her teeth. Found a nightgown. Then ran out of rituals.

Warm and relaxed, but not yet ready for bed, Marti checked on Christian again. He remained sound asleep. She wandered towards the stairs. Sat on the top step in the quiet of the dark hallway.

From this vantage point, she saw into Alex's office on the first floor. He must have used his own shower because he wore night clothes and a bathrobe. His desk faced the door and though he looked exhausted, he seemed hard at work. His focus concentrated on the computer screen.

She and Alex developed a routine over the past few months. Whenever Alex came to the nursery to spend time with Christian, Marti became indisposed, sleepy, under the weather, busy, or in need of something important from the store, like vitamins.

Alex, perceptive as always, cooperated. He made his plans for Christian through Mr. and Mrs. Dallas. They lived a life together far apart. Once, she brought Christian down to him and they shared their baby's first smile together. That day he looked so grateful that she felt like a criminal for treating him as though he were a shadow in her world.

Tonight, Alex pierced the shadows. He met warm topaz eyes with brilliant blue sapphires. She wanted to turn away. She didn't want to take a chance on what gazed back at her. Deep cool pools of blue, sharp crystalline flecks, or fierce bolts of lightning. She didn't want to see what he would show her, whatever it was.

But an electric current pulled her down the stairs. She always felt Alex's pull, even across a crowded room, a large conference table, a desktop full of paper work—even across the widest voids of anger, fear, hatred, and confusion.

He held out a hand towards her. Forgiveness? The last time he touched her was when they shared that quiet morning together in the hospital room. He held her hand then slept with his head on her shoulder. When he woke, she told him that the world he dreamed of could and should never be. If he found comfort in the arms of another since then, she didn't know. She didn't ask. He didn't tell.

He squeezed her hand now. He turned toward his computer screen. She followed his eyes.

"Sometimes," he began, "when I try to shut down my computer, I accidentally hit the logoff button instead."

Marti froze.

"And then when I sit down to use it again, I wonder why it's still on, waiting for me to put in a password."

She swallowed. Waited for his temper to spew forth it's volcanic verbal wrath upon her.

Instead, "Marti, I didn't tell you everything about Worth."

She put her other hand to her temple. "What didn't you tell me?"

"I told you Worth fell."

She felt a small knot of fear form. "Yes, that's what you told me on the phone." Her voice sounded unnatural to her ears. "That's what I told everyone else."

"Everyone else?" Alex stared at her for a long, uncomfortable moment. "Right."

He indicated a video icon on his computer screen. "The camera taped everything. I've been looking at it trying to decide if anyone else should see."

"Why?" Marti covered her mouth. "What happened to Worth, Alex?"

"It isn't pretty."

Marti thought a moment.

"I want to see."

He showed her. She shrank back in horror. Alex held her on his lap. Her twists flowed over his shoulders in a long curtain of ropes.

"I'm sorry, Marti. Honey, I'm so sorry. I didn't know he'd react like that."

"How did you expect him to react?"

He didn't answer.

She tightened her arms about him. "Alex, I do want to thank you for taking care of him down there."

"You don't have to thank me for that. Diving's about teamwork whether it's in a cave or the ocean. If it had been me—and sometimes it has—I'd want someone to make the effort, at the very least."

"It better not be you."

"What do you care?" His voice roughened with disgust.

She stiffened. For a long time, she didn't reply. The half-life, half-lie she and Alex lived together wouldn't work anymore.

She turned to face him. "Alex, even though I might have come across as a soul-sucking vampire bitch, I've always cared."

Alex stared at her. She saw the exact moment the realization hit him that she accessed his true feelings for her in his computer files. He leaned back in his chair.

She met his challenge head-on. "Apparently, I'm not the only one in this room who gets their feelings hurt. Right Alex?" she continued.

"I need you to watch the other tape from my camera."

"Alex, you don't have to..."

"Marti, just watch it. Please. I want you to know in your heart, for sure, beyond a shadow of a doubt what happened down there. Just watch."

This time she saw the heated exchange between Worth and Alex from the perspective of Alex's hard hat to which he fastened a backup camera. Worth swung away from Alex in preparation to deliver a hard blow. He took a step back to brace himself against a wall that wasn't there.

He slipped backwards. Alex reached forward with a shout. The horrible scream echoed up. Quint, Roger, and Dylan rushed into view.

Between fast forwards, she watched them figure things out with curt instructions to each other and Alex. Alex strapped on gear then climbed down to Worth's location. The men held him with rope and cable. Quint directed him from the top. Eight hours after the fall, Alex reached her brother. Worth raved with the pain from his broken body.

Alex tried to keep Worth calm. He pushed the stretcher underneath him. Mercifully, Worth passed out. Quint directed Alex to rig the rope and cable system in order to bring Worth's litter up to the main passage. Alex's sharp commands directed the team back to the surface. He called for an airlift.

"Alex, please delete the last part. I don't want anyone to see it and I'm pretty sure Worth doesn't either. He must have been so scared and angry. No wait." She held his arm. "Just cut the part where Worth's... where he...."

"Where he loses it?"

"Yes. That part. Give Worth the remaining copy. Let him decide what to do with it."

"I'll do it right now."

When he finished, Alex handed her the digital file. He got up without another word. Then he walked out his office door. She looked at the empty space he left behind. How he must hate her for doubting him. What was wrong with the two of them? When did the trust start and the hurt stop? Would it ever?

Were she and he doomed like her mother and father? Like his mother and father?

If this were a soap opera or made-for-television movie, his departure from the room was surely her cue to follow him to make a grand, passionate statement of devotion before the commercial break. But she waited too long. The violins cried out, but no one listened.

The moment was lost, gone forever.

◆ ◆ ◆

# 18 The Recovery

**J**ust as the sun rose, Marti answered the extension beside her bed.

"Marti!"

"Teresa? What's going on?"

"Chris and your father are in the same hospital as Worth."

"Visiting?"

"No. Last night, March took a turn for the worst. They called an ambulance."

Marti swallowed.

"Chris convinced the Reverend's doctor to do an emergency kidney transplant since Worth's injuries made it impossible for him to do it."

"They did the surgery?"

"Yes."

"How are they? Are you at the hospital now? Is Chris okay?"

"He's fine Marti. And Reverend March is recovering.

"Oh, thank God."

"I have to go home to get Mari and Kina off to school. I'll come back later for Chris."

"I'm coming to the hospital as soon as I'm dressed."

Marti knocked on Alex's bedroom door. She didn't hear a sound. She pushed the door open. Stepped in. Alex emerged naked from the shower in his bathroom. She tried, but failed, not to stare below his neck when she shared the news.

He wrapped a towel around himself. "Marti, I'm so sorry. But I've got some important meetings to chair at Celara."

"Well, almost my entire family's in the hospital."

"I'm sorry." Alex held up his hands. "Like I said, I've got to..."

"Never mind."

Brittle silence crunched through the air. Not enough oxygen remained in the room for both of them to breathe.

She left.

◆ ◆ ◆ ◆

She pushed Christian's stroller down white, antiseptic hallways. Not too long ago, she and Alex made their frantic midnight run down these same corridors after Christian's birth. She wondered if this was the same hospital where Alex's father died, where Lexa recovered from her near-fatal cry for help.

To her surprise, A.J. emerged from Worth's room.

"Marti," A.J. looked as though she got no sleep at all.

"A.J.," Marti covered her surprise. "Were you visiting with Worth?"

"Yes, Alex told me what happened."

"Oh."

"You know that he and I..."

"You and Worth?"

"Yes."

"I... I think you touched on it the last time we spoke?"

"Right." A.J. nodded. "He's going to make it all right the doctors say."

After an awkward pause, Marti asked, "Are you on your way out?"

"I'm stepping out for lunch, but I'll be back. Actually, I'm glad you're here so he won't be alone."

Marti nodded. A.J. walked down the hallway.

"A.J." she called.

A.J. turned around. Waited. Marti lowered her eyes to A.J.'s middle grown considerably bigger than at their last meeting.

"Welcome to the family." They smiled at each other a moment.

Marti entered Worth's room. She caught her breath at the variety of contraptions that held his limbs in place. He broke an arm and a leg, dislocated the other shoulder. A multitude of red scratches and dark bruises played tic-tac-toe across his face and upper torso.

"Well. Look at you."

Worth smiled at her. "You sure you want to see Frankenstein's monster up close? I just sent A.J. out of here screaming."

Marti laughed. "She was *not* screaming, silly." She saw the pitcher beside his bed. "Do you want some water?"

The bedside phone rang. Marti picked up the receiver for him, held it by his ear. She knew from what he said that it must be Beryl. Marti poured water for him with her free hand.

"She's coming back over in a couple of hours when her part-timer takes over the front desk," he informed her.

Marti sat in the chair that A.J. likely pulled closer to his bed. She held the cup to his mouth. He took a couple of swallows. She put the cup down

"Worth, Alex brought all your research and documentation to our house." She looked at her folded hands a moment and then glanced up. "He told me what happened to you out there. He showed me the tape from the main camera and from his."

Worth closed his eyes as if to shut out her voice.

"The whole thing?"

"The whole thing. I think... he was afraid I would think he'd done something to you."

"What? Like caused me to fall?"

"Something like that."

"Did you think that he did?"

Marti looked away from Worth's sympathetic gaze.

"No, Marti," his voice firm and clear. "No. I did it to myself by not paying attention to my surroundings—the biggest mistake a cave-diver could make. I was distracted because I lost my temper which was my own fault. You saw it."

"I saw that you really care about me. I appreciate that. I'm sure A.J. does too."

"Of course I care, Marti. You're my sister, but even before that, you were my friend. Well, you were still my sister all along but..." he shrugged, "you know what I mean." To no surprise, he let her A.J. comment go.

She nodded, gave him a faint smile. "When you get a chance, you might want to reassure Chris. His thoughts went to a similar place... and... well, Chris tends to follow through on his thoughts."

"My big brother, hunh?"

"That's right. I'm serious, Worth. He really cares about you too. And me. Please tell him everything, okay?"

"I'll talk to him."

"It's important."

"I will."

"Worth, I know you're in a lot of pain right now, so I'll make this brief. You're my brother and I love you. You mean so much to me. If anything ever happened to you, it would devastate my world." Marti couldn't stop the choke in her voice. "We already lost so many years."

She got up. Walked to a window. Leaned against it. Looked out on a beautiful, clear day in Lake City.

"Marti, I didn't tell you, but I did try to talk to him about things."

"Who? The Reverend?" Marti turned towards Worth. "What did he say?"

Worth tightened his jaw. "Nothing useful." He stared at the ceiling.

Where he lay broken under water and rock, in pain and darkness, Worth anticipated his death. In what he hoped would be his tomb, he unleashed a terrible diatribe about his not so immaculate conception against Beryl and the Reverend March. Worst of all was the weeping. He cried for the loss of all three children, the unfairness. He demanded that the universe finish the job and take him too. His only desire was to die alone in the cave.

Marti wasn't sure where to begin. "You cannot absorb the blame for what our father did to you. What he did to you, he did to me and Chris, as well. He did that to your mother and my mother. You saw and heard the whole thing when we were at his so-called welcome home shindig. You *know* how he is."

"I'm learning."

"Chris and I... I guess we got used to his abuse, and maybe that was a mistake because after a while, we both got to the place where we thought we earned it and deserved it. We excused him, and blamed ourselves. To anyone who didn't know him, the things he said would come as a shock. But keep this in mind. What he says isn't true for us and it isn't true for you either."

Marti moved back to fiddle with the flowers next to the pitcher of water at his bedside. She sat down again.

"We are not a perfect family. But please don't throw us away. And don't throw yourself away. Please, Worth. Don't ever do anything like that again."

A single tear escaped the corner of his eye. Marti bit her lip. Worth's fall put Alex in danger when Alex climbed down the steep, underground cliff. Worth lay half-submerged so Alex had to dive underwater to free Worth's leg before the water rose higher. The urgency in Alex's voice on the tape frightened her. Marti knew from the channel that Alex would push himself to the extreme when it came to the people he cared about.

"Worth, I'm so sorry for what happened to the children. So, so sorry. We never knew them and that means that we all missed out on something wonderful."

"They'd be about Mari and Kina's ages if they lived."

"I know." Marti nodded. "I know." She forced herself to continue. "Worth, your life is with the living. That includes the child that just walked out of the room with A.J."

His eyes flickered acknowledgement.

"Maybe, because you grew up alone you think that what you do doesn't matter to anyone else. But let me tell you something."

Marti leaned closer. "Listen to me, Worth." She used the same firm older sister voice she used with Chris. "You matter to us because you belong to us. Your life is not just your own anymore. Your life belongs to us because we are a family now."

More tears streaked from the hazel eyes that mirrored his mother's. But other than his lighter skin and hair, he looked more like Reverend Butler than Marti did since she inherited Christina's high cheekbones and clear, sherry eyes.

"That means you have a responsibility to stay here on Earth for as long as Beryl, me, Chris, Teresa, Mari, Kina, Alex, and yes, even Reverend March want you here. A.J. too. And I'll tell you right now. We want you forever. Do you understand?"

He faced her finally. "Yes."

"Promise me, forever." Marti lost the battle to her tears.

"I promise."

Marti took a moment to recover. "Alex and I decided to give you this." She showed him the digital player that held the middle portion of the video file—the part that revealed Worth at his most vulnerable. "The main part, before and after shows important parts of the cavern. That's locked up at home until you're ready to get back in the saddle. But we felt it should be your choice whether to show this section to anyone else or to destroy it."

"Burn it, Marti."

She looked around vaguely. Neither she nor he were smokers. She didn't have a lighter or matches. She crushed the case against his bedside table.

"Or... break it."

"There you go." She dropped the pieces into the bedside trash can. "So A.J. said she was coming back," Marti waited curiously for him to expand on their mystery relationship.

"She's a good girl," he said.

"Yes, she is." Marti decided not to push him further today. He was exhausted.

"So I'm gonna go, okay? I have to see about Chris and the Reverend. They're here too."

Worth closed his eyes. "The surgery, right?"

"He took a turn for the worse last night."

"Did..."

"No. It was before we got the news about you, Worth. It didn't have anything to do with that. But anyway they scheduled the surgery for tonight. Terry's watching the kids. I'll keep her updated and then we'll trade off."

"Marti, I'm sorry. Tell them..."

"Don't, Worth. It's fine. It worked out the way it was supposed to all along, I think. Chris and the Reverend have some things to work out too, you know. We all do. Just promise to get well soon."

"I promise." He smiled at her. "Tell that guy of yours that I appreciate what he did for me."

Marti nodded.

"I had my doubts, as you saw."

"I noticed."

"Is it going to work out?"

"Stranger things have happened." Marti stood up and walked to the doorway. "Especially lately."

"Marti, wait. There's something else."

◆ ◆ ◆ ◆

"He said Evan Lewis approached him out of nowhere and gave him a package of information. Evan told him the information would assist Save a Lake's fight against Celara. He said to use it only in the event that something happened to him."

Alex, home for a few mid-day hours away from Celara, glanced through a few pages, his mouth set in a grim line. He returned the pages to the package. "Did you read this?"

"No." Though his eyes frosted over, she met them with calm. "Worth opened it when he heard about Evan's death. He said he already knew what it was after he skimmed the first page. "

"Do you want to read it?" He held the thick package out to her. "Maybe you should."

Marti flicked her eyes towards the large bundle of papers, photos, and computer disks. Alex passed her the huge stack of Evan's final betrayal. Their fate lay in Marti's hands. After a long moment, Alex turned towards the door.

She toughened her voice. "Just where do you think you're going?"

He paused and then took another step. "I'm going back to work. I'm tired, Marti." She never heard him sound so defeated. "It's been a long day and I still have a lot to take care of at Celara."

"Oh. So that's how Alex deals?" She walked in front of him with the armload. "You just run away, is that it?"

"Marti, I can't do this with you anymore." He held his hands up in surrender. "I just can't." He brushed past her.

"Get back here, Alex!" He turned back, astonished that she raised her voice. "We're not done and you're still on the clock!"

Marti opened her arms. The portfolio fell to the wood floor with a loud *thunk* that sounded loud as thunder.

"You'd have to be a stone-cold idiot not to realize that that man," she pointed contemptuously to the floor, "is no longer this man," she jabbed her finger his way.

His eyes returned to cobalt.

"Burn it!" she ordered. He snatched her to him in an embrace that crushed the breath from her. He built a fire in the fireplace. Together, they banished the remains of the poisonous phantasm of distrust into harmless wisps of smoke that vanished into the night.

He threw his head back and laughed. "Marti..." He squeezed her tight to his chest and rubbed his face against her cottony hair. "You don't know how much I missed you. You must realize that I don't feel the same way about you when I wrote all that crap."

"I know." Marti chuckled, relieved to have him back in her arms where he belonged.

"After you asked me if I was okay, I thought about you all the way home. I couldn't wait to see you again."

She kissed him gently, at first. Then she devoured him. They surged against each other, pushed and pulled. They clutched frantically for handholds, lost balance, fell to the floor. He swung a leg to kick the office door closed.

"Marti." He held himself over her. "I want you tonight. I *need* you." She pulled him down.

They made up for time lost since the greenhouse. This time he punished *her*. He sent her to the edge then pulled her back over and over until she twisted beneath him as if to wring him dry.

"Tell me you love me," he insisted.

"Alex, Alex," she groaned. "Please, Alex. Do it now." She tightened her legs.

"Marti." His voice grew ragged. "Say it."

"No, no," she whimpered.

His voice rose to a shout. "Goddamit, Marti!" He worked her into a frenzied dance across the floor.

"Yes!"

"Yes what?" He stopped his movement, held her in place with an iron grip. "Say it. Say it right now!"

"Yes, I love you, Alex." Her world shattered into pieces. "I love you." She convulsed around him.

Alex forced the rest of his life into her then collapsed on top.

◆ ◆ ◆ ◆

The next evening, Teresa brought Mari and Kina back to Alex's house. Alex wasn't back from Celara. But at his request, Mr. and Mrs. Dallas returned, found a room for Teresa and the children, then served dinner.

Beryl's call came after Mari, Kina, and Marti's own sweet Christian, dropped off to sleep. All three of the men were fine. She would head home. Marti disconnected the speaker phone. She looked at Teresa.

"Can you believe this?"

"Never a dull moment, hunh Marti?"

"Lately, no." Marti laughed.

Teresa looked around Alex's office. Marti knew her friend had something on her mind.

"What is it, Terry. Are you worried about Chris?"

"Chris? No."

"Then what?"

"Do you love him?"

"Of course I love him. He's my brother. I've loved him all his life."

"No. I mean Alex."

"Oh."

Teresa studied Marti's face carefully.

"You do, don't you?"

Marti felt her face grow warmer. "Yes," she admitted. "I do. We've been through a lot."

"I *know*."

"I know you know," Marti laughed.

"So you're gonna stay here with him?"

"I am."

Teresa hugged her. "Marti, everything's going to be all right."

"Did Worth talk to Chris?"

"Yes. Chris came through the surgery just fine. I helped him to walk down to Worth's room. Neither of us could believe we thought that of Alex. It's over. Don't worry."

"Thank God. It's so amazing."

"What's amazing?"

"Even Worth warmed up to him."

"I'll bet he did after Alex pulled him out of that hellhole."

"The Rizal Caverns, Alex calls them." Marti laughed with her. "Alex won everyone over. I don't know how he did it, but he did."

"Are you the only hold out?"

"Trust me, I held out as long as I could. But then..." Marti's voice trailed off. "Life is full of surprises."

◆ ◆ ◆ ◆

The hospital released first Chris, then Worth, then Reverend Butler. Two weeks later, they held another celebration at the Reverend's retirement condo.

Marti helped Beryl to set things up. "We both failed her in different ways, Beryl."

"I know." Beryl bowed her head. "I loved her, Marti. I'd give anything to be able to go back in time and make different choices."

"I know. But then me and Chris wouldn't have Worth. Neither would you."

Beryl smiled. "I'm so glad it's a real family now. He spent too much time alone growing up, I think."

"Well, those days are over." Marti laughed. "We know exactly where to find him when we need him."

"And he knows where to find you."

"For always, Beryl."

"Marti?" Beryl still looked troubled.

Marti squeezed her hands. "Beryl. Let it go. For Worth's sake, my sake, and Chris's sake. Let it go. Life moves forward. Never backward. And it certainly doesn't stand still." Marti waved an arm towards the room full of people. "It's not so bad, is it?"

Beryl hugged her. "As a matter of fact, it's just fine."

More people pushed into the room. The door to the Reverend's condo stayed open so his neighbors could wander in and out. Her father's expansiveness allowed Marti the space to move quietly around the room without having to engage in small talk.

Beryl cornered Marti again in the kitchen doorway where Marti retreated to hide from the crowd and the Internet camera for a while.

"How are things with you and him?"

"Who?"

"Alex."

"Alex takes very good care of Christian. Christian loves him. He loves Christian."

"And Lexa?"

"Lexa is head over heels for her little brother. She's so good with him. She's like a mini-mother to him. To tell the truth, she's adjusted pretty well to me being in the house, though she stays so busy with activities, I hardly see her."

"So everybody loves everybody."

"Mostly." Though Marti told him, Alex never told her that he loved her.

They watched Chris walk over to greet Alex and Lexa.

"Chris always puts people at ease. It's like, within an instant, complete strangers fall in love with him."

"He turned out well, Marti."

"Yes, he did. He's so forgiving. I mean, whatever their past disagreements, as far as Chris was concerned, Alex became family when I had Christian."

They watched the Reverend circulate.

"It does make sense, you know." Beryl cocked her head to the side. "Worth inherited March's looks and my personality. But Chris is not only a dead-ringer for March, he has the Reverend's gift to draw people together."

"You're right. They've become closer ever since the surgery."

"Do you think they talk about," Beryl hesitated, "old times?"

"No." Marti shook her head. "Chris tells me that they mostly discuss Mari and Kina and their careers."

Beryl nodded. "It's funny. They're both counselors. Do you think Chris influenced Reverend March's transformation?"

"What transformation?"

Beryl shrugged. "Well, look at him. It seems like March decided to try on the wise family elder role for size."

"I hope it sticks."

"Time will tell."

*How very interesting.* As if she sensed Marti's scrutiny, inscrutable Beryl changed the subject.

"The real marvel is Alex."

"You think so?"

"He doesn't stalk and swagger about anymore."

"No, I guess not."

"I don't sense the aggression and arrogance that used to be there."

"Well, not around us, anyway. Not around me. Business is a different matter. Even I understand that."

"Yes, business is different." Beryl looked at her sidelong. "I guess there's no place like home."

"No." Marti didn't meet her eyes. "There's no place in the world like home."

Beryl studied the small group of men who spoke in low tones. She faced Martina.

"Your father and I talked it over."

"You talked with my father? About what? Why? When did you talk?"

Beryl raised her eyebrows. "He needed my help with an investment project. Naturally, we spoke about you, Chris, and Worth. Even though it hurts, you can't hide from life forever, Marti. You know that, don't you?"

"I know." Marti leaned against the doorway.

A.J. arrived with Worth who walked in with a cast on one leg and the opposite arm immobilized in a sling. Beryl headed their direction with open arms. She gingerly hugged her son. Marti waited a moment, then went to greet her brother and A.J.

Worth moved to greet the other men. Beryl circulated, leaving Marti alone with A.J.

"So what's up now, A.J.?"

"Oh, I don't know. The usual."

"The usual? Come on, A.J. Drop the mystery routine. This is Worth's older sister you're talking to."

"We're together."

"I know you're together." Marti laughed. "Are you in it to win it?"

"Oh," A.J. shook her hair that she allowed to grow longer, "I don't count the days."

Marti stopped smiling at the light dismissal. "A.J., normally I'd take the hint and politely change the subject, but not this time. You do know about Worth's first wife and three children?"

"Yes, Marti. I know."

"He barely talks about it anymore, but did he tell you what happened to them?"

"He told me."

"He lost nearly everyone he loved in one night. A.J., I love my brother. We all love him."

"I love him too, Marti."

Marti nodded. "I'm glad to hear it." She took a breath. "The thing is, even though I didn't know Worth at the time, I lost a niece, two nephews, and a sister that same night. It feels like a knife to the heart to think about them. I really can't... actually, I don't ever want to know what Worth went through. I only know that I don't want Worth to ever have to go through it again. For any reason." Marti searched her former co-worker's eyes. "A.J., are you in it to win it?"

A.J. hugged her, held on for a long time. "Yes, Marti. I'm in it to win it. Worth is the best thing to happen to me. I've been waiting for him for a long time—a man who doesn't mind how high I reach or how far I like to fly. In fact, he digs it."

"Yeah. He's like that. He's a good guy." Marti smiled. "Somehow, the two of you managed to keep your thing way under the radar. Was it ever since the convention?"

A.J. pressed her lips together and shook her head.

"The thing is, Marti, all the drama surrounding you and Alex absorbed everyone's attention. Me and Worth just went about our business. By the way, are you guys okay?"

Marti remembered just in time that no matter their personal relationships, Alex was still A.J.'s employer.

"We're light years from where we were."

As if he heard her words of hope from across the room, Alex looked Marti's way. She felt the familiar jolt ricochet throughout her body.

❖ ❖ ❖ ❖

Beryl waited until the last guest, including Alex and Lexa, left. "Marti, we're meeting now."

"About what?"

"Alex."

"He's not here. He had to take Lexa back to her mother's."

"That's why we're meeting now."

❖ ❖ ❖ ❖

# 19 The Boardroom

**B**y the time Chris and Beryl finished with her, Marti's head felt like a jigsaw puzzle. Apparently, the two of them compared notes to figure out the sequence of events the night of the greenhouse, the channel, the shredded red dress. The night of the spider and the spider's cocoon. The vortex and the gurgle of murky water.

Still in recovery and exhausted from the party, her father missed the whole discussion. He slept in his bedroom. So Marti sat for two hours and listened to her brother and Worth's mother hold forth at considerable length on Alex. Everyone knew what was best for Marti, but no one understood the ambivalence within her heart. Sure, they recognized his charm and sense of humor. They recognized that he extended himself to her and Chris, how he saved Worth. They also remembered what she told them about him.

"Are you sure? What about this? Are you sure? What about that?" they asked her again and again until she shrieked at both of them to leave her alone. Blindsided by Chris and Beryl's attacks, she left, upset and stressed.

They let her go.

Alex made everything all better at the house. She gasped for air during a long night of rock and roll. Before the sun came up, she crept back to her room. She lay alone in her bed to cry without a sound while Alex got dressed for work at Celara. She felt empty inside. Empty and ashamed though she didn't understand why. She pulled herself together in time to meet him downstairs for breakfast.

"Meetings, meetings, meetings," he told her.

"That's fine. I have my own work to do today."

"So," he asked her in an insinuating voice. "What are you going to do with yourself all day while I'm gone?"

"Research." She smiled mysteriously into a cup of tea.

"What kind of research?" He stroked her hair. "Anything I can help you find? Some place I can help you look?"

She shut down the dirty-talk before it began, because it looked as though he might change his mind about leaving the house.

"I have to check some facts in Worth's manuscript."

Alex immediately lost interest. "Well, enjoy it." He kissed her on the way out the door.

She flew upstairs to her office.

On her desk sat the huge stack of Worth's first draft inter-mixed with news clippings, brochures, and other bits of research. She prayed that truth might finally set her and Alex free.

One by one, she pulled out copies of the power plant stories from their hiding place deep within Worth's manuscript. She scanned through them once. Twice. A third time. She had to be sure.

No fatalities.

Each time, the buildings were cleared with not even a skeleton crew on the premises. It was "a miracle no one was hurt." The schedule mix-up was "a fortuitous accident." It was "lucky" and "so amazing." So said the reporters.

Until Lakeside. Until Augie.

She sat in her desk chair. He didn't intend for Augie to die. Tears pricked her eyes. That dark, evil night, Evan told her the truth. Evan was responsible for everything. Everything significant enough to matter, at least.

Distrust, Evan's evil legacy, remained between her and Alex. Maybe that was why Alex never followed through on the marriage proposal he brought up to her father. Her triumph in finding proof of Alex's decency was laced with guilt for her own lack of faith in him. She had to make it up to him.

◆ ◆ ◆ ◆

The next few weeks passed swiftly. Alex needed her research skills to knock down the final domino pieces that led to the super grid.

"Clean energy is a dirty business," he warned her.

"Make me proud," she countered.

Marti dropped an invoice for her consulting fee in the mail, almost as a dare. Alex had Celara cut her a check without a word.

Lost in the whirlwind with Alex, Marti sheltered their relationship. Inside their tighter orbit, Alex was the sun who drew her closer to his frenzied energy. Chris and Beryl, all their complaints, twinkled too far away in the distance to break through the gravitational pull that bound her to the father of her only child.

Sure, Alex exercised bad judgment in regards to Evan, but if anyone in her family lived a life without mistakes, then they should be the first to cast a stone at him.

Then at her.

◆ ◆ ◆ ◆

Tension in Celara's boardroom radiated in waves off the walls, the ceiling, and the table. Marti sat between Alex and Harlan. Across from them, three Lake City players, Alex's partners in "special projects" waited for Alex to convince them.

"The super grid is the Internet and Interstate for energy and power systems. Like satellite for radio and television, it would integrate local grids into a mega grid. In this respect, transmission and distribution of energy would flow both ways with digital systems serving as throttles. Whereas wind, solar, and hydro power can fluctuate individually, the super grid smoothes out the power flow by detecting imbalances and then accommodating for them."

Marti monitored the voice recorder and took notes. Once in a while, she slipped Alex a sheet of data if he needed it. Harlan took notes, as well.

"We have a growing labor force trained and ready to work. Even as we speak, they're getting certification on procedures and processes for green construction. In fact, through Lake

City's youth organizations, we've developed a strategic labor mix of skilled and unskilled workers—apprentices, interns, and work study students—at pay rates designed to offset the initial transmission costs."

Marti remembered Chris's meetings with Alex last summer. Alex was a master, actually a genius, of absorbing ideas.

"You have more information in your packets."

Alex met with the lead player, Derek, months ago. That meeting didn't go well, Alex told her. Still, Derek's voice could make or break the deal. So there he sat. His face, florid from excessive drinking, remained hard as stone.

After a long silence, the stone cracked open to reveal a dark cavern filled with yellowed stalactites and stalagmites.

"You got some nerve."

"Really?" Unruffled, Alex sat back in his chair. "What kind of nerve do I have exactly?" Marti recognized his challenge position.

She and Harlan remained silent. If Alex wanted their help, they knew to wait until he asked for it.

"The kind of nerve that acts like life is all hot dogs and apple pie. You can't believe this is going to work."

"Why wouldn't I believe it?"

"You think they're gonna let you?"

"Are *they* going to stop me?"

Marti felt her stomach tighten. This is what Alex wanted. This is how he liked it. He wanted the players out in the open where he could see them—where he could handle them better.

"Yes. They're gonna stop you, Alex."

Alex looked surprised and confused. "I don't think they will."

Marti held still. Derek's smile created fissures in the stone around it. One side of his mouth curled to a sneer.

"Any man, any real man who fathered children would do well to recognize that the most valuable asset in his life is *their* future."

Marti's heart skipped a beat. Harlan shifted in his chair. Alex perceived menace, but decided to get past it, back to the negotiation. "Clean energy is the future, Derek."

"Maybe for some, someday. Not for others. Maybe not for the children of others who have parents that don't recognize reality when it follows her home from school to ballet class."

*Lexa!* Fear slithered down Marti's spine.

"Or when it visits the pediatrician—Dr. Wintell—for healthy baby examinations."

Fear turned into a red mist of rage. She couldn't see, couldn't speak. She could barely breathe. White hot anger and fiery hatred spread throughout her body. It grew beneath her skin. It wanted to destroy the man that dared, *dared* to hurt something that she created inside her body. She heard Alex's voice, but she couldn't understand the words through the ringing of her ears.

*What did he say?*

She stood up, to walk over to the water pitcher on the sideboard. Alex would handle this. The voices in the room continued behind her.

She walked back to the table with a glass of water. She took a couple of breaths. She set the glass down on the table, tried to hear what the men said.

The other two players sensed weakness in Alex's position. They decided to join the dance. "How are you going to take on all those developers and the permits? There's no way."

They didn't know Alex like she knew Alex. He was the shark who slid like silk through the deepest, darkest water. He was the crocodile who smiled with rows of white teeth to invite the unsuspecting. He was the beautiful, velvety-soft panther who coiled with the epiphany that arrived one second too late.

"Save a Lake officially endorses the Midwest Consortium's plans for the super grid. They're working with Celara and various government agencies and organizations to expedite the permitting process."

"How the fuck did you do that?" Derek demanded.

Alex didn't miss a beat. "Every organization not already on board would do well to closely examine their overall priorities and to consider the long-term benefit of jobs, energy independence, and green technology right here in our own back yards. Save a Lake is prepared to state publicly that Lake City should and will be ground zero for the green revolution and that Celara should be part of it. Now is the time to join the Midwest Consortium, Derek."

"You're by yourself on this, Alex. You got some granolas on board with you, but that's not enough. You can't hold it steady without us and if you think the oil and gas boys are gonna lay down for this, you're barking at the moon. Your father never would have dared."

"Welcome to *my* world."

"Where's the money gonna come from? Are you gonna mortgage Celara?"

"Hell no."

"Well, why the hell not? I kinda like that big office you got with the big windows and the nice furniture."

Marti never wanted to see the smile on Alex's face directed her way. Ever.

"In the beginning, God created Heaven and Earth. Genesis tells us quite clearly that man is meant to be the park ranger for Planet Earth."

Marti wasn't surprised that Alex co-opted her arguments for himself. Alex would always be who he was. *Sell it, Alex!*

"Raising the necessary capital to cover the initial cost of transmission infrastructure throughout the Midwest has shown me how God makes the impossible possible."

"Alex," the third player finally spoke up, "I wondered how long it would take before the pressure of running your father's company would crack you up."

The players laughed.

Marti tried to disconnect from the horror show that she knew lay ahead. Alex held the room in a tortuous pause. His crazy-looking smile never wavered.

"The Midwest Consortium sold enough shares of its project through participants of a certain Reverend's Internet congregation, *the original E-vangelist of Lake City*, in fact."

Marti gasped. Beryl's project with her father!

"According to him, God is the One and only One we need to make things happen. The balance sheet seems to agree."

"Hallelujah and pass the ammunition!" Derek sneered again. "How much did you raise?"

"Enough."

"Then why are *we* here?"

Marti's mind scanned through the new information for the logical answer. *Power and control. Alex needed other investors to offset Beryl and the Reverend's economic intrusion.*

"You're here because the train is rolling. I want you on it with Celara. I owe it to you as a friend of my father's. Besides, if you're not on it, you're under it."

"Oh yeah? If I'm under it, then so is she," Derek yanked a finger Marti's way. "So is a tiny dancer who'll never see her tiny career take off. So is a certain young boy who can be vaccinated against the measles but maybe not an unfortunate turn of events along a lonely stretch of highway."

She heard Harlan speak over Alex's irritated voice. The entire room filled with voices and the ringing noise.

Marti heard enough. She switched off the voice recorder. She stood. She turned the corner. She stepped off the precipice and descended into darkness.

"But can a certain player in Lake City be vaccinated against syphilis? The word I hear from the stroll is 'no.'" She smiled. "That's 'no,' and 'no' again, friend."

She walked from one end of the room to the other, a moving target they couldn't hit. "How about the male prostitutes on the beautiful side of town? Oh, the stories they could, actually they do tell... no actually, they do *sell*, about certain events along certain lonely stretches of highway."

Alex swiveled his head, fascinated as always by sweet, secret little Marti. Harlan didn't look at her.

Marti contemplated the dry-erase board with interest. She made random notes on it. "Is there a vaccination for fathering children with your brother's wife, I wonder?"

"What the hell is the bitch talking about, Alex?"

She saw the outrage in Derek's eyes. He should not have let her see it because she liked that look on him.

"What kind of pill do you take for killing two people while driving drunk?" She made another note.

"And how do you top making extra-special anti-freeze-flavored slushies for your deceased wife?" She drew a sad face on the dry-erase board.

Marti stopped by Derek's chair, put one hand on the table, leaned into his personal space. Power! *She loved it!* All up in his face all up in the place, she was too angry to feel afraid.

"I wonder how *you* will stop him, Derek." She nodded her head towards Alex.

Derek grabbed her wrist which was all the excuse she needed. Marti twisted her foot around his chair leg, yanked it forward. Chopped his windpipe. His chair tipped back to the floor with a crash.

"Marti! Marti!" Alex yelled.

"Oh my God!"someone else yelled.

Derek coughed from the floor where he lay sprawled on his back. Alex yanked her hard towards him. "Marti, get back!" He thrust her behind him.

Harlan vaulted across the table, put an arm around her waist, held her tight against him. "Stay here, Marti. Stay here. It's okay now."

She felt dizzy from adrenaline. A few moments passed. Then she relaxed against Celara's counsel.

Derek struggled to pick himself up from the floor.

"Stay down until he's finished," Marti ordered with a cold voice.

Alex stood over Derek. He continued his presentation to the players with the same strange smile from before.

"Celara stands ready to go today. We have an amazing track record in renewable energy. We have the means, motive, and opportunity to offset fossil fuel dependence forever. We have labor in a strategic ratio to maximize profits. We have the research. We have the technology. We have numbers outlining the benefits of business development in Lake City. We know the environmental impact. We have public support and investment capital. There's nothing and no one to stop us."

Derek lay on his back on the floor. Marti drilled angry eyes through his forehead. The other two players remained still.

"Again, what we need today is a united front. That's what it's going to take to stand up against the oil and gas boys. They hate us because they're scared of us. They're scared of us because they can't control us. Right now, in the packets Marti gave you, there's a list of the agencies already on board as well as those who requested additional information or time to consider the consequence of not joining. Uniting as the Midwest Consortium will help the remaining agencies to make the right choice." Alex looked from one player to another. "Any questions?"

"Get me the fuck up off this floor," Derek growled.

Alex helped him up, dusted him off. Marti stood her ground. She couldn't move anyway with Harlan's arm locked around her waist. He didn't release her until everyone settled back down. Then he walked her to her chair, held it out for her.

Derek took time to adjust his hair piece. "Where did you find her, Alex?" He laughed with the other guys. "I want one too."

"Marti's one of a kind." Alex didn't bother to hide his triumph. "And she's all mine. Look, everyone's tired. Let's take an hour for lunch. Derek, you and you," he pointed at the players, "You're with me."

He left with the players. It was as if the sun set in the small world of the boardroom. Tired from the excitement, Marti sat with Harlan who moved papers around. She waited for his comment on her behavior.

Harlan set his briefcase on the table. Opened it. Took out a thick folder.

"Marti," he stared at the few sheets in his hands. "Sometimes when Alex says something, people find it so out-there or over-the-top, they assume it must be a joke, and that it can't possibly be true. I understand that your feelings for him are strong, but it's time you knew the entire truth."

He handed her the folder, then retreated to pour himself a glass of water. By now, she recognized one of Evan's many adventure stories. She read through each of the Lake City players' portfolios at Alex's house, didn't she? Memorized them for Alex. For Celara. For the future! What else did Alex need her to do today?

She opened the folder and found... her entire existence on display. Background from before Celara, during Celara, and after Celara. Her life with Alex.

How strange that Alex kept Evan's portfolio on her though she and he destroyed his together. She read through the information that Evan assembled on her. Then she read Alex's notes. The thorough follow-up. The frightening detail. The triumphant insults. The wicked plotting. Right up until this morning. Not only did he not destroy her portfolio, but he updated and expanded it into grotesque areas.

She kept her voice even. "Why... do you have this, Harlan?"

"Alex asked me to hold it for him. He was afraid that you, being a researcher, would find it if he left it at the house." Like she found his computer files.

"How long have you had it?"

She flipped back-and-forth through the pages, stalling the other questions that had answers she didn't want to hear. Answers that would destroy the false reality Alex built for her. The false reality that was her life with him.

Harlan didn't answer her.

"That long, hunh?" Marti swallowed. "Did you read it?"

"I read it."

"It... it looks like Alex's writing."

"That's because it is Alex's writing."

The knife through her gut hurt so much. Alex whistled for her. Marti came running. He snapped his fingers. Marti rolled over and opened wide. He pulled her chain. She barked. All this time, the whole time, *every* time, he was ten steps ahead. Marti closed her eyes.

Chris and Beryl tried to tell her. They sorted the details she refused to see. And when they presented it to her tied with a bow, she refused to listen.

"Why?"

The kaleidoscope shifted. Alex's stories about his father... Kate... Augie... Worth!

*Of course he'd say that.*

"Why? Harlan, I don't understand why he would do this." Her voice sounded like that of a small, frightened, confused child.

"Because he likes to win." Harlan's voice was calm, neutral, logical, and unemotional. He might have told her tomorrow's forecast.

A shower curtain separated her from the natural world. A clear bubble covered in gray film that only Marti could see. Something she would have to claw and fight through to escape before it smothered her to death.

Alex shredded her every intimacy and insecurity. Every confession of every secret fantasy that she whispered to him as tokens of her love, he wielded as a scythe to tear a path for him to stomp through the remains of her heart. It was all there on the pages in front of her. Everything!

Her mind still fought against the possibility of what it all meant. She sought a chink in the smooth wall of Harlan's reason. Harlan was jealous of Alex. He broke client confidentiality. What did that say about Harlan?

"Why did you show it to me?" She practically spit it at him. "Why now, if you knew all along?"

"Marti," Harlan sat beside her at the table. "Think very carefully about what just happened in this room. Do you see now that you have approached the point of no return?"

Marti bowed her head and closed her eyes. It was true. She was the new Kate and Evan all rolled into one. Two against the world, his new gun was Black and female, the unexpected sleeper he activated whenever he needed her. She blackmailed, she assaulted, she threatened—all to protect her master.

Her head was a funhouse mirror. Nothing she knew was real anymore. Up was down. Left was right. Right was wrong.

She watched an inner movie of her every encounter with Alex from a different angle. He admitted that he used Kate to keep tabs on Evan. Face it. Alex and Kate did sleep together. Kate had one or more moments of bad decision-making regarding Lexa. Alex ordered Evan to "take care of it." Augie rebelled against Alex's control. Alex ordered Evan to "take care of it."

During the car ride through hell with Alex and Evan, Alex... Alex... Alex... waited to see who would come out on top—Marti or Evan.

*Buckle up for safety.*

Evan came unhinged. Rendered himself useless. Alex jerked the steering wheel.

*I just told you Alex saved me.*

*I wonder why.*

She didn't want to see it. But behind her closed eyes, the horror played on. Worth stood with his back to nothingness in the cave. Alex showed it to her... between fast forwards. Alex and Worth argued. Alex waited for Worth to position himself in front of an empty space. Alex saw the danger that Worth did not. It took only one more provocation to make it happen.

*How did you expect him to react?*

Every time she challenged Alex, he distracted her, controlled her, manipulated her. He even used Christian to break down her defenses.

Marti couldn't look at Harlan. The sheer humiliation that Harlan knew the extent of her stupidity, exactly how Alex managed her, the vulgar things he knew she allowed Alex to do to her made her want to crawl away from the boardroom and hide.

She felt weary, so weary of Alex draining her life force to feed his own.

The ugly truth of the past few minutes shifted, clanged, and scraped against the duller edge of what she always knew from the first day she met Alex.

The edges of the jigsaw puzzle snapped into place. The kaleidoscope shifted to home position. The funhouse mirror shattered. She saw the wizard behind the curtain.

She saw everything. *Everything!*

A keening whimper escaped her throat. Harlan locked the boardroom door.

"How could he do this to me? How could he? How could I let him? I don't understand it."

Harlan took the seat next to her at the table.

"Marti, he did it because that is what he does. It's who he is. I would know."

"Because you helped him?"

"Because, I am where you'll be soon if you don't stop."

"What do you mean?"

"Marti, listen. My parents worked for Alex's father. They took care of the King household then. The way Mr. and Mrs. Dallas do now."

*Another puzzle piece.*

"Your parents?"

"Yes. After Celara left…"

"Celara left?"

"Mr. King's wife. Alex's mother."

"She was Celara?"

Harlan inclined his head. "Celara King. Once upon a time, he loved Mrs. King. When she left him the company became his new love. Mr. King cut off all contact with Celara. She begged my parents to help her stay in contact with Alex. My parents felt sorry for her. They passed on communications from Celara to Alex. Alex told his father which infuriated Mr. King enough that he fired my parents. We had to leave the King household. But he made it impossible for them to find work anyplace else in the city."

Marti knew this story from Alex but remained quiet. She needed to hear Harlan's version.

"They... we, descended into poverty. In the meantime, Alex pitched a fit about me being gone. See, me and Alex were about the same age. We played together. We were close. When Mr. King sent my family away, Alex protested, threw tantrums. Wouldn't stop. I don't think he realized the consequences of what he did to my parents would affect him as well."

"Gee, that doesn't sound like Alex at all."

Harlan smiled. "So Mr. King made my parents an offer they couldn't refuse. He told them that he would forgive the trespass, if they allowed me to grow up in Mr. King's house as a companion for Alex. Celara was gone. Mr. King had no plans to remarry. I would do as a substitute brother for Alex."

Harlan looked past the wall of the boardroom.

"It was a hard week of decision-making. A lot of pain and, yes, resentment. My parents gave me up to Mr. King. They didn't want to fight him. So I grew up with Alex. I went to the same schools. Participated in the same activities."

"So you were like a brother to him."

"Yes. *Like* a brother." Harlan sounded bitter when he said it. "There I was caught between two families and two worlds. I didn't belong in either, really. I never quite forgave my parents for the deal they made. Though they were able to earn a living again, they died two years later. After that, the King family was all that I knew. Mr. King put me through law school. I came to work at Celara the same year Alex did."

"But that doesn't answer the question of why you," Marti gestured at the portfolio, "kept all this about me for Alex."

Harlan let out a long sigh. "I was eager to prove myself. My ambition made me vulnerable to the Celara way. It took only one mistake, one wrong move. And then I was caught."

"And then what?"

"That's why I showed you this, Marti. What happened to me and Kate and Evan and the others doesn't have to happen to you. It's not too late for you to turn back."

"Others?"

Harlan inclined his head.

"You mean leave Alex."

"What I mean is you can't let him decide who you are. These pages are only *his* interpretation of your existence. It's really your decision, isn't it?"

"Is it too late for you?"

Harlan sighed. "Well, I just broke confidentiality which, among all the rest of it, is a sure path to disbarment."

"You can't let him decide who you are. It's your decision." She paused. "Isn't it?"

"Right back in my face, eh, Marti?"

"Harlan, you're more than what he or his father made you."

"You think so?"

"I know so. Otherwise, we wouldn't have this conversation. You helped build this maze. That means you know the exit."

"I always knew the day would come when I couldn't go any further." Harlan placed both of his hands on the table. "I do know the exit, Marti. And I do want to be free. Based on what you know now, are you willing to free yourself?"

She nodded.

"Marti?" He wanted her to say it aloud.

"Show me," she whispered.

He showed her with only seconds to spare before the boardroom door rattled. Harlan opened it.

"What're you guys doing?" Alex demanded.

"I needed to make a phone call."

Alex's eyes narrowed. Not before Marti saw the red around the rims from his lunchtime scotch, the drink of kings. *I'll deal with you two later*, the look said.

He and the Lake City players held draft copies of the Midwest Consortium agreement that Leslie typed up over the lunch hour. They discussed the details with Harlan, but Marti noted the cold attitude directed her way by the players. And why not? She did the dirty work after all. Alex kept his hands nice and clean. She could just imagine Alex's lunchtime conversation that expressed complete surprise that his researcher went rogue.

*I didn't tell Marti I was gonna throw her under the bus. If this blows up in our faces, I'll just tell everyone it was all her idea. She's in charge!*

She and Harlan took notes. Harlan reviewed the additions. Alex depressed the intercom on the boardroom phone.

"Leslie to the boardroom. Leslie."

They waited for Leslie to type up the second version. Harlan and the men talked sports.

"So is our team gonna make it?"

"Nah. Kidding me?"

"There's always next year."

"Next century maybe."

Marti sat in numb silence until Leslie returned. Marti and Harlan reviewed the documents again. Harlan asked a few innocuous questions, noted some additions. Alex received a text message, which he ignored. Leslie typed up the third version. Alex passed copies to the three players. His phone rang again. Alex decided to text a response this time.

He passed his own copy to Harlan. "Take care of that," he snapped, impatient with the details.

Marti knew the exact moment Derek realized what she and Harlan did. Derek exchanged a look with the other players. They knew too. Harlan passed Alex's copies down to Marti for another once-over.

"No, it's fine." Alex snapped mid-text. "We'll be here all day and I have someone to meet." He pulled out a pen. "Give me that." Marti wondered who Alex wanted to meet—the mystery person sending the texts. A woman.

Derek stared across the table at Marti with eyes that saw oil derricks on fire off the Gulf of Mexico, nuclear energies that glittered in the dark.

Marti thought she hit the low point of her life when she picked up trash out of the gutter with the ex-convicts to pay for school. But this place, this boardroom, was the sewer beneath the gutter where monsters hid to shed their human skins. She waited with unnatural calm. She wanted to know what a man with a face of stone might do.

That man watched Alex sign his copy. Alex put down his pen, continued texting. The other players, unsure, didn't move.

"Come on, what're you gay, Derek?" Alex didn't look up from his cell phone. "Are you the one visiting male prostitutes now that Cynthia's gone from too many... what did you call them, Marti? Anti-freeze slushies!" Alex laughed.

Marti felt prickles under her arms. Her skin cooled. She didn't react. She waited.

Captivated by personal triumph, Alex missed the look of sly malice on Derek's mottled face.

"Guess you got the best of me, Alex."

"Clean energy is a dirty business."

"Yeah. It's pretty filthy." Derek signed. The other players signed.

"Leslie to the conference room." Leslie notarized and processed the agreements. The players took their copies and stood. Marti, Alex, and Harlan stood.

It was done.

Alex dominated the room. He got what he wanted. He was in good spirits.

"When are you going to announce?" Derek asked him.

"The end of this week. Marti has the press release ready to go. We'll get some cameras in front of Celara."

"Sounds like you already knew how it would turn out today."

"You have to go green to get green, my friend. That's what we're doing. And now that's what you're doing." Alex tossed his cell phone on the table.

Derek looked Marti's direction. "We're certainly doing something."

Though she put the screws to him, Derek recognized that Alex got hit much, much worse—with Derek's full participation. The urban legend would become a story for the ages.

Under the cover of the men's backslapping and underhanded jabs at each other, Marti used the boardroom phone to make a call.

"Terry, don't ask. I need you and Chris to pick up Christian at Alex's house and take his things with you. Everything. All of it. Yes. Right now. It's important."

She hung up the phone. Picked up the receiver again. Looked over her shoulder to make sure no one overheard. No worries. Alex wrapped up the meeting with an obnoxious joke about a high-maintenance customer.

"Mrs. Dallas, Alex and I need some time alone together tonight, so I'm having my brother and sister-in-law pick up Christian this afternoon. You don't have to do anything. No. Yes. Yes. They'll take care of everything. Thanks."

Harlan met her concerned eyes. He kept the conversation going with the other men.

Marti dialed again. "Worth. Don't ask. Please. Just help me, if you can."

She heard her name. "Marti, get over here." Alex waved her off the phone, irritated. "Help me walk them out."

She disconnected.

Harlan faxed the paperwork. Leslie dropped the hard copies into the mailbox across the street.

The Lake City players left the front entry with furtive glances toward Marti and smug looks amongst themselves.

Alex noted the smirks. But his perception, usually so sharp, failed him terribly that day—the drinks at lunch. He pulled Marti into his office. Together, they watched the players drive away through the window.

"Look at them," he whispered against her ear, "They can't wait for the money to start rolling in. See how they waited for us to do the hard work? Then they jumped on board the gravy train. Take a good look, Marti. That's Lake City for you. Greed can move mountains." She felt his lips shift into a predator's smile of satisfaction on the soft skin behind her ear lobe.

"That's the old school type of religion we were up against." He squeezed her tighter. "But we did it!"

She felt him hard against her back. Conquests like this excited him. "I have to finish up here. Let A.J. and Kenneth know the deal." He bit her mouth. "I'll see you later tonight."

She danced with the devil in clear moonlight the night of the greenhouse. "I'll have Teresa pick up Christian for tonight so we can be alone together," she responded. She dared to dance again.

He nuzzled her neck in approval. Alex would reward her six ways to Sunday for a job well done, for giving him what he wanted most of all—the super grid.

She wouldn't be able to walk for two days.

◆ ◆ ◆ ◆

Harlan drove her back to Alex's home. Huge, vulgar, hideous. It devoured the landscape. She hated Alex's monstrous mcmansion as much as she hated him.

Harlan's phone rang. "Hold on." He parked. He took the call. "Kenneth," he mouthed to her.

Marti got out of Harlan's car. Her father sat in the back seat of Beryl's car parked nearby. He looked as though he were asleep.

Teresa emerged from the house with Christian in her arms, Mari and Kina carried his baby bags. Chris brought up the rear with the rest of Christian's things. None of them asked her any questions. They, including Beryl, knew far better than she that this day would always come. Marti was the last to figure it all out.

Harlan's phone rang again—A.J.

"Where is he?" Chris asked Harlan.

"He's still at Celara. We don't have a lot of time." Harlan disconnected. "He'll be coming soon." He waved Chris back towards the house with urgency. "He won't come alone."

"Get in the car, Teresa," Chris ordered on his way back inside.

Marti ran ahead to Mr. and Mrs. Dallas who stood in the doorway. "I'm sorry, Mr. and Mrs. Dallas, but something came up, and so..."

"Miss," Mr. Dallas cut her off, "Do you require our help?"

"No, its fine," she called over her shoulder. "Everything's all taken care of." No matter. They expected Teresa. Maybe Chris. Not her entire family. They would call Alex. They were loyal to him, not her.

She vaulted the stairs to her office. Beryl and Worth had just about everything packed. "Worth, Beryl!" She embraced them. "Thank you so much, both of you."

"Do that later, Marti. Get your things." Beryl never forgot the night of the shredded dress.

Marti grabbed a large suitcase from her closet. Threw clothes and shoes into it willy-nilly. Crushed everything down in order to zip it closed. Chris met her at the door with the last of Christian's belongings.

"Where's Christian?" she asked him.

Chris tightened his jaw. "Still with Teresa." She followed him down the hallway. "Harlan locked her in our car with the kids. I told him to stand guard, in case..." He took the suitcase downstairs.

Beryl and Worth emerged from her office, boxes and bags in hand. Marti led them out the front door. She halted just outside.

Alex and two large-sized, muscular men she didn't recognize blocked Harlan. Chris dropped her belongings to the ground. Male voices raised in anger. Worth strode forward. He dropped his armload.

The volcano erupted.

"Marti! You deceitful, low-level bitch!" Alex's face was so red, it was nearly purple. "What the fuck is wrong with you, you fucking degenerate slut?" His eyes blazed so that he appeared demonic.

She and Beryl moved fast to load the rest of her belongings.

"How many ways have you fucked her behind my back, Harlan, you jealous, low-life prick? Both of you are scum, fucking scum. Disloyal cowardly scum, both of you!" Alex took a step towards Marti. He stabbed the air with an outraged finger. "You let him fuck you in the ass, didn't you, Marti?"

Teresa raised her car windows so the children couldn't hear. Worth, Chris, and Harlan stood in front of the women. Alex and his goons would have to push through the three men to get to her.

"Did you get her in the mouth too, Harlan? Marti fucking loves that! Don't you, Marti?"

Chris started forward. Worth held him back.

Beryl got in the passenger side of her car. "Marti, get in!" She pulled Marti in after her.

Her father stirred in the backseat.

"What? Is that him?" In the review mirror, she saw her father fiddle around with his jacket. She wondered if he looked for medication. Was he about to have a heart attack? Why on earth did Beryl bring him out here?

"Marti!" Alex called to her in anguish. "How could you do it? How could you do that to me, you simple, dumb bitch?"

From the driver's side, Beryl locked all four doors, raised the windows. Marti cracked her window to hear what the men said. She heard metallic noises behind her, the Reverend fiddled with his seatbelt, or something. Maybe he thought she and Beryl would actually let him get out of the car.

"Don't listen, Marti," Beryl told her.

"Its fine, Beryl. I'm okay."

"It's over, Alex." Harlan blocked her view so she couldn't see Alex's reaction. "It's over. It's done. There's nothing you can do."

"You know better than that, Harlan, you goddamn fucking idiot! It's not over until *I* say it is. Didn't anyone ever tell you to dance with the one who brought you, you son of a bitch? You forgot who got you here," Alex pointed, "and you forgot who bought that fucking car and house for you. You had *nothing*. You *were* nothing but a piece of shit until my father found you and gave you fucking everything. And this is how you repay us? You're still a piece of shit! Fucking traitor!"

Harlan lowered his voice. She couldn't hear what he said in response. But she heard Alex.

"Harlan, if you and your new-to-you *bitch*," Marti flinched, "try to bring charges against me, or fuck with me in a public way, I'll take you, her, A.J., and Kenneth down with me. Is that what you want? Believe that it will happen *just like that*."

Chris moved closer to Alex.

"Chris, no!" she called. He couldn't go to prison a third time. He had the children and a future. Not for this. Not for her. Not for *him*.

This time, Marti recognized the metallic click of a gun safety from the back seat. She heard it once before when Christina...

"Chris, get back!" The back passenger car window lowered. She sensed movement from her father but dared not look away from the crazed, nightmare scenario in front of her eyes.

Harlan tried to reason with him. "You worked your whole life to earn Celara, Alex. You know the firm can't function without Kenneth and A.J. You would destroy Celara just to get back at us? Just for revenge?"

"Even the entire Earth." Alex stepped aside so he could see Marti. He made sure that she heard him from the car. "It's called mutually-assured destruction, dumbass! God, you're so fucking stupid!"

Marti turned around. Her father's aim was true. "Chris, get Christian out of here!" she screamed. Chris turned from Alex, saw the aim of his father's gun.

Teresa started her car.

"Get the kids out of here, Chris, please!" Marti was desperate. "Now!"

Alex's goons pulled back their jackets. Everyone had a good look at the pieces strapped to their sides. No one moved.

Car engine noises drifted around the corner. The police.

"It's okay, son," her father called. "We got it covered from here. Get all of them home, son."

Still, Chris didn't move. "Chris, go!" Marti pleaded.

The engine sounds grew louder. Two SUVs with dark windows pulled near the group. Everyone waited in a tense silence broken only by Mari and Kina's whimpers. Marti squeezed her fingers into fists when she heard Christian's wails.

The SUV's doors opened. Four men emerged from each car. Marti recognized two of them—Chris's friends from the Central District that she gave wide berth. The others she didn't know.

"Marti," one of the guys she recognized nodded at her. She nodded back. They slouched and swaggered into position between her family and Alex's group. Everyone, including Alex and his muscle knew what the bulky clothing of the eight men covered.

"Ya'll got this?" Chris asked them.

"Ain't nothin'," the guy she greeted shrugged. The other men didn't bother with words. At last, Chris got in the car with the children. Teresa burned rubber down the road. Marti sagged back in relief.

"Harlan, it's time for us to go." Worth got into the backseat of Beryl's car. "Do it!"

Emboldened by Chris's departure and Worth's retreat, but still mindful of the increased threat, Alex pointed Harlan off his property. "Get the fuck off my property, asshole. You are dead to me. You're a fucking loser, born of losers. Guess it runs in the genes. Get the fuck out of here you fucking prick!"

All eyes on him, Alex was in his element. Seething, righteous anger gave him the platform on which he thrived. He could do this all day, Marti knew.

"You motherfuckers step foot here again, any of you," he swept his arm around, "I'll have you shot dead for trespassing! Get the fuck out of here!"

Harlan got in his car, started the engine. The goons crossed their arms. Chris's group shifted position in response. Alex and his friends wouldn't try to follow.

"Don't darken my doorstep again. And bitch," he yelled to Marti, "Consider yourself back on the street where you belong."

Now she could leave, because Alex freed her. Any man who spoke to her the way Alex did in front of her child and her family had no place in her life. *Walk away from the man... walk away...*

But he wouldn't get away with it. His would not be the final word on the matter because by now, Marti knew how to hurt him too.

"You'll never be the man your father was, Alex!" she shouted out the car window to his purple face. "Never! Never! Never!"

Beryl whipped the car around, then fish-tailed, sending Marti, Worth, and the Reverend against the car doors.

"Never!"

Tires screamed behind them—Harlan. Her father's gun thumped to the car floor. Thankfully, it didn't fire.

◆ ◆ ◆ ◆

# 20 The Close

She cried for days. Teresa and Chris kept Christian for her while she took the time to pull her life back together.

Again.

Harlan allowed Marti to use a spare bedroom. She stored her belongings in his garage. Work would take her mind off Alex's final humiliation. Harlan helped her to retrieve the box that held Worth's manuscript.

"Marti, Beryl left a message for you. They're having a family dinner at the end of this week. They want to make sure you're there." He tugged the box away from her, walked back inside the house. She followed him.

"I can't face them right now. It's too soon. I can't bear to hear all that 'I told you so' commentary."

"Where do you want this?"

"On the table in my room?"

"Yeah. That's fine. Just a second." He dropped it off for her. "I didn't get the impression that any of them wanted to do that, Marti. Neither Chris nor Worth seem the type."

"That's not the only thing." Marti sat at his kitchen table. He followed her and got out frozen dinners. "I feel... so responsible for bringing Alex into all our lives. I can't believe that I did that to my own family."

"You didn't do it. He did."

"Still..."

"Marti, you didn't know what he was."

"I suspected."

"But how could you really know? Unless your mind works on that same deranged level, you can't understand it. Not completely." He looked at her while the microwave hummed. "It took me twenty years, after all."

"What are you going to do, Harlan?"

"I'm fine for now. My house is paid for. Plus, about ten years ago, I thought it wise to make some key investments. Those keep me comfortable. After that, I haven't decided yet."

"Harlan, you sacrificed your career to save me?"

"You saved yourself, Marti."

"I couldn't have done it without you. If you hadn't..." She bowed her head, unable to finish the terrible possibility aloud. He squeezed her hand.

"Actually, I couldn't have done it without you, Marti. I should feel afraid, but I actually feel free. I've never felt more alive, in fact."

"Why me?"

"What do you mean?"

"Why did you choose me instead of... the others?" He didn't answer her. "Harlan?"

He shrugged, turned back to the sink.

"Well, anyway, I think I'm going to skip the family get-together this week. I've fallen so far apart that it's going to take me some time to pull myself back together."

He ran water in the sink. "What about your son?"

Marti trembled. She also had to resolve her feelings of guilt for her role in bringing Alex into Christian's life.

"Harlan," she whispered, "it may not seem like it right now, but I am trying."

"I know you are, Marti. But don't turn away from the people who do love you because of the one who didn't."

Marti flinched but it was true. Alex did not love her. He didn't love anyone. Whenever she felt doubt or had second thoughts, she forced herself to focus on the last piece of Alex's plan to destroy her, and then rebuild her as his doll for hire.

Like Evan, he wanted her to "fix" his opponents. Like Kate, he wanted her to "fuck" them. That was the word he wrote in the last entry of the portfolio. If she could not convince Derek and the other players one way, he planned for her to convince them another. That was the one step too far she wouldn't go. She wouldn't have. Would she?

*Do it for me. Do it for Celara. Do it for the Midwest Consortium. For your family. For our son. For the green revolution. For the future!*

If not for Harlan...

How she wanted more than anything to reassure Harlan in a dignified tone of voice that she would never have consented. Never!

"After yesterday, I understood that I had to let him go."

Harlan got their meals out of the microwave. While they ate, he told her more about the man who played kick soccer with her heart.

"Alex's father, in his zeal to create a successor worthy of Celara and himself, broke something decent and human in Alex. I saw and heard a lot of cruel words and twisted actions in the King home while I lived there. Mr. King unleashed Alex upon the world with the power and access to break and twist the lives of others. One could say it isn't entirely Alex's fault."

Marti put down her fork. "That doesn't matter anymore. Alex tried to destroy my soul—the place where my heart and my mind and my spirit meet. The very essence of my existence." She lifted her chin. "He failed. So that's for him to work out." Marti picked up her fork. "For my own safety and sanity, and for Christian's, and to protect the people I love, I had no choice but to close the door."

Harlan nodded, waited for the rest.

"It's over."

◆ ◆ ◆ ◆

For the next few days, journalists made breathless reference to "The Bill Gates, Andrew Carnegie, Thomas Edison, James J. Hill, and Henry Firestone of green energy!" News media speculated whether Alexander King would pull off the deal of the century, or whether it would be the same old Lake City flim flam, runaround.

Anticipatory whispers and technical directions among the camera men signaled the start of the press conference. Lake City players in real estate, labor, environment, and energy stood three rows deep behind Alex. Kenneth and A.J. flanked the man who dominated Marti's thoughts and dreams for nearly two years.

Though open to the public, Harlan wasn't at the press conference, of course. He resigned as Celara's counsel. Marti wasn't present because she didn't want to breathe the same air as Alex. She and Harlan watched the festival that took place in front of Celara's building via the television in Harlan's kitchen.

Cool as ever, Alex flipped through some papers on the podium. He cleared his throat to unleash the carny magic of a speech similar to that from the boardroom. The newshounds held up their recorders and cell phones like cigarette lighters at a rock concert.

Alex added energy independence, national security, and the need for federal support to stand united against fossil fuel to the mix. Marti knew he saw the scowls from the audience. Nothing he couldn't handle. In fact, Alex reveled in the chance to press his case again and again and again.

"Celara's is but one voice to present the case for a green revolution in Lake City. All interested businesses will likely do the research to come up with their own plans to present comprehensive, workable solutions that satisfy all criteria."

In the midst of a cacophony of voices, Alex held up one hand for silence.

"Hold on. We've got a question."

There was no question, of course. Just Alex covering his flank.

"I'll go ahead answer it since it's important. Both Celara Solar and Celara Wind stand ready today to lead construction on the Midwest portion of the super grid where all transmission across the nation would converge. However, any talk or rumors that you may have heard about lake installations are inaccurate and untrue. That concept is not just unfeasible. It is literally, dead in the water."

Alex smoothly explained his decision to lobby hard against the misguided effort. He cited an insurmountable litany of logistical and environmental issues.

"Wind turbines in the lake don't make the least bit of economic sense. Not when there's abundant farmland just outside city limits, closer to transmission lines that would cost less than half. The Midwest Consortium secured deals with ten separate farms for exclusive wind energy initiatives."

Alex closed over the excited whispers.

"Overall, because of advances made by Celara in terms of research, business development, and installation techniques, the local economy would see significant job growth. Jobs are the crucial takeaway from this press conference. That's the sound bite, folks. If you don't remember anything else today, remember this: The super grid means jobs. Good-paying jobs that provide for families. Thank you, everyone!" He saluted.

The crowd applauded.

Harlan turned to her. "He pulled it off, Marti."

She nodded her agreement. "With Celara's focus on philanthropy—all the scholarships, technical and management training programs, and solar installations for low-income housing—how can they say no?"

"They can't."

"And they won't. Alex knew to tap into my family's networks—Chris, Worth, the Reverend. And they knew to invest in the Consortium. No matter how they felt about him using money and power like choke collars, they believed in his vision."

"Or... they wanted to keep an eye on him."

"Well, since they're part owners, including Beryl, they can balance out the big players. Keep things on the level, I hope."

Harlan looked doubtful. "One can only hope."

Alex took question after question from the press with forthright confidence. The camera moved in for a close-up. She noticed tiny lines at the corners of his eyes. Silver strands streaked across his hair though his brows remained dark and strong.

Today, his eyes did not glitter and slice. They shone. He got what he wanted. He was pleased.

He pressed the flesh, shook hands all around, stroked egos, and posed for pictures. He finished a round of impromptu interviews for various news outlets, delivered the requisite sound bites. Local news media were thrilled to have a ball to run in time for the six o'clock news cycle.

Later in the day, Worth, who did attend the press conference in order to support A.J., stopped by Harlan's home. A natural storyteller, Worth made the endgame seem so real.

"Alex's group headed inside Celara. He high-fived his staff all the way back to Celara's warehouse. They already cleared a large area to celebrate.

'Everyone,' Alex called out to the room in a strong voice. Then he tapped his fork against his champagne glass. 'Everyone, this party is to recognize Celara's good work. All of you should be proud of the time and effort you put in to make the super grid and the Midwest Consortium happen. We've come a long way, baby!'

The warehouse filled with applause.

'I'll take this time to announce a few changes in leadership at Celara.'

The warehouse filled with questions.

'No. No. Everyone stay calm, please.' Alex held up a hand for absolute silence. Then he held up his glass in a toast. 'If two heads are better than one, then three is best of all.' He turned to A.J. and Kenneth and he goes, 'You are my right and left hand at Celara. Kenneth, I know from experience that Celara will benefit from your steady, forthright, calm, and capable leadership. A.J., you've proven yourself a loyal, hard-working, and determined asset to Celara time and again. I'm pleased to have you both on my executive team.'"

Marti and Harlan exchanged a look. Only a select few in Lake City would know how she and Harlan dragged Icarus back to Earth.

Marti wrote a note to Leslie on the first contract draft to call or text Alex from different cell phones after she typed subsequent drafts. Leslie, for her own reasons, complied.

Harlan used Alex's distraction to insert the extra page of power-sharing conditions into the Midwest Consortium document. If Alex wanted the super grid, he had to relinquish decision-making power at Celara. Hand-cuffed to A.J and Kenneth, he couldn't make a move without A.J. and Kenneth's say so. Alex, ever-arrogant, impatient, and assured of his dominance, signed the agreement, unaware of the cold war waged around him in the boardroom. It made no difference to Derek. However, it did fascinate the old school player to witness Alex's take down from the inside.

Worth continued his tale.

"Under all the applause in the warehouse, Alex turned back towards the crowd.

'I'm also pleased to spend more time with my children during evenings, weekends, holidays, birthdays, and all that good stuff. In fact, my daughter and I will take a trip to Paris soon.'"

So Lexa would meet her grandmother and aunt. Alex's daughter would have support against her father's changeable emotions. Perhaps Lily and Mr. and Mrs. Dallas would help with the rest. Marti loved Lexa, but her main focus had to be Christian, younger and more vulnerable to Alex's designs.

"Alex closed the deal with his staff," Worth told them. "He goes, 'I know me, Kenneth, A.J. and all of you can make Celara a place that we all want to come back to every day. It's a new day for new ideas. We're looking forward at Celara. Never backward. And we're certainly not standing still.'"

Marti's heart skipped a beat to hear her philosophy adopted for Celara.

"He goes, 'What do you say?' And with that, he brought down the house. After this... electric pause, someone started to clap. Others joined in. Soon, the warehouse became the press conference melee all over again. It was pretty amazing." Worth sat back signaling the story's end.

The oily smooth panther, twisted mid-air, then landed on his feet.

Marti smiled slightly. She, Harlan, and Worth stood.

"Are you okay, Marti?" Worth asked her.

She hugged him. "I'm fine, Worth. Thank you."

Harlan shook Worth's hand. "So Alex is the face of renewable energy, the Midwest Consortium, Celara Solar, and Celara Wind these days?"

"Yes." Worth walked towards the door, "He's considered a hero in Lake City. He's celebrated all over the nation for his philanthropy. A.J.'s thinking that he'll do best as a figurehead for Celara and as an ambassador of clean energy for the Consortium. He already inspired a lot of other businesses that dragged their feet until now to follow the leader. He's good, actually excellent, with the politics and the public relations. That'll give A.J. and Kenneth the time and space to actually get the job done."

"How about that?" Harlan leaned against the doorway. "Woe betide the unfortunate soul who stands between Alex and any good deed he decides should be done."

They shared a laugh. Worth turned back to his sister. "We miss you, Marti. Especially Christian."

Marti blinked her eyes. Harlan, ever discrete, faded from the door.

"You're still hiding," Worth told her.

Marti shook her head, still unable to put nearly two years worth of pain, humiliation, and fear into words. Worth took her hand.

"Marti, we love you. It's going to be all right. I hope you believe that."

"Everyone saw me humiliated in the street. He smashed me to the pavement and everyone saw and heard everything. Even the kids. I never wanted to put Mari and Kina and, especially Christian in the middle of that."

"Well, since I was there, let me tell you what I saw. I saw you survive to escape a situation that would have broken someone else. You took hit after hit and came backing swinging. That's why everyone showed up when you called. We knew that if you called us that you were ready to make a move. That's what we saw. One of these days you're going to believe me when I tell you that you're so much stronger than you realize."

"Worth, I feel so... dead inside. Like he killed me piece by piece every day that I knew him. I feel absolutely destroyed."

"Nope." Her brother shook his head. "That's just you building muscle. And now's probably not a good time, but ah... you're behind on my manuscript, by the way."

"I can't believe you did it again." Marti laughed. "You always do that."

"What?"

"Make me laugh when I want to cry."

"You aren't alone, Marti. Your life is not your own anymore. You belong to us." Worth opened his arms. "Remember? Now promise forever."

"I remember." Marti hugged him as hard as she dared, since he was still in recovery from the fall. "I promise."

She looked across the room at Harlan who smiled in relief, then gave her the high sign.

"Worth, tell Beryl and my father that me and Harlan will follow you in half an hour. Okay?"

◆ ◆ ◆ ◆

Harlan helped her to close on a condo. She used her consulting fee from Celara as the down payment and the money she saved as Worth's editor to make six month's worth of payments.

She and Harlan looked out the window of her old-style brick home. Soon, her family would arrive for the house-warming and Marti felt so proud.

Her long, dark hair fell in a braid of twists that rested between her shoulder blades. Soft red-brown skin wrapped around high cheek bones that pulled back into the smallest promise of a smile. Marti's sherry eyes held Harlan's brown ones with quiet, welcome calm.

"Rumor has it that there'll be significant announcements involving A.J. and Worth, plus Chris and Teresa. What do you think?"

"I think families are a beautiful thing."

Marti squeezed his hand. "Life wouldn't be the same without them. Something tells me that the Reverend's going to perform at least two weddings this year."

Harlan's face flushed. "Possibly."

"It's so funny, Harlan. The Reverend and Beryl seem to have taken on the patriarch and matriarch roles of our family."

"Well, you never know what happens in a relationship between two people."

"No," she said. "You don't." Both she and Harlan knew the mountains each climbed to reclaim their better selves.

"Sometimes, I wonder if Beryl and my father ever get together to relive old times. Reba's long gone. Beryl's a widow. One family event or another will always bring them together," Marti speculated.

"Well, if the two of them ever find some type of happiness together, then we can only say, 'Congratulations.' Some things and some people have to take care of themselves." Harlan shook his head. "I still can't believe your father, the E-vangelist, packs a gun."

Marti didn't know how to answer that without dredging up memories of Christina. From now on, she wanted to remember only the good things about her mother.

Christian cooed in the next room. She couldn't wait to hear what wise words her son would surely say to her any day now. She leaned against the friend who stood by her in her darkest hours of doubt—when she teetered along the edge and nearly plunged into the abyss.

"You're so right, Harlan." She smiled. "Who would have thought you and I would end up standing next to each other?"

Harlan squeezed her hand again. He ran the other one through his brown hair. He took off his glasses and put them into his shirt pocket. He hesitated. "Marti, I practiced law for over twenty years."

"That's a long time." She searched his eyes, vulnerable without the glasses.

"Maybe too long."

"You think so?"

"I won't face censure or disbarment. A.J. and Kenneth smoothed things over. They're protecting Leslie too."

"They smoothed things over or did they play hardball with Alex?"

"Alex knows better than to under-estimate either of them. I traded my severance package to offset my law school tuition. The scales balance now." Harlan took a deep breath. "I'll begin teaching next fall."

Marti squeezed his hand hard. "Teaching is its own reward, you know."

"No, Marti." Harlan's brown eyes met her sherry-colored gaze. "This is."

Suddenly, Marti felt warm. "Harlan, when will you tell me why you chose me to take a stand instead of the others?"

"Clark. It's Clark."

Marti smiled. "Of course it is."

◆ ◆ ◆ ◆

# Author's Note

*The Green-Collar Economy: How One Solution Can Fix Our Two Biggest Problems* (HarperOne, 2008), defines a green collar job as, "blue-collar employment that has been upgraded to better respect the environment." Also, "family-supporting, career-track, vocational, or trade-level employment in environmentally-friendly fields."

Included as examples are, "Electricians who install solar panels; plumbers who install solar water heaters; farmers engaged in organic agriculture and some bio-fuel production; and construction workers who build energy-efficient green buildings, wind power farms, solar farms, and wave energy farms."

The concept of a super grid is not science fiction. It is a technological advancement that is real and achievable. A super grid would modernize the current North American electrical network. An intelligent digital system monitors electrical flow using superconductive transmission lines. Such lines lose less power which would increase energy efficiency. The super grid would also integrate renewable energy sources such as solar and wind.

Published in 2006, the short story collection, *Imaginarium*, contains an interesting entry titled, "Children of the Golden Ra." Sparse and tightly written, the story is only two pages long. Those two pages speculate the ambitions of a criminal enterprise that decides their economic future lays in solar power. This enthusiastic embrace of renewable energy becomes not only ingenious, it becomes *Celara Sun*.

Alexander, the Great was born Alexander III of Macedon in Pella in 356 BC. In 336 BC, he became king and ascended to the throne after his father, Philip II of Macedon was assassinated. In his lifetime, Alexander created one of the largest empires of ancient history. Though he died in 323 BC, his conquests had significant cultural impact. He is most remembered for his tactical abilities and for the spread of Greek civilization towards the Eastern empires.

Many thanks to the Writers' Workshop at the Des Moines Public Library and Jerry Hooten's Writing Group at Beaverdale Books for insightful feedback and critique, Drake University for use of facilities, Lisa Albrecht of Solar Service for access to research materials, and James McCain Jr. of Innovative Kinetics for providing the first review of the text. Thanks, as well, to my family and those countless individuals and organizations in energy, environment, and labor who shared their own visions of a blue and green North America.

# The Author

Iowa native, Lee McQueen's roots stretch deep into the world of books including libraries, bookstores, and publishing houses. Writing influences include Octavia Butler, Stephen King, Alice Hoffman, H.G. Wells, C.S. Lewis, Jules Verne, Edgar Allan Poe, among others.

Visit www.mcqueenpress.com for "The Manifesto" (the Alexander King short story), "Children of the Golden Ra" (the short story from *Imaginarium* that started it all), news and information, and links to Midwestern writing and greenery.

# Dreams

I took my dreams off the wall
So I would not see what I had not done

I took my dreams out of my mouth
So I would not voice those untruths

I took my dreams out of my ears
Because I did not want to hear them lie to me

I took my dreams out of my mind
While I slept, they tortured me

I pretended my dreams do not exist
And I breathed so free

I put my dreams on this page
Now I hold you captive to my dreams

www.ingramcontent.com/pod-product-compliance
Lightning Source LLC
Chambersburg PA
CBHW030023180626
46810CB00001B/186